The Iron Sword

Book Three of the Iron Soul Series

J.M. Briggs

Published by J.M. Briggs
www.authorjmbriggs.com

Printed in the United State of America
Second Printing 2017
ISBN 978-0-9967826-6-1

To Aunt Charlotte who loved to laugh and was a friend as well as family. I miss you very much and wish you could have seen these books.

1

Returning to Magic

Magic was waiting for her in Ravenslake. When the Welcome to Ravenslake sign appeared in front of her after the long drive from Spokane, Alex Adams hadn't been sure how she felt. On one hand she was excited to see her friends again, but on the other hand, life was so much easier in Spokane. There were no magic lessons, no battles at night with dangerous warriors from other worlds and no confusing reincarnations running around. During the summer her biggest concern had merely been showing up to work on time and living according to the rules and schedule of her parents.

Despite her doubts and worries, Alex hadn't stopped or turned around. She drove carefully through the streets of Ravenslake, keeping her eyes open for people out on their bikes and jaywalking pedestrians. The entire town was busy with new students arriving, parents running out to shop and campus staff trying to direct the traffic. Thankfully as a sophomore, Alex knew her way around and had managed to get a decent parking spot and check into her new room at Gallagher Hall without too much fuss.

Gallagher Hall was a four-story building right next to Alex's old freshman dormitory Hatfield Hall. While a little further from the arboretum, all the rooms on the northwest facing side had nice views of the South Santiam River. It was a newer building made of pale brick and greenish colored steel. Thus far Alex liked it; all the doors were opened by her key card, even the door of the suite. A large common area and kitchen downstairs were available to all residents and made cooking much more viable than the old tiny kitchen on her floor at Hatfield ever had.

The sound of boxes dropping in the living room made Alex sigh and grimace slightly. It made no sense that moving into a larger suite of rooms would be harder than moving into a small one room dorm. Yet somehow they'd managed it. Maybe, she considered thoughtfully, it was the illusion of having a lot of room. After all, she and Nicki both had stacks of boxes in the small square living room around the small blue sofa and ugly dark blue armchair that came with the place. Not to mention the 'hallway' which included a small alcove where the fridge, a sink with a counter and a mounted microwave stood as their kitchenette was very narrow. There were three doors in the hallway, one leading to a bathroom with absolutely no storage, one leading to Nicki's bedroom and one leading to Alex's.

Her bedroom was smaller than the dorm room she used to share with Jenny last year, but it was private. A key card lock on the door ensured that even Nicki couldn't enter the room without permission. Looking around the room, there was: a large wardrobe stood against one wall, a twin bed with a bad mattress, a desk that was more like a table, a small set small of drawers that she'd already shoved under the left side of the desk to give her some storage space and a short set of shelves set on top of a larger set of drawers. The result meant that she didn't have much free space to move, but she had a lot more storage than her old room. That right there was worth something.

"How the hell did I get roped into being your pack mule?" An aggravated voice called from the living room. "And why the hell are you guys on the fourth floor?!"

Another thunk from the living room made Alex stop organizing her new desk and head out into the hallway. The 'pack mule' Aiden Bosco looked over at her with a grin, his brown eyes glinting with amusement even as he brushed some sweating strands of dark brown hair out of his face.

"You volunteered to be the pack mule," Alex reminded him with a soft smile. "It was very gentlemanly of you and I'm sure your father will be proud. And as for the fourth floor, well that's on the university housing department, not us."

Aiden snorted at her remark and Alex barely held in a grin, glancing into Nicki's room. It had the same furniture as hers, but the room was more of a rectangle than the squarer shape of her own room. Nicki was already putting up curtains over the single window and humming along with her music player which was set to shuffle based on the odd mix of techno, hip-hop, and country that Alex had already heard coming out of the room. Her roommate's long auburn hair was styled in an elaborate braid that folded over her head, crisscrossing with another braid. Maybe once they were settled she could get Nicki to teach her how she managed to do that by herself.

"So how are we doing?" Alex asked Aiden, turning her attention back to him.

"That was the last of it actually," Aiden huffed, wiping some sweat off his forehead. "I notice your boyfriend managed to miss this part."

"He's not…" Alex trailed off uncomfortably, feeling a little better when Aiden shifted. "We haven't really discussed what we are," Alex informed him. "He asked me to go out with him when school resumed, that's all."

"Didn't you guys talk at all this summer?" Nicki asked, stepping out of her room behind Alex. It gave her the odd impression of being surrounded with Aiden in front, Nicki behind and no real room to maneuver in the tiny hallway.

"A bit, but it was kind of strange, to be honest," Alex admitted with a shrug. "Talking on the phone has never been my thing and you don't text about magic."

"I can see that," Aiden agreed with a small nod and pursed lips. "Didn't you video call?"

"That was the couple of times we talked, but our schedules didn't really work for that often. Lifeguarding kept me busy during the day and Arthur's job was mostly evenings."

"Behold the moments why I'm glad my summer job is working for my grandma," Nicki announced with a grin. "Scheduling time off just requires wide eyes and quivering the lip."

Aiden laughed and Alex couldn't contain her giggles; it was just too easy to see Nicki making that kind of expression to get her way. Shaking his head, Aiden pushed a stack of boxes out of the way with his foot.

"Not so easy for me, I was working at the bookstore, but in my case, a family operation means lots of hours with the benefits being mostly Mom's cooking."

A knock on the door interrupted the conversation and Aiden hopped around the scattered boxes to the front door. Alex couldn't see the doorway from the hallway and quickly moved down to look around the corner. She grinned as Bran stepped around Aiden and began to maneuver his way into the room. Bran's brown hair was a bit shorter than it had been in June and he'd gotten a bit more sun. His green eyes lit up when he spotted Alex and Nicki. His leg brace was still securely attached to his right leg, but he didn't seem to be leaning as heavily on his cane.

"Look who I found," Aiden called, grinning widely and throwing an arm around Bran's shoulders in a quick one armed hug.

Stepping forward, Alex waited until Aiden had finished his hug and Bran turned his attention to them. When he opened his left arm, Alex grinned and hugged him tightly for a moment before stepping to the side to let Nicki have her turn.

"Welcome back," Nicki greeted Bran warmly when she stepped back. "How was the drive?"

"Good and yes I already called my mother to let her know I got here safely."

"She's your mom, she worries," Nicki offered with a shrug and a smile.

"Yeah well," Bran sighed, "I doubt your parents are as bad."

"Actually I had to call when I got here," Alex informed him. "Mom and Dad were really upset they couldn't make it this time."

"Everything okay with them?" Nicki asked, leaning against the plain white wall of their living room.

"Oh yeah, just a scheduling conflict and Ed had his first football game this weekend for high school. I told them I'd be fine." Alex gestured around to the living room. "With this new suite, it's not like I needed to bring much besides clothes and books. We've got a fridge, a microwave, and even a sofa."

"Ours is pretty much the same," Aiden agreed as he glanced around. "Just on the first floor and a bit bigger."

"That's my fault," Bran remarked with a shrug.

"Hey our suite has much bigger hallways and more maneuver room, I'm not complaining about that," Aiden assured him as he nodded towards the small hallway that led off the living room. "The girls' place feels like a little rat maze."

"Thank you so much for that comparison," Nicki replied with a dramatic roll of her blue eyes. "Still the privacy will be nice," Nicki remarked calmly as she picked up a box and set it on top of a stack of boxes to clear the floor. "It's not like we don't come and go at odd hours some nights. Plus the living room does provide enough room to practice magic." Nicki gave Aiden a pointed look and added, "At least for those of us who don't throw fireballs."

"Hey, I'm getting better at other stuff," Aiden defended, crossing his arms over his chest. "I'm moving thing more easily and last week I even managed to fix a scorch mark that I made in my room."

Alex couldn't help but feel impressed and saw Nicki give a small nod out of the corner of her eye.

"I practiced a lot this summer too," Bran informed them with a small smile. "I'm able to lift and move much heavier things than before." Bran toyed with the top of his cane as he spoke. "I even did this weird thing where I saw into the next room in the house. I watched my mother baking, it was pretty cool."

"You saw something at a distance?" Nicki asked, her voice becoming higher in her excitement. "That is so cool."

"Yeah, teamed with your visions that definitely makes you the clairvoyant of this team," Aiden agreed with a grin before his features became more serious. "Speaking of which, any new visions or dreams?"

"Nothing clear," Bran told them with a shake of his head. "Sometimes I see the Sídhe tunnels and an Iron Gate, I think the one we made with Arthur in June, but I'm not sure. I can see their violet eyes down in the darkness and hear them laughing." Bran shivered slightly. "But I've only seen that big dark shape once since the summer solstice. I think Morgana and Merlin are right about it being an Old One, but I have no idea which of the old pagan deities that it could be."

"And being stabbed with the sword?" Nicki asked carefully.

Bran shook his head, a pensive expression on his face and slowly answered, "I hate to say it…but symbolically me being stabbed in the back just… makes me think about a traitor."

The room went silent and Alex swallowed down a rush of bile from her stomach. Her gut churned uncomfortably as the very idea of someone betraying them settled over her like a cold fog.

"But we already resolved the Jenny, Lance and Arthur love triangle," Aiden pressed almost desperately. "Jenny and Lance know now that they used to be Guinevere and Lancelot and Arthur is dating Alex now. He survived finding out that they were cheating last year, Alex saved him."

"That was a betrayal," Bran agreed, "But I didn't have the vision until that was over." Bran gave them all a forced smile. "But I might be wrong, it may mean something totally different or it might refer to something in the past or someone that we have yet to meet." Bran's shoulder relaxed slightly and he straightened up. "I trust everyone in this room and I trust Merlin and Morgana."

"So do I," Nicki declared with a raised chin and small smile. "We survived freshman year: learning about magic, attacks by vicious magical dogs, the Sídhe Riders invading to get slaves and discovering that the King Arthur mythos has real roots in events. We can handle whatever sophomore year brings."

"And now you've jinxed it," Aiden remarked with an easy going smile, earning him a glare from Nicki.

Alex shook her head and exchanged a look with Bran; there were moments that Nicki and Aiden fought worse than elementary school age brothers and sisters. Half the time if Alex hadn't known that Nicki considered Aiden her brother and was homosexual she would have teased her about protesting too much. But Aiden certainly had a point, last year had been a blur of magic lessons, dangerous discoveries and battling the Sídhe. It was their responsibility as mages to protect their world which was one part of a massive cosmos and multiverse spanning series of connected worlds known as the Tree of Reality. Unfortunately one of their closest neighbors were the Sídhe who'd already conquered seven worlds and had their eyes on Earth.

"So who is looking forward to hearing Merlin lecture about the legend of King Arthur?" Bran asked to break up the argument between Aiden and Nicki.

When they had stopped fighting, Bran raised his hand and stared at the heaviest of the blue plastic bins. There was a shimmer of yellow magic around Bran's hand before the box rose into the air and began to float down the hallway. Bran stayed where he was and a small triumphant smile took over his features. They all heard a soft thump as the box hit the ground and Bran exhaled loudly. Alex began to clap with a wide grin and Nicki and Aiden quickly joined in. Bran grinned and made a small bow, gesturing dramatically with his hands.

"Well I can't say that I'm looking forward to starting my Mondays off with a class like that," Alex admitted, turning her attention back to Aiden's question. "Still, Merlin said that it will give us a chance to put all our research to work and learn more about the Iron Soul."

"That's true," Nicki agreed thoughtfully. "He and Morgana haven't confirmed it yet, but in my research, I found a couple of other heroes that inspired the King Arthur legend and might be other incarnations of the Iron Soul."

"Such as?" Bran asked as he looked over at Nicki who was lifting a box onto the sofa to sort through.

"Well like I said I'm not sure yet, but for instance, in some Arthurian mythology King Arthur has a dagger called Carnwennan, which is from Welsh mythology and it shrouded the user in shadow. To me, that sounds a lot like a potentially real magical object."

"Maybe," Aiden agreed with a considering nod. "I just like how somehow we all managed to get into the class despite the wait list. Merlin was pretty serious about wanting us to take the class."

"Well we already know that he can use magic on people's memories," Alex pointed out, barely hiding a slight shiver. "He used it on the witnesses who came out of the Sídhe tunnel last year to mislead the police."

"True," Nicki agreed and the group was quiet for a moment. Nicki giggled and shook her head turning her attention back to the box. "You guys are taking Morgana's Enlightenment class right?" Nicki asked, pulling a rolled out wall hanging out of the box with a grin.

"Yeah, I'm using it as my upper-level social sciences class," Bran replied with a nod. "But you know we won't be able to share classes much longer. History and English classes aren't exactly related fields for my physics degree or Aiden's electrical engineering."

"Not unless you guys switch to the social sciences," Nicki answered with a grin as she tossed the wall hanging to Alex. "Come on, join us on the social science side," she said dramatically, holding a hand out towards Aiden.

"You don't know the power of the hard sciences," Aiden countered, deepening his voice. Nicki giggled and Alex shared a look with Bran as they both kept in their laughter.

"I think we left them alone too long this summer," Bran told Alex in a completely monotone voice that made Alex nearly crack up before he looked back at Nicki and Aiden. "We've all been focusing on the general education requirements so a switch wouldn't be too bad for any of us," Bran suggested before adding, "And you two are geeks."

"We know," Aiden and Nicki answered together, grinning widely at each other.

"Speaking of general requirements," Nicki remarked with a smile. "How did everyone do?"

"I did alright," Aiden replied. "Not as well as I was expecting when I started college, but then I wasn't expecting to have to worry about learning magic and being ripped about by magic hounds."

"Mostly As," Bran informed them with a shrug. "I honestly don't think that I deserved the A in Morgana's class."

"Yeah I get that," Nicki admitted. "I got an A in Merlin's Epic class that I'm not sure my final essay actually earned."

"Well, they are highly aware of the issues we're facing," Alex pointed out with a shaky smile. "And I'm sure that if we deserved to fail a class they'd still let us."

"I'm not nearly as sure about that as you," Aiden countered with a shake of his head. "But at least I'm still in good standing for pursuing electrical engineering."

Shaking her head at her friends' behavior, Alex unwrapped the bundle in her hand and smiled; it was a small woven tapestry with a unicorn, a copy of one of those old Middle Ages tapestries. Alex had to wonder where Nicki got it but certainly, wouldn't argue if she hung it up out here.

Another knock on the door made them all turn towards it almost as one. Aiden was still closest so he quickly pushed a box out of the way with his foot and opened the door. Arthur was standing in the doorway with a slightly nervous smile and his hands in the pockets of his jacket. His blond hair was a little longer than when Alex has last seen him at the end of June.

"Hey," Arthur greeted a bit awkwardly as he eyes swept over the room. He nodded to Bran and stepped inside the dorm room, closing the door behind him. "How are you guys?"

A chorus of good and fine was heard in the room as Arthur moved around the boxes to get into the living room. He stepped up next to Alex with a smile and his hand hanging at his side gently brushed her own.

"Do you have anything left that needs to come in?" Arthur asked quickly as he glanced around the messy living room.

"Nope," Alex informed him with a shake of her head. "Aiden just got the last of it.

"Sorry I missed helping you get your stuff in," Arthur apologized with a small sweet smile. "Coach wouldn't let us out of weight training."

"I understand," Alex assured him quickly. "We didn't wait for you so that's half our fault."

"Still, I'm sorry," Arthur apologized. "Last year we weren't even… and I still helped your dad get your things in."

That was true enough; Alex had first met Arthur, the tall blond hair, and blue-eyed football player last year when he'd been moving his then-girlfriend Jenny Sanchez's things inside. Of course, things had been very different at the start of last year.

"Well if you really feel that bad," Aiden cut in from near the doorway. "You can give me a hand helping get Bran's things in."

Arthur turned towards them sharply, a faint blush on his cheeks as he was reminded that they weren't alone.

"Course, uh, I'll be right there."

"Thanks," Bran agreed. "Meet you downstairs by the front door."

Arthur nodded quickly and Alex wasn't sure if she was nervous or relieved when Bran and Aiden headed out the front door. Behind her, Alex heard Nicki move down the hallway and the door to her room close.

"How was the drive down?"

"It was good," Alex told him with a smile. "Good weather and pretty pleasant." Alex toyed with a strand of her long blonde hair that had come loose from her ponytail. "I did think about turning around when the city came into view."

"I understand," Arthur laughed and his shoulders relaxed slightly. "When I finally got to go home after the solstice there was a part of me that didn't want to come back," he admitted. "Then I remembered that you agreed to go on a date with me," he added with a nervous little smile.

"I did didn't I?" Alex teased, feeling a bit braver after seeing that Arthur was nervous too.

"Think you can get away tonight for dinner? I know that once classes start we'll have magic lessons again together, but I'd like to spend some time just the two of us."

"Tonight sounds nice," Alex agreed with a widening smile. "How about Central Diner?"

"Okay, meet you downstairs at the front door at say… 6:30?"

"Great, that sounds good."

She was probably blushing bright red and grinning like an idiot now, but Arthur was smiling too. He leaned forward without a word and Alex felt warm slightly chapped lips press against her own. Her skin tingled with warmth and her heart jumped in her chest. The kiss ended quickly and Arthur stepped back with a silly smile on his own face.

"I'll see you tonight, better not keep Aiden and Bran waiting," he said in a rush, nearly tripping over a box as he moved towards the door.

"Yeah, but if you guys need any help just call," Alex reminded him.

He nodded and reached the doorway, pushing another box out of the way with his foot. Arthur gave her another wide grin and a small wave before vanishing out the door. It closed with a heavy thud and a small click behind him, echoing slightly in the room. Still smiling, Alex turned and stepped into the hallway only to find a grinning Nicki lingering in the doorway of her bedroom.

"What?" Alex asked, disliking the far too pleased look on Nicki's face.

"Oh nothing," her roommate replied in a sing-song voice. "Just you rescued the innocent children from a terrible fate as slaves to the Sídhe, protected the destined hero from dying due to the betrayal of his cursed reincarnated lover and friend and the finally secured the hero's love for yourself, freeing him from the chains of his cursed love triangle." Nicki grinned at Alex and added, "If this was a thousand years ago, they'd be writing songs about you."

Nicki ducked into her room and shut the door before Alex could find something to throw at her. A moment later Alex realized that she had a date tonight and had a lot of unpacking to do.

2

Date at the Diner

Alex was officially pathetic, that was all there was to it. It didn't matter that she could control magical energy and release lightning bolts from her hands, it was irrelevant that she had saved a bunch of children from slavery to the Sídhe, and completely immaterial that she'd protected Arthur from being killed by the Sídhe after he fled into the woods after discovering that Lance and Jenny were cheating.

No, Alex decided with a sigh, she was very pathetic. She'd changed clothes six times before finally deciding on a dark pair of jeans with low heeled black boots and she still hadn't settled on a top. Her dorm room was even messier than it had been when she'd started which was remarkable given she'd been unpacking boxes and bags of clothes all day.

"Alex it's almost time for your date," Nicki's voice called from the hallway. "Come on! Arthur's known you for a year, he's not going to judge. The guy has seen you bleeding with broken bones, from protecting him I might add."

Nicki wasn't the most inspiring speaker, but she did have a way of cutting to the heart of the matter. Mind made up, Alex grabbed a charcoal Ravenslake t-shirt and pulled it on, deciding for casual. She grabbed a small pair of silver hoop earrings and brushed out her hair, listening to Nicki whistle impatiently outside.

"Okay," Alex said as she reached for the door latch. Pulling it open, she gave Nicki a nervous smile. "How do I look?"

"Good," Nicki answered with an approving nod. "A bit fancier than normal, but not ridiculous. Trying, but not trying too hard. You don't want him to suddenly feel like he's dating someone else after all."

Alex relaxed at the words and reached over to grab her bag from atop the chest of drawers. Pulling it over her head, Alex adjusted the strap over her chest and reached inside to check that her dagger was in place. "My mom almost found this over the summer," Alex informed Nicki as she adjusted the sheath in the side pocket. "I made the mistake of asking her to grab my brush."

Nicki chuckled at the remark, but reached out and gripped Alex's arm and gently pulled her from her bedroom. "Get downstairs and have fun, I'm going to run out to the grocery store and get us a few basics."

"Okay," Alex replied weakly as Nicki ducked into her room, coming out with her keys and wallet. Alex took a couple of steps towards their front door, but her stomach tensed up and Alex thought she just might get sick.

"You'll be fine," Nicki promised as she joined Alex by the door. "You're friends, you saved his life and it is just a first date, nothing to worry about."

Nodding silently, Alex toyed with her hands and moved slowly as Nicki pushed her out of their suite, closed the door behind them and walked her down to the elevator.

"Alex, seriously," Nicki chided. "You can handle this; no need to be nervous."

"It's just I've had a crush on Arthur pretty much from the moment I met him," Alex confessed softly. "And after everything last year... I guess I just sort of settled into keeping

secrets and forcing myself not to bring my crush into things."
The elevator opened in front of them and both of them stepped
inside with Nicki pressing the button for the ground floor.

"And now it's okay, to be honest about your feelings for him,"
Nicki finished kindly. She reached down and squeezed Alex's
hand fondly. "You're beautiful, smart and brave Alex, you can
handle a date. You and Arthur are going to have a good time
tonight, settle into being boyfriend and girlfriend and help the
rest of us kick the Sídhe back where they came from." Nicki
released Alex's hand and crossed her arms over her chest as
the elevator dinged and opened. "And if he ever crosses a line
just let me know and I'll find a discreet way to kill him so
Morgana and Merlin never know it was us."

Nicki winked at Alex and stepped out of the elevator, heading
for the front door with Alex a few steps behind her. She
stopped in her tracks when Nicki pushed open the door and
she caught sight of Arthur waiting outside. He'd dressed up a
little too: he was in jeans, but his usual t-shirt had been
replaced with a dark blue button down shirt. Smiling, Alex
walked forward and grinned at Arthur as he straightened up
and smiled at her. Nicki chuckled and waved to them both
with a quick shout to have fun.

"You look nice," Arthur told Alex, holding out his hand to
her.

"You too," Alex replied, slipping her hand into his. She was
probably grinning like an idiot even as her stomach flipped
over.

"Shall we?"

"Of course."

18

They talked about their dorm rooms on the way across campus. Arthur was in a single in Upham Hall which was pretty nice according to him with newer furniture. Alex briefly wondered if come next semester he, Aiden and Bran would be comfortable enough with each other to consider moving in together. But his tone began more distant and sad when he revealed that Lance was in the same dorm as him; apparently, Upham was pretty popular with football players who weren't in fraternities. Arthur muttered something about a pool table and big screen television in the basement.

Central Avenue was very busy and Alex was glad they'd just decided to walk. The streets were packed with parked cars and the side streets weren't much better. Noise was spilling out of numerous restaurants and she could see several families out with their young college kids. She felt a small pang of homesickness, but before she could dwell on it the smell of burgers and fries washed over her. Alex looked up from the sidewalk and tensed as they arrived at the doorway of Central Diner.

Central Diner was the sort of place that had come full circle over the course of several decades. It started off in the fifties and hadn't changed much over the years meaning that the décor that had been boring and stale in the eighties had now become delightfully retro. Checkered black and white floors contrasted with the bright red of the booths and the red stools that were set up against the white main counter. A large menu with the specials hung over the counter near the cash registers and the dessert display. The only reason that a person would know they hadn't stepped back in the fifties were the big screen televisions placed around the main dining area and the modern pop hits playing.

"I've only been here twice with the football team," Arthur told Alex with a hint of nervousness as they waited for the waitress to show them to a booth.

"Me too," Alex admitted. "But it's hard to go wrong with basic diner food. Their burgers are good and they have these garlic and parmesan fries that are awesome."

"I had those last time I was here," Arthur replied with a widening smile as some of the tension drained out of his shoulders. "We'll have to get a plate of those."

"Those orders are huge for only two people," Alex protested as the waitress waved for them to follow her.

"I just came from weight training," Arthur reminded Alex with a grin. "I promise to do my part."

"Well… if you insist, they do go very well with burgers."

They slid into a booth near the back, Alex taking the side that let her have her back against the outer wall and keep an eye on the door. She'd never been this defensive and aware of what was happening around her before, but after last year it seemed like she always had to know what was going on around her. Arthur didn't say anything about her choice of side and slid into his side of the booth, accepting the menus with an easy smile. On the nearby television an action movie was playing; it looked familiar, but Alex couldn't think of the name and they couldn't actually hear the dialogue.

"So…," Alex faltered as she tried to figure out what to say. "Anything interesting happen since our last video chat?"

"Not really, things were pretty calm. Jenny avoided me, but that was the worst part of the summer so I suppose I can't complain. I did my best to stay busy, but I did practice my magic in the dining room whenever my mother was out." At Alex's odd look he shrugged and added, "The table is really easy to move and the china is kept in a side room so there's not too much fragile stuff."

Alex hadn't given much thought to Arthur's day to day life in the summer. Their waitress brought them their sodas and Alex took a quick sip, noticing Arthur's eyes move up to the television screen. Alex was just doing her best to stay calm and not be nervous. Dating in high school suddenly didn't seem like much in comparison to having her first real grown-up or at least college date. Her parents weren't waiting at home with a curfew and she was left wondering just when the adult rules of dating kicked in. Was college flexible or did the 'rules' start then? Why didn't they cover this stuff at orientation?

Arthur had already kissed her a couple of time and they'd talked over the summer so was this a first date or a second date counting Beltane Eve when they'd been out? Of course, that night had ended with Arthur finding out that Jenny, his girlfriend since sophomore year of high school was cheating on him with his football teammate and friend Lance and then finding out that he was the current incarnation of a magical soul created to protect Earth. Okay, she was probably not going to count that night as a date given she'd gotten broken bones out of fighting the Sídhe to keep him safe. Yeah, this was probably the first date. She didn't remember her first date with Thomas being this nerve-wracking.

"Nervous?" Arthur asked, his voice cutting into her thoughts and making Alex realize how long she'd been sitting there silently.

"A bit," she admitted with a shaky smile. "I dated some in high school, but I was too busy with classes and… everything last year to date." Alex knew she was blushing bright red, but refused to lower her eyes and settled for a little shrug. "I feel out of practice."

"I understand," Arthur told her with a warm smile. "I haven't dated anyone other than Jenny for years; I barely remember any dates I went on previous to her." He ran a hand through his blond hair and Alex relaxed, at least he was nervous too.

"How about we ask each other some questions," Alex suggested holding back a nervous giggle. "Things we don't know."

"Okay," Arthur leaned back in the booth and tilted his head as he studied Alex. "We've known each other for a year now so there's a lot of things I do know, but... what's your favorite color?"

"Blue, yours?"

"Blue also, but I like dark green too."

"Favorite food?" Alex asked, unable to think of something more interesting.

"I'd have to go with steak for that one. How about you?"

"I love cheeseburgers, they're my favorite."

Arthur nodded and they sat in silence until he shook his head and laughed, "This is ridiculous; we're friends and we like each other."

"I guess this is why most people go and see a movie or something before dinner, so they have something to talk about."

"We'll try that next time," Arthur agreed and Alex couldn't help but smile at the promise of another date.

"Okay how about this: what class are you looking forward to the most?" Alex asked.

"The Story of King Arthur," Arthur replied. "Professor Yates suggested it to me. I'm a little creeped out by the idea of taking the class, but I suppose it couldn't hurt to know more of the mythology we're dealing with."

"Oh, I didn't realize you were taking that class, it had a horrible wait list."

"I wasn't originally, but after finals were over and you guys left Professor Yates was able to get me into the class."

"Yeah, Bran and Aiden were originally waitlisted," Alex admitted with a smile. "Mer-Yates probably had something to do with that."

"We're crazy aren't we," Arthur remarked shaking his head. "Wanting to take an English class about the Story of King Arthur."

"A little weird to subject ourselves to it maybe," Alex agreed, "But not crazy. After all, that class isn't taught very often, but Yates brought it back for this semester. I daresay that our professor had a pretty stern expectation of us taking it."

"And hopefully he'll cut us some slack if we're late on a paper due to a Sídhe attack."

Alex nodded in agreement at that sentiment, but they both fell silent as the waitress returned to take their order. The diner was beginning to fill up more and more with students in large groups, young couples, and families who were in town to help students move in. Worried about being overheard, Alex asked Arthur about his favorite movies and they kept themselves occupied gushing over their favorite car chases. Arthur was grinning by the time their food came and the nervous knot in Alex's stomach had finally unwound.

"Don't get me wrong I lo- I still really care about Jenny," Arthur told Alex, stumbling for a moment with a guilty expression. "But it's kind of nice to know that my girlfriend wants to see action films instead of romance."

Alex smiled at the comment and pushed down the hint of jealously at Arthur's fumble. It made sense of course that he still worried about her; they'd dated for four years and she was the reincarnation of his wife and significant other in numerous lifetimes. Her jealousy also made a lot of sense, but Alex didn't want to dwell on that. Besides, he'd called her his girlfriend!

"Speaking of Jenny…" Alex trailed off with a small blush as she wondered if her question was a good idea or not. "She and Lance are still attending school here, so we're bound to see them around and they'll see each other… would it bother you if they got together properly?"

"No," Arthur replied with a sad smile. "In fact, I'd be happier if they did."

"You would?" Alex's heart skipped a beat when Arthur gave her a small smile and nodded.

"I think… I think they belong together. Jenny and I… what I felt for her was always there, always very… warm I suppose. It was never very passionate. I always thought that was what they talked about when they said that real love was a steady burning flame, but now I'm not sure if what I thought was love really was towards her." Arthur ran a hand through his hair in frustration and sighed loudly. "I care about her, I never want anything bad to happen to her and I want her to be happy, but I'm not sure that's really love. After everything came out I saw the way that Lance looked at Jenny and it… it kind of floored me. It was so much... more than I ever think I felt. So yeah if what was between them could have a chance, a real chance, then I think it would be so much more than Jenny and I had. Not to mention if they did get together and were able to be happy... then everything we went through becomes worth it."

Then he reached forward, took her hand and gave it a small squeeze. The tight ring that had been around her lung eased and Alex was able to breathe again. Arthur's thumb brushed over the back of her hand gently and she was able to smile.

"That might not have been the best answer to give my new girlfriend," Arthur admitted in a low voice without meeting Alex's eyes. "But it's the honest one." He swallowed thickly, a slight blush coloring his cheeks and added, "And for the sake of full disclosure you should know that I care a lot about you too and think about kissing you and...other things a lot more than I probably should."

Blushing brightly, Alex used her free hand to grab her soda and take a sip through the straw. It made a loud slurping noise that only made her blush redder, but Arthur laughed warmly and grinned at her. A moment later they had to release each other's hand when the waitress brought over their burgers and the order of garlic parmesan fries.

"Here you go kiddos," the waitress said with a wide smile as her eyes glanced between the two of them. "You two make a cute couple."

As the waitress moved away from their table towards another one, Arthur beamed at Alex and assured her, "Well just so we're clear Alex, I'd like us to go steady."

"Okay," Alex agreed quickly, her stomach flipping and her skin tingling.

"And I guess we'll just have to figure out date nights around protecting the Earth," Arthur added in a lower voice.

"The Iron Realm," Alex corrected with a teasing smile.

"Alright, the Iron Realm then," Arthur conceded, picking up his soda and holding it forward for a small toast. Picking up her own soda, Alex clinked the glasses together in agreement with a smile.

3

The New Warrior

806 B.C.E. Northern Cornwall

Arto stared out over the village that he now called home from
the doorway of his roundhouse. So much had changed in the
last few years that there were moments he felt adrift and
confused. He'd been born in this village long ago, the only son
of Uthyrn and Eigyr and younger half-brother of Morgana.
But he'd been born different from the other children; his soul
had been created by the power of the Iron Realm itself to repel
the invasion of the Sídhe. All his life he'd heard the tale of the
fierce magical warriors that came from another world,
capturing humans and taking them back into their own realm
to live as slaves.

His own sister had been one of their victims, taken at a young
age and replaced with a Changeling. Morgana had only been
returned to them in order to spy on him for the Sídhe. Merlin
had saved him from an attack and taken him away from his
family and this village to keep him safe. He'd grown up
traveling throughout the isles with Merlin, learning to control
his magic and preparing for the day he'd fulfill the reason he
was created. Now as an adult it seemed like he and the people
of the isles were finally making progress. The mages had
introduced iron to the isles and now Arto had discovered how
to use the iron to cut off the Sídhe advances, but there were
always more. Some days it felt like they could only hold them
back, never really stop them.

And it always seemed to come back to him, Arto mused as he
watched smoke rise from forges and fires throughout the

village and blow away in the morning sky. Breathing out slowly, Arto closed his eyes for a moment and tried to banish the darker thoughts trying to creep up on him. A soft breeze surrounded him, making his skin tingle and freshening the air.

"Arto," a soft female voice called from behind him.

Opening his eyes, Arto turned around with a smile to see Gwenyvar stepped out of the roundhouse with a quizzical look on her face. Her brown eyes were squinting against the rising sun and her long brown hair was in neat braids with small golden decorations. In her arms, she carried a light blue colored cloak and a bronze pin that glinted in the sunlight.

"Good morning Gwenyvar," Arto greeted warmly with a widening smile.

"Good morning husband," Gwenyvar returned with a brilliant smile.

In one movement, she swung the cloak around her shoulders. Arto reached out and gently caught the edges, bringing them together and using the pin to clasp them in place. His fingers moved up to brush against the soft warm skin of Gwenyvar's neck and he leaned down to kiss her. A soft laugh escaped his wife, but she met him halfway and pressed her lips against his without a word.

"Arto!" Another voice called sharply from nearby.

Pulling away from Gwenyvar, Arto gave her an apologetic smile. She sighed softly but gave him a small reassuring smile.

"And there's your sister," Gwenyvar observed with a shake of her head. "I wonder what she wants now?"

"Gwenyvar, Morgana means well."

"I don't think she likes me very much," Gwenyvar remarked with a frown. "She's always saying that your mother and my father shouldn't have let us get married."

"She's just worried we're too young," Arto assured Gwenyvar, ignoring his sister calling to him from down the hill. "We're younger than she was when she and Airril married. She's just protective."

"We're not children," Gwenyvar sighed with a small frown. "We're sixteen."

"I'm her younger brother," Arto countered with a small shrug and another apologetic smile. "In the end, I'm always going to be her younger brother, no matter how many warriors I lead, Sídhe I kill and iron gates I create."

Gwenyvar chuckled softly and gave him a warm smile with a small nod of understanding. Leaning up, she kissed his cheek gently and gestured down the hill.

"Well then, go on great leader," Gwenyvar teased gently as she gave him a small push towards the path.

Grinning at her, Arto started down the path and followed his sister's voice around the curve of the hill. His smile eased as he approached his sister and she stopped on the pathway. Morgana's green eyes were watching him sharply and she had a slight frown on her face. Her long dark hair was tied in a long braid twisted around the crown of her head. As usual, she didn't bother with much decoration, but the bronze pin she used to clasp her blue cloak around her shoulders was polished and gleaming in the sunlight. She'd mentioned that it had been a gift from Airril.

"Good morning sister," Arto greeted cheerfully.

"Good morning Arto," Morgana replied a bit impatiently. "You might be interested that Eaban's son Luegáed arrived last night after you retired for the evening. He insisted on not disturbing you and Airril and I hosted him, but you need to extend your greetings."

"Really, Luegáed is here?" Arto asked eagerly, his excitement making his sister's lips twitch into a slight smile.

"Yes Arto, he is with Merlin at the moment getting breakfast and touring the forges."

There was a hint of irritation in her voice, but Arto refused to apologize for spending time with his wife. He remembered too well the years that Morgana had traveled with him and Merlin and had not been with her own husband Airril. Since they'd settled here to oversee iron production, Airril was almost always in the village and traveled north to his home village only when necessary. His sister should understand better than most.

"I'll see him at once," Arto informed Morgana, straightening his shoulders.

Morgana nodded in approval and gestured towards the largest of the forging yards. Arto caught sight of an unfamiliar person moving through the yard and into a roundhouse with Merlin. As he started walking down the hill towards the roundhouse Arto couldn't help but smile with excitement. Eaban was one of the most powerful men on the western isle and had been a supporter of fighting the Sídhe since the very beginning. He'd been a comfort when the Sídhe had killed his father last year and promised to send his son to help them. Arto had been looking forward to meeting Luegáed for some time: he was a warrior near Arto's own age and if he was anything like his father Arto was sure they'd be good friends.

Arto followed the path down, greeting the villagers who smiled and bid him a good morning. His eyes scanned around for any sign of Merlin or the new arrival. Then he caught sight of them again on the path ahead, moving towards the village gate. With a burst of speed, Arto maneuvered his way around the people moving to start their days. He didn't want to rush up like an overly eager child so once he was clear of the crowd, he slowed his pace and called out Merlin's name.

The older man stopped, resting a hand on his companion's shoulder for a moment before turning to face Arto. Merlin was smiling widely and leaned forward on his staff as Arto walked up to join them. A hint of auburn in Merlin's graying hair shown in the sun and the older mage's brown eyes gleamed with amusement as he watched him approach. Arto had no doubt that Merlin could tell how excited he was.

"Good morning Arto," Merlin greeted warmly with a nod. "I see you've heard of our good fortune. Eaban's long awaited son has finally arrived to join us."

Arto nodded and turned his eyes towards the new arrival. Luegáed was intimidating. He was tall like his father, standing several inches above him with dark brown hair held out of his face by a woven band with small beads set into it. His brown eyes had the same softness to them as his father's. After a moment of studying each other, Luegáed bowed to Arto and lowered his eyes.

"It is a pleasure to join your service Mage Arto," Luegáed said formerly, his shoulders tight and his jaw muscles tense.

Shifting in place, Arto fought back the urge to fidget even while being slightly comforted by the knowledge that Luegáed was as nervous as he was. He'd heard a lot about Luegáed from Eaban before the older man returned to his home. Arto supposed it was only natural that Eaban had told Luegáed some stories about him and given the reputation that he was already developing despite only being sixteen the stories might have been a bit exaggerated. It didn't help that Merlin was hiding a smile behind one of his hand.

"It is a pleasure to have you join us, Luegáed son of Eaban," Arto replied with equal formality. "Please do not bow, we are all comrades here, all fighting to free our people."

"Thank you," Luegáed offered as he straightened up, a smile tugging at his lips. "Father has spoken very well of you, and I'm glad to finally be here."

Luegáed's eyes moved to Arto's shoulder and the other young man was looking past him at something. Arto turned slightly to look over his shoulder and smiled as Gwenyvar came walking down the path carrying a basket of reeds. She paused and met Arto's eyes with a smile. Holding out his hand, Arto gestured for her to join them.

"Luegáed, allow me to introduce you to my wife Gwenyvar," Arto said pleasantly as Gwenyvar moved to stand next to him.

He saw a flicker of surprise on Luegáed face, but that was understandable. He and Gwenyvar had been married for a very short time; that news probably hadn't spread very far. Luegáed once again inclined his head and smiled at Gwenyvar.

"A pleasure to meet you Gwenyvar. I trust that you are well?"

"I am very well," Gwenyvar replied with a happy little giggle. "It is wonderful that you have joined us at last Luegáed. Arto has been looking forward to meeting you for some time."

"Thank you both for your kind welcome," Luegáed responded with a widening smile. "I only hope that I can meet your expectations of me."

"I'm sure you'll do fine lad," Merlin assured Luegáed with a chuckle. "But let us get you settled into one of the roundhouses; one of the other warriors, a man named Rosid, has insisted that you move in with him. It's a rather large roundhouse, with just the two of you there will be plenty of room."

"Thank you," Luegáed replied turning his attention to Merlin.

"Luegáed," Arto called to regain his attention. "There is a meeting of the war council this afternoon, I hope that you will join us."

A look of surprise and excitement crossed Luegáed face and Merlin turned his eyes towards Arto. There was no disapproval at his hasty invitation, but some curiosity at Arto's action. Luegáed nodded and gave another small bow, barely containing his smile.

"Of course Arto, I would be honored."

"More reason to get you settled and find an iron weapon for you," Merlin added, touching Luegáed's shoulder again. "Come along."

As Luegáed turned to move down the path with Merlin, Arto heard his mentor ask the new arrival if he preferred swords, spears or axes, but couldn't hear the answer.

"What do you think about Luegáed?" Arto asked, turning to Gwenyvar.

She was looking after their new arrival with a small smile and a curious expression on her face. Hearing the question, she turned back to him with a widening smile.

"He seems very nice," she replied, taking his arm and squeezing it reassuringly. "It is a pity that Eaban couldn't remain; I know you were very fond of him, but Luegáed seems to take after his father and if he is half the warrior that he seems to be then he will be a wonderful addition."

"Do… do you think I was wrong to invite him to the war council?" Arto questioned, watching Gwenyvar's expression. "It just sort of popped out."

"It seemed very sudden," Gwenyvar agreed slowly, but quickly added, "but trust your instincts Arto. I'm sure that Luegáed is a fine young man and it might be a good idea to have the point of view of someone who hasn't been in the thick of things. He might see something that you and the other have missed or have new ideas."

Arto couldn't help but smile widely at Gwenyvar. Leaning down he kissed her quickly making her giggle.

"Thank you."

"You're welcome dear husband, but if you will excuse me, I have things to take care of. Don't forget that your mother wanted to see you for the midday meal."

"I won't," Arto promised, watching his wife turn and walk down the path with her basket against her hip. He sighed happily and glanced towards the forges. Maybe some work in the forges before he saw his mother and the war council would clear his head.

The morning passed in a rush, Arto losing himself in the crashing of hammers around him as he used his magic to pull forth the iron from a pile of stones. He could feel eyes lingering on him throughout the process but was becoming better at ignoring them with each passing day. When his hunger finally forced him to stop, Arto rinsed off his face and hands in the large basin of water kept in the nearby workshop roundhouse for that purpose and headed up the hill towards his mother's roundhouse.

Eigyr hadn't been thrilled when he and Gwenyvar had moved into their own roundhouse but had eagerly accepted his marriage. Pulling back the animal hide door, Arto glanced around the circular room to see if anything had changed. The large set of shelves across from the door now held a delicate bottle of perfume amongst his mother's necklaces and his father's old beard decorations that were still on display.

The fire pit in the center of the space had bright coals flickering gently with packets of leaf-wrapped food set at the edges. The roundhouse still had two beds, one on each side of the roundhouse which Arto doubted would ever change. Even when he'd lived here before his marriage he hadn't slept in his father's old bed, instead sleeping on a more temporary bed that had been taken apart and used for firewood when he was done with it.

"Arto," his mother called as she stood up from a short stool by the fire. A half woven basket in her hands was gently set to the side and she moved towards him with a warm smile.

Eigyr greatly resembled her daughter with the same long brown locks that Morgana had, but hers had streaks of gray. Her features were softer than Morgana's with wrinkles forming around her eyes and mouth and warm brown eyes.

"Hello mother," Arto greeted with a smile, grateful that it was easier to use that word now. When he'd first returned to the village it had been so difficult to connect with his parents. In truth, his father's death was probably the only reason he'd managed to build a warm relationship with his mother. The reminder that she could be taken from him had been a powerful motivator.

His mother's thin arms wrapped around him a moment later and Arto gently returned the embrace, careful of his mother's more fragile form. She stepped away from him after kissing his cheek fondly and gestured to another seat by the fire.

"Sit down Arto, your meal is almost ready."

Doing as she said, Arto sat down on one of the small wooden stools that his mother kept near the fire and watched her move about to tidy things up. Judging from the materials scattered about she'd been weaving more fabric on her loom. His mother handed him a mug of water with a smile and declined his offer of help. There was a lightness in her step and a smile on her face that put him at ease.

"How is Gwenyvar?" Eigyr asked despite the fact that Arto knew she'd seen Gwenyvar earlier that day.

"She is well, Mother," Arto assured her. "Gwenyvar and I are settling into our new roundhouse very well. Yesterday she completed a new blue blanket which adds a nice touch."

"That's lovely dear; I'm so glad you two decided to marry. I know that your sister had some concerns, but it is just so nice to see you happy."

"Well... our marriage did help solidify my alliance with Cailean and prevented me from having to juggle various marriage offers."

"Oh, I remember when Uthyrn was sorting our Morgana's marriage," Eigyr remembered with a laugh. "She had to marry someone who would help keep the family mining authority in place, but your father was very particular about who he allowed to meet her. I think he was relieved when she chose Airril as he was the closest to her in age. Not that the others weren't good men with good positions."

"I think I'm glad I was able to skip that," Arto agreed quickly. "It doesn't sound pleasant."

"Morgana and Airril turned out happy," Eigyr reminded him gently. "Even with your sister leaving him behind for so many years." Eigyr shook her head sadly and sighed loudly. "I just hope that being together now means that they will finally have some children. Morgana can be a little stern, but she'd make such a good mother and Airril is going to need an heir. Of course, it would be lovely if you and Gwenyvar had children soon as well. I'd love to have little children around again."

Arto remained silent and sipped the cool water; he wasn't going to share his theory that Morgana and Airril couldn't have children due to her Changeling half. His mother didn't even know about Morgana's Sídhe side and he wasn't going to risk her reaction to the news. He also didn't want his mother's desire for grandchildren focused on him and Gwenyvar. While he certainly didn't regret marrying her and sealing the alliance between the south and the north, he wasn't in a hurry to have children.

The Sídhe preferred capturing children, humans that they could train and mold to be obedient and accepting of the horrible things that the Sídhe did to them. Arto couldn't take the idea of his own children being targets and he knew Queen Scáthbás who had tormented and trained his sister for years would not hesitate to use his children to get to him. No, for the time being, it was better than he and Gwenyvar remain childless, but in time after the Sídhe were defeated then maybe they could have a real proper family.

His mother called his name, pulling Arto out of his thoughts of the future. Shaking his head, he smiled and apologized to his mother who sighed softly and handed him his lunch. Arto did his best to focus on his mother and answer the questions she asked, reminding himself that there was still a long way to go before the war was over. Starting with the war council and the many details of building a true opposition to the Sídhe.

4

Lunch with an Old Friend

The warm sun was shining overhead as Alex strolled towards Michaels Hall across the neatly trimmed green lawn. Many of her fellow students were out lounging on towels and tossing footballs around. She supposed it was wise of them since autumn would be here soon enough and then winter would hit. Alex kicked lightly at the sidewalk as her stomach grumbled. She and Nicki really needed to properly stock the fridge in their place and Alex needed to make sure that her roommate understood that bread, peanut butter, and grape jelly were necessities, not strawberry jelly. Of course, Nicki had been apologetic, not realizing that she was allergic to strawberries, but it had never come up before.

Walking into Michaels Hall, Alex was hit with a wave of noise and the smell of food which made her stomach rumble more adamantly. Alex handed her student card over to the cashier for a moment and then stepped forward upon its return. Grabbing a tray, she headed straight for the smell of burgers. Once there she placed her order and moved off to the side, waiting impatiently for her food.

Alex sighed softly as she drummed her fingers on the underside of her tray and glanced around. There was a crowd of students working their way through the large Michaels Cafeteria around her. The multiple sections of different kinds of food were all noisy and the smells of burgers, oriental, tacos and desserts were mixing together. School had only been back in session for a few days and already everything seemed to be settling back into the old routine.

"Burger and onion rings, number 22," a monotone voice announced.

Stepping forward, Alex scooped up the small plate with a burger and onion rings on it. She moved away from the booth quickly to let the next set of students step up. Alex glanced around to see if she recognized anyone in the cafeteria. Normally her fellow mages and Arthur would join her for lunch, but everyone had somewhere else they needed to be today. Nicki was having lunch with her grandmother, Bran had a doctor's appointment, Arthur was having lunch with the football team as some kind of bonding in preparation for the coming Saturday game and Aiden was at his family's bookstore so his parents could have lunch together.

A flash of long wavy dark hair teamed with a blue sleeveless shirt made Alex turn her head quickly. She caught a brief glimpse of the profile and inhaled sharply. It was Jenny. Alex was frozen in the middle of the room near the drink machines. Her chest felt tight and a wave of guilt crashed over her, making her knees shake.

Someone bumped her shoulder and Alex snapped back to reality as she instinctively balanced her tray. Alex moved forward quickly towards the carpeted half of the room where rows and rows of tables were laid out, all different sizes. Sunlight streamed in from the large windows on the far side of the cafeteria and Alex stopped and looked around. It took her only a moment to spot Jenny seated alone at a small table near the far wall, hidden back in the shadows.

Swallowing, Alex started to walk towards her former roommate before she could change her mind. Without meaning to she drummed her fingers nervously on the edges of her tray, threatening to spill her soda. The noise level dropped a little as Alex moved past the larger and more crowded tables near the food booths. To Alex's displeasure, she could see that Jenny was mostly just moving the lettuce around on her plate.

"Hello Jenny," Alex greeted nervously as she stepped up next to the small table.

Her former roommate looked up at her sharply, waving black strands of hair falling into her face. Jenny looked tired and stressed with dark circles under her eyes. She lacked the normal vibrancy that Alex had grown used to when they lived together even if she still looked beautiful. Alex suppressed a twitch of envy that Jenny still looked so lovely even when clearly so distressed. She gave Jenny a sheepish smile.

"How are you?" Alex asked softly, trying not to fidget.

"Fine," Jenny replied and Alex noted with relief that she sounded just as nervous. Jenny glanced around and then gestured at the chair across from her. "You'd better sit down."

Nodding, Alex slid down into the seat across from Jenny and carefully set down her tray of food. For a moment neither of them spoke and Alex mustered up all her courage.

"How are classes going?" Alex asked, pushing a strand of blonde hair behind her ear.

"They're fine," Jenny replied softly, picking up her iced tea and taking a sip. "It is nice to be taking more advanced classes. Last year... got a bit boring," Jenny said, her body tensing with her last words.

"It's the same for me I suppose," Alex told her quickly with a forced smile. "I'm finishing my science credits with astronomy this year. Nicki's in that class with me. I have the first lab class tomorrow and I'm not sure what that is going to be like yet."

"Do you have many classes with your friends?" Jenny asked, her voice tight and sad.

"I have a history class on the Enlightenment with Nicki, Bran, and Aiden; it's one of Professor Cornwall's classes. It's just me in Introduction to English Studies, it's a bit boring, but I have to take it for my major. Arthur and I are in the same Spanish class and..." Alex trailed off uncomfortably.

"Let me guess," Jenny sighed softly, "You're all in that Story of King Arthur class aren't you?"

"Guilty," Alex admitted with a grimace. "Mer- Professor Yates is teaching it so it seemed like a good idea."

"I suppose so."

"How about you? Any interesting classes?"

"Well I'm taking French for my language requirements and I'm also taking astronomy." Jenny shifted a little nervously. "What time is your lab tomorrow?"

"3:30 to 5:20 with Professor Clarke."

"Oh then I guess we're in the same astronomy lab," Jenny replied with a small shrug. "I uh... changed some of my classes over the summer."

"Why?" Alex flinched at her own question. "I see, you're... uh."

"Avoiding Lance is the phrase you're looking for," Jenny muttered as she roughly speared several leaves of lettuce. "Then I've got Macroeconomics class and a broadcasting and digital media class."

"Nice," Alex replied with a nod and a forced smile, mentally noting that Jenny wasn't talking to Lance either. "So where are you living this year?" Alex asked as she picked up one of her onion rings.

"I'm in Upham Hall, I've got a single room which is nice. My neighbor, a junior named Maria and I share a connecting bathroom." There was a small smile on Jenny's face. "I like it, I've set up the spare bed as a sort of sofa and the two wardrobes are really nice, I haven't had to use under the bed storage rollers for my clothes. And I get to keep my stuff in the bathroom instead of carrying it down the hall all the time."

"I know what you mean, Nicki and I are in a small suite together in Gallagher so we have our own bathroom. We've had to add some storage space, but it is nice not having to sort what I want each time I go to the bathroom. I don't miss having to wear flip-flops either."

"So you and Nicki are living together," Jenny observed with a slightly surprised expression. "Don't you worry that…"

"No, I don't worry about people thinking we're together. Sure Nicki's gay, but she's a really good friend and besides if people were going to think that then they would have thought it last May when I moved in with her. Thinking that now when we've got two bedrooms and I have a-" Alex stopped herself and then added with a nervous laugh, "Well it would be silly and besides, I think I'd be rather flattered by the assumption."

"Really?"

"Well Nicki is very attractive, smart and athletic, but between us she prefers brunettes. Of the two of us, you're more her type."

"Oh," Jenny replied with slightly wide eyes. She shook her head and laughed softly before taking a bite of her salad.

For a few moments, they ate in silence, both of them glancing at each other every now and again. Alex's stomach was twisting around on itself, making eating feel like a serious chore which was a shame since the burger was pretty good. Wiping her hands off on a napkin, Alex cleared her throat to get Jenny's attention and swallowed nervously.

"Jenny… look I feel that I should let you know that Arthur and I have started to see each other. As boyfriend and girlfriend. My responsibilities as a mage mean that I won't be around him with the football team too often, but I will be around and with you on the Spirit Squad-"

"Look, Alex," Jenny sighed uncomfortably, cutting Alex off. "If it's my blessing you want then you've got it. You were a good friend to Arthur, you clearly liked him and I'm not so petty as to think that you were always thinking of how to steal him from me. After what happened I'm glad that he has your support."

"Jenny I'm so sorry-"

"But understand that I'm not ready to be friends," Jenny said sharply cutting Alex off again. "All summer I was left rethinking almost everything I've done in my whole life. I've been trying to remember what started my relationship with Arthur and if I really ever wanted Lance. If I really ever wanted either of them or if it was always just some…. echo from another woman." Jenny inhaled deeply even as she trembled. Her eyes dropped to her plate. "So I'm not ready to act like I can play nice and put it all behind me, not yet."

"Okay," Alex agreed gently. "We're not friends, okay. But please Jenny if you ever need anything then maybe you can think of me as someone who feels they wronged you in the past and feels an obligation to help you."

"That might just be worse," Jenny grumbled, but she lifted her head and managed a small smile. "But alright, I'll give that a try."

Jenny's phone chirped at her making both of them jump in their seats. Pulling it out, Jenny hit a button on the phone and began to stand up. "I've got to go," Jenny apologized. "Take care, Alex."

"You too," Alex said biting back the urge to add for her to get some sleep. It wasn't her place anymore.

Jenny turned and began to walk away, but stopped and turned back to Alex with an odd expression. She took two steps to come back to the table and moved closer to Alex. Straightening up, Alex tried not to look surprised and seem friendly.

"One more thing, a friendly warning I suppose," Jenny remarked with a sad chuckle. "You're dating Arthur now and the distance will help protect you, but watch out for his mother."

"His mother," Alex repeated carefully.

"Elaine Pendred, very wealthy and very successful business woman who is known as the dragon in her social and business circles. She's a little… insane when it comes to her son. When I first started dating him she interrogated me several times over dinner and I'm pretty sure she had a detective check out my family. I suppose to make sure that I was good enough for her son."

Alex's eyebrows shot up and she really hoped that Jenny was kidding, but her former roommate wasn't done.

"She calls Arthur twice a day, has the decency to call around classes, but if you're with him when she calls then be warned that your job is being quiet while Arthur tries to calm her down and assure her that he's fine despite not living with her anymore. He tries to hide this of course, but if you're dating him then you'll find out about the dragon soon enough." Jenny shrugged and added, "I think it's cause his father died before he was born, but she is obsessive about her son." Jenny turned and started walking away, "Like I said, just a little warning."

Then Jenny was gone, lost in the crowd of students who were moving between tables with their trays of food. Slumping back in her chair, Alex exhaled slowly and closed her eyes. A moment later her own phone chirped and Alex pulled it out. Holding it up to her ear, Alex answered the phone with a tired greeting.

"Are you okay?" Arthur's warm voice asked, causing Alex to perk up slightly.

"I just… well, I sort of had lunch with Jenny," Alex admitted as she looked down at her half-eaten burger. "It was awkward."

"I'm sorry."

"It's not your fault," Alex reminded him with a shake of her head. "And it's not my fault. That's just how things are going to be for a while."

"How was she otherwise?" Arthur asked carefully.

"She looked tired," Alex told him, letting her own worry show to reassure Arthur that she wasn't jealous. "I doubt she'd been sleeping well since she returned."

"Damn," Arthur hissed on the other end. "Well, thanks for trying. Jenny probably just needs some time and space."

"I let her know that she could still come to me."

"Thank you for that Alex, even before we dated and all this happened she was a good friend to me."

"Of course Arthur."

"Well I've got to get back to the team," Arthur said with a chuckle. "I just slipped away for a moment. I'll see you in Spanish."

"See you in Spanish," Alex repeated before the call ended.

Picking up the last onion ring, Alex bit into it and smiled when she felt a flicker of appetite return. Alex polished off the onion ring and picked up the remaining half of the burger, biting into it with determination. She'd done what she could today and for now, that would just have to be enough. Still, Alex's free hand dropped to her bag and after a moment of fumbling traced the tip of the hilt of her iron dagger, safely secured and in reach. Alex realized with a sigh that she was becoming paranoid about things going too well. She was braced for something terrible to happen like the Sídhe or their mysterious new Old One foe attacking soon. She rolled her eyes at her own thoughts and forced herself to focus on the burger before it went completely cold.

5

Lunch at the Boscos

"This is going to be weird," Alex whined from the backseat of his truck behind him. "Your dad's a professor and he teaches our fencing club."

"And he likes you," Aiden assured Alex as he tapped the brakes as they pulled up to the bridge intersection by the campus. "Besides you're in astronomy, not his class. And spending time with Morgana and Merlin doesn't bother you."

"The Boscos are great," Nicki added from her spot next to Alex. In the rearview mirror, Aiden saw her patting Alex's arm. "You've met them before."

"Very briefly: they were on their way to a funeral and I've only interacted with your mom at the bookstore."

"Look my folks just thought a barbecue to celebrate the first week of school would be nice," Aiden reminded them. "They just want a chance to make you guys feel welcome."

"And let's not forget that because we're having a lunch time barbecue with Aiden's folks today that we don't have to start magic lessons yet," Nicki added.

"Still I sort of understand Alex's nervousness," Bran chimed in from the front passenger seat. "What if we let something slip?"

"Then something slips," he answered, gripping the wheel a little tighter. "We won't be able to keep our magical lives a secret forever." His truck full of passengers fell silent and Aiden sighed loudly. "Look, guys, I'm sorry-"

"We're all edgy about our families," Nicki interrupted. "It's natural, they are our families and we love them. None of us have ever had to worry about keeping secrets from them. But that's part of growing up, isn't it? Moving out and building your own life, natural and a little scary."

"Most people don't have to worry about the Sídhe and huge nightmare creatures," Bran muttered.

"The dreams still bad?" Nicki asked, leaning forward to put a hand on Bran's shoulder.

"No, I only have them on occasion," Bran assured Nicki with a soft sigh. "But I don't really have a good description for Morgana and Merlin yet. It's just a big dark shape, nothing that helps identify it. I know they're getting frustrated."

"Well it is hard to plan a defense for something you don't have identified," Alex conceded from the back. "But we appreciate the warning that your vision gave us."

Aiden nodded but didn't say anything more. Bran's last vision at the end of the school year had warned them that an Old One was heading for Ravenslake, but he'd also been stabbed from behind by a sword in the vision. Aiden knew he wasn't the only one worried about just what that might mean for them.

"We're here," Nicki called in a sweet tone. "Come on mages, smile and enjoy the food. Aiden's dad is really good on the barbecue and his mom told me that he was even going to make ribs."

Aiden pulled the truck up to the curb, noting that there were a few other cars he didn't recognize parked around on the street.

He saw Bran frown slightly and look towards a dark blue SUV parked across the street, but his friend just chuckled and shook his head. Everyone climbed out of Aiden's blue truck quickly.

Laurel Street was a calm street just off of Riverside drive, close enough to the university that his father usually walked when the weather was nice, but far enough away that there wasn't a lot of noise. The handsome two-story light yellow house that he'd grown up in had a decent sized front yard with a large crabapple tree. The dark blue door that his mother repainted every summer without fail was open with only the screen door securing the house. Even at the street, Aiden could already hear voices and people laughing.

"Who else is here?" Nicki asked as the group started up the sidewalk to the house.

"I don't know, but it sounds like they're out back," Aiden replied with a shrug, leading his friends towards the gate of the chain link fence that surrounded the backyard.

Pulling open the gate, Aiden waved his friends through and smiled when he heard the Bosco family dog Charlie barking happily. Alex gave Aiden a small smile as she passed him, but didn't move forward any further until Nicki took the lead. Aiden paused and closed the gate behind him once everyone was through and followed his friends onto the large back patio that took up a third of their yard.

"Mom!?" he heard Alex squeak loudly, her voice becoming oddly high pitched. "Daddy?"

"Surprise!" His own parents shouted, laughing loudly.

Aiden's eyes widened as he watched Alex launch herself towards a middle aged couple who were grinning at her. Bran was quickly pulled into a hug by a short Asian woman with a warm round face and black hair tied back in a messy bun and thick glasses. Samantha Russell was a lovely older woman with graying short hair, bright handmade jewelry and simple, but attractive clothing who quickly hugged Nicki tightly.

"Gran," Nicki laughed, pulling back from her grandmother's hug to look towards the strangers with their friends. "Did you help with this?"

"I may have helped Shannon organize this," Nicki's grandmother replied with a wink.

Aiden grinned, looking towards his father who was standing by their barbecue in a novelty apron. His mother was standing next to him with an equally wide grin and strands of her light brown hair falling into her face.

"I can't believe you guys came all the way from Spokane," Alex exclaimed, capturing his attention again.

"We've been waiting to meet your friends," the man he assumed was her father said, wrapping an arm around Alex's shoulder.

"Yes, so please introductions," the blonde woman next to her added.

Smiling, Aiden stepped forward and extended his hand to Alex's father.

"Nice to meet you, I'm Aiden Bosco, Shannon and John's son."

"I'm Elizabeth Adams," Alex's mother replied warmly as Aiden noted the strong resemblance between mother and daughter.

Alex's father took his hand and gave it a firm shake. Aiden noted that Alex's gray eyes seemed to have come from her father.

"I'm Michael Adams, good to meet you Aiden."

"Brandon Fisher, better known as Bran," their fellow mage said as he stepped up next to them. "Good to meet you both."

"Let's see Bran you're the physics major, right?" Alex's mom asked curiously. "And Aiden you're engineering? Uh, electrical engineering?"

"That's right Doctor Adams, on both counts," Bran replied with a nod.

"Oh Elizabeth please," Alex's mom told them with a smile before her eyes moved to Nicki who nearly skipped over to them. "And you must be Nicki."

"Nicole Russell at your service," Nicki replied with a beaming smile and a little bow. "Pleasure to meet you both."

Bran stepped back from them and moved over to his mother, putting an arm around her. Aiden noted with a chuckle that his friend rather towered over his mother. While he'd seen a photo of the woman in their dorm room up close like this he could see the subtle facial features that Bran had inherited from his mother.

"And this is my mother Jinsung Fisher," Bran informed them cheerfully.

The process repeated with all of his friends greeting Bran's mother, then everyone moved on to Nicki's grandmother although they'd all met her in passing at least once. His little sister Aisling was brought forward to meet everyone before she vanished inside with his mother to bring out the main course for barbecuing. Stepping away from the others, Aiden headed for the large folding table that was covered with a plastic blue tablecloth on the far side of the patio. Plates of crackers, chips, and cheese were set out beside a pitcher filled with red punch. Seeing nothing else to drink at the moment, Aiden poured himself a glass and leaned against the side of the house to watch the proceedings.

His mother's punch was a little too sweet, Aiden thought as he sipped the bright red liquid from the tall glass he'd grabbed from the table. That was probably due to Aisling helping with getting everything ready: his little sister did have quite the sweet tooth. Aiden was more than a little surprised that she'd managed to keep the secret that Alex and Bran's parents were traveling to Ravenslake for this get-together. Then again, it was possible that his parents hadn't told her that. Taking another sip, he had to admit it wasn't too bad and once the burgers, hot dogs and ribs were off the grill the barbecue taste would help dull the overly sweet tingling in his mouth. Aiden lingered by the door and observed the others with a small smile.

Alex was standing in the shade of his mother's lilac bushes talking with her parents and, judging from the smile on her face, Alex was more than happy to see them. The tension that had been in her shoulders since her lunch with Jenny on Wednesday was finally gone. Alex had been in such a knot that she'd let a new freshman member of the fencing club beat her at Wednesday night's meeting.

His father, Professor John Bosco, was engaged in a loud cheerful conversation with Bran's mother, Jinsung Fisher, who had driven down from Eugene about his chemistry classes at the college. But Jinsung's eyes kept flickering over to where her son was engaged in a conversation with his own mother Shannon Bosco about a book series that they'd both read with his mother promising to hold a copy of the latest book when it came in at their family bookstore. Aiden was beginning to see why Bran had been interested in going to a school a decent distance away from his mother as Jinsung wouldn't fully relax despite Bran being only a few feet away. He wondered how often she called and if she was as bad as Arthur's mother supposedly was.

Though when Bran moved and the metal of his leg brace clanged against the side of a patio chair, Aiden saw a flash of guilt on Jinsung's face. Grimacing slightly, Aiden remembered that Jinsung had been the one driving the car during the accident that hurt Bran. His friend's magic had manifested for a moment, giving him a brief vision of the danger. Bran had grabbed the wheel, saving his and his mother's life, but had suffered the injuries to his leg and groin so perhaps Jinsung's overprotective tendencies were understandable.

"I can't believe you didn't tell me you were coming," Alex laughed, her voice cutting into his thoughts as she and her parents stepped back onto the patio, heading for the punch.

"We wanted to surprise you," her father replied with a small shrug and a pleased smile.

"The look your face was brilliant," her mother added with a laugh as she put an arm around her daughter. "Besides we felt bad for not being able to come down when you moved in. Plus, like we said, we wanted to meet your friends. There isn't the opportunity to know your college friends like we did your high school ones."

"After all, despite having video calls the four of you got together in June," her father added with a curious glance towards him and Bram.

"Yeah well, you know just meeting up for a quick visit," Alex insisted nervously, her shoulder tensing slightly. "And Arthur was still in town then so it was nice to see him."

Aiden paused, noticing a curious expression being shared amongst the parents. He nearly flinched, recognizing the expression of worry coloring each of their expressions. Bran's mother was biting her lip, his father's smile had fallen away and Alex's mother was gripping her shoulder tightly. They knew that something was up, that much Aiden was confident about. Somehow parents knew when their children were keeping something from them. He looked towards his own parents as his mother brought a plate of cheese over to his father.

"Well it's nice that you've made such good friends," Elizabeth remarked with a smile, breaking the tension a little. "And it's nice to meet Samantha and the Boscos."

"Oh, are they going to spy for you now?"

"Spy is such a strong word," Elizabeth countered. "More like just keep an eye on things. After all, as much as I'd like to see Arthur again, this time as your boyfriend, your father and I can't stay more than tonight."

'We just want to be sure you're safe and happy," Michael added warmly. "It's important to be happy where you're at and with what you're doing."

"Well, you two shouldn't worry so much about Alex," Nicki's grandmother Samantha informed them as she and Nicki moved over to join them. "She and Nicki are such good friends that I consider her an honorary grandchild just like Aiden. If anything were to ever happen I'd be there in minutes. After all, she already stayed with us when the kids got together for that little visit in June."

Aiden chuckled as Nicki and Alex shared a look, but bit his lip to make sure that the girls couldn't hear him. He knew from experience growing up with her that Nicki could be very frightening and given Alex's record in battle against the Sídhe he wasn't interested in making either of them angry with him. After all, they lived together now and would have lots of time to plan their revenge, and Nicki would probably get Aisling to help.

"That's very kind of you Samantha," Elizabeth replied with a smile. "Not that I'm worried of course. Alex had a pretty good freshman year. Her grades were solid, she made friends, joined a club and intermural sports and now she has a boyfriend." Elizabeth turned her attention to her daughter with a teasing smile and added, "Pity he couldn't join us today."

"Like I said Arthur's off in San Diego with the team."

Aiden grinned, Alex sounded very relieved about that. Then again he couldn't blame the girl, she was probably still trying to explain how she'd ended up dating the boy that her parents had met last year when he'd been her roommate boyfriend.

"They're good kids," his father announced as he placed the cheese on the burgers. "Even if they are a bit secretive," he added with a dramatic wink to Aiden.

Raising his glass in a mock toast, Aiden gave his father a teasing smile and listened with relief as the conversations shifted back to questions about classes and professors. His father hummed loudly when Bran complained about not being able to really understand what his Modern Physics professor was saying due to his thick Chinese accent. With his own parents occupied with food, Aiden wandered over to refill his punch.

The others were laughing now, talking loudly with energy, but Aiden couldn't shake the split second look that had appeared on his own parents' face. There had been a shadow, a hint of nervousness and worry that he recognized from years back when Aisling had first gotten sick before they'd known how bad it really was. His parents were worried about something: they knew he wasn't telling them something. Sure he wasn't really lying to them, but he was hiding a huge part of his life.

"So what's going on?" Aisling asked, coming up behind him.

Aiden jumped at the sudden intrusion to his thoughts and turned to look at his little sister. The preteen girl was looking up at him suspiciously with the green eyes that they'd both inherited from their mother. Her long dark blonde hair was up in a more complicated French braid that made her look even younger.

"Hey sis," he greeted with a wide smile.

"Hello bro," Aisling returned, raising an eyebrow. "Again, what's going on?"

"A family barbecue with my friends and their families and me being a little worried about just how much professor authority dad threw around to get their contact information."

"Please, Dad didn't look them up I did. And no school records were necessary. There's this thing called the internet, I'm pretty sure you've heard of it."

"You're catty today," Aiden remarked, a smile tugging at his lips. "Any reason in particular?"

"You're hiding something," Aisling observed with a tilt of her head as she put her hands on her hips. "You and your friends.

Something is up and you're not telling. Mom and Dad have noticed, but they keep saying it's just college stuff."

"It is," Aiden insisted, straightening up against the side of the house. "I'm just trying to have a little independence despite just living across town from you guys."

Aisling gave him a doubtful look but slowly nodded as she sighed, "Fine Aiden, keep your secrets. Just don't get into trouble."

"I'm the older sibling, I'm the one who's supposed to say things like that," Aiden protested with a laugh. Aisling shrugged halfheartedly. Reaching over, Aiden wrapped an arm around his sister and tugged her closer. Her head barely came up to his chest, but she relaxed against him. "Don't worry so much Aisling," Aiden told her gently. "I know things have been changing, but I love you and mom and dad. I won't do anything that will cause this family to fall apart."

"I know, I just have a bad feeling," Aisling whispered, her words almost lost in the fabric of his shirt.

Not for the first time, Aiden was left wondering if his little sister might not have a touch of magic in her. He pushed the thought aside, not wanting Aisling's unease to have any impact on reality. Instead, he rubbed her back for a moment before setting his hand carefully on her crown of braids.

"Don't worry so much little sis, I'm right here and I've got good friends in addition to you and the parents. I'm doing great."

"Alright everyone," his father's booming voice called over the yard. "Come and get your burgers and hotdogs! The ribs need a couple of more minutes."

"Come on sis," Aiden called, bumping his sister's shoulder gently. "Barbequed food by Dad, what could be better?"

His sister gave him a look, letting him know that he wasn't off the hook just yet, but did smile at him. Aiden sighed softly in relief, catching Alex's eye and nodding to her. Without a word about secrets, magic or potential danger everyone gathered around to fill their plates and find seats around the patio for lunch.

6

War Council

806 B.C.E. Northern Cornwall

Arto's roundhouse was tidy with his most important treasures displayed properly on the stone shelves beyond the hearth. The only exception was Cathanáil which was strapped to his back as he never allowed the sword to be too far from him now. Gwenyvar was finishing a new basket, having already cleaned up the spare reeds and put away her weaving for the evening. She kept glancing towards the doorway, assuring Arto that she was a little nervous as well.

The war council meetings had been happening for months now. Naturally, he spoke with the others frequently about everything, but the village seemed to like seeing them gather together one night each week. He supposed it assured them that progress was being made, reassured them that the leadership that had emerged from the gaggle of regional leaders had a strong sense of what was happening.

In the end it hadn't been difficult. There was himself, Merlin and Morgana of course. His brother-in-law Airril had remained in the village as a representative of his area while his cousin oversaw things at home. Medraut was the official leader of their own village even if many did defer to him as Uthyrn's son. Thus far his cousin had been very patient and Arto made sure to direct anyone with concerns about their region alone to his cousin. His long absence from his father's life had made it impossible for him to remain his father's heir and so far he thought that Medraut was doing a fine job.

"They'll be here soon," Gwenyvar observed as she finished the top coil of the basket and set it to the side, just at the foot of her bed. She stood and brushed off her dress and brushed a strand of hair behind her ear.

Nodding, Arto rose from his place on his own bed and picked up the small stools they kept up against the wall of the roundhouse. While his wife pulled small packets of vegetables out of the fire, Arto placed the stools around the fire in a large circle. When that was done, he covered each stool with a small fur to make them a little more comfortable. Small mugs filled with water were placed by each seat and Gwenyvar nodded in satisfaction as she looked over the setup.

"Are you nervous?" Gwenyvar asked, looking over at him. "About Luegáed I mean?"

"A little," he confessed with a small smile. "But it makes sense; the western isle needs to be heard on these matters." Arto ran a hand through his brown hair making it tickle his lower neck. "We have you to speak for the north." His wife blushed, pleased at her position. "Ideally I'd like someone who is from the eastern lowlands as well, but we'll see what happens."

"I'm sure that it will be fine," Gwenyvar assured him with a soft smile, moving closer to him.

Her hands came up to rest on his chest and Gwenyvar looked at him, respect glowing in her brown eyes. Arto straightened up and smiled in return. His heart was beating a little faster as he brought a hand up to rest on hers and squeezed it gently. Gwenyvar nodded to demonstrate that she understood his silent gratitude. The sounds of people moving outside made them both pause for a moment before Gwenyvar leaned forward to kiss his lips quickly before she stepped away.

"Arto," Merlin's voice called from outside the house in warning.

Moving to the doorway, Arto quickly pulled back the animal pelt that kept the wind out of their home and gestured for Merlin to come inside. His mentor was holding a small glowing orb of magic in his hand and just behind him, Arto could see Luegáed eyeing the magical orb with a mixture of awe and nervousness. Containing a laugh, Arto reminded himself sternly that Luegáed probably had only seen magic once or twice in his life. While many priests had some abilities, the power and control at Merlin and Morgana's level were unheard of.

"Welcome, please come inside," Arto greeted with a respectful nod. He stepped back enough to allow Merlin and Luegáed inside while still holding the flap.

Luegáed had to bend over slightly to pass through the doorway but straightened up once he was inside. Once again, he gave Gwenyvar a small bow of greeting as Merlin greeted Gwenyvar with a soft kiss to her cheek and withdrew a small pouch from his belt which he handed to her. Arto didn't see what it contained, but Gwenyvar smiled pleasantly and thanked him.

"Luegáed and I met on the path here, Morgana and Airril should be only a short ways behind us," Merlin informed Arto as the animal pelt fell back into place over the doorway.

"And Medraut?"

"Oh, I'm sure he'll turn up," Merlin answered as he settled down onto one of the stools. He dug his staff into the crushed earth floor, creating a small hole for it to rest in before he leaned forward on it.

Arto shook his head and exchanged a glance with Gwenyvar. Merlin never sat in the same seat meaning that they had a ring of holes forming around the hearth. Arto privately wondered if Merlin had created some sort of new protection circle or seal against the Sídhe, but Gwenyvar was certain that Merlin did it just for a private chuckle. Either way, Arto had no interest in pestering Merlin about it.

"So Luegáed, how has your first day been?" Arto asked pleasantly, turning his attention to the newcomer.

"Very busy, but informative. Everyone in this village is very dedicated to the war and welcoming," Luegáed answered quickly.

"And your lodgings are comfortable?"

"They are," Luegáed replied with a nod. "I brought few things with me, but I am very comfortable."

The sound of more people coming up towards the house kept Arto from trying to calm Luegáed's nervousness. Moving back to the doorway, he pulled back the pelt enough to see his sister and Airril coming up the pathway with Medraut trailing behind them with a torch. He held back the door and his sister stepped inside gracefully, the light orb in her hand extinguishing as she walked closer to the hearth to give her husband room to join her. Medraut came inside after a moment, having extinguished the torch in the dirt outside. Arto reached forward and took the torch from his cousin, carefully placing it inside a clay pot where no embers could cause trouble.

There was a tension in the air that Arto couldn't quite understand. It was like everyone was braced for something, but no one said anything. Luegáed was shifting nervously, his eyes darting around and inspecting each of the other people in the room. Giving his new friend a small smile, Arto made a tiny nod and moved over towards his own seat. He caught Medraut eyeing Luegáed with a frown and nearly shook his head at his cousin's standoffish nature. Airril and Morgana moved across the Roundhouse together and Arto smiled when he caught sight of their hands linked together. He glanced over towards Gwenyvar who was on the far of the circle, opposite him, but she missed his look as she studied Luegáed.

"Welcome friends, sister, brother, and cousin," Arto greeted politely, giving his own family members respectful nods. "Tonight we welcome another member to this council, Luegáed son of Eaban. I have invited him so that the western isle has a voice in these matters."

That statement made Medraut press his lips, but his cousin said nothing. Satisfied that his cousin understood his actions better now, Arto looked around the circle, his eyes lingering on his wife for a moment.

"Is there anything to report?"

"The forges have successfully produced ten more iron swords and fifteen iron axe heads," Merlin announced with a small smile. "Unless there is an objection they will be sent east to the lowlands."

"What about other areas still in need of iron?" Airril asked with a hint of concern. "We're spreading the iron arms awfully thin."

"I'm afraid that we're still not producing enough to well arm all areas," Merlin conceded with a nod. "But there has been increased Sídhe activity in the lowlands. Nothing elaborate, just raiding parties grabbing humans and vanishing. I'm afraid the flatter terrain makes it easier for them."

"I have no objections," Arto said as he looked around the circle. "But I would note that I think the next supply should go to the western isle. We've barely sent any iron there and the Sídhe have always been active there."

"Indeed Arto," Luegáed agreed with a small relieved smile on his face. "Our priests are a little more adept at using blood signs to keep the Sídhe at bay, but we can do very little else against them."

"I remember," Arto replied as he briefly recalled the time he'd spent on the western isle with Merlin. The isle had some of the oldest sites of respect and it was said that the priests born to the isle were more powerful. Arto didn't believe that, but he knew their willingness to shed their own blood gave them an edge. "We almost have enough of our magic iron to create another gate, are there thoughts on which tunnel we should target?"

"One of the low-lying tunnels," Morgana insisted. "The Sídhe have created a tunnel near the Great Circles by the river. Even if they haven't taken many people through the tunnel yet having them so near such an important site is disgusting."

"I agree with Morgana," Merlin remarked with a nod of approval. "Rumors of this tunnel are spreading quickly and lowering morale. We finally have the population willing to believe we can fight the Sídhe, we can't allow this tunnel to undermine that."

There were nods of agreement around the fire and Arto tried not to let his relief show. The creation of gates was a huge process of magic and even some politics. Everyone wanted certain areas protected, even his war council. It was nice to have such an easy decision for once.

"I confess, though," Luegáed chimed in with a slight look of embarrassment. "My understanding of how these gates are made is very poor. We've heard very little of the process on the western isle and my father's knowledge was lacking."

Arto opened his mouth to speak, but Merlin had already begun to explain the process of making the gates. Falling silent, Arto did his best to stay still on his stool and listened to the discussion around the fire. Merlin and Morgana explained the process of infusing magic into the iron and then how Arto shaped it to form the gate over the Sídhe tunnels. Luegáed seemed disturbed to learn that he was the only one who could perform that magical task. This was followed by questions about his safety, a subject that Arto hated whenever it came up.

"This village is walled and despite the Sídhe knowing it is the site of the iron foundries they have pulled back from the area. I daresay even the Queen has trouble getting her Riders to attack a place where nearly everyone has an iron weapon. Arto leaves this village only with myself and Morgana," Merlin assured Luegáed. "When traveling to make a gate we stay very close to him even though Arto does have his own magic. His wife Gwenyvar and mother Eigyr remain in the village with warriors armed with iron to ensure that they are not captured."

"And I carry an iron sword and iron axe," Medraut added with a proud smile. "With them, I am capable of protecting myself."

Luegáed glanced towards Medraut, his expression completely neutral as he nodded, but Arto thought he caught a hint of irritation in Luegáed's eyes. He looked towards Medraut and nearly laughed at the petulant expression on his cousin's face.

"Is there anything more that needs discussion at this time?" Arto asked loudly to regain everyone's attention. "The decision for the shipment of new weapons has been made and the location of the next gate has been determined."

"I don't believe there is anything else," Medraut answered as he puffed up slightly. "Our forces here are settling nicely into their roles. There is talk of expanding iron ore production; we're having trouble extracting enough to keep up with demand. Food production has been going well and we have enough stored to make it through the winter months so I expect no problems."

"We may need to establish a second production village," Airril remarked with a glance towards Medraut before looking back to Arto. "Distance between us and other villages is becoming an issue."

"And should the Sídhe decide to launch a major attack then it would be best if there were multiple sources of iron," Morgana added with a nod.

"The western isle or the northlands would be good choices," Merlin said thoughtfully as he looked into the fire. "Travel between them by ship is fast and they have a high concentration of Sídhe tunnels there due to the terrain."

"It will have to wait a few months, though," Medraut insisted. "The best thing would be to send one of our masters to the new location to start construction of the smelters and forges. They could also start training men there. That way we don't upset our own production."

"Agreed," Arto replied with a nod of approval. "Medraut please start checking to see who would be willing to move either to the northlands or the western isle. We'll send out word that we need a location that can be protected and see what information we get."

There was a low chorus of agreement from around the fire and Arto did his best not to sigh. Meetings were almost painful, it was so much easier to just confront the Sídhe and fight them rather than having to talk about it all the time. There were moments he missed Merlin being in charge, simply being told when and where they were going.

"If there is nothing else, this meeting is over. Thank you, everyone."

Luegáed rose first, giving a slight bow to Arto once again before he moved over to the doorway. He stopped and lingered nervously, suddenly remembering that he'd come with Merlin and thus had no torch. Arto heard Merlin chuckle and rise from his seat. His mentor nodded in farewell to the others before moving to join Luegáed. Arto watched as Merlin created a new orb of light and Luegáed drew back the pelt, watching the sparking magic with fascination. Then Medraut stepped forward and extended his hand to him. The two of them gripped each other's forearms for a moment before Medraut stepped over to the doorway and retrieved his torch. Using the hearth fire, Medraut relit the torch and left the roundhouse.

"So," Arto asked, looking over at his sister eagerly. "What did you think of Luegáed?"

Morgana paused at the question, her eyes focusing on the now empty doorway with a pondering expression. Her lips were tight and Airril glanced towards Arto with a hint of worry.

"I'm not certain yet," Morgana finally replied. "He seems like a good and capable young man, but I caution you brother, do not trust too easily."

"Morgana, you don't even trust Medraut and he's family," Arto countered with a chuckle.

"He is your father's nephew," Morgana reminded Arto, her green eyes flashing in the light of the fire. "He is no relation of mine. I tolerate him for the sake of you and mother."

"Proving that we are truly loved by the ancestors to have her trust and love us," Airril added with a small forced laugh, gently placing a hand on his wife's arm. "We're not going to determine the value of Luegáed tonight Morgana; the only thing we can do is move forward and see what happens."

A soft sigh escaped Morgana, but she nodded in resignation. Leaning over, she kissed Arto quickly on the cheek, having to lean up a little due to his recent growth. Privately he hoped to grow a little more but knew that he was probably doomed to be shorter and smaller than his imposing father had been. Airril nodded to him and then he and his wife stepped out of the roundhouse, Morgana summoning forth a small orb of light to guide their way.

Letting the flap drop, Arto breathed deeply before he turned to Gwenyvar and asked, "And what did you think of Luegáed?"

"I liked him," his wife answered simply, giving him a sweet smile. "I think that he will be very pleasant to have around."

Grinning, Arto stepped forward and kissed his wife gently, pulling her into a warm embrace. As her arms came around him, Arto felt a little of the tension drain away. He exhaled gratefully, pushing away all thoughts of the Sídhe, gates, and alliances.

7

Training in the Hills

Alex inhaled deeply as she followed Aiden up onto a flatter piece of trail, catching her breath quickly and resisting the urge to turn around and check on Bran, knowing he wouldn't appreciate it. Her feet were beginning to ache a bit and she was rethinking this day hike idea of theirs.

"I'm sorry you couldn't spend more time with your parents," Aiden offered as he came to a stop in front of her and pulled out his water bottle.

All around them the trees swayed in a light breeze, their leaves sounding like the ocean over their heads as beams of sunlight found their way through. A few feet ahead, the leafed trees of the lower part of the hills started to become scarcer as pine trees took over the landscape. The smell of pine was filling Alex's nose and lungs.

"It's fine," Alex replied as she paused by a mossy rock and reached to her small backpack for her own water bottle. "But it was nice to have breakfast with them before they had to leave. Daddy had a meeting Monday morning that he had to prepare for, otherwise, they probably would have stayed longer."

"But it was nice to see them?" Aiden asked, sounding a touch nervous.

Laughing, Alex nodded and reached out to smack Aiden's shoulder playfully as she assured him, "Yes it was nice, a bit weird to have all of our parents together at once, but it was nice."

"Yeah," Aiden agreed, his smile a little sad and distant.

Alex didn't have to ask why, it was the same reason that she felt bittersweet about her parents visiting. It had been nice to see them again, the homesickness of leaving home after a whole summer of her mother's cooking, Dad's barbecues, family jokes and even just spending time with her brothers Matt and Ed, had been nagging at her for the last week. But it was wrong to have them in Ravenslake somehow. It was a part of her life, the magic and the danger posed by the Sídhe and whatever else was coming, that her family didn't belong in.

Maybe she was protecting them and keeping her parents from having to worry about her. Maybe she was just being selfish so that a part of her life remained calm and normal so that she had a place to go and not have to worry about being a mage. She wasn't sure and as Aiden started up the trail again, Alex shoved the question out of her mind, not really wanting to know the answer. It was a pretty day and she could pretend that they were just a group of friends out on a nice day hike.

The trail became steeper up ahead, twisting around the curve of the rocky hill and Alex had to wonder just how the Sídhe steeds were able to get down from here and into the city. Those large horses certainly seemed light on their feet and even in hiking boots, she was having some trouble keeping her footing.

"Almost there," Aiden called back to them.

"Why did I let you talk us into this?" Bran despaired from behind Alex.

Glancing behind her, Alex gave Bran a small supportive smile. Her friend was leaning heavily on a tall walking stick that Aiden had presented him when they'd arrived at the trailhead.

"Did you come up here last time?" Alex asked, turning her attention back to the trail.

"No, Nicki and I stayed down on the lower slope of the hill," Bran answered in a slightly winded voice. "Only Aiden went up to the tunnel with Morgana and Merlin."

"Which was good given how many of them got past us," Aiden added from the front.

"That was a rough night," Nicki groaned, her voice carrying a slight hint of a whine. "Stumbling around in the hills in the dark was not fun."

"That is the nice thing about daytime," Bran agreed. "You can see where you are going and the Sídhe can't stand the strong direct light of a sunny day."

"And here we are," Aiden called from ahead of them. "A lovely empty and flat place to practice our magic without any risk of hurting our dorm rooms or being seen."

Following Aiden up, Alex stepped over the crest of the slope. The side of the hill had been flattened by the Sídhe as they created their last tunnel. Already the old opening in the hillside had caved in, but Alex knew that a gleaming magical gate made of iron was hidden just below the surface and was keeping the Sídhe out. The flat area that had once been barren of plant life due to the alien magic seeping through from the opening was starting to show signs of renewal. Around them in the trees, Alex could hear birds and had seen insects flittering around.

"It's different than it was in June," Alex observed with approval.

"I swear that the hike wasn't that bad last time," Bran groaned as he came up behind them, leaning on the walking stick as a hand reached down to rub his leg carefully.

"Well last time we were all pretty tense and high strung," Nicki offered with a smile as she joined them. "After all we were marching up here to block off a Sídhe tunnel."

"And we did a great job," Aiden said, stepping further into the flat open area.

It wasn't exactly a glade, the sharp change from sloping woods to level surface far too sudden to be mistaken for natural. The vegetation was still rather spotty, but Alex suspected that by this time next year the little area would be discovered by hikers and become a favorite picnic or camping spot. Although she wasn't certain that camping was allowed up here, hopefully not or Aiden might get some really bad ideas into his head.

Aiden opened his backpack, a grin on his face that made Alex a little uneasy. A moment later a stack of large slim volumes was pulled out. The covers were brightly colored with images of dragons, wizards with a raised staff and sparks of magic filling up the space. Raising an eyebrow at the cover, Alex lifted her eyes up to Aiden.

"Really? This is your idea of training," she asked giving him a teasing smile. "I assumed you didn't just haul them here for the weight training."

"Come on Alex," Aiden huffed, raising an eyebrow in return. "We need to start doing more with our powers. Fireballs are great and all, but I'm a little limited in what I can do. Morgana and Merlin said that we can do a lot more with our magic if we focus and visualize. These can give us ideas. I know it seems a bit weird but these books are literally just lists of different ideas for spells and magical combat."

Alex looked down at the book that Aiden was offering her. She didn't recognize the name, but the subtitle proclaimed it a Grimoire full of spells. Sighing dramatically, Alex accepted the book and walked over to one of the larger leafed trees around them and settled down in its shade. If Aiden smirked victoriously behind her, Alex was content to ignore it. And if sitting under the tree in the cool shade, enjoying the soft breeze and the smell of the forest was much nicer than spending the day in her dorm room would have been then Alex wasn't going to mention that either.

Opening up the book, Alex skipped the book's introduction which covered the apparent game system it was a part of and instead moved directly into the spell section. The volume that Aiden had given her only had spells, but the first section had a lot of information and numbers that meant nothing to her. Then she found a section of fire spells and stopped to read the various descriptions. Some of them were very vague and conjured nothing in her imagination, but a few of them made her smile as new ideas began to spark in her mind. There were spells for water, earth, and air, but also spells to affect animals and even a few to affect machines. However, Alex had to note a distinct lack of spells that were just about energy in a raw form. There was the expected lightning bolt, but everything seemed to be split into a particular form.

She wasn't a student of physics like Bran by any extent of the imagination, but she had passed her physics class and lab with an A minus. That was totally due to Aiden helping her in the lab and Bran's help in understanding the class notes. Still, she knew that energy was all about affecting objects and conversion. It couldn't be created or destroyed, just changed.

She'd already managed to take over the magic of others: one of Aiden's fireballs and the light form of magic that the Sídhe used. Morgana had told Alex that her magic was raw energy that didn't take a particular form like Aiden's fire, Nicki's water or even Bran's visions and telekinesis. Of course, Alex realized with a smile, that didn't mean that it couldn't.

Groaning softly, Alex stretched out her legs and set the book down on her lap. She closed her eyes for a moment and reached for the small flickering spark in her gut that had become a familiar part of her being and tugged. A surge of warmth churned in her stomach for a moment before energy jolted up her arms. Seeing the magic as a small quivering strand of dark silver, Alex directed to her right hand and slowed its flow. Magical exhaustion was not something she wanted to risk, not with a hike down the mountain in the future.

Looking down at her fingers, Alex watched the small bolts of dark silver energy arc between her fingers like a surge of electricity. Her skin tingled with warmth, but she wasn't having difficulty breathing or keeping the energy contained in her hand. A small smile tugged at her lips and she stared at the sparks and forced herself to inhale slowly. The energy rippled slightly, reacting to her. Licking her lips, Alex thought about the light orbs that Morgana used and imagined the tiny sparks of lightning forming into a simple orb.

The tiny bolts arced again, but this time sparked up into the space just above her palm. Swirling together the random jolts slowed and formed a small orb of dark silver energy that hovered just above her skin. Then the dark silver color of the orb began to fade away, the color of the orb shifting as the energy began to thrum. She could still feel the magic radiating out from the orb, but it felt softer somehow, airier in a way that she couldn't explain. After a few moments, the dark silver color of Alex's normal magic had faded complexly, leaving a small glowing ball of pure light that she could barely stand to even glance at. The only similarity that Alex could discern was the shape and the sensation of magic still radiating into her skin.

Eyes dropped down to the book, Alex's eyes traced over one of the descriptions. It was apparently a simple spell just to shape an element like earth, but Alex couldn't help but think back to the demonstrations that Merlin and Morgana had done of magic when they first met. They created a beautiful tree in the center of the room made out of light but projected in place like a hologram. It had been that sight that had truly convinced Alex that magic was real and somehow she was a part of it.

Focusing on the small ball of light in her hand, Alex studied it for a moment before she thought about the light dimming. Instead of the bright ball in her hand, she wanted the normal form of her energy, the dark silver that barely glowed at all. For this to work, she needed to be able to see what she was doing. It seemed much faster this time, the light dimmed and transformed into the dark metallic shade of Alex's magic. She studied it for a moment; it wasn't kinetic energy: it had nothing to do with the movement of objects. It wasn't radiation either, and it wasn't exactly light. It wasn't really electrical either, even when it sort of looked that way, as it didn't behave like electricity.

Shrugging off her chain of thought, Alex chuckled at her attempt to explain the science of her own magic. After all, magic was something special generated by the earth to combat invaders. What was in her hand could be a completely unknown form of energy, something new and completely magical.

The magic expanded slowly, stretching out in front of Alex and twisting slowly into a new shape. Slowly the main pillar of energy lengthened enough to form the trunk that Alex was imagining in her mind. A small sound of delight escaped her and called the other's attention to her.

"Oh wow," Nicki whispered, but Alex didn't look away from the expanding magic.

Branches slowly began to grow out of the magic and sweat gathered at the edges of Alex's hair and on the nape of her neck. Her fingers were moving slowly, tracing the branches without conscious thought as her eyes remained fixed on the gradual growing form in front of her. A wave of fatigue washed over Alex and she quickly dropped her hands into her lap with a loud gasp for air. Her eyes closed in a moment of disorientation and she heard Aiden call her name, but a moment later she shook her head and opened her eyes.

Hovering just above the ground a few feet in front of Alex was a four-foot tall tree made out of softly glowing dark silver magic. Branches twisted out of the main trunk, growing up and around each other in the glade. Alex hummed in satisfaction and glanced towards Nicki and Aiden as they approached the tree.

"Wow Alex, it looks like what Merlin and Morgana did," Nicki observed as she reached the tree and moved around it slowly.

Aiden held out his hand and slowly touched the tree, his fingers shimmering as they slid through one of the small branches.

"Looks like it," he agreed, pulling his hand back quickly. "But it's not just light or like a hologram, I could feel... static when I touched it." Aiden looked over at her and grinned, "Your power is really neat Alex."

"Thanks," she replied with a small smile. "Now if I could just figure out how to control it properly. I think that I can transform it into different forms."

"That could be really important," Nicki said with excitement, clapping her hands together. "You've already been able to take over magic thrown at you and transform it a little, but think about it. You could turn a raging fire into something else completely with enough practice."

"Yeah," Aiden agreed with an eager expression, his expression becoming awed. "Or store up the magic and release it all at once. If you could do that, you could probably do anything."

"Let's not get ahead of ourselves," Alex insisted as a blush took over her cheeks and a wave of fatigue weighed down on her. Looking towards the tree, Alex noted that parts of it were beginning to disperse without her concentrating on it. "One step at a time okay. Let me get the basic conversion and shaping figured out before you want me taking over all the energy I come across."

"Fair point," Nicki conceded as she turned to watch the rest of the tree fade away, tiny sparks of magic floating away.

Leaning back against the tree, Alex held out her hand and tried calling some of the magic back to her, curious to see if she could. But the small sparks of magic just swirled around her hand until she sighed loudly and flicked them into the air. Nicki gave her a small smile and tilted her head, silently checking that she was okay. Nodding, Alex gave her roommate a small smile and after a moment, Nicki headed back to her own backpack and book.

Alex retrieved her water bottle and took several greedy gulps which made her feel a little recharged. Pulling out two cereal bars, Alex tore one open and closed her eyes. Her arms and legs were sore, but it wasn't too bad, just a lingering sense of doing too much. The rush of excitement was beginning to fade, but nothing could shake the sense of satisfaction that was thrumming in her chest. Listening to the soft rustle of the breeze, Alex nibbled on the first bar and sighed as she began to relax.

"I wonder if we'll ever be able to do some of these spells," Bran said some time later ending the silence that had fallen in the glade. "I mean we're supposed to visualize stuff happening, but how would that work on something that we can't see."

"Merlin has indicated that he can affect people's memories, which is something you can't see," Nicki pointed out, tugging a leaf from her hair. "So it must work somehow."

"Maybe it's only when we're still learning that visualization is needed," Aiden offered with a small shrug. "When you think about it, you'd need to have perfect control to affect someone's mind safely. I mean magic is a form of energy and if you used too much then you could really hurt someone."

"That's a fair point," Nicki agreed. "When I've healed it is exhausting and very difficult to keep control of my magic. And to be fair I don't know that much about biology or physiology so when I heal it's really the magic doing something that I've only given it a vague instruction for."

"So maybe when we've got more control we'll be able to do some of this other stuff?" Alex asked, glancing down at the descriptions of spells to help find your way, see through walls or move at faster speeds. "If we've got a strong connection to our magic then maybe it becomes a question of just willing something to happen or visualizing the final effect you want it to have."

"Maybe," Aiden agreed with a pleased smile. "Which is why coming out here today to experiment was a good idea."

"We're never going to hear the end of it are we?" Bran asked with a warm chuckle that made Alex smile.

"Oh eventually you'll hear the end of it," Aiden promised, his large smile still in place. "But come on guys, doesn't this feel awesome? Taking a step in our own direction as mages. Merlin and Morgana are great, but this is a different time! We've got potential of our own."

A laugh escaped Alex and she shook her head fondly. Aiden's love of being a mage, his energy was something that she'd never tire of. It was strange to remember that less than a year ago she'd been pushing him and his insistence about magic being real away.

"Guys," Bran called sharply, his voice tense. "There's something moving over there."

Glancing towards Bran, Alex saw him leveraging himself up on his walking stick and looking into the forest. Nicki and Aiden both turned to look over where he was pointing. Alex set the book to the side and pulled herself to her own feet using a low hanging branch on the tree. There was a strange shadow in the trees. One of the large nearby bushes snapped loudly making Alex jump.

"There's nothing there," Nicki told them, but her voice sounded a little unsure.

Then a shadow stretched out of the forest towards them. Glancing up, Alex's eyes widened as she realized the sun was directly overhead and her eyes flew back down to the strange shadow that was growing longer.

"There's nothing there," Nicki repeated, grabbing Aiden's arm and pulling him back from the forest. "Guys, nothing is casting the shadow."

It slinked out of the forest, a darkness over the ground with nothing casting it. Stepping away from the tree, Alex sucked in a sharp breath and opened her palm, summoning all the magic she had left as the shadow darkened to pure blackness, completely hiding the ground beneath it. Then it moved towards them.

8

Living Shadow

Taking a few steps away from the Shadow, Alex studied the shifting mass of .... blackness with a growing sense of unease. It slunk over the ground slowly. Her mind kept stumbling over that fact, trying to make some sense of it. Glancing towards the sky, Alex's stomach flipped when she saw nothing that could possibly be casting the shadow.

She didn't dare look away again but heard the others moving around her slowly. In the corner of her eye, she caught sight of Aiden moving around the thing on her right, positioning himself to flank it. In a moment a small ball of fire was floating over his open palm as he eyed the strange darkness. The surface of Shadow seemed to thicken and then it shifted upwards as if growing out of the ground.

Stepping back on instinct, Alex called her magic to her hands and waited. She could feel the crackle of the energy over her fingers, but none of her fellow mages were moving. The magic fluttered in her hands, but Alex felt the weight of exhaustion already creeping on her.

The Shadow solidified into a vaguely humanoid shape with two arms and two legs, but its body was all rough and jagged spikes. The air around it shimmered and seemed to darken as a pair of dark red eyes opened and stared at Alex. In the middle of its head, a tear seemed to open revealing bright sharp teeth. A hissing sound escaped the Shadow and it took a small step forward, hunching its back which made the spikes more prominent. Its hands were nearly dragging on the ground, but Alex stepped back once more as a terrible chill swept up her body. Her hands ached and she shivered. A low snarling sound escaped the Shadow.

It leapt forward, a blur of black, and Alex jumped to the right to avoid it. She hit the ground and rolled, nearly colliding with the tree she'd been reading under only moments ago. A loud half snarl-half scream reached her ears as she hit her knees and began to stand up. The sound sent a cold shiver do her spin, but Alex whirled around and backed up, trying to put some distance between the Shadow and herself.

Fire erupted against the Shadow's body thanks to Aiden's fireball, but the darkness of the form rippled and the fire vanished with the Shadow barely reacting. The heat of the fireball vanished and a chill hung in the air around them. Alex sucked in a painful breath, her lungs tightening as the cold air hit her throat. The glade seemed to darken with every passing moment despite the sun shining down on them.

A blast of water knocked into the creature's side, causing it to stumble and catch itself on its long arms. Raising its head, the red eyes glinted in the low light and it opened its mouth. A terrible roar, dull and long that made Alex's heart jump echoed around them. Her hairs all stood on end as goosebumps appeared down her arms and Alex fought back the desire to wrap her arms around herself for warmth as her teeth chattered.

Raising her hand, Alex pushed her magic out desperately, picturing a simple lightning bolt striking the Shadow. The energy lashed out from her fingers and struck the Shadow, knocking it backward and into the center of the glade. Alex's knees ached and her legs were starting to shake as a bead of sweat ran down the back of her neck.

In the corner of her eye, Alex saw Aiden summon another ball of fire letting the magic flare and grow stronger. The Shadow spun towards Aiden, its red eyes glowing as it crouched forward on its front limbs. Fire blasted through the air, sending a wave of delicious heat through the glade, but Shadow didn't even try to evade the fire. Instead, it raised itself up, allowing the fireball to hit it in the chest. The warmth in the glade vanished, the temperature dropped and Alex thought she saw her breath.

"Aiden stop!" Nicki shouted nearby, "The fire isn't helping, I think it's getting stronger!"

He swore loudly, his voice echoing as they all stopped and watched the Shadow. Leaning forward on its front limbs, it looked towards Aiden before its head turned all the way around to look at Nicki behind it. Alex shuddered and glanced towards Nicki who had a look of disgust and concentration on her face.

Nicki raised her hand, it shimmered blue with her magic as a long icicle appeared clutched in her hand like a dagger. In a graceful movement, Nicki threw the icicle forward; it shot through the air, a blaze of blue magic surrounding it. Howling in pain as the ice struck it, the Shadow twisted around and tried to dislodge the magical weapon. Ice crept over the creature's side, covering three of the black jagged horns on its body.

"Ice!" Alex heard herself shout. "Nicki hit it again!"

The Shadow roared and sprang towards Nicki, reaching for her with long claws. Then it suddenly stopped, suspended in the air with its claws less than a foot from Nicki's chest. Her friend stumbled back from the creature with a hiss. Looking towards Bran, Alex saw him glaring at the Shadow with one shaking arm thrust out in front of him.

"I can't hold it long," Bran groaned, his voice low and sharp.

Nicki nodded and Alex started to move towards her. She saw Nicki bring her hands in front of her, take a deep breath and close her eyes. Blue magic spun out of Nicki's hands, swirling in front of her like snowflakes on the breeze. Then Nicki's eyes snapped open and she shoved the swirl of magic towards the Shadow. Just before reaching the creature, the magic sparks shifted and formed three long lances of ice. The Shadow made a short cry of alarm before the lances struck it in the chest and belly.

The Shadow fell to the ground as Bran collapsed to his knees. Aiden rushed over to him and Alex ran towards Nicki, glancing at the fallen creature. It made a pitiful mewling sound as the ice lances began to expand, glistening ice spreading over the Shadow's body. Reaching Nicki, Alex wrapped an arm around her shoulder and pulled her back from the Shadow. The pained sounds had stopped, but the body was twitching and lashing about even as the ice continued to cover it. Then with one final twitch, the body began to fade away like a shadow gradually exposed to light. Nicki slumped against Alex and the ice crumbled to the ground, already melting in the warm sun.

Somehow they made it down the hill, Bran leaning heavily on Aiden and Nicki leaning heavily on her with Aiden and Alex each carrying two backpacks. By the time they reached Alex's car, Alex's knees were shaking badly and she'd broken out in a cold sweat. She tossed her keys weakly to Aiden and he nodded wearily. They didn't bother even putting their packs in the trunk, instead, they were piled into the backseat around the collapsing Bran and Nicki.

"Morgana's house is closest," Alex gasped as she fell into the front passenger seat and clutched her hands together, trying to stop the shaking.

"Right," Aiden wheezed as he started up the car.

As they pulled onto the small paved road that led up to the parking lot, Alex considered that she really should call Morgana, but her phone was in her backpack and she didn't have the energy to turn around and get it out. A weak glance over her shoulder revealed that Nicki and Bran were both dozing off against the stack of backpacks, their faces pale and distant.

"They don't look good," Alex muttered softly, shivering slightly. "Magical exhaustion."

"Will they be okay?" Aiden asked, keeping his eyes focused on the road even as his head started trying to drop.

"Yeah," Alex breathed, turning front in her seat again. "It's just… exhaustion. I was the same way when I got out of the Sídhe tunnels last year. Morgana will know how to take care of them."

"What was that thing?"

"It's probably connected to what Bran saw in his vision," Alex replied softly, her eyes searching the small turn off roads for Morgana's.

Aiden nearly missed the turn, pulling on the wheel sharply to make it. He shook his head and blinked twice as Alex looked in the back seat to make sure Nicki and Bran were alright. Their professor's Victorian style house was a welcome sight as they drove up the gravel road leading to it. The tower's white trim was gleaming in the bright sunlight and the front porch had several flower boxes perched along the rails. The sight of Morgana's red sports car parked in the drive filled Alex with relief and she breathed a little easier.

Aiden abruptly braked and the car fishtailed in the gravel for a moment before coming to a stop. Turning off the car, Aiden sighed in relief and collapsed against the back of his seat. Alex unbuckled her seatbelt slowly, her hands still shaking and kept telling herself to get up and out of the car. Someone needed to get Morgana, but she could barely move.

Then the heavy wooden front door swung open and Professor Cornwall appeared on the front porch. She was dressed casually in jeans and an old faded t-shirt with her long dark hair piled on her head in a messy bun. For a moment she looked irritated, but then her eyes widened and worry took over her face. Rushing down the front steps, Morgana ran over to Alex's side of the car and pulled the door open. The burst of fresh air made Alex feel a little more awake and she forced herself to sit up properly.

"Morgana, there was this thing in the woods, like a living shadow. We stopped it, but-"

"It's okay Alex," their professor assured her in a soothing voice. She placed a hand on Alex's shoulder and looked into the back seat. "Any injuries?"

"No, just bruising and exhaustion."

"Good," Morgana said with a visible smile of relief. "Let's get all of you inside and call Merlin."

Morgana helped Alex out of the car and said nothing when Alex nearly fell to her knees. Leaning against the car, Alex held the back door open so Morgana could gently shake Nicki awake. With gentle movements, Morgana helped Nicki climb out of the car and, supporting the girl, helped her up the stairs and into the house.

With a brief burst of energy, Alex reached into the backseat and started tugging at their backpacks in order to wake Bran. Next to her, Aiden was unfolding himself from the car. Bran woke up with a soft snort and looked towards her with glassy eyes.

"We're at Morgana's," Alex explained softly. "She's helping Nicki inside. She'll be out in a moment."

It took Morgana another minute to return, but when she came out she headed straight for Bran who was trying to shift himself around to get out. Aiden stumbled over next to Morgana and together they helped Bran climb out of the backseat. Through the car's windows, Alex watched as Bran carefully got on his feet and leaned on his walking stick to stay upright. Despite protests from him, Aiden kept hold of his left arm and walked him up the stairs and into the house.

Morgana watched them go inside the house before she turned her attention to Alex. Opening her mouth, Alex began to explain what had happened, but Morgana gently shushed her and wrapped a warm arm around her shoulders. Unable to resist, Alex fell silent with a relieved sigh and leaned against Morgana as they climbed up the porch and went inside.

The parlor was just as Alex remembered it with the large old fashioned looking red sofas and two large soft looking armchairs. Warm sunshine was streaming in through the three large windows, illuminating the whole room without the use of lights. Nicki was stretched out on the shorter of the two sofas and already snoring gently. Bran was stretched out on the longer sofa and Aiden was already sleeping in one of the armchairs. Morgana squeezed Alex's hand gently as she walked her over the second armchair. Sinking down into the chair, Alex moaned softly in relief and let her head fall back against the plush back. She closed her eyes but was aware enough to hear Morgana moving around the room, checking on all four of them before her footsteps headed away towards the back of the house. Morgana returned a few minutes later carrying a pile of blankets.

Protesting weakly, Alex told Morgana that she wasn't cold, but the moment Morgana tossed the blanket over her Alex felt a little better. Her fingers shifted, clutching at the soft and thick material and she felt her body relaxing further into the chair. Despite her intention to stay awake and explain what had happened, Alex's eyes closed and she sighed happily, drifting off comfortably.

Alex's eyes snapped open and her heart jumped when the front door opened and banged into the bench by the doorway. Looking towards the entry with wide eyes, Alex clutched at the armrests of the chair. She closed her eyes as something moved further into the house, trying to look asleep even as her ears strained to hear what was happening. Morgana's footfalls came quickly back into the living room.

"Quiet Merlin," Morgana hissed softly as she passed Alex's chair. "Honestly Ambrose have you no sense?"

Opening her eyes a little bit, Alex peered around the corner of her armchair as Professor Yates came around the corner with a sheepish smile. His expression turned serious as his eyes swept over the living room. Alex settled back in her chair but made no effort to draw his attention. A soft snore escaped Aiden as his head rolled to the side and snuggled his cheek into his own blanket.

"What happened to them?" Merlin asked Morgana in a low voice.

"Alex described it as a living shadow," Morgana replied in a sharp voice with barely concealed anger. "And given the dark form that Bran saw in his vision, it can only be Chernobog."

A series of strange words escaped Merlin, none of them sounded pleasant and Alex saw Morgana nod firmly in agreement.

"Of course he'd be the first one to fully wake," Merlin huffed, raising a hand and running it through his gray curls. "And he's already strong enough to be sending out his shadows."

"It seems so," Morgana replied slowly. She held up her hands to still Merlin. "The children are all alright; I'm not sure what happened, but they all survived the encounter."

"That's a good sign," Merlin agreed, sounding much more pleased. "We'll just have to defeat him again.

"Last time we had a lot more help," Morgana pointed out darkly.

"Ah Morgana, always the optimist," Merlin chuckled with a hint of sarcasm. "But I'll remind you that our current group has already managed to save the Iron Soul from the betrayal."

"This is different, and be careful of how much you demand from them," Morgana hissed in reply. "You asked too much of Arto and so many of the others. I won't have you putting too much on Alex… I mean all of them."

Merlin's chuckle was soft and warm and Alex shifted slightly so she could see more. Merlin was looking at Morgana with a soft and warm smile.

"I know you are very fond of the girl," Merlin said gently. "And that's alright Morgana. The first Iron Soul may have been your brother, but it is alright to love others too."

"That's never ended well for either of us when we've tried in the past," Morgana muttered. "We're immortal, kept alive by virtue of being neither human or Sídhe, kept alive to protect the Iron Realm. Everyone else, everything else, isn't."

"And yet we keep trying, regardless of how you act sometimes my dear I know how loving you can be. I've seen many times, even though you always try not to."

Alex couldn't see Morgana's face, but she took a step back from Merlin and calmly told him, "I've got hot chocolate brewing in the kitchen. They'll need something warm."

Alex closed her eyes as Morgana turned to head into the kitchen, trying to look asleep. There was a warm pulsing in her chest that made her smile underneath her blanket. Holding onto the sensation for a moment, Alex sighed softly before she yawned loudly and opened her eyes. Merlin was watching her with a small knowing look that made her blush. He stepped over to her and gently pushed a strand of her long blonde hair from her face.

"How are you?" he asked her in a low voice.

"Okay, this fight was harder on Nicki and Bran," Alex explained, grateful that she had the strength to speak.

"I'm not surprised about Nicole," Merlin remarked. "Her powers would have been invaluable in this battle, but Bran?"

"It tried to attack Nicki, but Bran stopped and held it in midair."

"Did he now?" Merlin marveled. "Wonderful."

The sound of plates and cups in the kitchen made Merlin look up towards the doorway. He stepped away from Alex and moved over to Aiden whom he softly tapped on his shoulder. Alex cuddled into her blankets as Merlin moved around the room and gently woke the others. They were barely awake when Morgana returned to the parlor carrying a large pot of hot cocoa and several mugs on a large silver tray. She set it down on the heavy wooden coffee table and began filling the mugs.

Alex's mouth watered as she inhaled the smell of the hot chocolate and she grinned happily when Morgana handed her the warm mug. Wrapping her hands around it, Alex breathed the steam in deeply before taking a sip. The hot chocolate warmed Alex's mouth and spread an instant feeling of warmth and contentment through her entire body. It was a little too hot and stung her tongue a little, but the last vestiges of the chill in her body from being near that creature finally vanished.

"So, what was that thing?" Alex asked after a happy little sigh. Her fingers tightened around the warm mug and she shifted back into the warmth of the armchair.

"Well roughly translated from what we used to call them… just Shadows." Merlin answered with a strained chuckle. "They are as you saw shadows that take the form of a creature which is immune to heat and fire. Rather nasty business. You assume that heat and light will deal with such a creature, but instead it makes them stronger. I'm pleased that you realized that in time."

"It wasn't that hard," Nicki replied with a small pleased smile. "It got colder whenever Aiden hit it with a fireball."

"Indeed," Morgana agreed as she handed Nicki her own mug. "But when you're fighting them in the dead of winter that can be a bit harder to determine."

"It took Morgana three fights with shadow creatures to figure out that her light attacks were useless. Then she tried fire. It wasn't until what? Fight number five that you tried ice."

Morgana gave Merlin a stern look, but he just smiled and sat on the armrest of the sofa that Nicki was stretched out on.

"Where did it come from?" Bran asked weakly before taking another deep gulp of hot chocolate.

"The Shadows are the creations and servants of the Old One Chernobog, an exile from Avalye. Gradually he lost his mind," Morgana explained calmly as she took Nicki's mug and refilled it. "In the tenth century the two of us, the then Iron Soul, Dobiemir, along with an alliance of several other Old Ones fought Chernobog, 982 C.E. if I remember correctly. He was forced underground and went to sleep under a powerful blast of our magic. Sadly the current rise in magic is waking up the Old Ones and it appears that Chernobog will be leading the charge."

"Chernobog," Nicki repeated slowly with a frown. "That sounds familiar."

"It should, he's become a rather popular evil god to reference in literature and film in the last few decades. Unlike many so-called evil gods, Chernobog really was evil given form. He didn't care much for worship or offerings, the only thing that he seemed to enjoy at all was causing devastation. He spurred on many famines and pestilences in early medieval Poland before he was locked away."

"The shadow form that you fought is one of the reasons he is so dangerous," Merlin added with a shake of his head. "Chernobog seemingly has power over cold, but in truth, his ability is to draw power from light and heat. He takes the power of heat and light and leaves the world cold in his wake. Darkness and cold are mere byproducts of his presence and his shadow forms are little bits of his power that he sends out in the world. His very own conjured army."

"Which we'll be seeing more of in the coming months," Morgana remarked with a sigh. "I suppose at least we understand that part of Bran's vision. The massive dark figure certainly matches my memories of Chernobog."

"At least until Chernobog himself arrives," Merlin added with a shake of his head as he glanced at them all. "I'm afraid that you'll need to be on your guard day and night now. Hopefully the Sídhe will remain trapped long enough for us to deal with Chernobog."

"Indeed," Morgana agreed darkly. "Wars on two fronts are never a good thing." She turned her attention to Alex and gave her a small sad smile. "All of you need to be very careful and protect Arthur. Unlike the Sídhe, Chernobog is not limited by anything as simple as a tunnel entrance. It's likely that his attention is fixed on Ravenslake as the focal point of the rising magic, but he can send his shadow forms anywhere."

"So going home is no longer safe," Bran said softly, a deep frown on his face. "Are our families safe?"

"They should be," Morgana informed them gently. "Chernobog doesn't know about them and they have no magic to draw his attention. He's powerful, but spying and clever plots are not his strong point."

"Great," Nicki sighed, clutching at her own hot chocolate. "At least the Sídhe only came out at night. Now we've got living shadows to contend with."

"Drink your hot chocolate," Morgana told them sternly. "You can stay here and rest this afternoon until you're strong enough to head for home."

"What about Arthur?" Alex asked, worry clogging her throat.

"I spoke with him earlier today to confirm his safety," Merlin replied gently with a small smile. "He'll be home tonight and we'll brief him on what is happening." Merlin gave them a wider forced smile and added, "Please keep in mind that Chernobog has been asleep for a thousand years: his powers are still returning to him. He won't be able to attack you all the time. Keep living your lives and protect each other. For now, that's all we can do."

Swallowing thickly, Alex managed a quick nod but dropped her eyes into her hot chocolate mug. A moment later she felt Morgana's hand drop to her shoulder and the older mage squeeze it gently. She raised the mug in a silent toast to her fellow mages and draining what remained of her serving. The chocolate lingered on her tongue, much cooler and tasting far bitterer than before.

9

The Plain of the Circle

806 B.C.E. Salisbury Plains

Traveling was the worst part of their mission and the worst part of the war in Arto's opinion. It was always a pain, even on the treks when they had some horses to carry them. He suspected that his sister had become as comfortable with their stationary life as he had because Morgana had insisted to Merlin that they weren't walking this time. Still, it was boring and tiring in its own way even if they made better time. Arto looked over to where Luegáed was sitting rather uncomfortably on a brown horse he'd been paired with.

"Not fond of horses?" Arto asked, trying to strike up a conversation.

"I'd only ridden one a handful of time before this," Luegáed admitted with a sheepish smile. "We mostly use them with carts for transport and sometimes in the fields."

"I've only ridden a few times myself," Arto told him with a chuckle. "Merlin and I traveled on foot most of the time when I was young, occasionally we borrowed horses from local villages for quick trips, but it's new for me."

"Why didn't you use horses if you traveled so much?"

"Lots of reasons I suppose," Arto answered with a small shrug. "We didn't have any way to protect them from the Sídhe, we would have had to stop to let them eat and keep them tethered all the time. They are pretty difficult to keep calm and we do have to fight a lot." Arto chuckled and glanced at the head of the party where Merlin was shifting uneasily on the horse he was riding. "Besides, I don't think Merlin likes them very much. He complains about them a lot."

Luegáed chuckled, sharing a look with Arto. The tension in Luegáed's shoulders eased slightly and Arto internally smiled, glad to see the newcomer adjusting. Luegáed had volunteered to come to the great stone circle with them but was still very uneasy around everyone. Arto could understand it: he'd grown up traveling so he was used to meeting new people and working with them, but he knew from Gwenyvar that most people did not live their lives that way. Everyone traveled a bit, usually to take part in the winter and summer celebrations and return their ancestors or tools to the earth, but Luegáed had come much farther than that.

"So what will happen when we get there?" Luegáed asked, breaking into Arto's thoughts.

"We should be there soon, I think you'll catch your first glimpse of the circle when we come over that hill over there," Arto replied, pointing at one of the sloping hills in the distance. "We'll be staying at a village near it. Depending on how late it is we'll review the protection from the Sídhe, make any changes that we can tonight and try to rest up. Beyond that.... well it just depends on if we can track the Sídhe back to their current tunnel and how long it takes to accomplish that."

"And if we find the tunnel?"

"Then we create a new iron gate with the iron we brought with us. That will help protect this area," Arto informed him with a pleased smile. "The magic radiates out and protects at least a few miles around it. I hope to someday have enough gates that the Sídhe can't even come through at all anymore."

"That's quite a dream," Luegáed remarked, "But one I hope to see come to pass."

"You will," Arto assured him with a firm nod.

An odd expression crossed over Luegáed's face, his eyes flickering for a moment. Then the other young man swallowed and nodded firmly. They both settled into silence, but it wasn't uncomfortable, just contemplative. Arto wondered if Luegáed was regretting his father's decision to send him off to the war. He wouldn't have blamed him, Arto was very aware that his life was difficult and dangerous, the sort of life that people didn't want to live. Honor and glory mattered to some, but they lived in a largely peaceful world except for the Sídhe, not like those in the south who seemed to occupy themselves with battle at all times.

The landscape around them was filled with gently rolling hills, patches of forest and farmlands. The southern plateau was home to many small villages, most with simple wooden walls and little else to defend them. Earthen walls kept livestock penned and small roundhouses were scattered amongst fields of crops.

Many people stopped to watch their small procession, hope in their eyes, but also nervousness. Arto couldn't blame them for that. He knew that failure on their part would just bring the Sídhe down harder in this region. His stomach clenched as the terrible thought of what would happen if he died crossed his mind. Merlin and Morgana would, of course, keep fighting, he had every confidence that his death would not stop those two, but would the others keep following? Arto glanced towards Luegáed with renewed curiosity. Mages were poorly understood, the people valued magic and their priests, but did not understand them. If he died then they'd need someone to keep leading the nonmagical side of things.

He shook his head; he was getting ahead of himself. Still, Arto conceded to himself, it was something that he needed to think about. His father was proof enough that great warriors could be struck down. Just thinking about the stab his father received in the back was enough to make him angry all over again.

They reached the crest of the hill and Arto grinned when he heard a soft gasp from Luegáed. A short ways ahead of them stood one of the largest and more elegant stone circles in the whole isles. There were larger ones, some with more stones, but Arto couldn't help but admire the great achievement of the circle. Large, tall stones stood in a circle with other stones perched carefully on them, forming great arches.

Also visible was the large timber circle, only two miles to the north-east of the great stone circle. Arto doubted that Luegáed could make it out that there was anything special about the site from their position, but he surveyed the area with a sense of pride. Their ancestors had built something truly great here. Beyond this site, Arto knew that the river and the circle of smaller stones completed the network of monuments that together served as the great funeral site. The place where the greatest of them were returned to the Earth.

"It's fantastic. We have funeral and celebration sites in my homeland, but nothing quite like this. I wonder how the builders managed to raise those stones so high," Luegáed remarked with a grin, looking over at Arto.

"It is the greatest of all our circles," Arto agreed with a nod. "There are many, but none match it. Traditionally anyone who can manage comes here at the Winter Solstice and there is a great slaughter of pigs. We return the dead to the Earth so they may guide us and help keep the realm safe and we celebrate their lives."

"Have you been here often?"

"A few times," Arto replied with a nod, his smile fading away slightly. "The last time was for my father."

"I'm sorry."

"It is the way of things, especially when the Sídhe ride," Arto muttered before he forced himself to smile. "But I have been here many times for the Winter Solstice celebration. You can't see it from here, but there is an avenue leading from that circle to the river where there is another circle made out of smaller stones."

They slowly made their way down the hill, turning away from the stone circle and heading towards a small village to the north near the edge of the river. Arto glanced up at the darkening sky and towards the head of the line of horses where Morgana was urging hers to speed up. He glanced toward Luegáed and noted that his friend had his hand on the hilt of his iron sword. A quick look around revealed that everyone had noticed that they were running out of daylight as thick clouds on the horizon clouded over the setting sun.

His horse whinnied nervously, shifting beneath him and Arto clutched tighter at the leather straps. The horse's nostrils were flaring, its ears were perked and its tail was high. Looking around, he tried to find the source of the beast's nervousness. He didn't know much about horses, but he could recognize fear and aggravation when he saw it. The sky was darkening fast above them as the clouds blocked the low sun from sight, but he could see no signs of a threat yet. Then his horse made a squealing noise and shifted backward, fighting against the leather straps.

A long eerie howl ripped across the plains, echoing against the low hills and the horse made a sudden jerk. Arto looked towards Merlin who was staring off into the distant hills. His own horse was moving and tossing its head. Merlin shook his head and swung down from the horse, planting his staff into the ground with a heavy thump. Scrabbling off his horse, Arto grabbed the leather bag on its back that held the iron. As his horse tried to pull away, Arto tore open the knot holding the bag and let the bag fall to the ground. He did nothing to stop it when the horse squealed again and backed away.

Then came another howl and Morgana was nearly thrown from her horse. She stumbled to the ground and glared at the horse as she grabbed the leather bag off its back. It hit the ground with a thunk as the horse pulled away from her. There was another howl just as the last of the warriors, a man named Aileen was getting off his horse. He fell to the ground as the horse pulled sharply away from him and took off running.

Pulling Cathanáil from its sheath Arto brought his sword up in front of him and looked around carefully. Magic shimmered down his arm and into the sword. Cathanáil's blade glowed a soft white color illuminating the terrain around them. He heard Luegáed gasp softly and resisted the urge to smirk, forcing himself to focus on the coming threat.

The Sídhe Riders appeared on the crest of the hill, the low light of dusk framing their gleaming silvery steeds. One of them held an orb of light that illuminated their golden armor and made their violet eyes glitter dangerously. There were seven in total, forming a straight line atop the hill, watching them as their Hounds rushed down the hill.

"Brace yourselves!" his sister shouted, her voice echoing over the plains. "Make them come to the flat ground!"

The Hounds reached them first, a wave of snarling shimmering fur and gleaming teeth. Swinging Cathanáil, Arto sliced into the one lunging at him, causing it to vanish in a brief flash of light while doing his best to stay aware of the others. In the corner of his eye, he saw concentrated light lashing around, striking two of the Hounds, Morgana's work no doubt, and heard the sharp cry of another Hound to his left. Spinning on his heel, Arto looked to his left where Luegáed was blocking the attacks of a snarling Hound. He stepped forward quickly and brought Cathanáil down on the Hounds back while Luegáed kept it distracted. The Hound began to turn on him, but it vanished with an animalistic cry of pain.

"Riders!" Someone shouted nearby and Arto turned back to the slope of the hill, raising Cathanáil as he scanned the Riders.

They were rushing down the hill, two of them gathering magic in their hands. A shout from Morgana gave the others enough warning to leap out of the way as a golden blast of magic shot past them. Dirt and small stones were launched into the air as the blast ripped into the ground. Arto turned his face away to protect his eyes but felt the debris rain down on his back. The other Rider released his blast, but a shimmering flash of green magic collided with it, sending sparks raining down on the ground. And the Riders were upon them.

There was a dull roar around Arto: the pounding of his blood deafened him to all but the loudest sounds. Cathanáil glowed in his hands, illuminating the terrain all around him. Three Riders pulled away, circling to the flanks of the group. Releasing his left hand from Cathanáil, Arto called forth his magic, envisioning fire erupting over the flesh and armor of a nearby Rider. He thrust his hand towards the Rider, pushing at the magic and commanding it to make his vision a reality. Screams tore from the Rider as flames erupted over his body and his steed attempted to throw him off.

Green magic flashed and Arto turned in time to see a section of earth rising up and surging in a wave of mud around the feet of a horse. As the beast tried to escape, two warriors rushed forward and pulled the Rider from its back before it could do anything. Arto saw silver blood splash in the light provided by the gleaming Cathanáil.

A cry of rage cut through the pounding in his ears and Arto spun sharply, finding a Rider bearing down on him. He brought Cathanáil up in front of him, barely deflecting the shining golden blade of the Rider. Spinning away, he slashed Cathanáil at the torso of the steed, the sword clanging on the metallic armor worn by the beast before the blade skipped off and sank into a small patch of exposed flesh. Twisting the sword, Arto pulled it out sharply and jumped back as the horse screamed and vanished.

The Rider leapt to the ground and swung at Arto. Ducking, he felt the air above his head being displaced by the blade. Someone called his name and he felt himself being pushed gently to the side. Luegáed swung his iron sword in a smooth motion across his body. Arto heard it scratch against the Rider's golden armor. It caught on the edge of the armor, just at the junction between the chest and arm protection. Shoving the blade forward, Luegáed made a loud cry as the sword was buried into the Síd's shoulder. The Síd screamed, clawing at Luegáed even as its body began to dissolve. The armor turned to dust as Luegáed stared at it in shock, his eyes looking down at the sword in his hand.

Arto nearly smiled, but a sudden crash to his right pulled his eyes away from his new friend. Another Rider was charging into Aileen, knocking the man and another warrior down to the ground. The metallic hoofs of the Sídhe's horse flashed in the light as the beast reared up. Eyes widening, Arto thrust Cathanáil forward towards the horse and pushed a burst of magic through. The sword shimmered for a split second as the horse began to fall back to the ground. Magic sparked off the metal, shooting forward off the sword like a solid beam of light, striking the Rider's steed in the chest. With a cut off scream, the horse vanished in a brief burst of light, sending the Rider crashing to the ground.

Aileen was on his feet, grabbing his iron headed axe back up from the ground. With a roar, the man brought the axe down on the Rider, the iron crashing into its skull. There was a brief splash of silvery blood before the Rider began to dissolve as Aileen cheered. His cheer was soon joined by others and Arto panted as he looked around. Raising Cathanáil high above his head, Arto pushed more magic into the sword and willed the light to become brighter. The beams of light stretched all around them, but the Riders and Hounds were all gone.

"Well done," Arto shouted over the din, swallowing to clear his ears. "Tend to the wounded and recover whatever you can from the horses."

The cheers turned to grumbling as everyone recalled that the horses had fled. Perhaps they'd find them and most of the supplies in the morning, but with the sun below the horizon and only a sliver of the moon, Arto knew it was a fool's errand to search tonight. Arto watched the others move about to check injuries and pick up fallen bags and blankets. His eyes went to the heavy bag of iron that he'd freed from his own horse and with a sigh of resignation he collected the bag and slung it over his shoulder. He started to make his way over to Merlin and Morgana, anxious to confer with them.

"That was an ambush party," Arto heard his sister say in a low angry voice to Merlin.

"Morgana, it may have simply been a raiding party," Merlin hissed in a low voice, glancing around and his eyes landing on him. Arto received a warning look and said nothing.

"Raiding parties are numbered three, four at the most: this was seven. That is a military group expecting combat."

"Perhaps they are increasing the size of their raiding parties due to areas being armed with iron," Merlin suggested, reaching towards Morgana.

His sister avoided Merlin's hand, flipping her long braided hair over her shoulder. Arto could see the anger and tension in her shoulders.

"Don't delude yourself, we've been betrayed. This was an ambush."

"Morgana, they may have anticipated our movements. This is the fastest route to the area they are now most active in. Routine can be predicted and planned for."

"I don't believe it," Morgana countered, shaking her head with a fierce look in her green eyes. "My instincts, my years of living with the Sídhe are saying that this was an ambush and they had help."

Arto saw Merlin sigh and shake his head while Morgana glared at him before she turned on her heel, her cloak fluttering behind her. His sister nodded to him before her eyes moved past him and settled on something behind him. Turning, he looked over his shoulder and stilled when he realized that his sister was looking at Luegáed. Irritation rose through him and Arto started to move towards his sister, but Merlin's large hand on his shoulder stopped him.

"Easy lad," Merlin told him in a gentle, but firm voice. "She'll not do anything rash, but you will not dissuade her from her anger."

"But she's wrong," Arto protested weakly. "She has to be, doesn't she?"

"Perhaps, perhaps not, but we'll not solve that problem tonight," Merlin sighed with a shake of his head. "Morgana's own... history makes her very inclined to see traitors, even when there may not be any." Merlin looked around, his eyes settling on the distance village. "And in the meantime, we aren't going to get those horses back tonight so it is time to start walking."

Arto sighed, but nodded and swung the heavy bag of iron over his shoulder. It thunked against his sore muscles and Arto huffed. Merlin chuckled in front of him as he shouldered his own lighter bag and called for the others attention. Everyone settled down quickly and in less than a minute they were working their way towards the village on foot, everyone looking forward to something to eat and a place to sleep.

10

Life and Love

With a soft sigh, Alex dumped her school bag on her bed and glanced at her laptop's clock. She had some time before her next class to relax which after spending Saturday worrying about her parents finding out too much and battling a Shadow on Sunday was a welcome relief for Monday morning. Opening up her bag, Alex ignored her tablet and pulled out the two paperback books that Professor Yates had assigned for them. As she put the books back onto the small set of shelves by her desk, Alex shook her head: The Story of King Arthur was a hell of a way to start off her Monday morning. Under other, non-magical circumstances she would have been thrilled to have the chance to read the old myths and discuss how the ancient Celtic tales had been transformed over the years. As it was, sometimes it was very very hard not to fall on the ground laughing as Merlin, currently going by the name Ambrose Yates, talked about the archetype that Merlin represented in literature.

"Life is weird," Alex muttered to herself as she grabbed her Spanish book and homework worksheet.

Walking out to the small kitchenette, Alex picked up a plastic glass and poured herself some water. She took a long drink and leaned against the hallway wall, enjoying the silence for a few moments. A knock on the door made her look up and blink in surprise. She set her glass of water on the counter and walked into the living room, turning into the small entryway. Opening the door, Alex's eyes widened slightly as she found Arthur standing there, backpack over one shoulder and a worried expression on his face.

"Alex," Arthur breathed, his blue eyes sparkling as he smiled at her and sighed in relief. "You're okay."

"I'm fine Arthur, we all are," Alex assured him, even as she melted more than a little and smiled in return. "I told you that on the phone," she reminded him, stepping to the side to let him into the living room and closed the door with a soft click.

"I know," Arthur replied, running a hand through his blond hair in aggravation. "I'm just sorry I wasn't there. Our next big enemy starts attacking and I'm at a stupid football game across the country."

"It's okay," she promised, both worried at his aggravation and touched by his obvious worry. "After all, I'm the one who didn't meet you for breakfast this morning. I just couldn't drag myself out of bed any earlier than necessary."

"But you're really okay, Bran and Nicki too?"

"We were just exhausted by the fight. We stayed at Morgana's house until after dinner to rest up and then came back to campus. No real injuries. Bran's leg is sore from the strain he put on it, but he's okay too and Nicki's bounced back to her usual self."

"And how are you?"

"Worried," she admitted with a shake of her head. "The Sídhe don't come out much in the daytime, but the light didn't bother this thing at all. We'll have to be on guard all the time now. Merlin promised he'd help us set up some protections for our dorm room. Apparently iron works okay against these things too. It doesn't hurt them like it does the Sídhe, but it slows them down so we've got that in our favor at least."

"Damn, I really should have been there, it isn't right for you to always have to face the threat."

Alex wanted to say something more, wanted to make sure that Arthur didn't blame himself for the insanity that was their life, but she couldn't because he suddenly pulled her closer, and Alex saw a flash of blue eyes before dry slightly chapped lips were on hers. Arthur might've meant it to be reassuring and life affirming, but without thinking about it, Alex tugged him closer and nibbled at his bottom lip. Arthur raised a hand to the back of her head, tangling his fingers in her long blonde hair as he opened his lips and responded perfectly to her.

There was a brilliant rush of excitement through Alex, washing away the fear and worry that had been lingering in her chest all last night. The nightmares of Shadows hissing and attacking her while Hounds howled in the distance were suddenly forgotten. She'd almost forgotten in the last year just what this felt like.

The large hand on her hip felt hot even through her clothing, but when Arthur's hand shifted just enough for his fingers to brush skin Alex thought the room might just burst into flames. Their chests were pressed together so tightly she could feel the outline of his ribs against her own. Groans and soft pants for air were the only sounds in the small living room. Their hands were everywhere, pushing up shirts and dancing over skin with eagerness that Alex barely remembered from her high school adventures. Arthur pulled his mouth away from hers and despite herself, a small whimper escaped Alex before his lips started caressing her neck. It felt like being punched in the solar plexus as her legs quivered and everything blinked away.

They somehow moved over to the small sofa that filled one corner of the living room. Alex's threw a leg over one of Arthur's as he returned to kissing her. She didn't even hear the sound of the front door's lock disengaging. The sound of the door opening and softly hitting the entry way wall barely registered as Arthur pulled her completely onto his lap. Forcing open her eyes, Alex glanced towards the entry lost in a heavy fog that lasted until Nicki stepped into view, turned red and squeaked.

"Oh god Alex, I'm sorry," Nicki gasped, averting her eyes from them.

"Nicki," she choked out.

Alex shifted away from Arthur on the too small sofa, nearly falling to the ground. Her roommate's eyes widened and a faint blush appeared on Nicki's face.

"Sorry," Nicki gushed as she rapidly headed to the hallway. "My class was canceled; I'll just be in my room-"

Arthur's phone beeped loudly, nearly echoing off the mostly bare white wall. Her boyfriend gave her a sheepish look and glanced towards Nicki who was hovering by the door to her room as she fumbled for her key card.

"I've got to get to class," Arthur muttered, bending over to pick up the backpack he'd dropped sometime during their little make-out session. "Uh, how about dinner tonight? Nothing fancy, but it would be nice to spend some time together.

"Okay," Alex agreed quickly, still very warm and embarrassed. With a tentative look towards Nicki, she leaned forward and caught Arthur's lips in a quick kiss, resisting the urge to drag him up against her again.

"I'll meet you guys for lunch," Arthur promised. "Just by the burger stand in the commons."

"Sounds good."

Arthur leaned forward and kissed her on the cheek before nodding to Nicki, a faint blush on his cheeks before he vanished out the front door.

"He's annoyingly perfect sometimes," Nicki observed calmly with a raised eyebrow. "But then again as Merlin's already pointing out in class the figure of King Arthur is a highly idealized figure who in his French courtly love retelling was in fact destroyed due to being too idealistic."

"I wonder how the French knew about Lancelot and Guinevere though," Alex remarked, grateful for the distraction. "I mean the names are different, but…maybe one of the French troubadours was a reincarnation or heard a folk tale that preserved the original story. After all, as Merlin pointed out, like Robin Hood, King Arthur is one of those heroes who is reinvented over and over to fulfill a need for a hero. He'd have to be modernized time and time again after all the Bronze Age was a long long time ago. And from what Merlin said about even the oldest Welsh texts there was already a lot wrong with the story by then. There doesn't seem to be much of the original Arto in the King Arthur myth anymore."

"True and Merlin did lecture about one of the local variations where Arthur had sons and a full sister. It's hard to imagine trying to find the original story in all of that," Nicki pointed out.

"I wonder what he was really like," Alex remarked. "If he was like Arthur, or Arthur is like him I suppose. Merlin and Morgana don't talk about him much, but he's the start of all of it."

"Well, Morgana and Merlin seem to like Arthur so there's probably some similarity between them," Nicki offered gently. "He's a nice guy: I understand why you like him so much."

Blushing, Alex smiled and nodded, looking down at the floor. "I still can't believe that we're going out. After he kissed me when the gate was created I was really happy, but part of me expected for Merlin and Morgana to forbid us dating or something or for him to change his mind. He's just so wonderful, he's smart, supportive and he forgave Jenny and Lance."

"Plus he looks good," Nicki pointed out and when Alex looked at her funny she laughed. "I'm gay honey, not blind. I can appreciate the aesthetics of the male form and your beau has an excellent male form."

"I've hit the jackpot," Alex agreed with a widely smile as a shiver of delight tingled up her spine. "There's this little part of me that's gloating," Alex confessed with a sly glance towards Nicki.

"You didn't date last year did you?" Nicki asked, raising her eyebrow and smiling.

"No," she agreed with a shake of her head. "I intended to, of course, figured once I settled in a little bit that I'd meet someone or at least ask out a cute guy from time to time. Things last year…. Well, everything just got a little insane for that."

"You could have done what I did; hook-ups are fun," Nicki observed with a shrug. "Although in my case you get a lot of bi-curious girls who aren't interested in more than once which can be sad if you want to date them." There was a flash of distaste on Nicki's face and she shook her head. "And then sometimes they are distinctly not fun."

"Hookups have never really been my thing," Alex admitted with a sheepish shrug. "In high school, I had a couple of boyfriends and had fun with them, but it was always after a few dates at least. I planned on finding a boyfriend since Thomas and I broke up, but after all the magic stuff started I just never seemed to have any free time and there was always the possibility of being attacked while out on a date."

"Plus you had that crush on Arthur," Nicki teased with a grin and small wink. "And then things got chaotic with the Sídhe and you having to keep an eye on the doomed love triangle."

Alex was grateful for the slight subject change even if the reminder of how the latter half of her freshman year had gone made her grimace. A stray thought crossed her mind, questioning if one of the reasons she hadn't tried to date last semester had been that she was secretly hoping that once everything was said and done that Arthur would see her as a potential girlfriend and not just his friend. She shoved it away: she hadn't done anything wrong last year and even if there had been a selfish little wish in there somewhere, she hadn't acted on it. Arthur had been the one to kiss her first and ask her out.

"I've got Arthur now," Alex said firmly with a pleased smile. "He's the Iron Soul, I don't have to keep secrets from him or lie to him about where I'm going. I can be totally honest, that's just perfect."

"I'm glad for you, it's nice that being a mage helped bring you two together." Nicki's expression turned a little sad. "And you're right about the secrets thing. Aiden and Sarah had a rough summer. The long distance thing was bad enough, but he didn't know what to tell her when she was home. Even when we all got together to make the gate she didn't meet you or Bran."

"That's horrible," Alex gasped as a wave of guilt crashed over her happy haze. She hadn't thought about how her friends' relationships were faring at all. "He hasn't said anything."

"Aiden not really the sort to talk about his feelings; he'll geek out on you no problem, but actually talking about something that's bothering him: no. Sadly I was surprised that they hadn't broken up by the end of summer."

"I thought Sarah was your 'true love' or something."

"Oh, I've moved on," Nicki laughed. "She may be beautiful and everything, just my type with dark hair and those awesome blue eyes, but bros before hos and all that. Aiden is my brother, has been since we were in grade school, and dating his ex would not be good, especially if he never told her about magic."

"I wonder how you do tell someone about magic," Alex asked thoughtfully, leaning back in the sofa. "I mean in modern times, who do you trust not to draw you to the attention of the government or some shadowy research corporation? It's just messy."

"I don't know, I wonder sometimes if Morgana and Merlin have revealed themselves to anyone other than mages in the last millennium."

"Maybe, but my gut is no," Alex admitted with a shake of her head. "Morgana... I don't know. Sometimes I get the sense that she's got a huge heart, but sometimes she's really cold."

"There are multiple sides to some people Alex; it isn't always straightforward. Morgana and Merlin are really old: they've seen and been through a lot. At a certain point, it is going to weigh on a person. At least they have each other." Nicki tilted her head in consideration and added, "I wonder if they've ever gotten together in the past, you know, just for comfort or something like that."

"Great, now I'm thinking about teacher sex," Alex groaned with a grimace and shudder of distaste that made Nicki laugh. "But I doubt it. Their relationship just doesn't seem like that to me. They're... I don't know equals, partners, friends... but I don't think they're lovers. I think Morgana would be worried about threatening their ability to work together peacefully."

"Well, you know her better than I do, after all, you're her favorite."

"I am not."

"Oh you totally are Alex," Nicki countered with a loud laugh. "Hands down, why do you think if there is something we really want to know we ask you so that you'll ask her?"

"Yeah well, I think you're Merlin's favorite."

"Maybe," Nicki said with a shrug. "But I don't think he's got a favorite; expect probably Arthur, mister perfect Iron Soul and all that."

There was an odd tone to Nicki's voice that confused Alex and she looked at her friend, trying to put her finger on it. But Nicki's expression was normal and she leaned against the wall with a growing smirk.

"So we don't need to have a birds and the bees talk, but you're up to three dates now. Just keep in mind that the logistics for college are a bit different than high school," Nicki reminded her with a chuckle. "Since he's got a single you'll probably be over there so long term plan on taking some stuff over. And stash a brush in your purse for tonight; the walk across campus is easier in the morning if your hair doesn't look like you just slipped out of someone else's room."

"Plus side no parents and fathers who glare at boyfriends," Alex added with a thoughtful expression, pursing her lips slightly.

"True, though I think my grandmother would prefer having one girl to glare at. She was a little disappointed to find out that I'm not interested in you."

"Oh?"

"Yeah, she liked you being here for me last year," Nicki paused and brushed a loose strand of red hair behind her ear. "But she likes me having a sister."

Alex smiled and nodded, her throat feeling too tight for words. Nicki returned the smile and winked at Alex before retreating into her room. Resting her head back on the top of the sofa, Alex stared up at the white ceiling and considered a small hole that she could see. It probably held a hanging plant in the past and for a moment Alex distracted herself with wondering if they should get something like that. Maybe they could even use it to practice magic on since those books of Aiden's did have a lot of plant spells. Merlin's magic affected the earth and some plants so it should be possible.

The distraction only lasted for a few minutes and Alex pulled out her phone to check the time. Arthur had probably been late to his class since Nicki had come home after hers had been canceled, but it wasn't time to meet for lunch. Pushing herself off the sofa, Alex walked down the hallway to her own bedroom and pulled a random Jane Austen book off the shelf, planning to lose herself in someone else's messy life until lunch.

11

Best Friends

The Michaels Cafeteria was fairly quiet as Aiden scooped up another ladle full of tomato sauce onto his tortellini and glanced around for his friends. They were ahead of the main dinner rush, with all of them wanting to eat before fencing club. Aiden watched Arthur and Alex head to the fountain drinks dispenser, staying very close to each other. A small smile tugged at his lips and he shook his head as he picked up his own tray and headed over to the corner where Nicki had secured them a round table. For a moment he nearly laughed at just how appropriate that was, even if Merlin had informed them that the legend of the round table came much later in the King Arthur mythos. Apparently, the closest Arto's council had gotten was sitting in a circle around a fire pit.

"Italian again," Nicki observed as he sat down with his pasta, salad, and a slice of cake.

"It's in my blood," he defended, raising his chin. "Besides this is one of the few Italian dishes that the staff here does well. The spaghetti or alfredo sauce has to be avoided at all costs."

"You don't get that defensive over Irish dishes."

"Well next time I see coodle, cottage pie or soda bread in the campus dining room I'll be sure to rate them."

"Touché," Nicki conceded with a nod. "Maybe on St. Patrick's Day."

"They probably just use green food coloring in the mashed potatoes like they did last year," he reminded her, curling his nose at the memory. "I know that Mom's people are known for the consumption of potatoes, but that was a bit much."

"To be fair I don't know if most college kids would be willing to try cottage pie, but maybe they could make up a good Irish stew. Your mom's recipe is really good."

"What are we talking about?" Bran asked as he set his tray down and sat in the seat between him and Nicki.

"Cultural foods of Aiden's family," Nicki replied without any hint of embarrassment.

"Mom would be glad to give you the recipes she's got," Aiden offered Nicki with a small smile to Bran, planning on wrapping up the conversation. "After all, you're part Irish."

"I think half the planet is part Irish," Nicki laughed. "You just give me a greater claim to it since I like your grandfather's stories."

"Hi guys," Arthur greeted cheerfully as he set his tray down.

He turned and pulled out Alex's seat earning a beaming smile and a slight blush from his girlfriend. Aiden heard a small chuckle escape Nicki and glanced towards her. She shook her head a little and rolled her eyes making him smile. He supposed living with one of the love birds meant that she had to see a lot of this.

"Hello," Alex greeted them all as she sat down and picked up her napkin. "Looks good Aiden."

"Oh don't get him started again," Nicki scolded quickly with a fake stern expression.

"Okay…" Alex said slowly with a confused expression. "I guess that's the cue to find a new subject of conversation."

"I've got a question for Bran if you guys don't mind," Arthur informed him, turning his eyes towards Bran.

"Shoot."

"Well, it's about how the Tree of Reality is supposed to work. I'm afraid that I don't get it," Arthur admitted, shaking his head. "How are the Sídhe so similar and yet different than us? They look so human. I'm just not sure that I understand."

"It is the multiverse hypothesis," Bran explained as he cut his sandwich in half. "The idea is that there are so many different universes that there is a probability of our world being fully recreated with other versions of us. Naturally, if replication like that is possible then it's easily possible that in one of those other universes another species evolved into a form very similar to our own."

"Isn't that just science fiction? The idea of other realities and stuff?"

"Once upon a time submarines and flying machines were just science fiction stuff," Bran replied with a small smirk. "Besides, traditionally alternate realities are branches off our universe. They are created by people making different choices causing variations in the timeline of the universe, but I don't believe in those. It doesn't really fit with Einstein's theory of space and time."

"Bran," Aiden said gently. "You're going to lose the non-science majors."

"Uh, right," Bran replied with a nod. "The multiverse hypothesis is something that has shifted from a science fiction trope to a viable explanation for many things observed in the world. Many physicists today accept at least to some extent the multiverse theory."

"But isn't it still just a theory?" Alex questioned.

"Technically it is a hypothesis," Bran corrected quickly. "People use the word theory wrong all the time: in science a hypothesis is an educated guess based on observations and in this case some very complex math. A hypothesis has to be testable in order to be considered scientific which with current technology the multiverse hypothesis is not, of course, we know better, but that's one of the reasons why so many physicists are still doubtful of it."

"But doesn't what we're doing prove it?" Arthur asked, tilting his head in consideration.

"Prove isn't the right word: proof only exists in a courtroom and in math. In this case, we know that the multiverse is a theory, not a hypothesis since it stands up to tests and can be observed. After all, gravity is a theory, evolution is a theory. Their effects can be studied and observed, but science isn't proven."

Aiden's eyes were beginning to glaze over now and he glanced at the others while Bran paused to take another bite of his sandwich. Nicki was blinking and she shook her head a little before straightening up.

"As for 'proving' that it is real to the scientific community, well we'd have to expose magic and the war between the worlds and as much as a part of me would love to be the one who brought forth evidence of the multiverse it wouldn't be safe."

"Okay Bran," Aiden cut in with a shake of his head. "I think you're going a little too much into technobabble territory."

"Oh… yeah sorry about that," Bran sputtered as he took in the vacant expressions of the others.

"That's okay," Alex assured him with a smile. "I go off on my own little rambles about literature and books."

"And I go off about history and just about anything I know anything about," Nicki added with a chuckle. "You're in good company."

"Okay," Bran said, still a little sheepishly before looking over at Arthur. "Uh, sorry about that, was there something in particular you wanted to know about?"

"Well… I guess will everything look so much like us?"

"Merlin and Morgana would be able to better answer that from experience, but I'd say no. The Old Ones are supposed to be energy beings, but I get the sense that they only resemble us if they want to. According to the Dark Matter hypothesis, they probably come from a universe with less Dark Matter, meaning that there is little pull on atoms to bring them together. In that kind of universe, matter isn't what… matters. They may not even come from a real planet in the sense that we'd understand it. Their universe may have very little matter."

"And that's why they're altered by coming here, right?" Alex asked, tilting her head curiously. Aiden wondered if she was even aware that she did that.

"Exactly: atomic particles gain their mass by traveling through our space. When they come into our world they are suddenly in a space that gives them mass and a material form. That's radically different than what they're used to. It changes their physical being and since they're energy than they probably also suffer side effects from at least one of the kinds of energy we have here. It's insane when you really think about it."

"I'm getting that," Arthur said slowly with wide eyes. "No wonder that ancient peoples just went with 'they're gods or from other worlds.' Without higher math, it must have been brutal to try and understand that."

"Well, it is very probable that the notion of gods predated human interaction with them," Nicki offered with a smile. "After all the creation and worship of a deity is a human response to fear and a desire for control. I bet in some places there were already local deities and when the Old Ones arrived they just took that identity."

"But do you think the big deities, the really famous ones, are Old Ones?" Alex asked her roommate.

Aiden chuckled and leaned back in his chair, listening with only one ear as Nicki turned the question into a little lecture of her own about some traditional deities that were more obscure. Personally, Aiden just hoped that the Greek Gods weren't real. While they were the most famous, they were a nasty and horny lot that he'd prefer never entered the equation. He looked towards Arthur who was listening to Nicki with a slightly bored expression on his face. It only took a moment for Aiden to notice that Arthur's eyes kept glancing towards Alex. Aiden smiled slightly: he was happy for them, and after everything Alex went through last year she deserved to be happy and have a relationship. They were lucky that they were both magical and could be honest with each other.

Inwardly he flinched at his own train of thought, a bubble of guilt rising in his chest. He picked up his soda and took a drink, staring into the liquid rather than his fellow mages.

Sarah's face popped into his mind, her wide pretty smile, bright blue eyes and long brown hair fluttering around her face. He'd been shocked in high school when she'd agreed to go out with him. Geeks were more accepted now in mainstream culture, but in his eyes she'd been one of the most beautiful girls in school. Putting down his glass, Aiden pushed thoughts of Sarah away except a small mental note to set up another virtual date for later in the week. Maybe just talking to each other about school more often would help.

"What do you think Aiden?" Nicki asked, her voice a little pointed and he knew he'd been caught.

"Sorry Nicki, I was thinking about something else," he admitted to his best friend.

"Merlin and Morgana have already mentioned interactions with the Norse pantheon," Alex informed Nicki, getting the conversation going again. "So at least some of them are real. Maybe that's how it works. Some of the core gods are real and then humans add stories, creating more and expanding the pantheons and making stories to go along with them."

"Maybe," Nicki agreed with a small nod. "Wouldn't it be cool if Thor's hammer was real?"

In the corner of his eye, Aiden saw Arthur straighten up and his eyes gleam with interest. He frowned, but the look was gone and he simply looked interested in the theory. Bran chimed in about which sort of gods might be Old Ones and if they'd even have 'domains' or if stories would add those later. That, of course, got Alex going on stories and how they developed and changed as if they didn't understand that being in Merlin's King Arthur class. Still, Bran and Nicki let her go off on her tangent without any interruptions.

"Guys," Arthur interrupted a few minutes later. "I hate to break this up, but didn't you guys say that you were helping to set up stuff for fencing club?"

"Shit, what time is it?" Aiden hissed as he pulled out his phone. "Nicki we've got to go. It's six twenty now."

"I'll get your trays," Alex offered as Nicki gulped down the last of her juice. "See you in a few."

"Yeah, you can help with the newbies this year," Nicki announced, thumping the empty glass down on the table.

"Maybe, but don't count on it."

Before Nicki could come with a clever last word, Aiden grabbed her arm and tugged her towards the doorway. His dad should already be waiting at the old gym for set up. All the equipment had already been cleaned and sorted from its summer in storage, but they'd have to get the mats down and get the registration table set up.

The old gym that the Fencing Club used wasn't too far to go. This side of campus was fairly quiet with most classes finished, professors gone for the day and students all back at their dorms or at Michaels for dinner. Aiden welcomed the silence as he and Nicki walked along the sidewalk in comfortable silence. It was something that he was grateful for; with him at least Nicki never felt the need to fill the silence. They were together and comfortable with each other; it was one of the constants in his life that he greatly valued.

A soft breeze was blowing the scent of the flowering trees in the arboretum through the campus. It wouldn't be long before the last of the flowers were gone and it became too chilly for students to spend time outside. September was well underway and the days were already becoming shorter.

"Have you given any thought to what you want to do for your birthday this year?" Aiden asked Nicki without looking at her.

"Bit early to be thinking about it don't you think?"

"Well I was thinking that maybe we should celebrate it early this year, I mean October 30th… sadly we're probably going to have something attacking us."

"Fair point," Nicki conceded with a resigned sigh. "But let's not worry about it just yet. I'll let you know if I think of anything in particular, how's that?"

"Okay," he agreed with a shrug. "Just wanted to bring it up."

"Don't mention it to Alex just yet; she's started stressing over Jenny's birthday."

"Oh?"

"Yeah her birthday is October 7th and apparently they've had a couple of civil conversations, but it is still awkward. Alex asked me if I thought getting her a present would be good or bad taste."

"Given her relationship with Arthur, I'm inclined to think it's a bad idea," Aiden remarked, tensing at the question with a slight hiss.

"Yeah, but… I think that Alex misses her," Nicki replied softly. "She really did care about Jenny, Lance too, but you remember how hard she was on herself last year trying to protect Jenny and Arthur. Alex really does care about Jenny."

"Maybe things will work out with them," Aiden offered gently. "I mean I understand Jenny needing some space, but maybe by the end of the year she and Lance will have things worked out and she and Arthur will be okay."

"That would make Alex happy, but I doubt it will happen."

"Don't be so negative, people can surprise you," Aiden reminded her carefully, knowing this was shaky ground.

"I know, but forgiving someone and giving them a second chance are two different things. I worry that Alex is too soft hearted and trusting sometimes."

"Then it's good that she's got us then," Aiden countered with a cheerful smile, looking ahead at the old gym. "We're a team that balances out each other's weak points."

"Ah, Aiden, always ready with some words of wisdom from a comic book," Nicki chuckled warmly.

"Or games, don't forget the games."

Their conversation was ended when a sudden crack of wood and the rustle of leaves in a nearby bush caught their attention. They both froze at the sound. Aiden felt his muscles tensing and bent his knees slightly, preparing himself for a fast movement. Next to him, he heard Nicki's breathing became fainter. The cracking in the bushes continued and a strange scraping sound reached his ears. Aiden licked his dry lips and took a slow step towards the bushes, grateful when he heard Nicki follow him.

A creature erupted from the bushes with a feline scream of alarm. The cat ran past them, its matted fur covered with twigs. It leapt over the sidewalk and vanished around the corner of the gym. A loud exhale escaped Aiden and he straightened up, shaking his head.

"I thought-"

"Me too," Nicki said as she squeezed his arm. "We've all been a little on edge."

"We're paranoid is what we are."

"It's not paranoia if there is really something after you," Nicki told him gently, tugging on his arm. "Come on. Let's go gets things set up. One of us is going to need to work with Arthur. He'll need to know at least the basics of using a sword."

"Unless he already knows it," he heard himself grumble as they started up the gym stairs.

"I don't think his reincarnation works that way."

"Who was talking about reincarnation, he just seems to be good at everything. A bit annoying really."

"At least you don't live with Alex; when she goes off on one of her 'he's my boyfriend now, I can't believing he's my boyfriend' moments it's a challenge not to roll your eyes."

"They're in the honeymoon stage; I'm sure she'll calm down in the future." Aiden offered as he opened the door and tried to hide his smile at Nicki's description of Alex.

"If the Shadows don't kill us first at least."

Aiden sighed and shook his head at Nicki as he followed her inside. She had a point, but did she really have to be so damn negative in her realism? Best friend or not, it got a bit irritating.

12

Fire Burning

806 B.C.E. Salisbury Plains

A tense stillness surrounded Arto and the others as they ate their evening meal. The roundhouse they'd been provided was dry and warm with a fire burning in the hearth. Their arrival in the village with news of more Riders having been destroyed had been met with cheers, but soon enough Morgana's silence and pensive expression had dimmed the enthusiasm of both the villagers and their own party. Morgana's insinuation of treason was hanging over Arto, like a stone around his neck, and the others had noticed. No one had asked, not even Luegáed.

He knew that Morgana's diplomatic abilities were wanting and she was suspicious by nature; her foster mother the Sídhe Queen had raised her as a weapon and to look down on humans. Arto feared that despite Morgana's decision to cut her ties to the Sídhe and help protect the Iron Realm, his sister would never fully shed the burdens of her childhood. Then again, he mused as he looked into the fire, perhaps no one ever did.

This village seemed no different than the many others he'd grown up visiting with Merlin. They all blurred together with names long forgotten. Even Gwenyvar's village was a hazy memory, lacking anything significant to him except meeting her while he was there. It bothered him that he took so little from the places he'd been, but perhaps that was the burden he'd carry from his nomadic upbringing by Merlin.

For a moment Arto wished that Medraut had come with them, before dismissing that idea. It was comforting to know that his cousin was back home and watching over things there. He'd only been away from Gwenyvar since their marriage began once before and it still felt uncomfortable. His fingers tightened around Cathanáil for a moment, a jolt of worry shooting through him for his wife and mother. But Medraut would keep them safe and plenty of warriors armed with iron had remained to guard the forges and the people. He was worrying for nothing. Besides, at times Medraut was more impatient, stubborn and harsh than even Morgana. His cousin was talented at saying the right things to people, he had diplomatic skills that Arto envied, but there were times when Medraut could be just as abrasive as Morgana. And right now he couldn't have handled it.

Sighing softly, Arto looked away from the flames and looked around the roundhouse at those gathered. Aileen was sitting near one of the four beds in the roundhouse on a mat of straw and blankets that would serve as his bed for the night and speaking in a low voice with Bradan. Drust and Maedoc were sharpening their iron swords with wicked smiles near the loom the owners of the roundhouse had left standing on the left side.

Luegáed was sitting on his own, his back against the wooden shelves on the far side of the roundhouse. His sword was sheathed and leaning against his chest and he stared up towards the ceiling. Lifting his own eyes, Arto watched the smoke twist and turn in the air until it seeped out the small cracks of the grass covered roof. It was beautiful in a way and he felt his muscles easing slightly. He glanced towards Luegáed and blinked in surprise as he realized that the other warrior was watching him with a small smile. Arto's lip curved up into a smile on their own accord and Arto nodded to Luegáed, urging his body to relax.

He rolled his shoulders and turned his neck, stretching his muscles out carefully. A small sigh of relief escaped Arto and he looked back to the smoke, watching a wisp twist into a spiral for a moment. He fancied that in enough smoke perhaps he'd see some amazing landscape or event. It made him think back to the description Morgana had once given him of the white tunnels she'd grown up in, where images of great Sídhe stories appeared and played out on the walls. While most aspects the slavery and selfish society of the Sídhe revolted him, Arto could admit to himself that Morgana's descriptions had sounded beautiful. He wondered if she ever missed the elegance of the Sídhe Court, the fine clothes or the pampering she enjoyed as the Queen's favorite, but he'd never ask such a question.

His eyelids were beginning to feel heavy and the lingering sense of being drained meant that he was already considering where in the roundhouse to curl up for the night. A glance towards his sister revealed her blinking her eyelids rapidly in an attempt to stay awake and Arto barely kept himself from chuckling and disturbing everyone.

Cries of alarm cut through the silence and Arto felt every muscle in his body tense as he sprang into action. Grabbing Cathanáil, he was on his feet in a moment and heading for the doorway. Behind him, he could hear Merlin and Morgana ordering the others to grab their weapons. The shouting and screaming outside was too chaotic, he could understand nothing that was being said and could barely hear anything inside the house as the noise level increased.

A sick feeling twisted in his stomach as Arto followed Luegáed from the roundhouse, nearly tripping over Aileen as they all sought to push their way out at once. Stumbling out into the cool night air, Arto gasped in alarm. The hillside was alight with flames, the trees burning brightly in the night and illuminating the darkness. He could hear the shouting in the village all around him and calls for water. Arto eyed the distance critically, it was over a mile between the outermost of the roundhouses and the edge of the forest, but fire could jump a great distance in the wind. As if answering his fears, a strong gust of wind ripped through the village, sending a chill up his arms and down his spine.

The group moved forward as one, rushing up the hill through the unfortified village and towards the fire. Above them, the flames were spreading quickly and making the sky glow, the light illuminating the clouds with a fierce red color. Even at the distance, Arto could see the shadows of animals and birds seeking to escape the inferno. Flames licked up the tall trees, reaching into the sky and Arto felt the heat radiating all around them. Ashes and burning leaves fell to the ground, sparking the grasses below as cries of fear and horror rippled amongst the crowd.

"Villagers back to your homes!" Merlin's commanding voice shouted above the dim. "The Sídhe are at work! Morgana, Arto and I will take care of this, the rest of you guard the village!"

"But-" Luegáed began to protest as he made a move towards him.

"Don't disobey!" Morgana snapped fiercely, her magic beginning to swirl down her arm.

In the low light, Arto saw Luegáed's eyes widen and the other young man nod nervously. He glanced towards him and Arto gave him a small nod and what he hoped was a reassuring smile. Luegáed spun on his heel, shouting to Bradan. Arto didn't linger to see what the others would do and raced forward with Morgana and Merlin.

They paused near the crest of the hill, keeping some distance between themselves and the flames, but the heat was almost unbearable. The shimmer of Morgana's magic distracted him and Arto looked over to his sister. She had a look of concentration on her face and her eyes were closed tightly. In front of her, Morgana was swirling her hands over and under each other as the silver magic danced in a cloud around them. Her eyes snapped open; he saw her exhale before pushing her hands towards the fire. The magic surged forward and changed form so quickly that Arto couldn't see the transition. A blast of water hit the nearest tree and carried over the ground, dousing a section of the flames.

Merlin's green magic illuminated his staff, creating a soft glow around the long length of wood that was brightest around his hand. His mentor raised the staff above his head and glared into the flames. The end of the staff crashed down against the earth and the green magic rushed down the staff and poured forth. Around them, the ground rumbled before the section in front of Merlin shifted forward in a wave of dirt and turf. It crashed into the burning grass and shrubs at the bases of the trees. The flames were buried in a rush of dirt, dimming and dying in an instant.

They didn't stop: Morgana kept throwing blasts of water towards the higher parts of the trees while wave after wave of dirt rushed through the forest floor. Arto looked around carefully, keeping his eyes open for any sign of danger and he glanced towards the village. More torches were visible and several outdoor fires were burning below which comforted him. Somehow he heard the growling over the cracking and groaning of the burning trees, the hiss of the flames being snuffed out with water and the thumps of earth being piled over the flames. Turning sharply to his right, Arto tensed as he caught sight of a Sídhe Hound moving along the edge of the flames.

Grabbing Cathanáil's hilt, Arto pulled the sword from its leather sheath with a smooth action and brought it in front of him, never taking his eyes off the Hound. It snarled at him, long and sharp teeth gleaming in the light of the fiery trees. There was another long howl from nearby, but Arto didn't dare take his eyes off the first Hound. Swallowing, he shouted a warning to the others just as the Hound leapt towards him. He swung Cathanáil in front of him, slicing into the torso of the creature. It vanished in a flash of light, but snarling from his right made Arto tense and begin to turn. He moved the sword, stumbling when a body hit him in the chest. There was a flash of light and a pained cry as another hound vanished, Cathanáil sunk into its neck.

His back hit the ground and his head slammed back against the rocky soil, his muscles twitching at the painful impact and darkness played at the edges of his vision. Arto felt Cathanáil slip from his hand and fumbled around blindly for the sword, his heart racing as another Hound snarled. He managed to raise his head only to see a flash of fur, teeth and gleaming violet eyes as the Hound launched at him. There was a blur of metal, a flash of light reflecting off a blade and the Hound screamed in pain. Arto heard a long whimper that faded away and blinked his eyes. He caught sight of the Hound dissolving into a cloud of gold.

"I'm here Arto," Luegáed shouted, his voice thick with determination. "Collect yourself, I'll protect you!"

His head was pounding, but the meaning of the words sunk in as he began to roll to the side. He felt Cathanáil's still warm hilt being pushed into his hand and tightened his fingers around it on reflex. Arto felt the magic in the sword thrum, reaching to connect with his own internal magic. He risked closing his eyes for a moment despite hearing shouting and more snarling in the distance.

"Morgana!" Luegáed shouted above the dim. "Arto is down! He's alive, but he can't fight!"

When he opened his eyes the world was a little clearer. The light of the burning trees had dimmed, but the smoke was much thicker making his eyes water as the flames were extinguished. All around them, smoke colored red by the flames was clouding their vision. Arto looked towards Luegáed who was standing less than a foot from his legs, sword drawn and at the ready. His fellow warrior was looking around with a determined and angry expression.

"I thought you were guarding the village," Arto managed to say, his throat dry and burning from the smoke.

"I organized the guard, but then we saw Riders approaching the fire and Hounds circling around your flank," Luegáed replied without looking at him. "I came to warn you."

It was an obvious trap and Arto wasn't sure if he was offended by Luegáed's thought that they didn't know, but not many willingly ran into a Sídhe trap. Near them the ground hissed as a fresh blast of water was thrown over it and Arto coughed as a new wave of smoke reached them. Luegáed shifted towards him as he climbed up onto his knees and coughed.

"Come on," Luegáed said quickly, kneeling down and putting one of his arms over his shoulders. Arto was pulled to his feet, Cathanáil still clutched in his hand and leaning heavily on Luegáed.

"I'm fine," he heard himself protest.

"You hit your head, hard from what I saw," Luegáed argued as they started walking towards the village and away from the fire. "You're in no condition to be up here!"

"I won't leave my sister and Merlin."

"Arto," Luegáed countered as they nearly fell over a rock. "There are Sídhe and Hounds all over the hills!"

"But they-"

"I'm sure they'll be fine," Luegáed insisted, guiding them around a pile of rocks. "Now come on." Luegáed turned and looked over his shoulder at the blazing trees and shouted. "I'm taking Arto back to the village!"

"Hurry and go!" his sister's voice called out from the trees a moment before she dashed out of the fire, her long cloak gone and ashes covering her clothes. On her heels was a Síd dressed in his golden armor and carrying a long gleaming sword. "Keep him safe!"

Pulling away from Luegáed, Arto nearly fell once again and stumbled for footing. His head was pounding, overshadowing the ache in his back as he raised Cathanáil. Morgana spun around magic curling around her hand just before she thrust her hand towards the Síd. Her magic wove together forming a silver spear only seconds before it pierced the golden armor of the Síd. It stumbled for a moment before its mouth fell open in a silent scream as it dissolved.

"Arto," Morgana gasped as she rushed up to them, carefully reaching her hand out and touching the back of his head. He flinched as her fingers brushed a large bump that was forming and his brain blacked out for a split second from the pain. "You shouldn't be here!"

"More are coming!" Merlin's voice called right before the older mage strode out of the forest waving his staff around him.

Waves of dirt and ash were sweeping up from the forest floor and over the trees, snuffing out the flames. The smoke was thick around them, but the light of the fires was fading fast and Arto could see only a few more burning trees. Morgana nodded to Merlin and moved away, giving a warning look to Luegáed who remained still and holding him in place.

The blast of a horn cut through the haze threatening to take him over. A burst of adrenaline raced through Arto and he straightened up to look around. Three Riders burst out of the smoke on their horses with a Hound racing along beside them. His sister's magic lashed out like a whip, striking one of the steeds and sending its Rider crashing to the ground. Another blast of magic made the Rider scream as it began to dissolve. One of the Sídhe threw a blast of magic towards them, but Morgana spun out of the way and Luegáed's rough hand hauled him to the side.

He stumbled, uneasy on his feet, but he managed to bring Cathanáil up in front of him. Arto's vision blurred, bits of black flickered on the edges, but he could see Luegáed ducking under a blow from one of the Riders. The other young man's iron sword flashed as he drove it into the side of the horse. It screamed, stamping its feet as its flesh began to dissolve. The Rider leapt down from the horse, gathering golden magic in its hand. Lashing forward with Cathanáil, Arto nearly tripped on a rock but brought the sword down on the back of the Síd's neck. It vanished in a flash of light and his stomach violently protested the sudden movement. Stopping, Arto nearly dropped Cathanáil as he struggled to breathe and keep himself from becoming ill.

Merlin caught his shoulder and held him steady even as the older mage raised his staff. Green magic glistened around the smooth wood and illuminated the space around them. The violet eyes of the last Síd widened and it took a tentative step back. Arto saw a golden orb of magic beginning to form in the

Síd's hand and opened his mouth to warn Merlin. But his mentor waved his staff forward, sending a cloud of green magic sailing through the air. The Síd stopped moving as the cloud of magic surrounded it, a look of confusion apparent on its unearthly face just before the magic tightened around it. There was a scream before the magic completely enclosed the Síd and hid it from view. When the magic settled, the Síd was gone.

The Hound snarled, leaping forward in a flash of teeth and fur towards Merlin. Arto couldn't move properly as he saw Merlin begin turning to face the Hound, a bubble of fear in his chest that Merlin wouldn't be in time. There was a flash of silver magic in the corner of his eye and he saw Morgana's hand move. The Hound's snarl turned into a long pitiful cry as it dissolved into a shower of golden dust and faded into the night air. All around them the scent of charcoal, ash and smoke lingered and Arto looked towards the trees with a sad look. Many of the trees were black and still radiating heat. The ground was now ash mixed with dirt and no sign of plant life. Yet, there were still some trees that were nearly untouched with their branches swaying gently in the wind. It would grow back, Arto told himself firmly and there was still enough of the forest left to shelter the animals and provide forage for the village.

"I think," Merlin said slowly as he gasped for air. "That is the last of them and the fire is out. I'd call this a success."

He looked over at Luegáed and nodded with a small smile. Arto relaxed but felt his legs start to shake badly. His sister made a quick move towards him, but Luegáed caught his arm gently. It may have been childish, but as Luegáed carefully took his weight and started walking him back towards the village, Arto grinned at his sister as the nerves that had been fluttering in his stomach at the thought of betrayal were driven away by a sense of peace and triumph.

13

Homecoming Events

Raven Stadium echoed with cheering, screaming and talking around Aiden as he blinked to keep the wave of disorientation threatening to overtake him at bay. The stadium was nothing special in Aiden's eyes. It had been built over twenty years ago and always looked like a soda can on its side to him, but he'd attended plenty of games in it over the years with his father. That was just natural for the child of a professor, but he hadn't bothered with it much as a student thus far.

Next to him, Alex was on her feet clapping and cheering along with the rest of the crowd as their football team thundered out of the locker room and onto the field. Aiden barely heard Bran laugh at their friend's excitement for the homecoming game, but he heard Nicki's loud snort as she bit back her giggles. Alex didn't care; she just kept cheering and shouted good luck to Arthur as if he could hear her. With their fellow mage, the Iron Soul and Alex's boyfriend on the team, Aiden supposed it was only natural that attending football games would become a normal thing for them.

"Bit excited isn't she?" Bran asked, having to shout the question.

"A bit," he answered with a shout of his own before he noticed Bran shifting uncomfortably and toying with the button of the loose black jacket he was wearing. "You okay?"

"I'm not a huge fan of crowds," Bran announced as the cheering began to die down slowly around them. "This is actually my first football game here and I only attended a handful in high school."

"Well just let us know if you need anything."

Bran didn't say anything, but smiled and nodded telling Aiden that he understood and appreciated the gesture. Aiden felt himself relax slightly; he always worried about offering help to Bran, not wanting to suggest that his technically disabled friend couldn't handle something. He knew that he was probably a little too careful about it, but Aisling had gone on more than one rant about hating people treating her like she was fragile when her cancer had been at its peak. Aiden knew that Bran was tough; he'd refused to let the car crash that had injured his leg keep him down. Plus, Aiden was certain that the dreams and visions that his roommate had would have left him shaking.

They still had no answer for what Bran's vision last year had meant. Sure they knew that Chernobog was coming, but in the vision, Bran had been stabbed with a sword from behind. The very idea of experiencing that, even for only a moment, made Aiden shiver. He wouldn't wish it on his worst enemy, okay yes he would on his worst enemy like the Sídhe Riders and Chernobog, but not on his friend.

"I hope there isn't the stupid homecoming court thing like in high school," Nicki called from the other side of Alex who was still standing.

"I don't know," Bran shouted down to her. "Was there any kind of vote?"

"Don't know," Nicki replied with a shrug as she grabbed her soda. "I wasn't paying attention. I started ignoring school politics about sixth grade."

"The little parade was good, though," Aiden offered. "Not the best, but not the worst one they've ever done."

"Yeah, I remember three years ago when that float toppled over!" Nicki snorted into her drink.

"I remember," Aiden replied with a mock shudder as he looked towards the confused Bran. "You can find it online. It set off a chain reaction, sort of like dominoes, but much funnier in hindsight once you knew that no one got hurt."

"Guys!" Alex called, clearly irritated. "Come on, football game!"

"I'm not much of a football person," Bran told her. "Unless you remember that soccer is called football in the rest of the world."

"And I can never get past the quarterback licking his fingers and then putting them under the butt of another player," Nicki added with an evil little smile. "Plus, you know, men bending over in really tight pants."

Alex looked over at Nicki with a horrified, angry and threatening to burst out laughing expression. Lowering his face, Aiden covered his mouth and snorted into his hand. He didn't have to watch the girls to know that Nicki was being glared at and that Alex was probably getting a stupid grin in return.

"Why am I friends with you guys again?" Alex asked, huffing slightly as she sat down on the bleacher seat.

"I'm pretty sure you know the answer to that," Aiden answered with a grin.

"And I'm pretty sure that you damn well know that there is homecoming royalty. They were a part of the parade today, between that cool dragon and the marching band."

"Oh… right… the formally dressed people in the cars."

Alex gave him a look that made him flinch back in his seat, but he could see the corners of her lips trying to curve up. Sometimes she was just too much fun to mess with. Plus, he was really sure that Alex didn't care about this stuff half as much as she pretended to.

"That was yesterday," Nicki chimed in. "We can't be expected to remember everything. After all they've been throwing homecoming events at us all week." She tightened her jacket around her. "You even made us go to that prep rally that started three hours before kickoff."

"It was Jenny's first rally," Alex replied without looking at them, her eyes fixed on the football game below. "I wanted to support her."

No one teased her about that. Aiden saw Nicki make a small nod and Bran turned his focus to the field.

"How'd she do?" he finally asked.

"She was great and she looked genuinely happy and excited," Alex announced with a wide and happy smile as she looked over at him. "Jenny's even agreed to go out to lunch with me next week for her birthday."

Aiden couldn't help but smile and he exchanged a look with Nicki who was also smiling. No wonder Alex seemed in such better spirits. He figured the Lance issue was still probably bothering her, but she had Arthur and now things were normalizing with Jenny. A loud scream from Alex made him flinch and cover his ears as the offense rushed out onto the field.

"This is going to be a long game," Aiden muttered as he gingerly lowered his hands from his ears and ignored Nicki laughing at him.

In the end the game was more interesting than he had expected. He hadn't been converted into the fan base of the game or anything like that, but by the end with the scoreboard reading Ravens 45 and Vandals 17, even he could admit that it had been fun. Aiden always enjoyed sports more when he was in the thick of the energy. Plus there was a lot to be said for knowing someone on the team and cheering for them.

"That was great!" Alex cheered, her voice sounding rough and raw.

"Okay honey," Nicki said to her, pulling her down into her seat and handing her a bottle of water. "You need to stop with the screaming."

"Thanks," Alex replied sheepishly as she took the bottle of water and took a drink. "Maybe I did overdo it."

"I think everyone around us thought you were having a fit," Bran teased with a grin.

Alex was her usual mature and well-spoken self; she stuck her tongue out at Bran. Nicki laughed and shook her head at them.

"Let's wait here until the crowd thins a little," Nicki suggested as she glanced at Bran.

"If coming to see football games is going to be a thing now we're going to need something with more support than just blankets," Bran observed, straightening up and rolling his shoulders. "Otherwise I'm afraid I'll have to beg off and watch on television."

"We'll grab some of those little fold out chairs with the backs," Alex suggested, giving Bran an apologetic smile. "But thanks for coming with me guys."

"It was actually kind of fun," Aiden told her warmly. "Don't worry about it."

Alex's phone beeped and she pulled it out in record speed, almost dropping it. She had to pull off one of her gloves in order to manipulate the screen and grinned a moment later.

"Arthur says hi to you guys, he's just going to grab a quick shower and then he'll meet me by entrance C."

"We can hang around for bit," Bran remarked, beating Aiden to it. "I don't want to leave you out alone, just in case."

Alex nodded in agreement and grinned happily as she texted Arthur back. They lingered in the stands for a few more minutes with Nicki asking them about how their midterm essays for their King Arthur class were coming. The topic was an analysis of the Arthur, Lancelot and Guinevere love triangle and looking at other love triangles from the same courtly romance period for comparisons. Remarkably, Aiden hadn't even started it yet. It was just too weird, writing about the supposed legendary and totally fictional figure when you knew his reincarnation and had even observed part of the love triangle play out. He glanced over at Alex who was frowning into her water bottle.

"Alex?"

"I actually got permission from Mer- Professor Ambrose to write about the French creation of Camelot as the setting for their Arthurian stories," she admitted with a grimace. "I just couldn't… not after Jenny and Lance."

"That was good of him," Nicki announced with a smile, shifting to wrap an arm around Alex. "Besides, your essay sounds more interesting than our topic on the love triangle."

"Well the research is pretty dull," Alex replied with a shrug. "Camelot is after all basically a medieval utopia for the upper classes: their perfect courtly world. I'm worried about having enough for a proper essay."

"I'll take a look at it," Nicki offered with a smile. "Maybe I can suggest a few areas to expand upon."

"Thanks, that'd be helpful."

"Guys," Bran called. "Things are clearing out."

There were still lots of people near them, but the packed and racked crowds were gone. Standing up, he stretched out his hands and wiggled his fingers in the empty space. They gathered up the blankets they'd borrowed from Nicki's grandmother to pad the seats and headed for the doorways.

Parking Lot A was a mess, full of cheering students and families trying to find their cars. Aiden knew that the other two parking lots that served the stadium had to be just as bad. At least parking lot C was across the street and thus would be a little calmer.

"This way," Nicki called, grabbing Alex's hand and steering her around the massive stadium.

Aiden and Bran followed along behind as they walked around the curved sidewalk that connected the various entrances. Then up ahead, Aiden caught sight of Arthur leaning against the side of the stadium near Entrance C. His blond hair was still slightly damp and he looked exhausted but grinned as he caught sight of them.

Alex rushed forward and Arthur caught her up in a tight hug. Stepping away from the building, he swung Alex around twice before setting her back down on the ground. Aiden raised an eyebrow; he'd never seen anyone actually do that in real life, but Alex was grinning and Arthur looked just as silly happy.

"Good game Arthur," Aiden shouted.

"Thanks for coming guys," Arthur said, turning towards her and putting his arm around Alex's shoulders. "Hope you had fun."

"We had a good time," Nicki replied with a smile. "But we've seen Alex to you and I feel ready to drop."

"I get that," Arthur agreed with a nod. "Thanks for walking her over here," Arthur added more seriously.

"'Course," Nicki answered. "Just make sure you get her home okay."

"Yes ma'am," Arthur assured her with a small salute even as Alex rolled her eyes. But she lost interest in them and looked up at Arthur with a wide smile.

"Come on," Aiden told the others. "Let's go."

They got stuck in the flow of people heading away from the stadium as they crossed the street into Parking Lot C. The noise around them consisted of people talking and car horns honking as everyone tried to leave the area all at once. Turning away from University Drive, Aiden led the others down the sidewalk that connected the collection of buildings together. The parking lot was still full and cheers could be heard echoing in the dark night. Aiden glanced over to a red car with a pair of students perched on the top, beers in hand. Shaking his head, he sighed 'freshman' softly. The police would find them soon enough he reassured himself.

A long sidewalk stretched out of the parking lot and led into the small lawn area between the Music Building and the Math Building and continued beyond. It was a quiet route, away from the honking horns of football fans and the risk of careless drivers. Plus after being stuck in the large shifting and noisy crowd, Aiden figured they'd all be grateful for the peace. Aiden walked along beside Bran, moving at a slower pace to match the rhythm of Bran's own steps. Nicki was just behind him and he heard the soft beeps of her cell phone.

"Anything interesting?" he asked her, seeking a topic of conversation.

"Nah, just Alex telling me she won't be home," Nicki replied before a small sound escaped her. "Uh, I probably shouldn't have told you that."

"Don't worry about it," Bran said calmly. "You didn't mean to and it's not like we'll give her a hard time about it."

"You'd better not," Nicki replied sternly before she made a shivering sound. "Man, winter is trying to move in quickly."

"It is October," Aiden remarked, but he shifted slightly to zip up his own jacket. "But it does seem colder than before."

"We're out of the crowds now," Bran remarked. "And closer to the lake; that's probably helping us feel colder."

"Yeah..." Nicki said slowly.

Aiden was suddenly aware of how alone they seemed to be. The sidewalks stretching towards the dorms were empty despite the football game just ending. It wasn't late enough on a Saturday night to explain the strange absence of other people. He exhaled slowly, trying to calm down only to see his breath wisp out in front of him.

"Guys," Nicki whispered with a slight quiver in her voice. "I think we have a problem."

"Sídhe or Shadow?" Bran asked carefully, adjusting his pace and looking around carefully.

"Shadow, we're suddenly cold," Aiden decided. "Do you think we can make the dorms?"

"I doubt it," Nicki answered in a low voice. "But keep moving."

They rushed from streetlight to streetlight in small bursts of speed that had Bran panting. Aiden was stepping forward again; the Holmes dorm parking lot was in view ahead of them with the lights of Holmes Hall just beyond that. He hit what felt like a wall of icy air that forced the air from his lungs. Gasping, he stumbled back and shivered.

"Shit!" Bran huffed, pointing into the darkness just outside the streetlight.

Then Aiden saw movement in the shadows as the air rippled. The Shadow slinked towards them, its movement deliberate and slow as its glowing red eyes were fixed on him. Aiden struggled to stay upright as he stumbled back. On instinct, he called a fireball to his right hand, the burst of heat thawing the chill that was threatening to take over him.

"Aiden no!" Nicki shouted nearby, her voice ringing in the air. "No fire!"

The words cut through the confusion that was settling over him, replacing the disorientation and fear with terror. His most natural form of magic was useless and suddenly he couldn't remember how to use anything else. Aiden felt his fingers twitch painfully, an icy sensation crawling over them and making them ache and difficult to move. It was getting hard to breathe all of a sudden.

This must have been like what fighting the Sídhe was like for Alex before she could use her magic, he suddenly thought. The stray realization gave him a burst of energy and he reached to his back, pushing up the hem of his jacket enough to reach the holster of his iron dagger. He had no idea if the iron would affect this thing at all, but the terror eased slightly as he gripped the weapon in his hand.

The Shadow wasn't deterred by the sight of the iron dagger as Aiden brought it forward. It lunged towards him and Aiden felt his body begin to shift, ready to jump to the side. Something cold and hard slashed across his side making him flinch in pain. A blast of icy air hit his face and hands just as a spear of ice thrust into the side of the creature.

"Get back Aiden!" Nicki shouted before another ice spear embedded itself in the Shadow's neck.

The Shadow screamed at the impact, stumbling to the side as its front limbs began to give out on it. As before, Aiden could see ice crystals spreading over the creature's body. Then it began to vanish, the cloak of darkness that was surrounding them lifting and exposing the Shadow to the light of the streetlight. It was gone in a second, so quickly that Aiden had barely seen it vanishing. He looked down at his side where the creature had gotten him and realized with surprise that he was bleeding.

"Everyone okay?" Aiden asked, gripping the gash in his side carefully.

For a moment he lamented the destruction of his jacket but was also grateful for even the limited protection it may have given him. Maybe it was time to invest in a leather coat; it was always worth an armor point in the games. A hand on his shoulder pulled him from his thoughts just as he was realizing that he wasn't altogether there anymore.

"It's okay Aiden," Nicki told him gently. "You're hurt, but it isn't too deep. Come on let's get to the dorms and I'll patch you up."

"I'll call Morgana," Bran said from nearby, but Aiden couldn't see him. "She can help Nicki heal you."

"It's been awhile," Nicki muttered distantly.

"You can do it," Bran told her, encouragingly.

"I trust you," Aiden heard himself say as he smiled softly. "You're a natural at it."

"That's sweet of you to say," Nicki replied even as she shook her head. "But it is stressful, kind of scary and exhausting. I hope you never have to do it."

In the corner of his eye, Aiden finally caught sight of Bran as his friend made an odd little shiver with a look of confusion. Bran shook his head and stepped up next to Aiden, ready to support him on his shaky feet as they headed for the dormitory. Aiden sighed gratefully as the icy chill around them faded away, but internally lamented how useless he'd been in that fight. He'd just have to learn to call on his magic in other forms while in a stressful position. He wouldn't freeze like that again.

14

Catching Jenny Up

Brushing a strand of hair behind her ear, Alex stepped inside Central Diner and fought off a sense of unease. The loud fifties style diner was crowded with students and the sound of laughter filled the air. It was so normal and non-threatening that Alex was able to relax a little as she looked around.

"Can I help you honey?" an older waitress asked as she moved over to her.

"Uh I'm meeting someone," Alex told her just before her eyes landed on Jenny sitting alone in a small booth. Her old roommate was busy tapping away on her cell phone and hadn't noticed her. "I just found her, thanks."

"Okay, someone will be over to take your order in a few minutes," the waitress told her before rushing off to a rowdy table.

Alex shifted the small gift bag in her hand and took a deep breath before she forced herself to smile and start walking. The diner seemed strangely long, but all too soon she was at the table and slid into the bench seat across from Jenny. She was a little touched when Jenny slipped her phone into the pocket of her purse, out of sight. Alex noted that Jenny was wearing her favorite autumn shirt, a good sign, but the nervous knot in her stomach was still there.

"Hi, Jenny, happy early birthday," Alex greeted with forced cheerfulness.

"Hi, Alex," Jenny replied giving her an uneasy smile. "Thank you."

Setting the bag down, Alex relaxed as a spark of interest and excitement flashed in Jenny's eyes. Jenny tentatively reached for it only to pause and withdraw her hand. Her former roommate looked at her and chuckled softly, a resigned look in her eyes.

"It's weird isn't it?"

"A bit," Alex admitted with a nod, shrugging out of her jacket. "But I suppose that's natural."

"Maybe, but let's force our way past it," Jenny suggested, tossing her long dark hair over her shoulder. "How are you?"

"Good," Alex replied with a small nod. "I'm staying really busy between fencing club and the intramural soccer team and the other stuff. Soccer will be wrapped up next week, but we've had a good run and gotten further in the tournament than we did last year. And I think I'm going to do okay during midterms so I can't complain. You?"

"About the same, I love my broadcasting class and I'm excited for the more advanced stuff. I hate macroeconomics and can't wait for it to be over. Spirit squad is keeping me busy. It's harder than it was in high school since we can do more difficult techniques, but I like the training. A lot of the girls are really nice and one of them, Amanda, and I go shopping together every other Saturday. It's nice to have friends to hang with again." Jenny's eyes widened as she realized what she said and Alex did her best to hide her own flinch. "But... uh, I'm a little worried about the astronomy test. Otherwise, I think I'm going to be okay in midterms," Jenny finished with a brave face and charming smile.

Alex inwardly grimaced; she'd lived with Jenny for months without separate rooms. She was more than capable of seeing past Jenny's little acts, in fact, her former roommate seemed to be losing her touch.

"I'm taking astronomy too, I could help you study. I'm doing well in that class" Alex offered with a cautious smile. "Who's your teacher?"

"Professor Chohan, he's nice, but I just don't get. Who's yours?"

"Professor Clarke. Listen, Nicki and I are in the same lab so she could help too if you wanted."

"Well if you think she'd be okay with helping me," Jenny answered carefully. "I'd appreciate the help. I really want to do well and get my science requirements out of the way. But I don't want to make things hard on you with the others."

"Jenny, look Nicki understands that what happened... a lot of things were happening outside your control. You can't keep beating yourself up for that. I'm sure that Nicki would be glad to help you study if you needed it. But we can start with just the two of us."

"Thank you," Jenny replied in a softer voice with a small smile. "You're a good friend Alex. I know that last year must have been hard on you too."

"It's the past now," Alex insisted, not wanting to dwell on it. "I'm just glad to be able to talk with you again. I know we weren't the best of friends, but it always seemed like we... I don't know, clicked."

"Yeah," Jenny agreed with a real smile now. "I know what you mean. I'm sorry, I didn't mean to shut you out and if I ever gave you the impression that I blamed you-"

"I blamed myself," Alex interrupted. "But that's just me Jenny, that's not on you."

They barely noticed their waitress walk up. It was a girl about their age who looked frazzled. Pausing the conversation, Alex looked over the menu she'd neglected since her arrival. There was nothing new since the last time she'd been here with Arthur and she settled on her usual. Alex ordered a burger while Jenny ordered a salad and sandwich. As their waitress nodded and vanished into the bustle of people, Alex gave Jenny a teasing look. In her opinion, it was a serious waste to come to a classic burger diner and not get a burger.

"I'm on spirit squad; we've got a healthy diet and workout system, just like the football players," Jenny informed her, cutting off her teasing.

"Speaking of football players-" Alex started to ask before she thought better of it and slammed her mouth shut.

"Lance says hello when he sees me," Jenny informed her in a calm voice. "After the homecoming game, he actually asked me out."

"What did you say?"

"I said no," Jenny told her firmly, shaking her head and appearing much more relaxed with the topic than Alex was. "Lance just... he accepts all this. It doesn't bother him at all from what I can see."

"Jenny, he might just want to be with you regardless," Alex offered gently in a soft pleading voice.

"I have no intention of letting a former lifetime control this one," Jenny informed her with a darkening expression. "I let it happen once and it cost me Arthur and nearly got him killed." Jenny grimaced at her own words and sighed loudly. "I'm sticking my foot in my mouth tonight, aren't I? Please understand Alex, that I don't regret Arthur and my relationship ending. It was time, we'd both changed, but I regret the way it ended. In all honesty, I think that's part of why things happened the way they did with Lance. I loved Arthur, still do in many ways, but the passion I had for him in high school just started to fade away. I know that it isn't responsible and mature, but in hindsight, it probably turned out about as well as I was willing to let it back then. I just couldn't commit to ending the relationship."

"Of course," Alex assured her, trying to not look too relieved. There was a little part of her that pointed out how beautiful Jenny was and how much history she and Arthur had far too often. She forced herself to smile and cleared her throat. "But he and I both would like to know that you're happy and okay. Arthur still loves you in some ways and I consider you one of my friends."

"I'm getting there, one day at a time," Jenny assured her. "I've got activities I'm taking part in now, I'm volunteering at the soup kitchen, I'm making more friends, you and I are talking again and I… I guess I've almost forgiven myself."

"You should forgive yourself."

"I'm Catholic," Jenny replied with a short laugh. "Forgiving myself takes some time."

"Gee, makes me glad I'm not religious," Alex muttered incredulously. "'Course I don't know how I'd figure all the stuff I see now with that."

"It's a bit weird, I'll admit, knowing that there are different worlds, but I have faith so it doesn't bother me."

"Okay I guess, if it works for you," Alex said, still slightly stunned before she laughed. "But anyway it's good to hear that you're doing okay."

"I am. How are the others?"

"Arthur is good: his classes are going well despite his football schedule, and you saw homecoming, it was awesome."

"Yeah, but it wasn't just Arthur I was asking about," Jenny reminded her. "How are the others?"

"Nicki is doing well, it was an adjustment living with her, but we've got everything worked out even if it is odd finding long red hair everywhere. Bran seems to be alright and Aiden is doing well. We've been working on getting better at our…" Alex glanced around and lowered her voice, "Talents lately."

"Has something happened?"

"Sort of, there is this thing from another world sort of like the Sídhe that is coming towards Ravenslake. It has minions; the others were actually attacked right after homecoming. They're okay, but we're being really careful now. Nicki actually drove me over here just to be on the safe side."

"Shit," Jenny muttered under her breath, her eyes wide and nervous. "Sorry about that then."

"No, I wanted to see you and talk properly," Alex reminded her with a genuine smile. "One thing I've learned in all of this is that you can't just give up your day to day life." She pushed the gift bag closer to Jenny. "Happy birthday Jenny, I hope that things keep looking up for you."

"Thank you," Jenny told her with a real smile.

Jenny handled the bag gently, pulling out the two small gift boxes. A small squeak escaped Jenny as she recognized the logo of the local candy shop. She opened that box quickly, setting the other to the side. Alex smiled when the small individual chocolates were revealed and her roommate popped one into her mouth.

"What about that healthy diet?"

"Hush you, it's my birthday," Jenny scolded lightly with a blissful expression. "Just lovely, there's one thing I taught you: how to shop for the best chocolates."

"For what they cost they'd better be good," Alex replied with a loud tisk.

Jenny carefully closed up the box and slipped it back in the gift bag as their drinks were set down in front of them. Alex took a sip of her soda, enjoying the burst of sugar and caffeine as Jenny turned her attention to the second box. It was a plain small white box without any marks that jangled slightly when Jenny moved it.

"Jewelry?" Jenny guessed with a glance to Alex.

When she merely shrugged, Jenny gently opened the box and grinned. Inside was nestled a small pair of glass and ceramic earrings made in different shades of purple that Alex had bought at the Russell Gallery. Nicki had directed her there to find something distinct for Jenny's birthday and she was pretty sure that Samantha Russell had given her a big discount given the pricing on the other jewelry.

"Alex these are just perfect," Jenny cheered as she held the up against the sleeve of her purple turtleneck shirt. "They'll go great with my fall stuff."

"When I saw them I remembered how much you wear that shirt in the autumn."

"I look great in purple," Nicki replied with a shrug as she carefully put on the earrings. "How do they look?"

"They look great on you," Alex assured her, inwardly very pleased with herself.

Their food arrived only moments later, the rather large plates being set down in front of them along with a bottle of ketchup.

"So to address the elephant in the room," Jenny said calmly as she sliced her sandwich into quarters, "How is the other stuff?"

"Slow going," Alex admitted as she poured ketchup on her plate next to the fries. "Our new enemy means that we have to learn to use our abilities in new ways. All of us have a more natural manifestation of the energy that we use easily. In theory, since all the energy comes from the earth then it can take any form, but it is pretty hard."

"You'll get it," Jenny said encouragingly even though Alex could tell she didn't really understand what she was saying. "So your power comes from the earth; that's what makes you… you know?"

"Yeah, that's how it works."

"So do you think that the earth is actually alive? Some of this stuff makes it sound like it is…"

"Well…" Alex paused and frowned slightly. "It's weird. I think it is a living changing system, but does it have a consciousness… I don't know. Then again, it made the Iron Soul and that seems like an intelligent act to me."

"What do… the professors think?"

"I'm not sure; we haven't really talked about that. There's always other stuff to do. We have to practice or discuss how to protect ourselves." Alex frowned and toyed with a French fry. "I guess there's still a lot we don't know, but Nicki and I looked up Bronze Age Britain one night. It seems that back then they may not have had deities like we think about, but rather that they revered the earth and their ancestors who joined it. I know Nicki wants to ask, but we're not sure how sensitive Merlin and Morgana are about discussing their past."

"I don't know how you do it," Jenny admitted, shaking her head. "Deal with all this; just knowing a little bit about it has really thrown me off."

"Knowing that magic is sometimes real or something specific?" Alex asked, taking a sip of her drink. "To be honest it throws me sometimes."

"I think what bothers me the most are the religious implications of it," Jenny admitted with a slight frown. "Since I found out I've been trying to understand it in terms of my religion; it's important to me and in light of… everything else I didn't want to lose that."

"I don't understand you still being religious," Alex admitted carefully. "Knowing that magic is real and that there are other universes doesn't exactly fit most religious views, at least not ones that are still around."

"But clearly souls are real, Lance and I wouldn't have-" Jenny cut herself off, but recovered with a smile. "There is clearly something significant about them and that holds with my religious ideas."

"Sure souls are real, but it might have nothing to do with a deity," Alex reminded her with a shrug, searching her head for something to say. "It could be a collection of memories given form by magical energy or something like that. And after all, the problems we have are because of different universes coming into contact."

"But that could mean that it was God who created magic and gave mages their power. From the little I was told the power you have comes and goes, it isn't constant."

"I suppose that is possible," Alex conceded carefully. "But if it was some kind of real deity, not just a being from another universe that has a lot of power, then it still doesn't match up with most religious visions."

It was Jenny's turn to frown, but she shook her head and straightened up. Despite their differing opinions, Alex had the sense that Jenny was enjoying the little debate.

"Do you really not wonder about this?" Jenny pressed. "Wonder if it is proof there is a God and a plan?"

"Of course I wonder," Alex scoffed, toying with the straw in her drink for a moment. "Sometimes when I'm lying in my bed it is all I can think about. The repercussions of all of this, all the questions I want to ask the professors and how it's affected my view of the world. But in the end I need sleep and this war needs to be fought. There are always more important things to worry about and those concerns override everything else."

"What is it like, being like you are and doing this?" Jenny asked, nibbling at her bottom lip lightly. "Nicki told me about what you do, but at the time... well, I was thinking more about what it meant for me and Arthur and Lance. But what is it like?"

Alex froze as the question sunk in, her mind suddenly feeling like it had stalled. Then there was a rush of a million tiny little thoughts, images and even smells that pushed their way to the front of her mind. She had no idea of how to respond and felt herself swallow awkwardly. The answers that should have been on the tip of her tongue were: terrifying, frustrating, confusing and overwhelming. Yet those weren't the words that were trying to come forward.

Since she'd actually started using her magic and become a part of the team something had changed. She'd changed: it had crept up on her, but she had changed in small little ways that blended with her normal life. Alex's throat felt tight, but she managed to swallow, becoming aware of how Jenny was watching her and waiting for an answer.

"It's strange. Sometimes it's very scary and I feel the urge to flee, but I don't and I know that I won't. Sometimes it is frustrating because there just so much that I don't know and sometimes it is overwhelming because there is just so much that I need to know. The professors are teaching us slowly, just what we need to know, but I know that there are literally worlds out there that I'll discover one day." Alex realized that she was waving her hands around as she spoke and tried to still them. "But I'm not alone and I know that it matters, I guess. I never saw myself as a hero, just figured I was a decent person, but I was never going to be anything great. Now I know that my life matters; I've done something important." Alex smiled, feeling a warm flutter in her chest that she hadn't felt often in her life. "I saved those kids from the Sídhe, I turned around to help them and risked my life to help them.

They don't remember me or what happened, but they are out there living their lives because of me. It's strange but wonderful. It might not always be that way, but for now… it feels like something to be proud of."

Jenny nodded vaguely, an expression that Alex couldn't quite read on her face. The conversation focused on particulars about their classes and teachers after that. Alex focused on eating her dinner and asking Jenny for more details about her journalism classes. The tension drained away from Jenny and her eyes lit up as she talked about her broadcasting class. She was so excited by the material and it struck Alex that she might be watching her friend on the evening news one day. It certainly wouldn't surprise her, as long as her friend kept in mind that reporting on magic was a bad idea.

Eventually, they finished their meals and began to get the 'time for you to go' looks from the waitresses as more people came into the diner. Alex paid for dinner up at the main counter while Jenny said a quick hello to a student from one of her classes. She didn't pay much attention as Jenny made the quick introduction, her eyes drawn to the front door as a group of young men entered, Lance among them. Next to her, she heard Jenny suck in a sharp breath, but otherwise, her friend retained her composure.

They began heading for the main door, but Lance stopped them. His shoulders straightened and the smile on his face became fixed and tense. Alex stopped just in front of the doorway, glancing nervously between Jenny and Lance. Neither of them said anything, even though Lance cleared his throat and opened his mouth to speak, but nothing came out.

"Hello Lance," Alex finally greeted with a forced wide smile. "We were just finishing our dinner."

"Uh great," Lance replied, stumbling over his words even as his eyes remained locked on Jenny. "Happy birthday."

"Thank you, and thank you for the card, it was sweet," Jenny told him, her eyes wide and her smile faltering. She gripped Alex's hand, squeezing it tightly.

"We're blocking traffic," Alex announced, getting the help signal from Jenny. "Have a good night; we'll see you around."

Without waiting for Lance to respond, Alex pulled Jenny towards the door. As her roommate slipped outside, Alex glanced over her shoulder and gave Lance what she hoped was an apologetic look. His expression was too much like a kicked puppy for her to bear and she followed Jenny outside. Taking a deep breath, Alex tensed up at the sudden temperature change.

"Yikes," Alex groaned, zipping up her jacket and shoving her hands into her pockets. "It's freezing out here."

"My car is around the corner," Jenny told Alex, gesturing down the street. "Come on, I'll give you a ride back so you don't have to disturb Nicki or walk home alone."

"Thanks, that'd be great," Alex replied, shifting on her feet in an attempt to warm up.

"It's the least I can do." Jenny sounded sad and distant. "Sorry about Lance, that was weird."

"A little, but it's normal or as normal as things are for us," Alex said, trying to lighten the mood.

"Yeah," Jenny agreed weakly with a small shrug.

The street was filled with parked cars crammed into every little space they could manage along the streets of downtown. Alex frowned as another shiver worked its way down her spine. Despite all the cars it was really quiet on the street. They were some of the only people out she noticed, watching an older man scurry into the small lounge and casino across the street.

"It's really quiet out here," Jenny whispered nervously. "Come on. I don't like this."

"I know," Alex told her, trying to understand what was happening. Then her teeth chattered and she tensed up with realization. Her chest tightened and Alex pulled her hands out of her pockets.

"Jenny, you should go back inside, quickly," Alex ordered as she glanced around. "A Shadow is here."

Looking around, Alex tried to find where the creature was as Jenny slowly backed away from her. Alex could see that she was conflicted and forced a smile.

"You can't help Jenny so please go get safe. I'm not sure, but it seems like people are repulsed by these things without even knowing it."

"But you're on your own," Jenny protested weakly.

Then Alex heard a soft growl down the alley behind the diner. She backtracked up the sidewalk past Jenny quickly and looked down into the narrow gravel alley. A bright light hung above the backdoor of the diner, illuminating the small open space between the door and the trash bins. Just beyond the radius of light, Alex saw a ripple in the darkness. Her chest tightened as a Shadow slinked into view. Around it, the light dimmed leaving the creature's glowing red eyes as the brightest things in the alleyway.

15

View from a Hillside

804 B.C.E. Northern Cornwall

It was a perfect day, Arto decided as he inhaled the fresh air and looked out over the valley. From the hill he could see the pastures with their earthen boundaries where men and their dogs worked to move the livestock, he could see the fields were the crops for the coming year were growing and he could see the wisps of smoke rising from the roundhouses safely tucked in the fortified village. The wooden walls and gate did little against the Sídhe, but even now he could feel the soft pulse of his blood spell. If he closed his eyes, Arto thought he might even feel the magic of the nearby Iron Gate that sealed off the area.

Lying back in the grass, Arto let out a soft sigh and stared up at the bright blue sky. A few wisps of clouds were scattered high above him and the summer sun was beaming down. The grass under his back tickled his bare skin, his shirt discarded next to Cathanáil beside him. Breathing deeply, he could detect the scent of livestock and a hint of the coming harvest. Nothing was ready yet, but the indications were for a good year. It was just as well; trade routes were being disrupted more and more by the Sídhe and two weeks ago Medraut had put men armed with iron weapons on guard duty for the fields and pastures. Morgana had approved of the precaution; in fact, it was the first things Medraut had ever done that his sister had approved of. Her disapproval of him had become something of a running joke in the village.

"This is nice," Gwenyvar observed with a soft sigh on his other side.

Turning his head, Arto smiled at the sight of his wife sitting contently in the soft grass with a half-finished reed basket in her lap. A pile of reeds soaking in a bowl of water was at her feet and her long hair was only half bound up, blowing in the gentle breeze. On the other side of her was Luegáed who was lounging back on the grass and chewing on a long blade of grass, his sword nearby along with the whetstone he'd been using only minutes before. There was a sense of calm surrounding the three of them that made Arto feel safe and happy.

"I wish it was like this more often," Gwenyvar added wistfully. "You're gone so often."

"I wish things were different too," Arto told her gently, reaching out and brushing her hand as she reached for a fresh reed. "But I am needed out there. There are more gates every season and soon the Sídhe will have nowhere to go. The end of this war is coming fast, I can feel it."

"He's right," Luegáed called to Gwenyvar, an easy and happy smile on his face. Arto was struck by it for a moment, remembering only a few years ago when his friend had just joined them, nervous and unsure of his place. "Arto has created gates in the northlands, the plains, by the white cliffs and even in my homeland! There's little more the Sídhe can do."

"Cornered and wounded animals are the most dangerous," Gwenyvar reminded them, her frown deepening as her eyes dropped to the basket in her lap. "I worry about you both when you are gone; I know that you look after each other, but it is not as reassuring as knowing that you are home."

"We are both good warriors Gwen," Luegáed assured her gently. "I won't tell you not to worry as it is your nature, but please remind yourself of that when you do worry."

"Gwen?" Arto repeated, raising his head to look towards his best friend and wife. "When did that start?"

"Oh a while ago," Gwenyvar replied quickly, a blush staining her cheeks. "If it bothers you-"

"Of course not," Arto assured her with a wide smile. "It's wonderful that my wife and my best friend get along so well. But speaking of wives Luegáed, are you ever going to marry yourself?" He sat up and looked back Gwenyvar, noting an odd expression flash over Luegáed's face.

"I'm not sure," Luegáed answered with a shrug. "We travel so much that I'm not sure I could properly provide for a family. I mean, wouldn't it be harder to leave if you and Gwenyvar had children?" Arto barely caught his wife's flinch in the corner of his eye, but he saw it and saw Luegáed blush and lower his gaze from them. "I didn't mean…"

"It's not a concern: we're both young and as much as my mother begs for grandchildren it can wait," Arto said cheerfully, taking Gwenyvar's hand. "You do have a point; it is hard enough to leave Gwenyvar, even on the long trips when I know that you're here protecting her for me. If there were children it would be even harder."

"There, you see," Luegáed announced in a forced cheerful tone. "I'm busy enough either guarding you or protecting your mother and wife. I haven't got the time for a wife of my own."

"Don't let my mother hear you say that. Once she wears Medraut down enough to consider marriages she might turn her attention to you." He paused, tilting his head slightly in thought. "It would do him some good, of course, maybe help him calm down and relax a little. Even Morgana knows that you have to stop and breathe in the fresh air every so often."

"Airril is here a lot lately," Gwenyvar agreed with a small smile. "It makes her very happy."

"Yes it does, he's actually going to officially hand control of their village to his brother after the summer celebration."

"What?" Gwenyvar asked with wide eyes. "You didn't tell me that?"

"Morgana told me only two days ago," he replied with a wide smile. "I've been waiting until there was a good moment. But yes, Airril will no longer be making those long trips. He's even offering to join the main force."

"That would let him stay with Morgana," Luegáed observed with a small nod.

"And you wouldn't have to worry about who is guarding my back when you stay to protect the village," he couldn't help but add. "I trust Airril completely."

"Not to mention he is a very pleasant man," Gwenyvar approved. "He does make Morgana so happy. She always sulks when he's gone."

"I wonder what Medraut will make of that?"

"Who knows," Arto replied with a shrug. "My cousin is a mystery to me sometimes."

"Medraut did seem very upset with the trader yesterday," Gwenyvar observed calmly, her deft fingers continuing to work on the small reed basket. "Any idea why? He's been very tense and short tempered lately."

"I'm sorry he snapped at you yesterday," Arto apologized to her gently with a soft smile, reaching over and brushed her exposed ankle gently. "It wasn't really you, he's just preoccupied."

"Why, though?" Luegáed asked with a frown, rolling over to face them. "What's got him so worried all of a sudden?"

"He's concerned about the recent traders' attitudes towards bronze," Arto replied with a loud sigh. "Iron is starting to take hold in the southern lands. It isn't common yet, but it is being produced a little more there and traded in from other areas. People have heard about it and are more interested in it. I'm afraid that iron is starting to replace the demand for bronze."

"But-" Gwenyvar stared at him with wide eyes. "That's our primary currency! If bronze isn't-"

"I know," Arto told her calmly. "But the fact is that knowledge of iron is getting to be more common. We've done very well off of bronze because our lands contain the materials needed to produce it, but things are changing now. My brother in law Airril has known that for years. Medraut will adjust in time."

"No wonder Medraut was unhappy," Luegáed observed with a frown. "His prestige comes from controlling most of the southern bronze trade."

"Exactly," Arto agreed with a nod. "But I think he's worrying too much; it will take time. Sure there is a little less demand for bronze and it isn't as valuable. But three bronze axe heads still got us wine, that jet necklace, and some other things. There's no need to panic."

"I suppose not, but still Arto Medraut-"

"If you haven't noticed my cousin worries a great deal about what people think of him. He's always reorganizing his shelves even before I visit his roundhouse," Arto observed with a laugh, shaking his head. "It's silly. I hope he'll grow out it."

"My father wouldn't mind it if you worried a bit more," Gwenyvar reminded him with a teasing smile.

"Your father wanted you to marry me believing that I'd become a powerful lord over the islands," Arto sighed with a shake of his head. "I love you darling, but your father is a bit too concerned with position. He and Medraut would get along."

"No they wouldn't," his wife disagreed. "They'd both be too occupied about who was considered more important."

A loud laugh escaped Arto as his mind provided an interesting image of his cousin and father in law glaring at each other. Gwenyvar was right of course, but it was tempting to see if he could introduce the two someday. Cailean's position as a regional priest kept him in the northlands and Medraut rarely went too far from the village. If he did, he might miss a chance to inspect a shipment of tin or copper before it went to the smelter.

"Still, aren't you worried about the changes?" Luegáed asked him once he'd stopped laughing. "It will affect the isles."

"No," Arto admitted. "My life, almost my entire life, has been nothing but constant change. It is natural. I worry about how the people will react to the changes, but not the changes themselves."

"For instance?" Luegáed pressed, a frown marring his features.

"If we lose trade with the south then I fear that the wealthy will seek wealth by other means. War is not something we have a history of suffering in these lands. We have always fought the Sídhe, not each other, but if bronze stops having value then that may change."

"Unless there was someone strong enough to keep the peace," Gwenyvar said softly.

"I am not going to seek dominion over the isles, Gwenyvar," Arto snapped. He didn't mean to sound angry, but her father was too fond of having this conversation for his tastes. "No matter what you father says."

"He might have a point," Luegáed remarked in a soft and cautious voice. "The leaders and priests already look to you Arto. They respect you as a warrior and a leader despite still being young. You have powerful magic and the loyalty of the two most powerful mages in the lands. Perhaps it wouldn't be such a bad thing. What do they call such men in the south?"

"They call them kings," Gwenyvar informed him, her eyes darting between them. "They are great men according to the traders who make law and protect the people."

"That is not our way," Arto reminded them as he laid out once more and stared stubbornly into the sky.

"But things are changing," Luegáed said in a low voice with a sigh. "I understand Arto that you would prefer to lead a quiet and peaceful life. I understand that my friend, but that is not what you were born for."

Arto had no words to say to his friend that he had not already said before. Merlin had said much the same thing to him as had Gwenyvar's ambitious father Cailean. His own mother often made noises about him being too content as a guest of his cousin. She knew he'd never try to take Medraut's place, but made no secret that she believed he could have more. Arto told himself not to be angry. They just did not understand. He loved Gwenyvar and merely wanted a happy life with her. He would have been content to have never been the Iron Soul, for his sister to have never been taken. Only Morgana seemed to understand that.

"A rider," Luegáed remarked calmly as he nodded towards the village. "For you or for Medraut?"

"No one comes to see Medraut," Arto answered with a resigned sigh as he sat up.

He reached for his shirt and pulled it on quickly. Looking towards the village he could just make out a dark horse entering the village with someone on its back. They were alone, that was rarely a good sign. It usually meant a call for help from a far off village being plagued by the Sídhe.

Standing up, Arto smiled at Gwenyvar as she handed him Cathanáil which he strapped around his shoulder without a word. The weight of the sword settled on him, both a welcome reminder of his power to create such a thing and a bitter token that his life wasn't his own. It was selfish and as Gwenyvar looked up at him, Arto felt a twitch of guilt knowing that he'd caused plenty of grief for his wife.

"You stay," he told his wife and friend. "No need to spoil your day. If it's nothing I'll return straight away."

"We'll be behind you," Luegáed promised with a pointed look.

Arto smiled fully this time and nodded in resignation. Good and loyal Luegáed was never too far from him or Gwenyvar. Shaking his head, Arto moved down the slope of the hill, a faint memory of playing here with a dog when he was young tugging at his mind. He pushed the memory away as he squared his shoulders and brushed off his tunic. Arto just hoped that there was no grass in his hair just in case the rider came from someone important.

The guards at the wooden gates of the village snapped to attention as he approached despite him waving for them not to worry. Arto barely contained his sigh as he headed into the village and scanned for signs of the rider. A dark brown horse was being led to a watering trough near his mother's roundhouse. Arto allowed himself a small sigh before he headed up towards the roundhouse.

Stopping just outside the door he heard a frantic voice say, "Please, I must speak with Arto! He's the only one who can help us!"

Arto straightened his shoulders, took a deep breath and pulled back the pelt that covered the doorway. It seemed that duty called once more and the day of rest was over.

16

Darkness Rising

The darkness moved with the creature as it slinked through the alley. Alex's eyes widened as a layer of ice appeared on the side of the large dumpster and spread over it with a creaking sound. Ice began to form in the gravel and even the light coming from behind her seemed to dim. Growling echoed off the brick walls as the Shadow took one slow step forward at a time, its footfalls shifting the gravel.

Alex's chest tightened. The Shadow was trying to frighten her; it was making each sound deliberately. Those red eyes were calculating as it watched her try to recover her senses. It felt like ice was creeping up her legs from the ground, locking her into place. Then the Shadow stepped into the dimming light of the street in front of Alex and she saw just how large the thing was. It reminded her far more a great bear than a man or a hound. Massive shoulders and thick front limbs with low claws put images of being ripped apart at the front of her mind.

There was a squeak of fear behind her from Jenny and Alex jumped to the side, the sound from her roommate breaking her fearful trance. A blast of cold hit Alex in the chest, making her gasp in pain as the air was forced from her lungs. In front of her, the breath twisted into misty shapes that spun off into the night as the creature lunged at them. Alex was pulled back by Jenny so quickly that both of them stumbled. The Shadow snarled as ice radiated out from where it touched the ground. Alex watched in a mixture of horror and awe as frost began to spread onto the bricks of the buildings.

With a sharp movement, Alex pulled at her magic and pushed it forward. The small blast of magic struck the Shadow in the chest. It shuddered but did not budge. Pulling away from Jenny, Alex dashed past the creature, allowing more magic to flow into her hands. Another blast to the side caused the creature to hiss and fix its glowing red eyes on her. The darkness of its form rippled and seemed to absorb her magic, but its attention was on her now. Alex darted back into the alley and reached into her bag with her left hand. Her fingers tightened around her dagger and she pulled it free, bringing it up in front of her.

The creature slunk towards her, the light of the lamp dimming as it passed and the temperature dropping further. Swallowing, Alex struggled to remain calm. She needed ice to hurt this thing, which was so stupid, but she needed it now. Magic glided over her cold fingers and Alex did her best to focus on that feeling. The urge to close her eyes tickled at the back of her mind as Alex tried to remember what Nicki's ice attacks looked like, but nothing came.

A sudden snarl was all the warning she received; the shadow sprang forward like a great cat striking her in the torso in a flash of darkness and sharp pain. Alex hit the ground, the gravel digging into the back of her torso and arms. Her lower back throbbed, but the pain flashed away as the low growl above Alex pulled her attention back to the danger. The Shadow shifted its weight, holding down her shoulders with the weight of its body. Terror clawed at her chest: Alex could barely breathe as the creature exhaled an icy mist across her face.

This close to the Shadow, Alex could see the swirling shades of red that made up its eyes. There was no pupil, just a socket filled with spinning colors, all reminding her of blood. The darkness of its form wasn't simply black, but rather a shimmering void that Alex thought she might reach right through. Had she not felt its weight and seen the flash of its long teeth, she might have thought it some sort of ghost.

There was a rush of noise, someone moving against the gravel. Above her, the Shadow paused and raised its head. A blur of brown collided with the Shadow, knocking it off of her and to the side as it shrieked. Turning her head as she sucked in a greedy breath, Alex saw the large Shadow fall against the dumpster with a metallic thud. Jenny was looming over her, a piece of short lumber clutched in her hands and breathing heavily with wide disbelieving eyes. Alex began to sit up, but the Shadow was faster. With a snarl, it was up and lunged for Jenny with a deafening roar.

Jenny avoided one long arm reaching for her, the claws swiping her hair as she pulled back, but in her haste, she lost her footing on the now icy and slick gravel. Everything slowed down as her former roommate hit the ground with the Shadow looming over her. It roared once again and rose off of its front limbs, stretching itself up on its back legs. The darkness of its form filled the entire alley and only the slight flickering of the nearby lamp betrayed its real location. Beyond the darkness, she could hear Jenny whimpering and could hear gravel shifting as she tried to move away.

Ice lance ice lance ice lance Alex kept repeating in her mind as she reached for her magic. Not daring to close her eyes, Alex glared at the Shadow as the small warm spark of her magic in her gut fought off the chill threatening to immobilize her. She had to make her magic take on the new form. Raising her shaking hand, Alex pushed her magic towards the Shadow and risked a glance at Jenny. Her former roommate groped at the gravel and dragged herself back across the ground from the creature just as the dark silver magic blasted forth.

The Shadow howled, its cry echoing off the walls of the alley. Alex had to blink before she could properly see the spear of shimmering magic that was plunged into the creature's side. A wave of despair began to well up inside of her, even as she tried to force her mind to see the shining spear of ice that she wanted. The Shadow was wailing and thrashing about, knocking into the brick wall and spinning, trying to dislodge the spear and completely ignoring Jenny.

Then the magic spear pulsed with a soft light and the shadow creature fell to the ground. It shook as the light in the spear intensified, only for a moment and Alex stared at it, completely dumbstruck. Magic was being pulled into the spear out of the creature and in the light of the doorway lamp, Alex saw the creature begin to fade just as the spear flickered out of existence.

Alex sighed in relief, collapsing to the side and dropping her head onto her outstretched arm. Below her, the ice on the ground remained firm and she inhaled the chilled air, but couldn't quite bring herself to move just yet. Alex closed her eyes for a moment, easing the painful dryness that had been setting in. Then with a soft exhale she opened them and looked down the alley towards the street where Jenny was staring at her. Alex forced a small smile and one was returned. It was a silent conversation of mutual gratitude that allowed Alex to breathe easier and start to sit up.

Then there was a low rumble from the street and Alex sat up quickly in alarm. Beyond the edge of the alley the lights were dimming rapidly and all distant sounds of people on the main street around the corner faded away. Alex exhaled and her breath danced as mist in front of her.

"Jenny," Alex choked out. "There's another one!"

Scrambling to her feet, Jenny started to run away from the end of the alley, her eyes locked on Alex as she moved towards her. Alex twisted her body, bringing her knees under her as she fought to stand up.

It lunged into the alley, a lithe fast moving form that screamed something that almost sounded like a word. Alex shivered as the Shadow launched itself at the brick wall. The darkness shimmered and a pair of glowing red eyes appeared just before a long human-like limb reached out and gripped the bricks. Then another limb appeared and the creature moved towards them, creeping along the wall like some kind of spider. Horns formed a twisted crown atop its head and the Shadow snarled revealing rows of long gleaming white teeth. Jumping towards them, it twisted in midair and landed with a barely audible thump in the middle of the alley.

Jenny was right in front of it, looking right at Alex with wide pleading eyes. The Shadow lashed out an arm, its hand grabbing Jenny's leg and pulled her down.

"Jenny!" Alex shouted, a rush of fear jolting through her body and overwhelming every conscious thought.

Alex felt her hand shoot forward, magic blasting off of it as she desperately tried to hold onto the desire for an ice spear. The words repeating in her head weren't enough; she couldn't see the spear that she needed. Her friend's scream cut through her concentration.

A strange laugh erupted from the Shadow as it tugged Jenny towards it as she frantically grabbed at the ground. Anger surged through Alex at the thing toying with her friend and she barely felt the magic jolt up her arm before it blasted away from her skin. Dark silver magic arched off her fingers and struck the Shadow's head like a bolt of lightning. There was a roar of rage and pain as it clutched at its head and in the corner of her eye, Alex saw Jenny scramble away.

The surge of magic dropped off and Alex gasped, sucking in air as quickly as she could. She tried to remember just what it looked like when her magic had killed the first Shadow. But she couldn't hold onto it; fear was prickling at the back of her mind, jarring her attempts to concentrate. The Shadow stalked towards her, Jenny forgotten.

Alex threw another bolt of magic, slowing the creature down, but the darkness of its form just seemed to swallow the magic. She released another bolt and another bolt, trying to form the ice, but it wasn't working. Then there was a dull cry that echoed in the alley, and the Shadow tensed and began to turn around. A body struck the creature from behind, releasing a loud scream of anger and alarm. Alex blinked in shock at the body that was suddenly pinning the Shadow, holding its front limbs down with bare dark skinned hands. Then the face of the person turned up towards her and while it did not shock her to see Lance's face, she could barely believe it.

"Alex!" he shouted in a blend of alarm and pain. Water dripped off Lance's fingers where the ice of the Shadow and his own body heat warred.

She moved quickly, pushing herself off the ground and half standing. Ice crackled beneath her feet just before the slickness sent her falling forward to her knees. Alex grit her teeth in pain and outstretched an arm. Magic sparked violently, darting off around her in swirling untamed sparks of dark silver as the pain in her knees overwhelmed her senses.

"Alex!" a pained half-shout half-groan called, cutting through the ache.

Alex gave up on the words ice spear; gave up on trying to control how her magic killed the creature. Instead, Alex allowed everything to pinpoint on the frantic, fearful wish for the Shadow's death. Magic erupted down her arm: her skin felt like it was burning through the layers of her coat and shirt. The ice around her no longer mattered and Alex hissed in pain but kept pushing the magic forward. There was a shout of pain from Lance, as ice began to crystallize over his fingers, but his grip didn't loosen.

Dark silver sparks surged forward, vanishing into the darkness of the Shadow. The blackness before Alex shimmered and then rippled like the surface of a still pond. The Shadow howled beneath Lance, a sound, unlike anything Alex had ever heard before. Half human, half animal, and filled with terror and pain. Light tore through the darkness of its flesh from within and dark silver magic surged out like a stream of water, twirling in the air before diving back into the glowing silver wound. Another wound opened and the Shadow convulsed beneath Lance who rolled off and slammed into the brick wall next to Alex.

Her wide eyes met Jenny's on the other side of the alley as the Shadow twisted and released another terrible scream. It gurgled something that again almost sounded like words, rolling over and reaching towards the night sky. Then it was silent as another wound ripped open its flesh and her magic spun out and dissolved into the air. Without another sound the darkness fell apart, forming tiny shreds of seemed to be black cloth blowing in the wind before those too vanished.

"What did I just do?" Alex gasped, staring at the empty space as her body threatened to collapse despite the adrenaline pumping through her.

Above them, the lamp above the doorway hummed and the level of light increased so suddenly that Alex slammed her eyes shut. It took her a moment before she dared open her eyes and check for signs of any more Shadows. In the distance, she could once again hear the sounds of people on the main street and past the end of the alley, Alex saw a car drive by. She exhaled loudly, breaking the silence in the alley and allowed a small relieved laugh to escape her.

Rising to his feet, Lance stumbled towards Jenny. He had to grip the wall, the ice under his feet making him unsteady. Jenny was trying to get up as Lance stepped over to her and extended a hand down to her. Alex froze, staring at the scene right out of the tales of Camelot as Lance helped Jenny to her feet. She dropped her gaze to the ground, but even the rapidly thawing sheet of ice couldn't distract her. Lance had tackled one of the creatures, been exposed to its magical cold and she should really be checking that but…. perhaps she was a coward after all.

"Lance," Jenny breathed, her voice sounding weak and overwhelmed making Alex look up sharply with worry. She rallied quickly, raising her chin and straightening her shoulders. "Thanks for the help."

"Jenny are you okay?" Lance pressed, reaching for her face.

Alex climbed to her feet as quietly as she could, using the brick wall behind her. The melting ice beneath her feet threatened to send her sliding, but she managed to stay upright. Under other circumstances, she might be tempted to shout out that she was alright and complain about the lack of concern for the person who actually killed the Shadows. But under the current circumstances, Alex actually regretted that she could clearly see both Lance and Jenny's face and hear them.

"I'm fine Lance," Jenny answered in an almost cold voice, but there was a slight waver to it.

She couldn't help it; Alex studied Jenny's profile, trying to read her emotions and expression. Lance was staring at her longingly with a soft and worried frown. It hit Alex like a punch in the gut.

"Jenny, I mean it. That thing didn't hurt you did it?"

"I'm a bit bruised," Jenny replied with a soft sigh. "But nothing more serious."

"There aren't any problems from exposure to them," Alex announced, reminding them of her presence and trying to calm Lance. "Well, I suppose if you were around them too long, but other than the cold nothing."

"See Lance?" Jenny said, giving him a stern look. "I'm fine."

There was a moment where Jenny hesitated, her eyes dropping to Lance's hands as he rubbed them together. There was no sign of any ice or discoloration. The hesitation was gone and Jenny started to step around him, tightening her coat around herself. Lance moved to catch her arm, his worried expression still in place.

"Lance stop!" Jenny snapped, pulling her arm away from him.

Lance stepped back as if burned, swallowing thickly. He nodded and quickly answered, "Of course, I'm sorry."

"No, I meant...stop trying so hard," Jenny sighed, as she turned back to him. She suddenly looked exhausted and her shoulders slumped. "Please. Every time I see you.... The way you look at me, it's just too much. I realize that what happened between us wasn't just our past lives. I know that we made certain choices too and those were the result of a real... attraction, but I'm just trying to sort my head out. You've sorted yours out, but I'm still trying. It means a lot knowing that you care and that you want to protect me, but you've got to back off. This isn't something that can be fixed overnight."

"Okay," Lance agreed softly, nodding as he took a step back. "I'm sorry Jenny. I didn't mean to be that guy-"

"You're not," Jenny insisted, interrupting him urgently. "But I need time," she added in a softer and sadder voice. "Finding out that you're the reincarnation of a famous adulteress who caused a lot of pain, even if by accident, isn't something I can just bounce back from. I've known Arthur for years and I hurt him through my selfishness, through being something that I never wanted to be, never dreamed I could be."

"I know," Lance answered in an equally soft voice. "I know that Jenny, it's the same for me, but..." He shook his head slightly and forced a small smile. "Anyway, if you need anything... you know my number," Lance finished awkwardly before he glanced over at Alex who had been trying to fade into the brick wall. "You two going to be okay?"

"Well... you could walk us to my car," Jenny offered with a tentative smile.

Lance smiled right back at her, his shoulders relaxing and he nodded. He moved as if he was going to offer Jenny his arm, but thought better of it. Instead, he lingered near her side. Alex held back a smile and walked over to join her friend, examining some slices in her coat. Soft feathers and stuffing were floating onto the ground like snow. As she stepped next to Jenny, her friend linked their arms and gripped her arm tightly. Alex made no move to stop Jenny and gritted her teeth to hide a flinch of pain as Jenny's grip became incredibly tight.

As they stepped back out into the street, Alex breathed a little easier as she caught sight of people moving in between buildings, talking in small crowds and heading to their cars. For a moment she felt dizzy but forced herself to keep moving. The light from the neon signs spilled onto the side streets and nearby people were pulling away from the curb in their cars. She could smell food, car exhaust and a hint of frost in the air. Normalcy had returned to Ravenslake, at least for the rest of the night.

17

Spears

Inhaling deeply, Aiden rolled his shoulders and did his best to ignore the ache in the side of his right knee. A cold blast of wind made him shiver, despite the Ravenslake sweatshirt he was wearing. He leaned back on the browning grass of Merlin's back yard with a sigh and looked over towards Nicki who was trying to coach Bran through making an ice spear with his magic. Judging from the look on Bran's face, he was having about as much fun as Aiden was having. The only difference was that a small shard of ice was floating in front of Bran, surrounded by a swirl of yellow magical sparks, something that he had yet to achieve.

Scattered about on the lawn were ice spears of different lengths that Nicki had created when they'd started this process. In theory, it was supposed to help them visualize their own ice attacks. Aiden wasn't sure if it was really helping or not. He'd lived in Oregon all of his life so he knew what snow and ice looked like. His mother had stopped him and Nicki from fighting with long icicles more than once after all. Still, Nicki was being very patient about all of this he considered as he watched his friend coaching Bran. The small shard of ice was slowly expanding, becoming longer and thicker with each passing moment.

Realizing that he was staring, Aiden turned his eyes away from Bran and Nicki before he made them uncomfortable. His eyes landed on the other pair of mages who were working on the ice magic problem. Alex and Arthur were sitting on the ground together nearby, their knees touching while both of them were focusing intently on softly glowing balls of magic in their hands. Alex's was a shimmering dark silver color while Arthur was a brilliant white color. Tilting his head, he wondered if there was any significance to the color of a person's magic. His own was red and he used fire most easily while Nicki's was a light blue color and ice was her thing. Of course, Bran's magic was yellow and he had telekinesis and visions so maybe it didn't mean anything.

A sense of exhaustion was weighing on him and Aiden chuckled to himself. Maybe he and Bran shouldn't have stayed up so late playing video games. Still, it was nice to have another guy to hang with, Nicki had been his best friend for years, but her interest in playing video games had waned over the years. A flash of light reflecting off of ice caught his attention and he grinned as he saw a small ice spear appear in front of Arthur. Alex grabbed her boyfriend's arm happily, grinning like a maniac.

"Great job Arthur!" Nicki called over with a wide smile.

"Nice!" he shouted to them, giving Arthur a thumbs up.

Arthur had a pleased smile on his face, but a moment later the spear fell to the ground and began to melt along with the others. The sound of the back screen door swinging shut made Aiden turn to look back towards the house. Morgana was walking away from the door, looking more relaxed than Aiden thought he'd seen her in some time. Her long dark hair was in a simple braid over her right shoulder and she was smiling as she surveyed their limited progress. In her hands she carried a large tray of sandwiches and Merlin was trailing after her with a fresh pitcher of iced tea and a small bowl.

"Time for a break," Morgana called to them. "Come and eat some lunch."

Pushing himself off the ground, Aiden looked down at his hands with a small frown. His fingers felt stiff and awkward, crunching softly as he flexed him. Nicki shot past him, cheering about the break and food. Alex followed at a more sedate pace, giving him a tired look that he was certain was reflected on his own face. Arthur smiled at her and wrapped an arm around Alex's shoulder, making her smile as they got to the table.

Aiden almost fell into his chair, his back and arm muscles aching like he'd been lifting heavy boxes all morning. When he used his fireballs, he often felt a bit tired, but nothing like this. It was annoying and more than a little worrying.

"Why can't any of us get it?" Alex asked, leaning on her elbow and looking over at Merlin as he sat down in his chair next to Arthur.

"We'll get it," Arthur assured Alex, reaching over and covering her other hand with his for a moment. "It's just hard learning something new."

"Arthur's right. You shouldn't worry about it so much," Morgana informed them calmly as she set the tray of sandwiches down onto the wrought iron patio table. "Magic doesn't respond to your thoughts like that. Worrying about it has very little effect."

"It's just you use light magic, but you also heal," Aiden pointed out, flexing his fingers in frustration. "You've said that we can move beyond our initial form of magic. Nicki can already heal too."

"You can; it is a natural progression, but for you, for instance, fire will always be easiest to use and when you've under stress the most likely form that your magic will take," she told him calmly as she pushed the plate of sandwiches toward him.

"Some of you will learn other forms of magic more easily than others. That is natural."

There were some looks exchanged around the table while Morgana watched them with a knowing look. Obeying the silent order, Aiden grabbed one of the sandwiches and set it on his plate before taking a few of the apple slices.

"Don't worry about it so much, guys," Arthur said with a wide smile. "You're all great at magic; you've even started practicing new ideas from books." Arthur grinned at Aiden, causing a spark of irritation. "I bet you're only having so much trouble with ice because your natural thing is fire. If I can learn how to make an Iron Gate in only a few months then you guys can do ice spears."

"Well we're not all perfect like you," Bran muttered, shifting in his chair. Aiden looked at his friend with a touch of alarm, wondering how badly he was hurting. Bran's facial muscles were tight and his hand was in a fist.

"I am not perfect," Arthur huffed, running a hand through his hair and looking over at Alex. Thankfully, she seemed to notice Bran's discomfort and said nothing.

"I'm inclined to agree with him Arthur," Aiden chuckled, hoping to pull the attention off Bran. "You are a little too perfect."

"Oh come on," Arthur protested, frowning slightly even as the others around the table perked up slightly. Aiden thought he saw Morgana chuckle, her mouth mostly hidden as she took a sip of her iced tea.

"I'm serious," he laughed, leaning back in his chair and enjoying the banter. "It's like you're not even a real person Arthur. You became quarterback for the football team in your freshman year, look like a pretty boy model, no offense, get good grades, are generous enough to forgive your ex-girlfriend for cheating and are from a wealthy family. Oh, and you're also the chosen champion for the entire planet Earth against beings from other universes."

An odd look crossed Arthur's face, one that Aiden couldn't read fast enough before it was gone. Arthur turned to look at his girlfriend who was trying not to laugh, a hand over her mouth and her eyes sparkling with amusement. Then a sheepish smile appeared on Arthur's face and he turned back to him, shrugging helplessly.

"I guess it is a bit much, maybe being part of the Iron Soul is being blessed with great luck," he offered without looking at Merlin who snorted in response. "And in my defense, I was only the quarterback last year because of two injuries; coach wasn't too thrilled about having to use me at first," he added a bit more defensively. "Though, I'll admit that it was thrilling the first time I played in the games."

"I didn't mean any insult," he assured Arthur, wondering if he'd hit some kind of nerve. He raised his glass of iced tea in a slight toast. "It's just a little funny sometimes, well funny and irritating."

"He's got a point," Nicki chimed in with a laugh and Aiden felt relieved at the rescue. "You're one of those overly perfect people that everyone wants to hate, but can't."

"I think that's a compliment," Arthur replied slowly, glancing over at a smiling Alex. "But I certainly hope that none you hate me. I'm grateful for you guys, I can't imagine trying to confront all of this without you."

"Particularly Alex," Nicki added with a sly smile. The girl in question blushed slightly but said nothing so Nicki turned towards Merlin. "Are the Iron Souls always like that?"

"No," Merlin answered calmly, looking far too amused at the conservation. "Arthur's life thus far has been rather pleasant by the standards of the Iron Soul. In truth, there is nothing that sets the Iron Soul apart from other humans unless magic is active."

"That said, the Iron Soul does seem to demonstrate leadership abilities and has been intelligent," Morgana added with a soft smile, looking at Alex and Arthur with pleased eyes. "This may simply be due to the reincarnation that it undergoes. While Merlin and I's knowledge of such things are limited, I have observed that old souls seem to have a natural inclination towards certain behavior."

"So if there isn't anything obviously special about the Iron Soul then how do you know it when you find it?" Nicki asked, tilting her head curiously as she glanced between Arthur and Morgana.

Merlin chuckled and smiled at the question before answering, "Well Nicki, we know certain things about the Iron Soul that allows us to keep an eye out for it. Morgana is very talented at scrying which steers us towards the proper location. Although in many of the Iron Soul's incarnations magic has remained at a low level and we barely interacted with them."

"In this incarnation's case, I saw the town sign for Ravenslake nearly twenty years ago," Morgana continued, slipping into lecture mode. "Thus Merlin and I moved here and built our current lives while we waited."

"And the summer before last Morgana saw visions of battles leading to us checking on the status of the iron gates in Great Britain and the status of the sleeping Old Ones."

"How does scrying work?" Bran asked a curious and thoughtful expression on his face, replacing the earlier look of pain. "Does it take a lot of magic or is it like the stories suggest?"

"Many people can scry, even those with very low levels of magic, and it is something that I can do even when almost all other magic is impossible," Morgana informed him with a small smile. "That's one of the reasons why there are scrying traditions all over the world."

"But how does that work?" Nicki asked. "I mean what do you see that is so exact?"

"As someone with full magical abilities, my scrying is a bit more complex than most. I still use a bronze polished mirror that shows me glimpses of the future. In a town like Ravenslake that I am very familiar with it is very simple to recognize where certain things are going to happen," Morgana explained as she poured herself more tea. "As for dates and times… that's a little harder. There isn't anything to tell you when something is going to happen exactly so you have to keep an eye out for little clues like the phase of the moon, position of the sun, signs of the season or if you're really lucky a sign showing the date."

"Sounds messy," Bran remarked looking discouraged.

"Seeing something beyond what is around you is always difficult, but I suspect that you'd have a strong talent for scrying Bran," Morgana assured him gently. "Once this episode with Chernobog is over I'll start teaching you, but you have to tightly control your magic for it to work. Too much power into your scrying instrument and you destroy it, but too little and nothing is clear."

"So basically back to practicing ice," Bran sighed, looking rather dejected.

"I'm afraid so," Merlin said kindly. "But really, all of you are already doing so well. It wasn't until I'd been training for years that I was able to use my magic in different ways. Yes this is hard, but soon enough you'll get it and once you do even more things will be open to you."

"That will be nice," Nicki remarked with a smile to everyone around the table. "After all we've already started trying to experiment."

"Things will get easier," Merlin told them firmly. "You can do one major form of magic each and some of you have had some success with other forms of magic such as healing or mending objects. Just be patient and practice."

"And don't forget to be careful on Halloween," Morgana added quickly. "If you want to spend the night at my house that will be fine, but otherwise stay at least in pairs and remember that carved pumpkins can help keep you safe."

"Will jack-o-lanterns help against the Shadow Creatures?" Nicki asked with a frown.

"No they won't, but there is a chance that the Sídhe might be able to push through on Halloween so just be cautious."

"That would be great wouldn't it," Aiden muttered with a frown. "Sídhe and Shadow Creatures."

"Yeah but maybe they'd fight each other," Nicki offered with a tentative smile.

"I doubt it," Aiden scoffed. "So you've gotten Bran to form some ice, care to coach me?"

"Alright," Nicki agreed with a nod. "Come on fire boy; let's teach you how to use ice."

Aiden nodded in agreement as he pushed his chair back and stood up. He was feeling a little better with some food in his stomach and was ready to give it another try. The others followed his example, pushing their plates in and standing up. Arthur offered to help Morgana and Merlin take everything in and Alex quickly joined the cleanup crew.

Aiden walked back over to the small patch of grass he'd been parked in earlier. He was taking in a deep breath with his eyes closed when he heard a low growling sound from nearby. Opening his eyes, he jumped to his feet and looked towards Merlin's blacksmithing workshop.

"Aiden?" Nicki questioned softly.

"Listen," he hissed, his eyes darting around.

There was another long deep growl that rumbled through the air and made the hair on his arms stand up. Around them, the sky seemed to darken as if a cloud had covered the sun. A chill crept over his body and Aiden took a tentative step back, moving closer to Nicki. She was alert now and watching the dark corners of the yard.

"Shadow monster," Nicki whispered, shifting her weight and bringing her hands forward.

Aiden was about to agree and call the others when the low growl turned into a snarl. Above them, there was a thump and Aiden's eyes jumped up. On the slanted metal roof of Merlin's workshop was a massive shadow creature built like a great panther with glowing red eyes and jagged dark spikes growing along its spine. It opened its mouth exposing two rows of shining white teeth and roared. The sound echoed against the metal walls and roof and through the yard. Behind him, Aiden heard clamoring as the others rushed out of the house.

The air turned colder as another shadow leapt onto the workshop roof. This one was standing on two long legs with long arms hanging down in front of it. Spikes grew all over its body, protruding where its joints seemed to be. Large red eyes narrowed at them and a high pitched hissing sound escaped the new creature.

"Nicki!" Morgana shouted from behind them. "Fall back!"

"What?" Nicki called back in shock.

"I want the others to handle this fight. They need to be capable of defeating these without you."

"But-"

"Alex," Merlin called, "You too."

"I can't do ice yet!" Alex shouted behind him.

"Your energy draining spears do just fine; let the others work on these two."

Aiden flexed his fingers and refused to look away from the two strange creatures before him even as his stomach churned with unease. He did not like where this was suddenly going.

"Well," Merlin called to the monsters. "You've found the mages, what now?"

His words spurred them on. Both leapt from the workshop roof, the panther-like one towards him and the two legged one in the other direction. Risking a glance over his shoulder, Aiden saw Arthur standing a little in front of Bran and glaring at the creature. Aiden swung back to the large shadow beast that was watching him and exhaled slowly.

"I can do this," he whispered to himself and tried to ignore the fact that the others were watching him.

Pulling on his magic, Aiden swallowed as he felt the small warm point in his gut expand. A wave of warmth spread through his body, fighting back the chill. The shadow beast roared and lunged for him, but Aiden leapt to the side, avoiding the massive paws complete with sharp claws. His magic jolted up his body and down his arm like an electric shock. There were the sounds of another battle behind him and it took all of his focus not to turn and look. He had to trust that Arthur and Bran could take care of it. The snarling of their Shadow beast blended with the roars and growls of his own.

"You can do it!" Nicki shouted behind him and Aiden inwardly growled.

The cheerleading was not helping the situation. In fact, it made it worse, just reminding him that he wasn't really in danger and fighting for his life. No, he was fighting because his professors were nasty and terrible and-

The shadow beast roared and swiped one massive paw towards him that he barely dodged. Above him the shadow creature roared once again, sending a shiver of fear up his spine. The red sparks of magic gathering in his hand felt cold against his skin, he realized with surprise.

"I can do this," Aiden muttered to himself. "Just think about it as a game spell."

There was an animalistic scream of pain behind him and then cheering from Nicki and Alex. A moment later Bran and Arthur's voices joined the cheers for him, but he told himself to ignore it. Neither he nor the shadow beast moved, his brown eyes staring into the swirling red eyes of the shadow beast. The chill was forcing itself through the warmth of his magic and Aiden could feel goosebumps up and down his arms. He bit his lower lip softly, envisioning a shimmering spear made of ice in his mind.

Done with waiting, the shadow beast leapt towards him with a roar. For a split second all he could see was those long sharp glinting teeth, but he pushed on the magic. The red sparks blasted away from his skin, coming together in a long reddish beam of magic right in front of him. Icy air exhaled by the roaring beast hit his face, but Aiden didn't move. His magic spun together into a shining red spear, visible to him for only a moment before it struck the inside roof of the shadow beast's mouth.

A deafening scream of pain filled the yard and Aiden dove out of the shadow beast's way. Hitting the ground, he rolled out of the way as the shadow creature lashed around for what seemed like forever, tossing its head around. The spear still lodged in the creature was shimmering with magic, glowing so brightly that red light was spilling out of the shadow creature's mouth. Then the shadow creature stopped spinning around, gave a weak cry and fell to the ground near him.

Climbing to his feet, Aiden watched as the darkness that made up the shadow creature's body faded away in front of him. It vanished gradually, leaving ribbons of black behind that lingered for a few moments before they too vanished. He sighed in relief even as a rush of satisfaction and pride warmed his chest. The others were cheering for him and he couldn't help but smile. Hearing someone coming up behind him, Aiden turned quickly to find the smiling Merlin standing next to him. The professor looked down at the vanishing remains of the shadow creature and nodded.

"Uh so did I pass Professor?" Aiden couldn't help but ask with a wide smile.

Merlin grinned at the question, his brown eyes shining with amusement as the last vestiges of the creature vanished. Aiden breathed a little easier as the light around him brightened and the chill vanished from the air, at least as much as was reasonable for late October.

"Well it wasn't exactly an ice spear," Merlin remarked, rubbing his chin thoughtfully. "I'm not even sure what it was, but it did the trick so I'd say that yes you passed."

"Good," Aiden sighed loudly, relaxing his sore muscles. "It is nice to know that I can kill them on my own."

"Indeed," Merlin agreed, reaching over and putting a hand on his shoulder. Merlin let the weight of his hand just rest there for a moment before he removed his hand. "I think that you've practiced enough for this weekend; go finish your homework and have some fun."

"We won't be practicing on Halloween," Morgana reminded them, looking remarkably calm. "But remember to stay safe and stay in contact with us. I'll be scrying to keep an eye on things, but it isn't perfect so watch yourselves."

Nicki looked like she wanted to ask more questions, but he was sore and tired and one look at Bran assured him that his roommate was a similar state. As Arthur put his arm around Alex and asked her if she wanted to do anything special for the afternoon, Aiden walked over to Bran. His roommate was leaning on his cane more than normal and had a small scowl on his face.

"Back to the dorm, order pizza and have a game marathon?"

Bran smiled, chuckling softly and he nodded and replied, "Yeah, let's go and kill some things without having to do anything more than push a few buttons."

"Amen to that," Aiden sighed as the two of them waved goodbye to the others and headed for the gate. He needed some video games, preferably nothing to do with magic, at least for a few hours.

18

Homecoming Fears

803 B.C.E. Northern Cornwall

Urging his horse forward, Arto felt a coil of anticipation tightening in his chest. Behind him, he could hear the soft murmurs of the other warriors on their own horses. The sun was almost completely set and long shadows stretched out around them creating a dark and gloomy atmosphere, but Arto wasn't bothered at all.

He glanced to his right where Morgana was swaying gently on her own horse. In her right hand, she held an orb of light which was providing them enough light to keep going despite the twilight. Airril was on her other side, one hand twitching, ready to steady Morgana if she did try to nod off. Arto smiled softly at the look that his brother-in-law was giving her which made him miss Gwenyvar even more. He turned as much as he could manage and looked back at Merlin who was in the rear of the small party, speaking with one of the warriors in a low voice, his staff laying across his lap.

Taking another long breath of the chilly night air, Arto searched the darkness as his horse made it to the crest of the rolling hill, and he grinned at the sight of the village below. Fires and torches illuminated a few roundhouses and even at their current distance, he could hear the sounds of the people below. Beside him, he heard an audible sigh of relief from Airril.

"Come on," Arto called to the others breaking the silence. "We're almost home! Just a little further."

"At last," Gareth groaned behind him. "I request not having to get on a horse for at least a month. I need to recover from this mission."

"I agree," Arto called back as they started down the hill towards the village, using their own torches to navigate the slope of the hill. "This trip was far too long."

"It was necessary," Morgana reminded him sternly, now sitting up a little straighter on her horse. "Even if four months was a bit much."

"And I thought you grew up traveling," Boisil remarked, sounding very tired to Arto's ears.

"I did, but I've decided that I like having a home to call my own," Arto admitted, a small smile playing at his mouth. "Even if it makes traveling harder."

"Well at least there are two more Iron Gates now," Merlin reminded them with a chuckle. "We'll probably have a few months rest at least for winter. The Sídhe have very few areas of access to our world now, and even they cannot travel easily in the winter."

The idea of not having to make another Iron Gate for a few months cheered Arto up immensely and he had to resist the urge to force his horse to go faster. The poor beast was due a long rest of its own at this point. They settled into silence, all of them focusing on the village which was getting closer with each step.

The wooden walls that surrounded most of the roundhouses looked dark red and streams of smoke gleamed orange in the last light of the sun. Arto guided his horse on the small path that ran between the livestock fields and towards the main gate of the village with a grin. The day of riding had been hard on them, but it was worth it now with home so close.

Arto looked towards the doorway of the village as they drew closer. It was a narrow opening in the walls that provided only a little protection and was a constant point of worry. Two warriors were stationed by the gates, tall torches burning next to them illuminating the surrounding area. Both men grinned as they rode into sight, one turning and shouting that they had returned to the village. People rushed out of their roundhouses and called eagerly to them, but to Arto, all the voices blended together in a mess of noise.

Cheers rippled through the gathering crowd as they rode into the village and were swarmed. Thankfully, someone stilled his horse and gave him a chance to dismount. Arto wondered if he needed to say something to the crowd, but the exhaustion in his bones was too much. His head was hazy and he didn't imagine that he could manage more than a few words. In the corner of his eye, he saw Airril dismount and help Morgana down. Merlin gracefully dismounted and smiled widely at the crowd, looking far too relaxed and awake for Arto's taste.

"Arto!" a very familiar voice called over the crowd which thankfully began to part. Gwenyvar rushed forward, Luegáed right behind her, both of them smiling.

His wife jumped forward, wrapping her arms around and almost sending him to his knees. Arto laughed and returned the embrace, closing his eyes for a moment, willing the rest of the world away. The moment of peace didn't last long with Bosil's booming voice greeting his own family behind them. Questions erupted from many people about their trip, but Arto ignored them, feeling relief when Bosil began happily answering them.

"Welcome home," Gwenyvar greeted in his ear before she released him and stepped back.

"Good to have you back," Luegáed greeted, clapping him on the back.

"I see the village is intact," Arto remarked loudly so he could be heard over the crowd of people.

"Yes, I did my part," Luegáed replied with a laugh. "Although it was horribly boring without you here."

"Sorry to hear that," Arto remarked with a laugh, wrapping an arm around Gwenyvar. "I missed you both," he told them before looking at Gwenyvar. "You most of all."

"I'm glad you're back safely," Gwenyvar told him in a soft voice with a faint blush on her cheeks. "I worry when you're gone."

"I worry about you too," Arto informed her. "The only thing that kept it at bay was knowing that Luegáed was here."

"Welcome home cousin," another familiar voice said from behind him.

Arto twisted to look back at Medraut who was standing calmly behind them, regarding Arto with a blank expression and dressed in fine woven robes.

"Thank you Medraut," Arto replied with a nod. "It is good to see you well."

"Indeed. I am sorry to ask, but may I speak with you?"

"Now?" Arto asked, frowning at the request.

"I know it is late, but please," Medraut answered, looking at Gwenyvar for a long moment.

"It's alright Arto," Gwenyvar assured him. "I'll stop in and wake your mother; she made me promise to tell her the moment you returned."

"I'll see her home," Luegáed promised, looking at Medraut with open curiosity. "Goodnight Medraut," Luegáed added as he gently touched Gwenyvar's arm.

Arto sighed and watched his wife and best friend slip away from the crowd. Medraut cleared his throat loudly, making Arto think about just walking away. With a small sigh, he gestured for Medraut to lead on and they quickly extracted themselves from the crowd, a feat made possible only because Bosil was entertaining them all with a recounting of their last battle against the Sídhe.

Leaving the crowd behind them, Arto followed his cousin up one of the two gently sloping hills that the main village was built around. He turned and looked over his shoulder at the top of the other hill where his own roundhouse stood near the roundhouse occupied by his mother. Medraut cleared his throat again and Arto sighed once more, following his cousin into his roundhouse.

It was a large roundhouse, built for Medraut when he became the leader of the village. A large set of shelves opposite the doorway displayed signs of his wealth: several bottles of perfume, a plate of jet and gold beads, vases from Rome and other trinkets that the traders brought with them. A low fire burned in the hearth and his cousin took a moment to stir up the flames.

"What is it that you wanted to talk about?" Arto asked, rolling his shoulders and barely holding back a yawn.

"Yes, of course. It is very important that we talk," Medraut said even as he frowned deeply, his hands behind his back as he paced across the roundhouse for a moment.

Arto shifted uncomfortably, his aching muscles protesting being kept from his own roundhouse and, more importantly, his own bed. He was unsure of what to make of his cousin's hesitation as in his experience, Medraut spoke his mind.

"Medraut," Arto cut in, finally losing his patience. "I have been away for four months, been in more than twenty battles with the Sídhe and made two new Iron Gates," he reminded his cousin, leaning wearily against the wall of the roundhouse. It wasn't comfortable, but it took some of the pressure off his lower back. "What is bothering you? Tell me or let me go home and spend some time with my wife."

"Of course cousin," Medraut replied quickly, stopping his pacing and wringing his hands. "I'm sorry, I'm just not sure how to tell you."

"Tell me what?" Arto demanded, worry churning in his stomach at Medraut's wording. "Is my mother-"

"Oh she's just fine," Medraut assured him quickly. "I have no doubt that she is waiting for you in your roundhouse."

"Then what is it?" Arto asked, his impatience and exhaustion returning.

"I fear that Gwenyvar has betrayed you with Luegáed," Medraut informed in a rush, his eyes gleaming oddly in the firelight.

"...What?" Arto asked slowly, his mind not fully comprehending what his cousin had said.

"I've observed them spending a great deal of time together, especially when you are gone. In the last four months... this time together became more frequent. It is not uncommon to find Luegáed at your roundhouse late at night and slipping in and out of the roundhouse at odd times in the day. Whenever he finishes training with the warriors, he always goes to see Gwenyvar."

"He is my best friend and I entrusted him with Gwenyvar's safety whenever he doesn't travel with me," Arto replied coldly, narrowing his eyes at his cousin. His heart was beating faster than normal and his hands tightened into fists of their own accord. It was all he could do, not to lash out and strike his cousin. There was a smug little look on his face that threatened to enrage him as if Medraut was internally betting on what his reaction will be. "It's natural that Luegáed is spending time with Gwenyvar, he's her friend as much as he is mine." Glaring at Medraut, Arto couldn't help but add, "He's the closest thing I have to a brother."

Medraut didn't seem bothered by the last remark, but then again he'd never seemed to care much about their relationship beyond making sure that they remained allies.

"Arto I know this is hard for-"

"You will not speak of this further," Arto ordered, straightening up and using his great height to glare down at Medraut before turning towards the door.

His cousin moved in front of him, a firm expression on his face, to block the doorway. Arto was surprised and impressed by the move. His cousin had never struck him as a brave man: the only battle he even remembered Medraut ever being a part of was the Sídhe attack that claimed his father's life. The very reminder made his scowl deepen.

"Arto, some of the warriors are already talking," Medraut insisted. "Your influence is based not only on your magical powers and martial skills, but also your marriage to the daughter to an important northern priest. If news about her having an affair gets out then it could impact-"

"And your position is partially based on being my cousin," Arto retorted with a small snort. "You're worried about yourself, not me. I don't believe this for a moment and you are foolish to believe it. Leave these rumors be."

"But Arto-" Medraut protested, but Arto pushed him out of the way and quickly left the roundhouse.

Stepping out into the cool night air, Arto strode away from the roundhouse, confident that Medraut wouldn't follow him. His cousin would want to keep such conversations away from the ears of curious villagers. Arto breathed in the air deeply, taking in the smells of his home village and began to calm down. Medraut was seeing something where there was nothing; his concern over appearances and power dynamics driving him to new levels of concern. It was something that Arto didn't understand and preferred not to.

Looking around, Arto surveyed the slight differences in the village. The eastern wall had been partially rebuilt and a new roundhouse had been constructed near it. Otherwise, it was much the same, the roundhouses scattered about with small yards containing a few livestock or supplies. Smoke wafted out of the houses and he could smell the remnants of dinner. On the far side of the village were the smelting forges and the iron storehouses. Nothing had really changed.

He walked down the path from Medraut's roundhouse and towards his own, his movements sluggish as his feet dragged against the dirt. There was an uncomfortable sense of doubt seeping into his mind that he did his best to ignore. But it was persistent, like a little voice whispering to him. Shaking his head, Arto summoned the image of Gwenyvar and Luegáed's smiles upon seeing him and relaxed. A small smile came to his own face at the mere memory of their expressions.

Stopping in the middle of the path, Arto closed his eyes and inhaled deeply. Beneath him, he could feel the solid well-beaten soil of the village and could smell the chill of autumn on the wind. He opened his eyes and looked up into the night sky. With the sun gone, he could see countless twinkling stars. For a moment Arto felt as if he was falling into the darkness, falling towards on the lights. He lost any sense of time, listening to his own heartbeat and feeling the soft pulse of his magic within him.

Arto jumped when a young couple walked past him, each of them smiling at him even as they gave him curious looks. They vanished into their roundhouse and Arto became aware of the silence in the village. No longer could he hear Bosil or the sounds of questions down the path. Instead, everything was still, save for the livestock in the nearby yard. Shaking his head, Arto chuckled to himself and resumed walking up the hill.

"Arto," his sister called, causing him to stop suddenly and look around for her.

She was right up ahead of him, standing next to a torch. He'd only been a few steps away from walking into her, Arto realized with a flush of embarrassment. Morgana frowned at him, the long thick cloak fluttering softly in the wind. From the look on her face, she had something to say to him and she knew that he wasn't going to like it. Arto sighed softly, hoping that Medraut hadn't run off to tell his sister his suspicions while he took in the village.

"Sister, I would have thought you'd have gone to sleep now. Surely you and Airril are pleased to be home again," he greeted, hoping that if he seemed relaxed and content that she'd let him be for the night.

"Arto, I need to speak with you," Morgana informed him, wrinkles between her eyebrows deepening.

"Can it wait for morning, Morgana?" Arto asked, nearly whining. "I'm exhausted."

"I know what Medraut told you," she told him bluntly, stepping closer to him. "And you should consider his words."

"I don't believe it, Morgana," Arto replied firmly, raising his chin. "I trust them and I don't blame them for spending time together when I'm gone. Medraut is just obsessing over nothing."

"Arto, I know that you value Luegáed, but I'll remind you that we have never identified who is passing information to the Sídhe. We suffered that ambush-"

"Morgana, those attacks are random! The Sídhe's power is weakening with every new gate, they have patrols everywhere and orders to destroy us on sight," Arto insisted, throwing his hands up in the air. "There is no real evidence beyond your suspicions that there is a traitor. Besides, even if there is a traitor passing information to the Sídhe and Medraut is right, which he isn't, that hardly proves that it is Luegáed. There is a huge difference between what Medraut is suggesting and what you are suggesting."

"Arto-"

"No, you don't like him because of that ambush right after he joined us. That wasn't his fault and your grudge is ridiculous.

And you have never liked Gwenyvar, but she is my wife and is your sister as much as Airril is my brother. We cannot simply accuse them of wrongdoing. We are at war and I will not cast suspicion on our allies and warriors without true cause."

"Arto, I only want to protect you," Morgana insisted softly. "Please, understand that. I spent so long worrying and feeling guilty."

"I know Morgana, but I'm not a child," Arto offered in a gentle voice. "Luegáed is not a traitor, please trust me on that. He would not risk the war effort. He doesn't care about power or position, he cares about people."

"And what of Medraut's suspicions?"

"I do not believe them and even if they are true, it is my concern and I will deal with it."

"What affects the Iron Soul affects us all," Morgana reminded him before a deep sigh escaped her. "But for now, it will be as you wish. Sleep well brother; we will speak in the morning."

Staying in place, Arto watched his sister turn and walk towards her own roundhouse. Even from here, he could see Airril standing by the doorway waiting for her. He huffed softly and shook his head, looking up the hill at his own home. The animal hide protecting the doorway was down, but he could see traces of light escaping around it. As he approached, he could hear the soft voices of Gwenyvar and his mother. Smiling at the sounds, he pulled back the flap and stepped into his home, putting Medraut and Morgana's concerns out of his head.

19

Slice of Life

Holding back a yawn, Alex glanced over the options for dinner as she balanced the tray in her hands. She set the tray down on the edge of the serving bar and reached for the tongs, grabbing a small piece of meatloaf that didn't look overcooked. Hearing people walk up behind her, she paused and tensed slightly.

"I still can't believe that they did that," Aiden grumbled, setting his tray down next to her own. "Making us fight the shadow monsters without help," he huffed, spooning up a large helping of mashed potatoes. "I mean sure they were standing right there, but fighting one of those things solo is intense."

"Gee," Alex muttered with a raised eyebrow, giving him a pointed look. "I wouldn't know."

"Seriously Aiden, let it go," Nicki remarked with a roll of her eyes as she came up on Alex's other side. "You're just pouting about not getting the ice spear spell to work."

"Alex hasn't done an ice lance spell yet," Aiden whined, his bottom lip sticking out a bit further than usual.

"Leave me out of this," Alex replied with a shake of her head. "I can't believe you're talking about it again."

"He's been whining about it all day," Nicki muttered as she snagged a baked potato wrapped in foil. "It's getting old."

"Yeah, it is," Alex agreed, giving Aiden a pointed look as she picked up her tray.

The others followed her over to the small dessert bar that oddly enough shared space with the fresh fruits and salads.

"There is a serious lack of chocolate today," Alex pouted, surveying the selection of carrot cake and tarts.

"Well we are eating late tonight," Nicki replied with a shrug, grabbing a slice of carrot cake and examining it. "Do you think this counts as healthy?"

"No chance," Aiden snorted, picking up some kind of tart that Alex couldn't identify. "Even the carrot flavor cannot overcome the sugar content."

Alex was ready to leave the dessert bar with her friends in disgust when a cafeteria worker suddenly appeared with a small tray of chocolate cakes slices. With a victorious smile, Alex grabbed one of the small plates and ignored the expressions on Nicki and Aiden's faces. She led them over to get drinks and then paused at the edge of the tiled area and checked the seating area for the others.

It only took Alex a moment to spot Bran and Arthur in the mostly empty space. They were at a small round table in the back of the dining hall near one of the large windows. The sun had set more than an hour ago and most of the cafeteria was empty, feeling a little deserted. A few students were coming in and out to raid the dessert bar and ice cream dispenser. One girl was sitting at a far table with what looked like a bowl of sugary cereal and a pile of books. There were only a few people actually eating from full dinner plates.

As she approached their table, Alex slowed down upon catching sight of the scowls on both Arthur and Bran's faces.

Her internal alarm began going off and she nervously glanced at Nicki who'd slowed down as well. Aiden didn't falter, stepping around them and striding towards the table. He sat down next to Bran with a calm expression.

"Hey guys," Alex greeted as warmly as she could manage as she sat down next to Arthur. Hoping to ease the tension hanging over the table like a bad smell, she leaned over and kissed her boyfriend's cheek. "What are you talking about?"

"Bran doesn't approve of me seeing Lance yesterday!" Arthur damn near growled, glaring at Bran. "Despite me reminding him that it isn't his business and Lance is still my football teammate. I have to get along with the guy!"

"You're the Iron Soul," Bran said softly in a very calm voice that sent a shiver down Alex's spine; it was almost unnatural. "And he has a history of betraying you, even if he doesn't mean to it is dangerous."

"Look, he and my ex had a thing together," Arthur replied after taking a fortifying breath. "It may not have been something that was easy, sure I would have preferred them just being honest and dating after Jenny and I broke up, but that is hardly a real betrayal of the sort the Iron Soul should be worried about."

"It's Arthur's decision to spend time with Lance," Alex added with a small frown towards Bran. "No one has questioned me spending time with Jenny and trying to mend our friendship. It does take two after all Bran."

"It's different for Arthur," Bran protested with a deepening frown. "You might not be there next time Lance and Jenny's actions trigger a disaster." Bran stopped and held up his hand to halt her protest. "Look, I'm not trying to be a pain, but that vision I had… well, I've been having reoccurring dreams of the same thing: being stabbed in the back."

"What? You haven't said anything," Aiden cut in with a worried look. "How often?"

"Once a week lately, I told Morgana after our lessons," Bran replied, waving his hand dismissively. "But I can't get it out of my head and I'm sorry, but being stabbed in the back means being betrayed in my book."

"So you think the dreams mean this betrayal is getting closer since you're dreaming of it more often?" Alex couldn't help but ask, feeling sick to her stomach. She leaned closer to Arthur who looked distinctly unimpressed and huffed.

"No one is going to betray me! You're mages of the Iron Realm and good people. And I don't believe that Lance and Jenny would harm us, Jenny still feels guilty as sin over what happened and Lance just wants another chance with her."

"I agree," Alex cut in with a firm nod. "I told you guys about how Lance tackled that shadow monster. He put himself in harm's way to help."

"Maybe, but we still have to be careful," Bran insisted. "Something is going to happen, I can feel it!" He shivered slightly, a sad expression replacing his impartial mask for a moment. "So please don't make assumptions about what is happening."

"Suppose you're right and the dream is a warning," Nicki offered gently. "It doesn't mean that it's one of us or Jenny and Lance. After all, there are a lot of things about the Iron Soul that we don't know. The betrayal could be from another ally like the Lady of the Lake, or someone from another life of Arthur's."

"Maybe it's Mordred," Alex suggested hesitantly as she looked around the table, her dinner long forgotten. "Merlin and Morgana have never been really clear on if he ever existed."

"He is a big part of the Arthur mythos," Nicki considered with a frown and a tilt of her head. "While Merlin and Morgana have been clear that Camelot didn't exist, a lot of the elements of the oldest Arthurian legends are true. Hell, in some old stories, Mordred features before Lancelot returned to the mythology."

"That's a stretch," Bran replied with a shake of his head. "You're supposing that Mordred was real, at least in some form, was reborn and is capable of attacking us. Jenny and Lance were reborn, but they had no knowledge of what was going on until we told them."

"It might be-" Nicki began to say before being cut off.

"And even if that all was true, it still isn't an actual betrayal. That requires trust," Bran argued as he toyed with his fork. "I'm sorry, but I think we should be concerned about the worst."

"Maybe," Arthur conceded with a sour look. "But maybe not. Your vision could have been sent by Chernobog to confuse us and cause us to turn on each other and your dreams could just be honest normal dreams about your fears," Arthur told Bran. "There's a lot we don't know about magic. After all, Merlin can alter people's memories, maybe Chernobog can send visions to confuse or is working with someone who can."

"My visions are not being hacked!"

"I can't believe you just said that," Aiden muttered, shaking his head at Bran.

"My point is that we don't know enough," Arthur insisted, waving his hand to silence argument. "Let's not turn on each other."

"But we're never going to learn anything more if you won't even allow the conversation," Bran snapped at Arthur. "Sure it's uncomfortable, but so is dreaming about having a sword shoved through your back!"

"Let's change the subject," Alex cut in quickly. "We're not going to agree on this and I'd rather not ruin what's left of dinner fighting."

"That won't-" Bran began to protest.

"We'll keep our eyes open and Morgana and Merlin are certainly doing the same. Arthur is only with Jenny and Lance in public," Alex added, giving Arthur an apologetic look and feeling a twitch of guilt over the statement. "For now, we're all okay so let's drop it."

There were a few grumbles and pointed looks exchanged, but the subject vanished. Nicki glanced at her and Alex tried to think of something to talk about, it occurred to her that it would have been easier to change the topic if she'd had that figured out.

"So Halloween is Saturday," Nicki reminded them with a smile. "Any plans?"

"Well Alex and I are going to a party on Friday," Arthur volunteered with a hesitant smile. "We decided against going to any on Halloween itself."

"And we're signed up to take kids around on Saturday afternoon," Alex added with a much more comfortable smile

216

than her boyfriend's. "They need more volunteers if you guys want to join us. Costumes are required, though."

"Sounds like fun," Nicki agreed with a grin. "I was thinking that we could grab lunch on Saturday and then carve up some pumpkins. Just in case, so we're ready for sunset."

"It's a bummer that the seasonal days starts at sunset instead of midnight," Aiden remarked, leaning back in his chair. "I've always loved Halloween."

"Yeah, but don't forget that the period of weakness starts at sundown," Alex reminded them firmly. "I made that mistake and got taken into the tunnels." She shivered at the memory and Arthur reached over and rubbed circles on her back.

"Anyway, I haven't got any set plans yet, but maybe one of the Friday night parties would be fun," Aiden continued with a glance towards Alex.

"You should come with us," Arthur offered quickly. "The guys throwing the party are cool; a couple of the team live there and said I could bring friends."

"Will Lance and Jenny be there?" Aiden asked, flinching slightly as soon as the words were out of his mouth making the glare Alex shot at him a bit redundant.

"Maybe, Lance is a part of the team and was probably invited and Jenny is part of the spirit squad," Arthur answered calmly, meeting Aiden's gaze evenly.

"I'm going as a druid this year," Nicki informed them with a smile despite the tension. "Well not actually a druid, but I have this great long dark green cloak that I'm going to wear with some Celtic jewelry. It won't be as good as my costume last year, but I figured I'd want something I could move in.

I've got some leather riding boots that I think will work with it."

"On that same train of thought I'm doing a basic adventurer look," Aiden remarked with a smile. "You know loose shirt, jeans, cargo jacket, fedora hat and some fake weapons, plus my real iron dagger."

"I'm going a simpler route: zombie," Bran told them with a shrug, still eying Arthur a little. "Pull out some old clothes, put a little fake blood them, do some fake wounds and you're good to go. Plus it works with the leg."

Alex offered a slightly uncomfortable chuckle at Bran's joke while Aiden actually laughed. She was never going to be comfortable joking about his disability like Bran and apparently, Aiden was.

"We're doing pirates this year," she heard Arthur say next to her as he squeezed her hand, pulling her back into the conversation. "We were thinking the same thing. I know that there's no reason to expect trouble on Friday, but I wanted a good way to keep my dagger on me. Especially after hearing about Halloween last year."

"Yeah, running from vicious hounds from another world in heels, not fun," Nicki sighed dramatically. "But we're ready this year or at least we know it's coming this year."

"True, but at the same time Halloween was sort of a beginning for us all last year," Alex offered with a small smile. "After all, I was avoiding several of you."

"No, by Halloween you'd mellowed out some," Nicki reminded her with a laugh. "And Aiden had stopped stalking you."

"I did not stalk her!"

"You totally did, I'm lucky she stayed on the soccer team!"

"I was just trying to get her to think about magic being real! I know I sound crazy when I say that, but come on! She was totally ignoring us," Aiden argued, gesturing towards Alex and Arthur.

"Can you really blame her?" Arthur asked a slight smile on his face now. "I mean we live in an age of science and reason... magic is mythology and superstition."

"It is interesting that something like magic has a real explanation," Bran remarked, leaning on his hand with a thoughtful look. "I mean sure the multiverse theory is still widely debated and probably will be for decades more, but it actually provides an explanation for mythology and folklore."

"True, at least for some of it," Nicki said with a nod, pushing her empty plate back. "But I'm not going to suddenly say that all of human mythology has factual roots. I'm sure that most of it is still made up. Like, humans encountered a being from another world and then told stories about it that grew in the telling. After all, modern fairy tales distantly trace back to the Sídhe.... Very very very distantly."

"Yeah, the fairy godmother will help you go to the ball and get a prince, but the Sídhe will drag you underground, make you a slave, rape you and force you to bear more slaves," Alex muttered with a shudder. "That's a pretty big change."

"But that's what human stories are, especially oral ones: a living explanation of the world around us," Nicki reminded her. "They change and adjust based on what we know and understand. Thousands of years ago we didn't understand lightning and thunder so the tale of Zeus was created, maybe there was a real being, but since people don't actually interact with him, he's given a history to explain his existence."

"Not the best example I've heard you use," Aiden said with a smirk.

"Yes well… I don't know how religious Arthur is so I decided against picking on the Bible," Nicki shrugged.

"Probably a good move," Aiden agreed with a nod and a smile. "How did we get on this subject again?"

"Somehow we went from Halloween to this," Alex said with a small laugh and a shake of her head. "I'm not sure how that happened, to be honest."

"Segways are amazing things," Nicki informed her solemnly, sounding way too serious for the situation.

"You are terrible Nicki," Alex chuckled. "Absolutely terrible."

"I know, but I'm just so good at it."

"On that note," Bran said, pushing back his chair and reaching for his cane propped up against the wall. "I have some homework to wrap up."

"Wait, pumpkin carving? Yes or no?" Nicki asked, waving her hands about to get everyone's attention.

"Sure, I'll join you girls," Arthur answered with a smile towards Alex. "Sounds nice; I haven't carved a jack-o-lantern in years."

"Sounds good," Aiden added with a nod. "Do we have any guidelines from Morgana about what works because, I hate to say it, Nicki, I don't know if your masterpiece two years ago of the dragon encircling the castle would hold back the Sídhe."

"Actually if all of you want to carve pumpkins then we should call Morgana and see if we can do it at her place."

"Fair point, we'll be awfully crowded in our living room," Alex agreed with a nod. "And that way we can make sure that our pumpkins will keep the Sídhe back."

"Agreed, but you call her," Nicki told her with a grin. "She likes you best."

"Oh, not this again."

"She likes you more than me," Arthur told her seriously. "But don't worry about it."

"And for the record, I'm going to carve a fun pumpkin too," Nicki informed them all solemnly, straightening up in her chair. "I am not going to let the Sídhe take that from me."

"I don't remember a jack-o-lantern at your dorm room last year, other than the ones Morgana and Merlin gave us," Bran remarked with a thoughtful frown.

"It was at Gran's shop," Nicki explained as she curled her nose. "I didn't think it was important and as much as I love planning and carving them, I don't really like the smell."

"Okay so dress up and party on Friday night, take kids out on Saturday and hopefully meet up at Morgana's place for jack-o-lanterns," Bran summed up. "Are we going to stay there for the night?"

"Well if we're all in one place, then if the Sídhe or the Shadows do attack we'll all be together and away from prying eyes," Alex pointed out carefully.

"Although," Nicki sighed as she pushed back her chair and stood up. "It is Halloween, the one night when anything is supposed to be possible."

"Why is it that when you say that it sounds ominous instead of exciting?" Aiden asked as he stood up and collected his tray.

"That is just the life we lead Aiden: dark mythology, twisted evil fairy tales, and horrifying Halloweens. Ah, the glamorous and magical life of a mage."

"I hate you sometimes," Aiden grumbled as they walked away, Bran shaking his head and trailing after them. "I really do."

Alex laughed at them as she and Arthur collected their own plates and headed for the dish drop off.

"No," Nicki half sang, "You really don't."

20

Jack-o-Lanterns

Aiden grimaced; the slimy guts of the pumpkin were sliding over his bare palms as he lifted a handful of the innards out of the orange shell and dumped them into a large bowl. Pale seeds stuck to his skin and the slimy fibers seemed almost tangled with the hair on his hands and wrists.

"I am now remembering why I stopped doing this," Aiden groaned, shaking his hand to get rid of the last of the seeds. "It's gross and hard to scrap all this stuff out."

"Stop whining!" Nicki's arm half inside the pumpkin she was cleaning out. "It's not so bad and the better a job you do now then the easier it is to carve the pumpkin later."

"I haven't done this in years," Alex laughed, even though she had a slight look of distaste on her own face as she dumped a load of pumpkin guts into a bowl.

"My mother hated the smell of pumpkins," Arthur added as he turned his own pumpkin around and examined its sides. "I never did this as a kid."

"Really?" Bran asked, "Never? At all? Not even at school?"

"At my school, we drew on little pumpkins with markers; they weren't going to let us use knives," Arthur replied with a laugh. "Which I don't blame them for." He tapped at the surface of the pumpkin. "What I don't get is how something like this holds the Sídhe off. I mean, it's a pumpkin and a candle. How is that anything special? The Sídhe aren't stupid."

"No idea," Nicki remarked with a shrug. "But Morgana says that a carved face in a pumpkin or something similar does the trick."

"Does it work on other seasonal nights?" Arthur asked making them all look at him with odd expressions. "What?"

"I… haven't asked that," Nicki told him with wide shocked eyes. "Why haven't I asked that?" She asked, throwing her slimy hands around and sending orange fibers flying. "It could be that it's freshly harvested or the chill in the air or-"

"Calm down Nicki," Aiden said, reaching out to grab her hands. "You're making a mess. You can ask later."

The large dark wood table of Morgana's formal dining room had been covered with a thick layer of newspaper and a plastic tablecloth. To Aiden's left, the curtains were pulled back on both the tall windows and allowing sunlight to stream into the room. He suspected based on the table's position that it had been moved further away from the tall china cabinet than it normally was.

The smell of pumpkin pie was already wafting out of Morgana's kitchen, making Aiden's mouth water. He had to admit that it was pretty impressive that Morgana was using the pumpkins to bake pies. His eyes moved over to the plate of treats that Morgana had put out on the buffet for them to snack on along with a stacked pile of their favorite sodas. She had something for all of them. It was actually kind of funny how well she took care of them whenever they were over. She intimidated him in class and at magic lessons, but at the same time, there was a very caring side to her that she showed in little ways. Aiden frowned and stopped scraping the inside of his pumpkin as a strange thought occurred to him.

"What is it Aiden?" Bran asked from next to him. "You have a weird look."

"I was just wondering if Morgana ever had kids," Aiden answered in a low voice, glancing towards the kitchen doorway. "Sometimes... I don't know, she just seems like she'd make a good mother."

"I don't know," Alex said slowly, a slight frown on her face. "I mean she's immortal so if she ever did have kids then she outlived them."

"That would be very hard," Nicki added sadly. "But it doesn't mean that she hasn't. Merlin too; maybe they've both had a few families over the centuries."

"Do you want to ask her?" Arthur asked, glancing almost fearfully towards the doorway.

"I can say no in five languages and that still wouldn't tell you just how much I am not going to ask her that," Aiden replied quickly his back straightening.

"You speak five languages?" Alex asked him, looking rather impressed.

"I can speak three languages: English, Spanish and some Gaelic," Aiden told her with a small smile. "And I know how to say no in German and Arabic."

"Arabic and Gaelic?" Arthur repeated, raising an eyebrow.

"Gaelic from my grandfather, he's not fluent, but he likes to use the language and taught Aisling and me what he knows.

And I learned some Arabic a few years ago from an Egyptian exchange student that my family hosted for a semester."

"Oh I remember him, Hamid was his name!" Nicki added with a smile. "Nice guy, I wonder how he's doing?"

"Don't know, we fell out of contact," Aiden answered with a shrug, mostly for the benefit of the others since Nicki already knew that.

Picking up one of the smaller knives he began making a few guiding cuts on the surface of the pumpkin, just deep enough to see as he marked out the face he was going to make. Next to him, Nicki had a marker and was carefully outlining a much more elaborate face. She had the whole thing planned out on a sheet of paper and was looking back at it every few seconds. Alex wasn't as diligent as Nicki, but she was also drawing the face she wanted on the pumpkin's surface. Arthur glanced over towards him with a smile and shrugged at the antics of the girls. Bran shifted his pumpkin around and scrapped another large scoop of innards out of it with a small grunt.

"I wonder if Morgana gets trick or treaters up here?" Alex asked, breaking the silence. "It's a bit out of town."

"Probably not," Nicki answered, turning her pumpkin from side to side and studying her work. "There aren't many people up here when trick or treating you have to keep to the high-density areas to get a good candy-time ratio."

"Do I even want to ask how long you trick or treated?" Bran remarked to Nicki with a smirk.

"I trick or treated until I was ten," Nicki informed him, raising her chin and trying to look put out.

"And then she volunteered to take younger kids around and got candy that way," Aiden informed them with a grin.

"You did the same thing Aiden: when we finished with the kids today don't think that I didn't see your bag of candy."

"I only take candy when the people insist," Aiden countered seriously.

"I'm not sure if watching and listening to the two of you makes me sad I never had siblings or happy that I didn't," Bran cut in, shaking his head and chuckling.

"How is it going?" Merlin asked as he strolled into the room.

Professor Yates was dressed casually in jeans with a black t-shirt with a white skull on it and was carrying an iced tea in one hand. The combination looked off on an older man with curly graying hair, but somehow Merlin made it work. Perhaps, Aiden thought, simply due to the fact that at this point nothing about the three-thousand-year-old mage surprised him.

"So far so good," Nicki replied, pausing in her work and wiping off her hands before securing a stray strand of red hair into her ponytail. "None are done yet."

"Well with these five and the three that Morgana and I made earlier we should be safe," Merlin told them. "Oh, I pulled out sleeping bags for all of you and Morgana has put extra blankets in the living room."

"Why did you have so many sleeping bags?" Bran asked curiously.

"When you're as old as we are, you tend to collect all sorts of things," Merlin answered with a laugh. "But these are actually a fairly recent acquisition; I got them at some fundraiser a few years ago. I forget which department it was for, but one of the auction items was a rather large camping set with tents, sleeping bags, and cookware. I've actually never used most of it."

"Really?" Arthur said, sounding interested. "Maybe we'll have to borrow it at some point."

"Oh, do you like camping?" Merlin asked Arthur with a glint in his eye.

"Actually I've never gone," Arthur admitted with a laugh. "Well other than summer camp, but that's not the same as pitching a tent and cooking over a fire."

"No, it isn't," Merlin agreed with a nod. "Honestly I haven't been camping in years, I confess that I rather like the age of modern plumbing. It was so sad when the Roman system fell into disrepair. But electricity is nice too and the internet is wonderful. I often wonder how I got any research done before it came along."

Aiden glanced towards Nicki who was working very hard at not laughing and then he looked back at Merlin who was watching him with a sly smile.

"Are you teasing them again?" Morgana called from the kitchen before appearing out of it a moment later. "Honestly, you keep this up and they're not going to know what to believe from you."

"Ah, but it is so much fun, my dear Morgana."

"Sometimes I think you don't remember what is real and what isn't anymore," Morgana said, giving Merlin an appraising look. "Now go and finish chopping up the vegetables. They need to finish at least one jack-o-lantern a piece."

"Oh wait!" Nicki called, shaking some pumpkin guts off her fingers. "Do jack-o-lanterns work on other seasonal days? Why do they work in the first place on Halloween?"

"I believe that the real power of the jack-o-lantern comes from the freshly harvested nature of the vessel it is carved into," Merlin explained calmly with a smile as he studied the bowl full of pumpkin guts. "Add to that a source of light that radiates out... well, it all comes together with a strange magic. The truth is children that what Morgana and I understand and know about magic is dwarfed by what we do not understand."

"So the faces may not be necessary?" Nicki asked with a considering look on her face as she looked at her pumpkin. Morgana shook her head fondly and vanished back into the kitchen, giving Merlin another look. Merlin nodded to her quickly before looking back at Nicki.

"I'm not sure, but then again I doubt that we'll ever have a good chance to test it with a real Sídhe," Merlin reminded her. "This trick wasn't even well known during the first war. We stumbled across it in a small Irish village, but they didn't use pumpkins."

"So how did you discover that pumpkins worked?" Bran asked. "If the Sídhe have been gone for so long."

"The Sídhe are gone, but during the final days of the war many of their slaves escaped into our world and they share most of the same weaknesses. While most of them aren't usually interested in causing trouble for humans, the seasonal days are too much to resist for some of them. Thus humans have been protecting themselves from them for centuries."

"Morgana mentioned that," Alex added thoughtfully. "I guess I haven't thought about it much, that things like brownies are real."

"Brownies? You mean those helpful household spirits?" Aiden asked with a grin. "It would be awesome to have one of those around."

"Potentially, but keep in mind that our magic reacts very strongly towards them."

"If they live in our world then why do magic levels go down?" Nicki questioned Merlin as she drew a face on her pumpkin.

"They are not a threat," Merlin explained calmly. "Simply put, the Earth can't seem to sustain magical levels all the time and thus activates the protective measure of magic only when really needed. Otherwise, we'd have a constant battle with visitors and it would be exhausting."

"Is it really that simple?" Alex asked, picking up her finished pumpkin carefully in her arms. "Aren't there short invasions from time to time?"

"Occasionally on the Indian subcontinent. They have an odd, almost permanent connection to a particularly troublesome world, but the Old Ones who live there are very fast to deal with these problems. So fast in fact that Morgana and I usually don't even find out about them until later."

"Old Ones in India... wait, do you mean the Hindu gods?" Nicki asked, her voice going higher in her excitement.

"Indeed: Shiva was a good friend of Lokpal, a previous incarnation of the Iron Soul," Merlin told them, looking to Arthur fondly. "Lokpal created the Trishula just as Arto created Cathanáil - forgive me Excalibur and entrusted it to

Shiva. In fact, I believe that one of Shiva's names to his followers is Lokpal, no doubt a way of honoring that incarnation of the Iron Soul."

"Seriously," Arthur asked with wide eyes. "One of my previous forms was friends with an honest to goodness god?"

"Well depending on your definition of god then yes," Merlin told him kindly with a smile. "Of course one of your other incarnations was married to an Old One."

"I thought he and Jenny-" Bran started to ask.

"Gwenyvar and Luegáed are only reincarnated some of the time," Morgana said as she stalked into the room, a pensive expression on her face. "They are not a problem in every life. But enough about that, the sun will be going down soon so focus on finishing those pumpkins and let's get them outside."

Aiden glanced at Alex who had a strange little frown on her face as she looked at Morgana. She caught his eye and shrugged quickly. Warm beams of sunlight illuminated the room through the window as the sun dipped lower in the sky and Aiden forced himself to focus on cutting out the eyes that he'd drawn on the pumpkin. The room lapsed into calm silence and Merlin headed back into the kitchen, no doubt to finish the vegetables for Morgana.

Alex finished her pumpkin first; a relieved sigh escaped her as she flexed her fingers. Aiden grimaced, feeling the strain in his own fingers. He just wasn't used to carving pumpkins. With a burst of determination, he sliced into the thick orange skin to create a couple of jagged teeth. He put the knife aside and picked up the pumpkin while Alex did the same and went off towards the front door.

Twenty minutes later, the porch was an odd sight; anyone looking at it would have thought that a whole slew of kids lived at the house. Some were wonderfully precise with mouthfuls of sharp teeth and fierce jagged eyes like Nicki's while his own pumpkin was much more on par with a kid's. Its three squarish teeth looked more humorous than frightening. But Arthur's was the most frightening with narrow long eyes that curled down slightly at the edge and a long narrow mouth with teeth that looked more like tears in fabric. It gave him the distinct impression of an evil scarecrow for some reason. In the corner of his eye, he saw Alex shiver slightly at her boyfriend's jack-o-lantern as the candle flickered for a moment.

"I hate to say it, but Arthur's is the best," Nicki admitted next to him. "Seriously creepy."

"I'm kind of sad that we changed out of our costumes," Bran remarked as he glanced over at the setting sun. "Feels a bit odd to be surrounded by jack-o-lanterns and not be dressed up."

"Well after last night's party and trick or treating with hordes of kids today, my costume was getting a bit smelly," Arthur replied with a laugh and shrug. "I don't know about you."

"Yeah, but it was fun to volunteer with the kids and nothing weird happened," Aiden pointed out as he followed the others up the porch steps.

"Even if getting out of bed was a pain," Nicki sighed dramatically, gently moving a pumpkin to the side so that the porch steps were flanked by two jack-o-lanterns.

"Nicki, trick or treating wasn't until two in the afternoon," Aiden reminded her, chuckling at the scowl on her face.

"Yeah, but after last night I was tired and my head was killing me."

"You were the life of the party," Arthur teased with a laugh and a smirk at her expense.

"You kids really shouldn't drink," Morgana chided them, gesturing them into the house with a frown. "If you lose control of your magic it could be very dangerous."

Nicki turned bright red, wilting under Morgana's gaze and she nodded her understanding quickly before darting inside. Morgana's expression softened and she exhaled softly.

"In her defense, the punch got seriously spiked," Alex explained quickly. "We were trying to be responsible."

"I know, and I am pleased with all of you," Morgana replied with a nod. "But caution is necessary for our kind. There are still places in this world where those accused of magic are killed and all the magic in the world can't hold back a mob of frightened and enraged mortals."

The jack-o-lanterns placed around the house cast an eerie light into it through the windows. None of the curtains were drawn and strange shadows flickered on the walls. A tray of food had been set out on the coffee table along with a tea service. Alex lingered by the doorway until Arthur took her hand and pulled her into the room. He sat down in the large armchair and tugged Alex down next to him, squeezing them both into it. Morgana sat down on one side of the loveseat and pulled a round object that Aiden thought was a mirror for a moment. It caught the light from the jack-o-lanterns and gleamed. In Morgana's hand, it began to shimmer and he was struck silent and still.

Aiden leaned against the wall, watching as Morgana held the small polished bronze disk in her hands. It had been a year since he'd seen the disk last, having only vague memories of seeing it on her desk last Halloween after being rescued from Sídhe hounds. The surface of it shimmered in the light but did not provide a clear reflection like a mirror would have. Bran was leaning towards Morgana, a look of intense curiosity on his face. Then Morgana smiled slightly and shifted her position to give Bran a better view. The disk began to glow more brightly and Aiden realized that Morgana was pushing some of her magic into the bronze disk.

"It is a subtle thing," Morgana said in a low voice, speaking mostly to Bran. "All it takes is a small spark of magic that you sustain. You allow your magic to reach out and connect back to the Earth itself, the source of your magic. Sometimes you'll see nothing and sometimes you'll see something very important."

Stepping forward, Aiden looked at the bronze disk around Nicki's head as she crept forward as well. Bran reached out and carefully touched the edge of the bronze disk, his breath catching for a moment. Aiden wondered what it felt like or if he was seeing something strange. There was an energy in the room, an undercurrent of nervousness and excitement beneath the silence. In the armchair, Arthur was watching Bran with wide and nervous eyes while Alex nibbled at her bottom lip. Nearby, Nicki was almost vibrating. No one said anything, but Aiden knew that everyone was thinking about Bran's last vision.

"I see…" Bran frowned deeply, his eyes narrowing as he stared at the bronze disk. "I'm not sure what it is."

"What is your first impression?" Morgana asked in a low voice, her tone calm and even. "Trust your instincts."

"Blood," Bran whispered, swallowing thickly. "It's blood…"

"That's not necessarily a bad thing," Merlin told him gently, his voice soft, but cutting in the silence. "Anything else?"

"No- wait," Bran said, twisting and gripping the bronze disk in both of his hands. "There's a sword!"

"Cathanáil," Morgana breathed, her own eyes wide as she looked at the disk before a wide smile spread across her face. "Merlin, it's Cathanáil!"

"Are you sure?"

"I'd know that sword anywhere," Morgana told him with a nod. "But I don't see the blood, just water."

"You can see different things?" Arthur asked, almost knocking Alex to the floor as he leaned forward suddenly. "But I thought-"

"This is a tool Arthur, one that responds to each mage a little differently," Merlin told him, stepping forward and putting a hand on Arthur's shoulder.

"Children! Get ready!" Morgana ordered sharply, releasing the disk and standing up. "The shadows are coming."

21

In the Shadow of the Mound

802 B.C.E. Newgrange Ireland

The small opening into the hill was shadowed even as the sun shone down across the grassy plain. From his place several feet back, Arto tried not to fidget. His back muscles were tense and his legs were sore making it hard to stay still. He bit back a sigh and swallowed the saliva in his mouth to relieve his thirst. Glancing up towards the sun, he tried to calculate how long he'd been standing like this.

"Have you been here before on the winter solstice?" Luegáed asked in a low voice next to him, shifting slightly in his discomfort. His friend sounded as bored as he did which made Arto feel a little better.

"I have," Arto answered in a soft voice, watching to make sure that no one was looking at them. "When I was much younger, Merlin wanted me to meet with the regional priests and see the inside of the complex."

"It's impressive when the sun can shine inside," Luegáed replied with a tiny nod. "My father arranged for me to have the honor shortly before I went to join your efforts. He hoped that I'd carry some of the power of the ancestors with me that way."

"It is an honor to be here once more," Arto agreed even as his joint ached. It was unusually cold for the spring and he thought he could smell rain in the air. "But it isn't the solstice today and I could do with some rest, not an honor."

Luegáed chuckled softly beside him, adjusting his cloak with small movements so it covered more of his torso. Arto frowned, wondering if he could manage that on his own, but part of it had been tossed back over his shoulder to make Cathanáil easier to draw. So while he could get to his sword quickly, his right side was freezing in the early spring wind.

"I'm not sure what the priests are doing," Luegáed admitted softly, still keeping his eyes locked on the figures who were moving around the entrance. "I may have grown up nearby, but I've never understood the ceremonies here."

The mound was amongst the largest in the isles, a piled hill of earth that had been constructed generations ago. Arto doubted that anyone knew exactly when it had been completed and he'd already been regaled with many local stories about its creators. But it was more than a simple hill; a long passage led inside from the small entrance that aligned with the sun on the winter solstice. There were three small chambers at the far end of the passage that only priests and special guests could enter. Only the ashes and bones of the most honored were brought here.

When he'd been here as a boy, Merlin had taken him inside and he had run his fingers over the triskele carved into the stone at the far end of the passage. His mentor had spoken to him in a low voice about the power of the symbol, its meaning for the world. Arto shivered and exhaled nervously. This had been where Merlin had first told him about his power and his destiny to protect the Iron Realm.

"You alright?" Luegáed asked, glancing towards him with a worried expression.

"Just remembering an unpleasant conversation here," Arto told him, grateful that his voice remained steady.

Unable to keep looking at the entrance, remembering the long corridor that to his younger mind had gone on in the dark forever, Arto glanced at the standing stones that surrounded the complex. They were smoother and more rounded than the ones at the great circle in the plains where his own people celebrated the winter solstice. Yet they were stunning; the triskele and other symbols carved deeply into the stone. These were newer, having been added only a few generations ago, similar to the large timber circle nearby.

"Do you think you will be placed here?" Luegáed suddenly questioned. "After the war?"

"My people have always been cremated at the plain stone circle," Arto reminded him calmly, looking at his friend in the corner of his eye. "My father was cremated there."

"I know, but my people place the honored dead here after cremation," Luegáed told him. "I thought that maybe you would be included."

"I am not from the western isle," Arto answered carefully. "I do not believe that would be the case. Besides… I think that Morgana might have something to say about it and Gwenyvar of course."

"But not too soon I hope," Luegáed added quickly, a strange tone to his voice. "Many years from now when the war is over and you die an old man."

Arto chuckled, but nodded in agreement, forcing himself to look back to the entrance into the mound. A priest stepped out of the dark passage and into the light of the sun, nodding to one of his fellows. They nodded in return and stepped away from the entrance. Arto straightened up as the men approached them and internally debated if this was the right moment for a smile or not. Thankfully, the priests merely nodded deeply to him. Neither of them were smiling and Arto kept his expression as neutral as possible.

"May the ancestors be with you," one of the priests said in a very dramatic voice. Arto barely kept himself from chuckling.

"Thank you," he replied with a deep nod of his own.

"We wonder, Arto, if we might speak with you in greater detail about the Iron Gates?" the other priest asked, a glint of curiosity shining in his eyes.

"Caisid!" Merlin's familiar voice called. "Mochan."

Arto turned to see his mentor walking towards them, a small smile on his face as his staff gently hit the ground with each of his steps.

"Merlin," one of the priests greeted with another nod. "Thank you for being here."

"Of course," Merlin said kindly, glancing quickly towards Arto. "I wonder if I might have a word. It is so rare that I am able to speak with you."

Next to him, Luegáed chuckled softly as Merlin distracted the two priests. Luegáed gripped his shoulder and started leading him back towards the nearby village. The gently rolling hills surrounding them were dotted with trees, but it would be a short enough walk.

"Remind me to thank Merlin," Arto grumbled, reaching back to adjust his cloak.

"I suspect you'll remember," Luegáed replied with a smile. "Of he'll remind you himself."

"Did I look that panicked?"

"Your discomfort wasn't obvious," Luegáed assured him, sounding a little too amused for Arto's taste. "I just know you well enough to notice it."

"I sorry, I don't mean to be offensive. I know that these are your people, your family, and friends."

"I know that you don't mean anything by it," Luegáed told him firmly, looking over at him quickly with a small smile. "You're tired. You created a gate before the sun rose this morning, killed two Riders and then they promptly took you off to the mound. I'm impressed that you are being so calm and collected. I'm exhausted and I don't have any magic that I used."

Arto felt himself flush slightly even as the knot in his stomach eased. He would hate to have his best friend think that he was ungrateful towards his homeland. The reassurance let him release the breath he'd been holding as yet another man moved towards them to congratulate them on the latest victory he found it a little easier to smile and nod.

"They mean well," Arto said, mostly to himself. "I'm a point of curiosity, I know that."

"You think that's bad: just imagine what it will be like when you win the war and seal the Sídhe out of our world forever," Luegáed laughed, reaching out and squeezing his shoulder. "Life will be really interesting then."

"When this is all over…. I want seven kids," Arto said. Sighing, he stooped down and picked up a small forked stick. "Maybe I'll get a small herd and a dog. I haven't had a dog since I was a kid." He frowned and shook his head. "I wonder what happened to that dog."

"You haven't asked your mother?" Luegáed asked, his voice suddenly thin.

"No, there never seemed to be a good time. Besides, he probably just died of old age. At least that's what I'll hope for. I don't really remember him, but every so often something comes to mind and it makes me smile," he remarked with a shrug, twirling the small stick between two fingers for a moment before tossing it away. "Gwenyvar wants kids."

"I know."

"But I'm never around right now. I don't know if I'd be a decent father."

"I think you'd be a very good father," Luegáed assured him with a small sad smile. "You care about everyone Arto, you are patient-"

Arto snorted at the remark only to get a stern look from Luegáed that nearly made him fall over laughing. "You just reminded me of my sister," he gasped, stopping in his tracks and throwing his head back laughing.

"You don't give yourself enough credit. Sure you complain... a lot, but you don't let it stop you," Luegáed continued before gesturing behind them. "And you stand through ceremonies even when all you want to do is sleep."

"Maybe, hopefully, Gwenyvar and I will have the chance to see how we'd be as parents. We haven't talked about it for... years," he said, trailing off with a frown. "Has it really been that long since we talked about kids?"

"She knows you have work to do," Luegáed told him quickly. "I'm sure she doesn't want to upset you by talking about something that just isn't possible yet."

"It's possible… we could have kids, but I wouldn't be around much. But my mother would be there and most of the time you'd be there. We could make it work."

"Arto…" Luegáed said slowly, his voice shaking slightly. Arto looked at him, concerned by the sudden odd color on his face and the tone of his voice.

"What is it Luegáed? Are you alright?"

"Arto!" another voice suddenly called, drawing his attention to his right.

Eaban was striding towards them, a heavy fur cloak draped over his shoulders and a wide smile on his face. Arto straightened up and smiled. The older man still stood taller than Arto, but there wasn't as great a difference as there had been a few years ago. He looked back at Luegáed, but his friend's expression had returned to normal. Luegáed caught his look and gave him a small and rather forced smile. Arto frowned and was about to ask once again what was wrong, but Eaban reached them and laughed loudly.

"Ah the young heroes!" he boomed, his gaze locking on his son. Eaban's eyes darkened for a moment as he took in Luegáed's expression, but he merely set his hand on his son's shoulder and turned to look at Arto. "How are you faring in our land Arto?"

"I'm doing very well," Arto replied politely with a respectful nod. "Everyone has been most welcoming."

"Diplomatic as ever; you get it from your mother," Eaban informed him with a small smile. "Your father was never quite so... delicate with his words. Not like that cousin of yours."

"Medraut is very good with his words," Arto agreed, unsure of what else to say.

"How is your mother?"

"She is well, sir," Arto replied, relaxing at the well-meaning question. "She worries of course, but she remains healthy and I am grateful for her presence in my life."

"That's good to hear: your father's death was a terrible thing," Eaban said, his frown deepening. "It still troubles me that a Síd got behind him. Uthyrn was an excellent warrior and in that crowd... it shouldn't have happened."

"Father," Luegáed interrupted sharply. "I'm sure that Arto doesn't want to discuss that right now."

"It's alright Luegáed," Arto said quickly, glancing between the father and son.

"No," Eaban conceded with a nod. "My boy is right; he usually is. He takes after his mother too. Though from the reports I hear from the traders, he has maybe more than my skill in battle."

"I'm grateful that you sent him to us," Arto said sincerely with a small smile, watching with pleasure as Luegáed flushed at the praise. "He has become a fine commander of the warriors and I trust him to look after things whenever I leave the village. Luegáed himself has slain many Sídhe."

"That's my boy," Eaban agreed with a grin, squeezing Luegáed's shoulder a moment before he released him and looked back to Arto. "Come," Eaban said in a warm tone, clapping him on the shoulder. "You've more than earned some rest."

"Thank you," Arto told him, meaning the words more than he had all day as Luegáed's father steered him towards the roundhouse they'd provided him with two days ago when they'd arrived.

"Of course Arto," Eaban replied with a chuckle. "I'll send my son along later, but I'd like some words with him myself."

"I understand", Arto said quickly, looking over at Eaban as they reached the doorway. "We don't have to hurry back, no matter what Luegáed may tell you. And if he wants to stay here for a time I would understand."

"Thank you Arto, but it is clear to me that my son is proud of his service in the war. I would not seek to keep him from it."

Nodding, Arto took a step away from the pair. He lingered for a moment, watching the father turn to speak with his son. They started talking in low voices and Arto felt a small pang of wistfulness. He had barely known his own father Uthyrn: there had been such a short span of time between his return to the village of his birth and his father's death. Shaking his head, Arto mentally chided himself of thinking of 'what ifs' and focused his attention back on the nearby village.

It was unfortified like most that he'd seen over the years. Several large roundhouses were mixed in with small roundhouses and yards with animals. Arto reached up and rubbed his neck as he headed straight for the roundhouse he'd been given for his stay. All he wanted now was some sleep, and then he'd get something to eat and find out what was next from Merlin. He just hoped it was a return trip home.

22

Halloween Anniversary

"So…" Alex asked slowly as she looked out the window at the dark sky. "Uh… how soon are the shadows going to show up?" She fingered the hilt of her iron dagger gently, admiring how snug it was on her belt as she toyed with the small metal clasp that held the dagger in the sheath.

"My knees are hurting," Nicki muttered from the next window over, her bottom lip sticking out a bit further than usual. Alex barely kept herself from laughing; it wasn't often that she saw Nicki pout. Her friend was holding her own iron dagger and eyeing a nearby piece of wood furniture.

"They'll be here," Morgana said in a stern voice, but it wavered slightly, betraying her own boredom. She was sitting in a small chair at the far side of the room near the kitchen doorway, her bronze disk still in hand. "My scrying indicated that they were close."

"But not yet upon us," Bran finished thoughtfully from across the room where he sat in the armchair. Alex looked back at him, noting his irritated expression as he eyed his cane. Morgana had suggested against him sitting by the windows with them. She understood both Morgana's reasoning and Bran's irritation, but at least he was in a position that would let him help just about any of them.

"They might be circling the house," Arthur offered with a frown from his place by the doorway that led to the entry way. Alex looked over to see him eyeing the front door with a frown. "Looking for a weak point to attack us or waiting for more of them to arrive."

"Aren't you a ball of sunshine," Aiden grumbled, shooting Arthur a dark look.

"Everyone calm down; sniping at each other will do us no good," Merlin told them all, sounding far too cheerful before he popped a piece of candy corn into his mouth. "We all figured we'd be attacked tonight and Morgana and I just aren't sure if the jack-o-lanterns will hold the shadows back."

Alex nodded at Merlin's statement, her eyes sweeping the porch just outside of her window. The jack-o-lanterns were still in place. She turned and looked back into the living room where small jack-o-lanterns sat in each doorway leading out of the room. Between the walls and the jack-o-lanterns, if the shadows were affected by them, they'd be safe. But Alex felt a twitch of alarm for the state of Morgana's house if the things came crashing through a different window and tried to claw their way through the walls. From what she'd seen, some of them probably could do just that.

"Let's talk about something," Nicki suggested, giving herself a small shake in the corner of Alex's eye. "Just sitting here in silence is going to put us all to sleep or at least make us start daydreaming."

"I don't know if everyone daydreams as easily as you do," Aiden chimed in, earning himself a stuck out tongue from Nicki.

"What would you like to discuss Nicole?" Merlin asked with a soft, amused smile from his place

"What about water travel?" Nicki asked Merlin, glancing towards him and pouting at the sight of his bag of candy corn. "How does that work?"

"Water travel is very dangerous Nicole," Merlin scolded.

"I'm not going to try it," Nicki insisted, straightening up and almost hitting her elbow against the window frame. "I'm just curious. We've still got a lot to learn and it seems like you guys add more to that list every time we talk."

"I suppose it does seem that way," Merlin admitted with a small nod, setting the bag of candy corn on the small corner table. "Water travel is the only magical means of transportation that I know of. There is no teleportation or anything similar, not like you see in the movies or read about. In truth, moving your body which is matter through energy is a very dangerous prospect. A mage who uses water travel creates a magical tunnel linking two bodies of water," Merlin explained carefully, a pensive expression on his face.

"We are not even sure if this tunnel passes through the Earth or works on a different level than the physical world," Morgana added, looking at them all in turn. "We've only used it a few times ourselves due to the amount of magic needed to form the tunnel and keep it in place long enough to reach your destination."

"Exactly: it is not an easy feat for us. Some of the Old Ones are able to do it; in fact, it is probably how Chernobog is traveling towards us without being seen."

"So it is a magical tunnel," Nicki clarified with a nod. "Is it actually made of water?"

"It seems to be to the user," Merlin agreed. "In order to use water travel, a mage must have a clear mental picture of the body of water they are traveling to. You have to pour in a tremendous amount of magic into the water you are using as the starting point, all while keeping a clear image of the place you are going in mind. Sadly, I lost a student of mine almost five hundred years ago because they did not focus on their destination. They entered the water tunnel and never arrived or returned."

"They just vanished?" Aiden asked with wide eyes.

"I suppose that they probably washed up on some shore somewhere," Merlin told him with a sigh and a grimace. "But it is a huge world and it was impossible for me to know that for certain. Water travel is fast; it gets you where you want to go in moments, but it takes a great deal of magic. One slip and the tunnel will collapse around you. When Morgana and I have used it in the past it has left us drained."

"And of course you have to know the place you're going," Aiden remarked with a frown. "That limits its usefulness."

"The only being I know who is truly skilled at water travel is Cyrridven, but she is an Old One who never leaves the water. She has become connected to it in a way that is beyond most of them. As for Chernobog; he sees through his shadows and if he is using water travel, has most likely seen the lake through their eyes."

"When Cyrridven wakes up, do you think she'll come here?" Nicki asked, her voice soft, but excited. "Like rise out of the middle of the lake?"

Alex smiled at the eagerness in Nicki's voice and couldn't help but wonder what it would be like to see a person emerge out of the water itself. She briefly wondered if she looked like

the Lady of the Lake in the stories or if she looked like
something else completely.

"I am certain that Cyrridven will come here," Merlin assured
them. "I just do not know if she knows the waters of this lake
or if she even requires such knowledge to water travel."
Merlin paused and chuckled. "And for all I know, the lake is
where she is sleeping."

"You think that's possible?" Aiden questioned, leaning
forward with a frown.

"Cyrridven has many gifts and the power of the Iron Realm
has revealed many things to her. I put very few things beyond
her."

"But she's an Old One," Bran remarked thoughtfully. "Why
does she know so much?"

"Cyrridven was shown many things so that she could instruct
Merlin," Morgana informed them calmly. "To be honest, she's
never had that much interest in me. I suppose to her, I'm
merely another mage, but Merlin is her responsibility."

"Just as the first Iron Soul was my student and I have sought
to teach the different incarnations in times of need, so she
taught me," Merlin explained with a small pleased smile. "As
to why her and why an Old One, I do not know. Perhaps the
magic simply knew that she could be trusted."

"You make it sounds like the Earth is alive sometimes," Alex
told him, an odd feeling twisting in her stomach at the idea.
"Is it?"

"I do not know," Merlin replied gently. "I am not inclined to
believe in the western monotheistic idea of a God, but my
experience indicates that there is something guiding the mages

of Earth. Perhaps it is sentient or perhaps it is some kind of chaos that just seems to put the right people at the right place at the right time. Perhaps Cyrridven's original connection to the magic of Earth was not her being chosen, but rather an accident like getting hit by lightning, something quite possible but rare."

"One more thing to wonder about," Aiden chuckled. "As if there wasn't enough already."

"Oh lighten up," Nicki scolded him lightly. "After all, today is sort of an anniversary for us."

"Ah yes," Alex sighed dramatically. "It was a year ago that we were chased and cornered by vicious Sídhe Hounds looking to rip us apart."

"At least it's also the anniversary of the day you were reassured that you weren't crazy," Bran added with a grin.

"True, not crazy, but stuck in a magical story that got me dragged underground."

"Hey, you got Arthur out of the deal," Nicki reminded her with a smirk, nodding towards the boy in question. "Not all bad."

"Yeah, okay not all bad," Alex agreed with a glance towards her boyfriend who was smiling at the banter.

They quieted again and Alex leaned against the wall, trying to stay awake. The initial rush of fear that the shadows were coming was fading away and being replaced by boredom and the reminder that with the party last night she hadn't gotten much sleep.

It was a low growl that brought Alex back from the fuzzy haze that she'd fallen into. She tensed as the sound grew louder and looked out the window. In the darkness beyond the lights of the house, she thought she could see something moving. A chill seeped through the window and she shivered. Shifting to her feet, Alex glanced around at the others and noted that everyone was stirring and moving.

The front door rattled and Arthur's eyes widened in alarm. He glanced down at the jack-o-lantern in the doorway and took a cautious step forward to look around the corner. A moment later he sprang back and moved away from the entry way as the front door rattled louder and louder. Moving away from the window, Alex quickly moved towards Arthur as he backed away.

Then there was an odd sound, almost like a blast of water and the air turned even colder. In the entryway, the lights flickered and dimmed. Something rippled just beyond the jack-o-lantern and a shadow appeared out of the darkness. The shadow twisted in midair, floating over the ground like a black ghost. Long arms jutted at awkward angles out of the black form looking disconnected and almost hazy, but the long claws at the end of the arms were perfectly clear. The head shifted and came forward on an unnaturally long neck that curved into an arch as it looked at them with large round red eyes. The inky blackness that made up its face rippled in the low light until two rows of sharp teeth flashed into view. It growled but came no closer to her and Arthur as her boyfriend moved beside her.

Another snarl made her turn to look towards the doorway to the kitchen in alarm, her heart racing and her legs tensing to move. A shadow that bore a strong resemblance to a wolf with a long muzzle and glowing red eyes was just beyond the jack-o-lantern. The flames inside the jack-o-lanterns flickered and Alex held her breath, wondering, watching and waiting.

"Stay calm," Merlin's commanded, his voice filling the silent room.

Alex looked back at the misshapen shadow creature looming in the doorway. It was watching them as it took a small step forward. The fire in the jack-o-lantern flared wildly, casting strange shadows across the walls. Alex glanced down at the fire and swallowed fearfully as she noted the flame shrinking. She exhaled slowly to calm down, only to have her breath dance in front of her in the chilled room.

More sounds of snarling, growling and groaning echoed through the windows. Glancing over her shoulder, Alex saw Nicki looking through the window cautiously. Her friend opened her mouth to say something, but then thick black liquid began to seep in from under the windows. The windows rattled and the temperature plummeted.

"They're getting in!" Morgana shouted right before a whip of silver light flared in the corner of Alex's eye. "Take out the fully formed ones! Bran, Nicki keep an eye on the windows!"

The jack-o-lantern cracked open, the shadow snarled and the flame extinguished. It lunged forward, entering the living room with a snarl. Behind them, Alex heard movement, banging and Bran shouting something, but it all masked by the overpowering sound of her own heart racing in her ears.

Gasping, Alex barely kept herself from stumbling back as the long head surged towards her, the long jaws open. She darted to the side, sending a blast of magic out of her left hand towards the creature on reflex. The dark silver magic swirled in the air before colliding with the exposed roof of the shadow's mouth. With a shriek, the shadow slammed its jaws shut and recoiled from Alex. Using its distraction, Alex planted her feet against the wooden floor and braced herself.

The shadow shrank back, shaking its head as a high pitched sound escaped it. In the corner of her eye, she saw Arthur gather his own white magic in his right hand. It slowly lengthened into a shining spear. The shadow creature saw it and began to move towards Arthur who was still focusing on the growing spear.

Alex tugged at the warm spark in her chest, pulling her magic forwards roughly. It was hard to breathe as the dark silver spark shot down her arm and followed the path of her hand, gathering on the end of her pointer finger. The shadow creature was bearing down on Arthur just as the burst of magic sprang off Alex's finger and struck it in the face. There wasn't enough focus or magic to do any damage, but the shadow creature snarled and spun towards her. The distraction was enough and a moment later a spear of ice was thrust into its odd head. Red eyes widened and a terrible gurgling sound escaped the creature as it lashed its head around for a moment. A warm hand gripped Alex's chilly arm and tugged her back as the shadow creature began to fade away.

As the last dark remnants of the shadow creature vanished, Alex turned her attention to the rest of the room. Another humanoid looking shadow creature with long limbs was facing off against Merlin as the oldest of the mages' green magic swirled around it. Morgana was occupied with a shadow that looked like some kind of floating snake as it twisted and dodged her whip of silver magic. Then a large bulky shadow creature hit the far wall, knocking a painting onto the floor and Alex caught a flash of bright yellow magic as the creature tried to move. Bran was still sitting in his chair, one hand raised and glowing softly while his other hand gripped the top of his cane tightly.

"Nicki!" Bran shouted, drawing the attention of Nicki who was still near her window. The vestiges of another shadow creature were vanishing. "A little help!"

Aiden moved first, a red glowing spear sputtering in his hands as he tried to form it into something useful against the Shadows. A roar from the pinned creature seemed to shake the room. Ice formed along the floorboards and Alex shifted towards Bran. It broke loose with another roar, a wave of cold flooding the room. Alex stopped short and panted, hearing Bran coughing across the room.

"Bran!" Aiden shouted as he lunged forward to intercept the huge bear-like creature moving for Bran. It swiped out a large paw, striking Aiden in the chest. His red magic surged into the shadow creature and it released a sharp hissing roar.

Alex heard a growl escape Nicki as Aiden slammed against the floor with a hideous crunch. Before she could even move, Nicki's hand glowed a light blue color as her magic gathered. Nicki didn't even let it fully manifest before she waved her hand towards the shadow creature. A bright blue glow surrounded the beast as it stumbled back, but then it stilled in its place as ice formed around it, made of jagged shapes and freezing it solid. As Nicki swung around to look at the last of the shadow beasts, the wolf-like one that Arthur was hurling magic at with little success, Alex surged forward and dropped to the ground next to Aiden.

"I've got him," Alex told Nicki quickly as she reached out and felt the skin of his neck. It was cool to the touch, but she could feel it warming up and his pulse racing beneath her fingertips. A sigh of relief escaped her and Alex scanned him quickly for any signs of injury. There wasn't any blood on his chest and arms were the creature had struck him and there was no blood on the floor beneath his head.

Across the room, Alex could hear a soft scraping sound and felt a wave of cold brush over her skin as Nicki went to attack the Shadow. She didn't look up, reminding herself that Nicki was the best suited of them all to fight the Shadows and instead focused on Aiden. There was a fierce animalistic cry from the corner of the room and a moment later Morgana was kneeling next to her. Alex shifted away to give the former doctor more room and finally risked a glance over towards where the Shadow had been.

Arthur was panting slightly and already moving towards her. Nicki had a murderous expression on her face and her fists were tightly clenched. A soft groan from Aiden made Alex looked down at him. She grinned as his eyes fluttered open for a moment before closing. He shook his head slightly but then grimaced at the movement. Aiden tried to open his eyes again and slowly focused on them as they crowded around.

"You're alright Aiden," Morgana assured him, reaching out and touching his cheek for a moment. Then a soft ball of light appeared in her hand. Aiden blinked at the light and Morgana smiled before the light vanished. "A slight concussion judging from your eyes."

"But… he hit the ground so hard," Arthur protested with a frown before flinching at his own words. Standing up, Alex put a hand on his arm and forced a small smile.

"He's fine," Morgana repeated, helping Aiden sit up. "Come on, you'll be more comfortable off the floor."

Working together, they carefully helped Aiden to his feet with Nicki hovering at Morgana's elbow. Alex kept glancing at her, wanting to make sure that the usually cheerful and collected girl was okay. By the time Aiden was settled in a chair and Morgana was checking his eyes again, Nicki's shoulders had relaxed and her expression had softened. Of course, she stayed at Aiden's side and her hand crept over to his shoulder.

Alex stepped back and sank down into the nearby coach with a sigh of relief that Aiden was alright. Arthur walked over and placed a hand on her shoulder, giving it a quick squeeze. Merlin withdrew to the far side of the room and glanced out the window, nodding to himself.

"How are you feeling?" Nicki asked Aiden as Morgana stepped back and vanished into the kitchen.

"Actually, I'm already a bit better," Aiden told them all with a smile. "And I've had concussions before and this doesn't feel anywhere near those. You remember that time I slipped on the wet gym floor and smacked my head, Nicki?"

"Yeah," Nicki replied with a rather pained smile. "You crawled off to the side and I could barely get you to understand a thing I was saying."

"Good times," Aiden joked with an easy grin before shaking his head. "Really though guys, I'm okay. Honestly, I'm surprised too."

"Your magic gradually makes you more resistant to physical attacks," Morgana said calmly as she walked back to Aiden and handed him a sack of frozen peas. "It is a slow process and one that we don't control, but we slowly become harder to hurt."

"Your skin can still be pierced of course," Merlin added quickly. "But I haven't broken a bone in more than a century."

"Seriously? Why didn't you tell us this before?" Nicki demanded with a frown, arms crossed over her chest with her earlier anger returning.

"Because it is hard to plan for," Merlin replied calmly, not at all affected by her tone.

"In layman's terms; we didn't want you rushing off and doing something stupid on the mistaken belief that you are invincible," Morgana told Nicki, giving her a stern warning look that deflated the irritated red head slightly. "Think about some of the fights you've been in. Some of you have been thrown around and yet haven't broken any bones, but still, get cut and bleed."

"It's just a little manifestation of your magic to help you stay alive through trauma," Merlin concluded with a shrug. "We did a little bit of testing on it in the 70s, but we haven't really looked at it in a while. We found it is harder to break our bones and a little harder to draw blood, but certainly still very possible. After all, Alex and Arthur routinely give blood and Alex has certainly had her fair share of injuries."

"Testing?" Arthur repeated with a startled expression, looking torn between curiosity and horror.

"I was a medical doctor," Morgana reminded him with a shrug. "And there isn't exactly a manual for us. We've spent the centuries gradually learning more and more about what our magic can and can't do and the limits to our physical abilities."

"Of course, each mage is a little different," Merlin added quickly with a smile as he tied off Arthur's bandage and patted his shoulder. "So one of you might go beyond what we know one day or achieve something that we cannot."

"The point is, don't panic if you get tossed around a little or someone else does," Morgana announced. "You'll probably be fine after some rest and a touch of healing magic, but be careful because there isn't a clear threshold for mages."

"Maybe that's why I haven't had a paper cut in ages," Bran muttered with a smile, trying to ease the tension, but Alex caught him glancing down at his leg.

"Guys," Nicki called over in a tired voice. "The sun is starting to rise."

Twisting around, Alex looked over towards the east facing windows and sighed softly in relief as the first glow of the sun could be seen just above the mountains.

"Thank god," Arthur groaned, reaching back and rubbing his neck carefully. "This is definitely the worst Halloween ever."

"Even though last Halloween Jenny and Lance started cheating on you?" Aiden asked, exhaustion clear on his face until he realized what he'd said and it was replaced with horror as he grimaced.

Alex looked over at her boyfriend, noting his shoulders slump for a moment before he took in a deep breath. "I wasn't aware of that," he muttered before shaking his head. He collapsed on the couch next to her a moment later, putting his arm around her shoulders. "But, yeah I'd still say this one wins."

"At least we can sleep today," Nicki announced, stretching her arms up into the air. "It'll really stink when Halloween isn't on a weekend."

"I suppose so," Arthur agreed, tugging Alex closer to him. "But maybe we'll have everything resolved by then and we can have a nice normal Halloween."

Whatever the response was, it was lost on Alex as she leaned against Arthur's warm shoulder and snuggled up against him. She closed her eyes and firmly ignored the ongoing conversation, preferring sleep and the warmth of her boyfriend until it was safe to go home. The last thing she remembered hearing was Aiden chuckling and saying "happy anniversary"

23

Home Again

Being home was a blend of wonderful and horrible. It was a reality that Alex couldn't adjust to smoothly anymore. She'd heard from other students that going home was weird, fun and odd. Living under the parents' roof, sharing a bathroom with both of her brothers and adjusting back to their schedule were all normal oddities that threw her off, but the real problem was in the silences.

Matthew, for instance, was three years older and in his senior year of college with his graduation with a communications degree coming up fast. He'd had so much to tell their parents as he ruffled their younger brother Edward's hair. There was his new girlfriend Tina who was a psychology major, the interviews he had lined up for internships in the spring and his plans to go on one last spring break adventure before the real world. Alex knew all about his classes by the end of his first day home but hadn't said much about her own.

Eddy, on the other hand, talked about high school and had admitted his worry for upcoming tests. Alex nearly laughed at the idea of being scared of the ACTs but remembered the feeling all too well. It seemed like an eternity ago. Eddy wasn't dating anyone at the moment; he'd always been more of an introvert compared to her and Matt. It was all so normal.

It all came crashing down on Alex the day before Thanksgiving during dinner. Her parents were chatting about work, Eddy was complaining to Matt about recent changes to the high school graduation requirements and asking for advice about what volunteering he should do for college applications.

She didn't know what to say or talk about. Sure she had classes and she was doing fine in them, but that wasn't what consumed her thoughts. It wasn't classes, homework, tests, friends or even boys that kept her up at night. It was worries about a magical war. She almost burst out laughing.

"You've been quiet Alex," Matt observed, "Everything okay?"

"Yeah," Alex told him with a forced chuckle. "Just can't get my brain away from school I guess."

"That good or that bad?" Matt asked with a glance towards their father who was frowning with worry lines furrowing his brow.

"Nothing like that," Alex assured them in a rush. "We just did scheduling and midterms and I guess it's a bit weird being back."

"Well forgive your father and I, but we'll take advantage of having you come home for Thanksgiving for as long as we can."

"True, after all, Matt may not be able to come home next year," her father observed. "He could have a job in Chicago or Seattle or who knows where and not be able to make it back."

"Or he could have plans with a girlfriend or fiancé," her mother added with a little smile. "It's hard to say so try not to worry about school, Alex. Focus on being home with your family."

Smiling at her mother, Alex nodded and dished up more of the salad. The conversation turned to her own classes and Alex did her best to think up little stories to tell. It was hard since the most important class she was in was about Arthurian mythology which she and others used to build their knowledge about what they were dealing with.

"We spend a lot of time debating what elements influenced the stories," Alex told her family with a slight smile. "Nicki loves mythology and Aiden actually knows some of the old Irish stories thanks to his grandfather. Apparently, the story of King Arthur is probably the combination of a lot of ancient hero stories from all across the British Isles. In some versions, they have a slightly different name and Arthur has a dagger in some of the stories that has magical powers. Mer- Professor Yates liked the class discussion so much that he actually allowed us to work together on a project about some of the other myths that could have influenced the King Arthur story."

"That sounds really boring," Ed observed with a curled lip.

Chuckling, Alex, pushed a strand of hair behind her ear. "I suppose a bit, but like I said thankfully Aiden and Nicki had some good ideas of where to start. Aiden's mother was able to point us to a bunch of good stories too; she knows even more than Aiden."

"That's nice," her mother observed. "Sometimes I wish I knew more about my heritage."

"You've got Vikings and the Norse gods, Mom," Matt pointed out, waving his fork with a piece of steak on the end about. "What more could you ask for?"

"There's a lot more to Swedish stories than just the old Norse culture," their mother reminded him firmly. "My grandmother used to talk about them, but I just don't remember many of her stories."

262

"Is there anything you do remember Liz?" her father asked kindly with a soft smile.

"I do remember her talking about trolls," she answered slowly with a growing smile. "There was one story with a young man outwitting a troll who had a pet bear…" She shook her head, "I just don't remember, but I enjoyed the stories as a girl."

Alex frowned slightly, making a mental note to ask if trolls were real. Maybe they were from one of the Sídhe branch worlds or from somewhere else completely. Or maybe they were completely fictional and she was jumping ahead of herself. It was hard to tell nowadays.

"Sounds neat," Alex told her mother with a smile. "My classes certainly have me more interested in mythology and how it has influenced modern literature."

"Well it certainly has, after all, you only have to look at Tolkien and J.K. Rowling to recognize that they use mythology as a cornerstone for their worlds," her mother agreed. "It could make an interesting focus area for you as a literature student."

"Sure Mom, 'course I still haven't got a clue about what I'm going to do with my literature degree."

"Maybe you'll become a college professor who teaches these classes," her father offered with a grin. "Just focus on grades and maybe a part-time job or internship for now. The key is to have a college degree."

Alex nodded and sipped on her water, trying not to think about how that job would fit in Nicki's plan for all of them to achieve 'total genre Savviness'. Her roommate was a little frightening sometimes and had recently gone over the evil overlord rule list with her. Alex had personally gotten a lecture about going off alone as if the time she was captured by the Sídhe that had been her intention. If Nicki ever got the idea that they needed to make a master list of mythology and confirm what was real and what wasn't it would be a dark day. Alex nearly shivered at the very idea of having to create a database with appearances and weaknesses. Course, she'd probably regret her dislike of the idea one day; she was... genre savvy enough to know that.

"Alex?" her mother called. "Are you finished?"

"Yeah," Alex said, nodding and setting her fork down. "It was really good Mom and Dad."

"Well thank your dad on this one. I just made the salad."

"Thanks, Dad," Alex told her father with a grin.

"You're welcome sweetie," he looked up at her mother. "Liz, I'm going to steal the boys to move that plywood into the garage before it gets too dark."

"Alex and I will handle dishes." Her mother gave a quick nod, ignoring the groans from her brothers. "Boys, help your father."

"What are you building this time dad?" Ed moaned as Alex stood up and started to collect the dishes.

"I'm replacing some of the shelves in the study; after that water leak some of them have started to warp more than I like."

Walking into the kitchen, Alex ignored the rest of the conversation and started handing the plates over to her mother who was filling up the sink with water. She cleared off the table, fed some of the scraps to the golden retriever puppy Anne that her parents had gotten two months ago and packed away the leftovers quickly. Anne barked cheerfully at her feet and nearly tripped her as she brought the last of the plates in.

"Careful!" her mother called, catching her arm. "Are you alright?"

"I'm fine; she's just a tripping hazard."

"Give her a few months and she'll be big enough to knock you over," her mother replied with a chuckle, taking the plates from her. "But she's a good girl."

"I kind wish Nicki and I could have a dog, I miss it."

"Well… I wouldn't recommend getting a large pet until you're more settled in a place. I know that it's tempting and having a dog is wonderful, but moving is hard on them."

"Yeah, I know. Maybe Aisling will wear her parents down. If Aiden had a dog then we could all go over and play with it."

Her mother chuckled at her statement and submerged another stack of dishes in the water.

"Things seem to be going better this year," her mother remarked casually, but Alex heard the hint of a question in her mother's voice.

"They are: I'm used to living away from home now and I've got good friends," Alex replied with a smile, looking down at the dishes as she dried them. "Plus Arthur of course."

"And Jenny?"

"Things are still a little weird with her," she admitted with a grimace. "But we're working on it. We've met to talk a few times and I think she and Lance may actually go somewhere now."

"Well... I suppose that's a good thing," her mother said doubtfully.

"I know that a cheater is always a cheater and all that," Alex said quickly jumping to Jenny's defense. "But there really seems to be something between Lance and Jenny. I'm not around them both very often, but when I am... it just seems like something that could be real. The sort that stories are written about." She almost laughed at her own words, they were a little too true, but she really did live in hope that maybe, just maybe the story could have a happy ending this time.

"I'm just glad that it hasn't caused any serious problems for you," her mother replied a bit doubtfully. "Anyway, you and your friends seem to be taking a lot of classes together."

"That won't last much longer. We've all done most of our general education classes now so gradually we have to take more of our field classes. But we're going to try and have a fun class or something together each semester."

"That's not a bad idea," her mother agreed. "It's great that you are in fencing club together, though Bran can't really take part and you and Nicki have soccer, but there is a lot to be said for taking a class just because it is different and interesting."

"Yeah, but the real challenge will be deciding which class and figuring out the scheduling."

"Well you've done scheduling for next semester already, what did you decide on?"

"We were all able to get into Professor Yates' the Bible as literature class. He's pretty much our favorite professor."

"That certainly sounds interesting; just don't tell your grandmother that you're taking a class like that," her mother cautioned. "You've mentioned Professor Yates often, what's the name of the other one you really like? Cornwelsh?"

"Close Mom, it's Cornwall, like the region in England."

"I'm surprised you know that," her mother told her with a bemused smile.

"Nicki's mind is a frightening warehouse of weird information, especially history or mythological information," Alex told her mom as she carried a stack of dry plates to the cabinets.

"She's been a good friend for you, but is it ever strange?"

"'Cause she's homosexual? No, not really. Actually, it's nice to have a friend who doesn't assume that I want to talk about boys, 'course, she has a lot of fun with Arthur and I dating. She teases me a bit, but she's been really supportive of the relationship."

"I'm glad, when you told us you and Arthur were dating I was a little worried."

"I thought you liked him?"

"We do, but I was afraid that you were just going to be a rebound," her mother confessed with a soft smile. "I'm glad I was wrong."

"Me too, I don't think I could have handled that," Alex admitted with a shaky smile. "But things are better. I guess I'm getting used to this grown-up thing."

Her mother snorted in amusement as she handed her the last of the dishes. "You say that now, just wait until you're paying rent, student loans, and a car payment each month. We'll see how you like the grown up thing then."

"I'm in college, I get to delay that."

"That's not what it's for missy."

"Whatever you say," Alex couldn't resist adding, dodging a handful of soap suds and rushing out of the kitchen. Downstairs she could hear the boys moving the wood for her father, complete with Matt groaning about having to work while home. Smiling, Alex shook her head and headed down the hallway to her room.

Stepping inside, Alex looked around her room carefully as she closed the door. There were still some posters from her youth here and there on the walls. A small collection of prized stuffed animals sat on a high shelf above the small desk in the corner where her laptop was set up. Galahad was of course on the pillows of the twin bed that she'd slept in since she was three. The room felt familiar and foreign all at once. There were so many reminders of her childhood interests, dreams, and hobbies. But there were also classics on the bookshelf, her graduation tassel hanging off the mirror and a few other subtle reminders that the room belonged to an older teenager.

She sat down on the edge of the bed and sighed, her eyes tracing a pair of photos on the nightstand. One was of her family; it was a formal photo in a photography studio that had been taken just before Matt went to college. Her elder brother now had stubble and longer hair, her younger brother was almost a foot taller than he had been when the photo had been taken and both her parents had more gray in their hair. And the younger Alex in the photo had a wide smile and no cares in the world. She snorted at the idea of her younger self finding out that in a few years' time she'd be a mage and fighting against Shadows and evil fairies. That would go over like a ton of bricks. This wasn't exactly the fun and wonder filled magical life that she'd envisioned as a young girl. For one there were too few unicorns and dragons and so far pretty much everything was hostile.

The other photo was of herself and her high school friends, all gathered together in a park during a school picnic. Everyone was smiling, eyes covered with sunglasses and hair blowing in the wind. She'd always liked the photo since her best friends were in it, but now she was hard-pressed to remember the last time she'd talked with any of them. Amy and Betsy were at the University of Washington and she'd seen them a few times last summer but hadn't called since. Becky was at Washington State and thanks to an internship she hadn't even seen her last summer.

Alex flopped back on the bed and looked up at the white ceiling, telling herself that she was being melodramatic. She didn't have a bad life. Sure her connections to her family were strained by the secrecy, but she had her fellow mages. She couldn't complain: Morgana and Merlin only had each other, and they'd watched generation after generation of people they cared about pass away. What right did she have to feel sorry for herself?

But still…. It was hard not to tell them. There were reasons on both sides of the argument: if her family didn't know then they didn't have to worry about her as much and they didn't have to live in fear of what might be out there. She got to come home and just be their daughter without any complications, but… she had to keep secrets from them. It was tempting to see how they'd react; she wondered what they were would say. She could show them magic easily enough even if her powers weren't as flashy as the others; Alex was getting better at doing simple tasks. She shook her head; this wasn't something she was going to sort out here and now.

A knock on her door made Alex sit up and look over as the door opened. Ed poked his head in with a smile.

"Hey sis, Mom wants to know if you'll join us for Yahtzee?"

"Full card?" Alex asked, a small smile tugging at her lips.

"Anything else is a waste of time," Ed replied with a raised eyebrow and a very serious voice. "Come on."

Nodding, Alex stood up, stretched out her shoulders. She told herself to smile and headed out to the living room to spend some time with her family. Maybe someday she'd tell them everything, but for now, she just needed to focus on them as people that she loved and who loved her.

24

Future Draws Near

801 B.C.E. Near the shores of Loch Torridon

Violet eyes glared hatefully at him as Arto swung the softly glowing Cathanáil in a smooth arch in front of his body. The blade impacted the shining gold armor, sliding over it with a sharp hiss and scraping sound. Stumbling back, the Síd tried to gather some magic in its hand, but he moved too quickly. With a quick step forward, Arto brought the sword down on the creature's arm, spilling silvery blood across the ground which began to fade away in mere moments. The Sídhe released a terrible scream of pain mixed with a curse. Without hesitation, Arto stepped closer, thrusting Cathanáil forward and forcing the Síd to dodge. He pushed more of his magic into the blade, causing the soft white glow to intensify and fully illuminate the area around him and the Síd.

Around them, the steep hills were slick with snow and rocks were shifting beneath their feet. They both paused and Arto glared at the Síd who met his look with one of equal hatred. He noted with satisfaction that the Síd's eyes were now squinting in the bright light of his magic. Down the hill, Arto could hear the clanging of swords and there were flashes of light behind them, reflecting on the snow.

Not waiting for the Síd to make the first move, Arto swung Cathanáil again, this time releasing some of the magic in the sword. Magic flashed off the sword like a burst of lightning and struck the Síd in the chest just before the sword collided with its armor. Arto grinned as the golden metal buckled under the double attack. It began to crumble into dust as the Síd retreated.

Arto allowed himself a moment of satisfaction at the look on the Síd's face. It knew it was going to die; that much was clear from the way its violet eyes turned murky and its face muscles twitched. But it didn't try to run. Arto almost respected it for that. He tightened his grip on Cathanáil and steadied himself on the rocks.

Sounds of battle rang up the side of the mountain and Arto had to resist the urge to look around for signs of the others, but he knew better than to turn his back on a Síd. Maybe they weren't all brutal enslavers who favored children that they could train to be obedient and serve their every need, maybe they weren't all vicious warriors that killed and enjoyed it and maybe they weren't all able to quickly summon forth and release their magic, but enough of them were. If there were Sídhe who weren't like that, Arto imagined they were probably slaves of their own kind.

An orb of golden magic blasted past him into the darkness and left a burning sensation dancing over his cheek. Snarling, the Síd jumped forward and swung its golden sword in a last violent assault. Arto twisted to the side to avoid the wild thrust and brought Cathanáil up over his head as the Síd fell forward on the rocks. Bringing the sword down, Arto closed his eyes momentarily as the sharp edge of his blade impacted with the back of the Síd's neck. There was no resistance as the iron blade sliced into the flesh. His eyes opened and the body was already vanishing before the sword had passed all the way through its neck.

Arto nearly slipped on the icy rocks as he backed up. Using Cathanáil as a support, Arto caught himself and shook his head at his own foolishness for chasing a Síd so far up the hills. Carefully, he kicked at the ground to solidify his footing and raised Cathanáil up, pushing more magic into the sword. It glowed brightly and shed light over the entire rocky hillside.

Arto looked around with a small thoughtful frown which turned to a deep scowl as he caught sight of the archway opening in the rocks up ahead. For a moment he struggled to contain a surge of anger. They'd just been attacked after sealing one entrance and here was another less than a mile away. He was almost impressed with the Sídhe, it was clever in a way and he hated it.

"Fine," he grumbled, kicking a rock into the darkness stretching into the ground. "I'll be back."

Arto didn't dare turn around, all too aware that a Síd might be lurking just beyond his view. They were creatures of a much darker world and had the advantage at night. Stepping carefully, Arto walked down the hill sideways, his eyes darting between the opening and his footing. It took longer to descend the slope than it had to run up it after the retreating Síd. Arto kept looking back towards the fight, illuminated by both Sídhe and Morgana's magic. He nearly slipped several times on the ice covered rocks, but soon enough found himself nearing the valley floor. Arto could see Airril and Boisil further up the valley with a Síd and Gareth swinging at a hound that was snapping at his legs. Another flash of Morgana's silvery magic against the snow drew Arto's attention over to his sister. She was facing two Sídhe, one of which was trying to circle around her while she swung her magic like a whip at the other.

The snow slushed around his feet, but Arto forced himself to keep moving towards Morgana. She spun around, throwing a blast of silver magic against the Síd who'd been trying to flank her and sent him to the ground. The Síd didn't vanish and Arto glanced towards Airril who was still occupied as another hound came rushing out of the darkness and attacked him. Bosil shouted something and crashed his iron sword against the Síd's head. It began to vanish and they both turned their attention to the hound.

Looking back to Morgana, Arto began to gather white sparks of magic in his free hand. The Síd she'd attacked was standing up while she sent the other crashing back against a boulder and calmly sidestepped its own blast of magic. Magic crackled off his sister's fingers and struck the Síd with a satisfying ringing. It was vanishing just as Arto ran up to join Morgana.

"Arto," she greeted calmly, turning to study the remaining Síd.

It eyed them both and Arto raised an eyebrow as it brought its golden sword up in front of it. Glancing towards his sister, Arto relaxed at the look in Morgana's eyes. She wasn't worried; instead the sharp cold look in her eyes was one that he was familiar with at this point. Morgana knew that she was about to destroy one of the race that had enslaved her and Arto wasn't going to get in the way of that wrath.

His sister's magic flashed through the air with a sharp crack and crashed into the Síd. It howled, head thrown back as its golden armor crumbled. Another blast of magic, this time in the shape of a simple orb caused the Síd to dissolve into a golden mist. Smirking, Arto watched the softly glowing flecks darken and blow away in the wind. In the corner of his eye, he saw his sister shake herself quickly, like a dog shaking off a layer of water.

"Are you alright?" Morgana asked, stepping towards him as she scanned the area.

"Morgana?" Airril's voice called, causing them both to turn as her husband moved into view. He relaxed in visible relief at the sight of her, his brown eyes warm as he moved towards him.

"I'm fine," Morgana assured him, a soft smile on her face and her eyes softening. "And you?"

"Boisil and I teamed up against one so it couldn't focus on harming either of us," Airril told her before he looked over to Arto. "What about the one you chased? It didn't hurt you?"

"No, it didn't and yes, it's dead," Arto informed him with a nod. "But while I was looking around I found another entrance up the mountain," he gestured up the valley towards the slope where the entrance was. "It's higher than they usually build, but it's there."

"You sure it's one of theirs and not a cave?" Airril asked, grimacing at his own question and running a hand through his brown hair in aggravation.

"I'm sure: it's straight up the hill from a large stone up that way," Arto said, pointing back from he'd come.

"They must be getting desperate," Morgana remarked with a pleased, slightly vicious smile. "This is a terrible place to put an entrance. They can't use their steeds."

"It's not going to be easy getting back up there to close the gate and we'll need more iron," Airril reminded his wife, stepping up behind her and putting a hand on her shoulder. "Two entrances in this area were more than we were expecting."

"I suspect that they figured we'd only find one of them and leave the other," Arto added with a nod. "But you're right about the iron; we'll have to return to the village and come back later."

"After you get some rest," Morgana told him firmly, looking him over quickly with a frown.

"I'll be fine," Arto insisted quickly, preparing to argue more, but the look on his sister's face made him stop.

"You just made a gate before we were attacked," Morgana reminded him with stern green eyes. "After you rest then we will return with more iron and take care of it."

Arto exchanged a look with Airril, pleased to note that the older man was smiling softly. Giving up the fight, Arto nodded and allowed his sister to reach out and straighten his cloak before leading him down the ravine.

"At least we travel with a lot of iron these days," Airril chuckled as he fell into step beside Arto. "And Merlin will be joining us with more soon."

"True, but I'll admit I sometimes wish we didn't travel with so much. It would give us an excuse to go home more often," Arto grumbled as they found the small path that would lead them back to the village.

Airril reached out and put a hand on Arto's shoulders, squeezing it gently and Arto felt himself relax a little. His brother understood duty keeping him separate from family all too well. After all, during the years when it was just himself, Morgana and Merlin, Airril and his sister had barely seen each other. Smiling, Arto nodded to his brother in law and looked ahead to where his sister was creating another light orb as the other warriors joined them on the path. Everyone was silent, the exhaustion of the day weighing on them.

Dawn was breaking as they climbed the last hill between them and his wife's former village. Even at a distance, they could hear the sounds of people beginning their days and Arto sighed in relief. Hopefully, that would mean some warm food would be available before he collapsed into bed.

As they drew closer, however, Arto could see a crowd gathered near the edge of the village, clearly waiting for them. He couldn't back a sigh of resignation that earned him a wry chuckle from Morgana and Airril. They exchanged a knowing look and Arto nodded to her after their silent communication.

"I'll deal with Cailean then," he concluded.

"And I'll inform Merlin of the situation," Morgana agreed. "Just as well he stayed here to protect the village. He'll have some energy to see to things."

"Good, that means we can get some sleep," Airril chimed in with a soft smile for Morgana and a sympathetic one for Arto.

Sure enough, as soon as they were a few yards from the village an older man with gray hair and using a walking stick decorated with gold strode out to them. He passed Morgana and Airril, moving to intercept Arto with a beaming smile. Forcing a smile, Arto nodded in greeting to his father in law and wondered, not for the first time, how his calm and sweet wife was this man's daughter.

"Arto," Cailean said warmly, stepping up to grip his shoulder, all the while smiling proudly at the assembled villagers. "You are the greatest of warriors my son."

"Thank you Cailean," Arto replied, trying to sound pleased and just as warm, but he couldn't manage it, not even for Gwenyvar's father. "If you'd excuse-"

"Quite a man my daughter married, isn't he?" Cailean continued, speaking with the crowd and tightening his hold on

Arto's shoulder. For an elderly man, he had a surprisingly strong grip.

"Cailean," Arto said through a forced smile. "I'm afraid that we located a second tunnel entrance in the area. I need to rest while Morgana and Airril collect the iron necessary to build a second gate."

"Another tunnel!?" Cailean gasped, his pleased expression falling away. "Truly?"

"We believe that they intended to let us seal one tunnel and then continue their raids with the other one once we departed," Arto announced, well aware that the gathered crowd could hear them. "But we'll deal with it quickly. Once we are rested up and the iron is collected." He looked at the crowd and added, "So continue to be cautious and keep the children in the village."

There were murmurs in the crowd and many quickly turned to collect their children or rushed back to their homes to check on them. As Arto walked forward, the remaining people began to disperse and make room to let him and the others pass. Arto smiled and nodded to the people who looking at him curiously and sighed softly in relief as he cleared the crowd. His relief faded quickly as Cailean caught up with him and walked along beside him.

"You have no sense for a crowd," Cailean berated him, his brown eyes flashing with irritation and his lips thinned. "That was no way to announce the tunnel. You should have returned victorious and then patrolled the area. You could have easily said you found the tunnel then. Tell me, boy, what do you think is going to happen once the Sídhe threat is no more. What will you do with yourself then?"

"Cailean," Arto said as calmly as he could manage through gritted teeth, trying not to hiss at the use of the word boy. "You seem to have a very different idea of the future than I do."

"With the Sídhe gone, our lands will finally be able to fully enjoy our riches!"

"Our riches are based in bronze, which as you've no doubt heard is declining in value. The demand in the south is shrinking with the spread of iron. They won't need us to supply them with metal much longer.

"Exactly why a strong leader will be needed," Cailean insisted with a nod. "Someone who can keep us strong and prevent chaos. Someone who can build a new future and power base."

"Already I have about had my fill of conflict," Arto grumbled. "I don't know what the future will bring, even though I know it is marching closer, but I'm not interested in trying to take power." He turned and began to walk away, hoping to avoid making a scene.

"Arto, my son, listen to me," Cailean called as he raced after and grabbed his arm. "In the south, there are kings and emperors. Our land is rich, fertile and enjoys natural protections, but perhaps it could be much more."

"Our land is home to regional leaders, not kings and not emperors," Arto reminded him calmly. "The population isn't large enough to require conflict amongst ourselves beyond family feuds. This is a good thing. I don't want to see that changed by war."

"War might not be necessary," Cailean told him firmly. "The regional leaders respect you; they might not all like you, but they know your magical power and the importance you hold.

The people love you: there are stories about you scattered throughout the lands."

"Yes," Arto laughed. "I've heard some of them; they get more wrong than right."

"That doesn't matter," Cailean insisted with a shake of his hand and dismissive wave. "What matters is that you won't need to fight for rule over the isles. You will be a hero when this is all over; the greatest man the Isles have ever had. All the power can be yours; the people will give it to you. When the time comes you just need to accept it and be careful in your dealings with the regional leaders. As you say, bronze is fading and so is their influence and wealth. Be careful and you will have the chance to decide the future."

Arto didn't know how to respond, something that must have been clear on his face. Cailean sighed softly and patted his shoulder. "Just think on it lad; what you want may matter very little and I know you think this war is nearly won, but never underestimate what can surprise you. Be ready for anything and take advantage of any chances that you get."

His father-in-law walked away, leaning a bit more heavily on his staff than Arto had noticed before. Frowning, Arto shook his head and rubbed his hands together as he tried to ignore a flutter of nervousness in his gut. He kept walking towards the roundhouse and entered it with a grateful sigh. Walking over to the small bed, Arto sat down and carefully set Cathanáil to the side, but within arm's reach and laid back. He closed his eyes and pushed Cailean's concerns from his mind.

The future would come soon enough and he had more immediate issues to worry about, including yet another iron gate.

25

Warnings

Alex zipped up her winter coat with a soft smile as Arthur opened the front door of Gallagher Hall for her. The lights from the dorm made it difficult to see the stars, but it was a clear night and Alex shivered at the reminder that it was only going to get colder as she tightened her scarf. Next to her Arthur chuckled and reached over to take her gloved hand with his own.

"Damn, it's getting even colder," Alex muttered, her teeth chattering.

"Winter does that, and December is the darkest and coldest month of the year," Arthur replied in a teasing voice.

"December just started!" Alex protested with a pout, kicking at a nearby pile of snow that had been shoveled up by the dorm.

"We don't have to leave campus if you don't want to."

"No," Alex replied quickly, shaking her head and tugging him away from the doorway. Nearby another student swiped their keycard and dashed into the dorm building. "We need to get away for a bit."

"If you insist," Arthur said warmly, picking up his own pace and falling into step with her. They were quiet; enjoying the company and the soft crackling sound of their feet against the packed down snow on the sidewalk.

"Are we going to need to dig out your car?" Alex questioned, glancing towards Arthur as they headed into the parking lot. His grip on her hand tightened to keep her from slipping, earning a pleased smile from Alex.

"No, I dug it out earlier today when I went on a grocery run."

"Please tell me you got something other than hotdogs and those terrible microwave burgers."

"Sure, I got cereal, milk, bacon and apples," Arthur told her with a grin as they drew closer to his car which was now alone in the corner of the parking lot.

"Bacon? Are you actually going to cook something in the main kitchen?"

"You can do bacon in a microwave," Arthur informed her with a look of superiority.

"Can't be as good," Alex protested, stepping back so Arthur could unlock her side of the car first.

"I'm not saying it is," Arthur replied with a grin as he walked around to his side of the car. He beamed at her and added, "It's nice to be having a silly conversation. Feels like it's been forever."

"Yeah," Alex agreed warmly, tugging the door open. "How long has it been since we went on a real date?" Alex asked, knowing she had a silly smile on her face as she climbed into Arthur's car. "Three weeks?"

"At least, we went out for dinner and a movie right before Thanksgiving break," Arthur reminded her with an equally silly smile as he climbed in and buckled up. "Otherwise we've either been on campus or at one of the professors' houses."

"Or you've been off with the team," Alex added as they pulled out of the parking lot. "I know you love football, but I'm really glad the season is over."

"Me too," Arthur agreed quickly. "I do love it, but classes, training, games, traveling and magic lessons are a lot to juggle. I'm just happy I don't have a job too."

"Yeah, I remember figuring I'd get at least a part-time job when I came to college, but obviously that didn't happen."

"You could babysit or something like that," Arthur reminded her gently as he steered them out into the Friday night traffic. "Just to get out and about a little."

"I'd be too worried about attracting the Sídhe to some helpless kids," Alex told him, unable to stop a small shiver going down her spine. "I don't want to go through that again."

"I wish I could have helped you then."

"I know," Alex told him gratefully. "But it's okay and we'll get through this."

"Yeah," Arthur muttered, his jaw clenching for a moment. "Is it terrible that I wish Chernobog would just get here already?"

"No, I totally understand, it's hard waiting and dreading something. I was worried that he'd show up during Thanksgiving break."

"Morgana and Merlin would have been here."

"Yeah, but so were Aiden and Nicki and I don't want them to have to face him without us," Alex countered quickly. "We're a team; it's better that way."

"You're right of course," Arthur agreed with an easy going smile. "So how is final prep going?"

"It's okay, though I do wish that Thanksgiving wasn't so close to the start of Christmas break. I have a week to calm down and try to relax only to come back and have all the professors talking about finals."

"Is Merlin giving you a hard time?"

"A bit yeah, I mean he just wants me to do well. Unlike all of you, I'm actually studying one of the professor's subjects as my major and Merlin is my advisor. We actually had tea yesterday to go over my classes and my studying schedule."

"Tea?" Arthur laughed, "He and Morgana aren't actually British you know. At least I don't think they consider themselves to be."

"They predate the idea of British by like a thousand years," Alex agreed with a laugh. "I don't know, maybe they lived there recently. It would explain the slight touch of an accent that they have."

"That sounds like stretching to me," Arthur informed her doubtfully.

Alex was about to retort, trying to come up with something witty when her phone rang. Alex wrestled her phone out of her jean pockets with a soft huff as the seatbelt dug into her shoulder. Without glancing at the caller, she raised it to her ear. "Hello?"

"Alex. Morgana," the older mage greeted quickly. "I need to speak with you and Arthur. Nicki said that you're together."

"Uh yeah, we are," Alex said.

She was aware that Arthur was pulling the car over and stopping them at the side of the street just past Central Diner. On a Friday night, it was a coveted parking spot, but Alex was getting the feeling that they weren't going to be using it.

"Excellent: come to my home immediately. Merlin will be here shortly." The call ended and Alex looked at her phone with a frown. After a split second, she stuck her tongue out at it and then sighed loudly.

"That was Morgana," Alex informed Arthur with a sigh, leaning her head back against the headrest. "She wants to talk to us. Immediately."

"Us as in us or us as in we need to call the others?"

"Don't know; she talked to Nicki so they know," Alex groaned, reaching up and massaging the side of her head lightly. "Damn it! Was it too much to ask for one Friday night off?"

Arthur gave her a soft smile before he returned his eyes to the road and carefully pulled them out in traffic. He made a right hand turn to start them in the opposite direction towards Morgana's house. Alex looked out the window and bitterly noticed all the students walking out on Main Street and vanishing into restaurants and shops.

"Sorry honey," Arthur apologized gently, sending a flash of guilt through Alex.

"It's not your fault, sometimes I just wish…"

"That we could be normal sometimes," Arthur offered with a smile.

"No, not normal exactly," Alex admitted, playing with a piece of her blonde hair. "I mean I do enjoy magic and I'm not so ungrateful for the chance to be a part of something so important. Plus I got to know you, Nicki, Bran, and Aiden because of it. But it would be nice to be able to schedule time off without feeling worried about leaving Ravenslake or a crisis happening."

"You're a better person than I am," Arthur admitted with a laugh.

"Why's that?"

"I felt no guilt when I got on that plane to go back to California for Thanksgiving," Arthur told her with a grin. "I got to see my mom and I felt like I was away from this chaos for a little bit. Maybe that's selfish…"

"No, it's human," Alex assured him with a soft smile. "When the time comes you'll be right there with the rest of us and that's what matters."

The smile Arthur gave her made Alex feel warm and her head a little light. She basked in the warmth as they crossed the river and followed the road into the hills. The houses rapidly became further and further apart from each other until only lighted windows gave away their positions beyond the fences and trees. Finally, the well-lit Victorian style house of Morgana came into view and they turned onto the gravel drive. Through the windows, Alex could see Merlin pacing in the living room. By the time Arthur turned off the car and the headlights went dark, the front door was open and Morgana was waiting for them.

"Thank you for coming," Morgana called out to them as she pushed the screen door open, sending light across the snowy front yard. "Come in."

Only Morgana could make an invitation sound so much like a command, Alex internally grumbled as she climbed the porch stairs. The professor was dressed in jeans, slippers and to Alex's surprise a very comfy looking flannel shirt that was at least one size too large. As they stepped into the house, Alex was greeted with the smell of fresh cookies and a hint of some kind of tea. A bit of her irritation melted away as she unwound her scarf from around her neck and shrugged out of her coat.

Arthur stepped into the living room ahead of her, his shoulders tense and straight. Looking around him, Alex spotted Merlin sitting on the sofa with a small plate of chocolate chip cookies in front of him along with a map that was spread out over the coffee table.

"Ah Arthur, Alex thank you for coming," Merlin greeted them kindly as he waved them over. "Please sit down."

"What is this about?" Arthur asked, taking a few steps forward and glancing towards Morgana who had moved over to join Merlin on the sofa.

"I've been scrying regularly for Chernobog, trying to track his location and movements," Morgana explained, gesturing towards the armchairs in the room.

With a glance towards Arthur, Alex sank into the nearest one and tilted her head slightly to get a better look at the map. It looked like it might be a map of the town of Ravenslake, but it was much too large, showing the whole of the lake, part of the South Santiam River and up into the forest hills.

"Any luck?" Arthur asked doubtfully.

"Yes and no," Morgana admitted, giving Arthur an irritated look, clearly not impressed with his tone. "I haven't been able to pin down his location, but tonight I got a sense that he is very close. We have to be ready for him to attack any day now."

She'd deny the small whimpering sound she made forever. Arthur reached over and put his hand on top of the one that was clenching at the fabric of the armrest. A glance at him helped her relax a little. His blue eyes were dark and sharp as he studied Morgana.

"Close? Any sense of how much time we have?"

"I'm afraid not," Morgana admitted, shaking her head and giving Alex a soft look of apology.

"For all we know he could be in the lake right now and simply gathering strength for an attack," Merlin informed them, gesturing at the map spread across the table. "Morgana and I are planning to check the area daily for any signs of change."

"Is there any good news?" Arthur demanded with a sigh.

"Yes, there is in fact," Merlin replied brightly, straightening up on the sofa. "Morgana's scrying has indicated that Cyrridven is awake and coming closer to us."

Alex perked up at those words and couldn't help but ask, "Cyrridven. She's the Lady of the Lake right? She has the sword?" She glanced towards Arthur and smiled as his eyes brightened and a pleased smile appeared on his face.

"I'll have the sword soon?"

"Hopefully," Merlin agreed with a nod. "We can only assume that the sharp rise in magic and the threat of both the Sídhe and Old Ones has woken Cyrridven. Under those circumstances, she'd know how urgent it would be to get Cathanáil to the Iron Soul."

"So what do we do in the meantime?" Alex asked, smiling at the notion that Arthur would have his sword soon. There was a nervous excitement in her chest at the idea of seeing the sword and seeing what kind of power it really had.

"You kids need to focus on staying safe," Morgana told them, giving Alex a firm look. "Stay with other mages as much as possible or at least nearby. Keep your phones on you and charged and your daggers in reach. Chernobog and the Old Ones don't share the Sídhe's great weakness to iron, but it is a symbol of the raw power of this realm and helps repel them."

"What about if he doesn't make a move before we go home for Christmas?" Arthur questioned with a frown.

"I'm not sure you going home for winter break is wise," Morgana informed them, her green eyes dark with regret. "The danger is just too great."

"We went home last Christmas," Alex protested.

"Yes, but that was the Sídhe only and Merlin and I are very experienced in dealing with them. But the potential threat of Chernobog is much greater. It took us and several Old Ones working together to put him to sleep last time."

"If Cyrridven is on the move then it means that something very important and significant is about to happen," Merlin added in gently as he looked between her and Arthur. "I know that it is difficult to be away from your families, but Morgana and I are simply unwilling to take chances."

"Chernobog has the power to level Ravenslake," Morgana said softly, looking very tired and suddenly very old to Alex. "And the concentration of people in modern cities…. Ravenslake isn't huge, but there are thousands of people here and if we can't stop Chernobog quickly then he could hurt them."

"Or kill them all outright," Merlin added ominously. "Aside from his power and his shadow creatures, Chernobog is physically large."

"So he could just crush the city?"

"Well… he's not Godzilla, but yes he is capable of doing a lot of damage."

Alex wasn't sure if she should laugh at Merlin referencing Godzilla, stamp her foot in frustration or start crying at the idea of missing Christmas with her family. She settled on clenching her hands into fists and trying not to meet Morgana's eyes."

"If Chernobog attacks sooner then we will be able to reevaluate this of course," Morgana told them carefully.

"Great, that would put the attack during finals week," Arthur grumbled, giving Morgana a sharp look. "That's not much better."

"I understand that juggling the two parts of your lives aren't easy," Merlin said quickly, drawing Arthur's attention. "But don't shoot the messengers."

"I understand what you're saying," Arthur told them. "And thank you for giving us the heads up that this is an issue. But if you'll excuse us then I'm going to take my girlfriend out on an actual date and we're taking tomorrow off."

"Arthur, I'm not sure that's a good idea," Morgana interrupted, looking towards Merlin with a nervous expression that made Alex worry.

"Look Morgana," Arthur said quickly, a nervous expression on his face. "I know that you just want to keep us safe and make sure that we're prepared for whatever is going to happen, but we've been practicing every weekend; you even had us over on Sunday night after we all just got back from Thanksgiving. We've taken out seven shadows since Halloween and we're doing okay on magical lessons. Finals are coming up fast and to be frank, we all need a weekend off. We need to study and recharge."

"Arthur, when Chernobog gets here-"

"I know he's very powerful and more dangerous than what we've faced before, but if we're completely wiped out then we won't be any good against him. He could be here tomorrow night and if we've used too much magic then we won't be able to do much."

"They have been working very hard," Merlin reminded Morgana, setting down his tea and looking at her seriously. "And if they do badly in school then it will draw attention to their out of school activities. We can't afford to have the other professors asking about how frequently they visit us."

"But Arthur-"

"You've warned us," Arthur cut in quickly, straightening up and meeting Morgana's gaze. "And we do understand: I won't cancel going home just yet as we still have a couple of weeks, but I will do so if he doesn't come in that time." Morgana opened her mouth to say something, but Arthur cut her off once more. "You are not my sister anymore Morgana."

The room was still as Morgana struggled for words. Looking towards her boyfriend, Alex resisted the urge to punch his arm. She understood his points of course, but seeing Morgana look so lost was disturbing. Alex glanced towards Merlin and found him watching Morgana with a sad look in his eyes.

"You've made good points," Morgana managed a few moments later. "Very well then; I will call the others and give them the news and cancel lessons until after finals. Should Chernobog not appear until after you have all had to stay over winter break then we will set up a new training system to make sure that no more than one of you is exhausted at a time. Does that meet your approval, Arthur?" Morgana asked the last question with more of her usual confidence in her voice and one raised eyebrow. There was an almost audible shared sigh of relief in the room at the display.

"It does," Arthur agreed with a nod as he stood up from the armchair, pulling his hand away from Alex. "And thank you for taking our concerns into account."

Alex nodded in agreement, gave Morgana a small smile and tried to ignore the awkwardness still hanging in the room like a fog. Arthur held out a hand to her and Alex accepted it, letting him pull her out of the armchair. He squeezed her hand quickly and with a nod to Morgana and Merlin, he led Alex towards the front door.

"Wait!" Merlin called, stopping them both in their tracks. He stood up and darted over to them, holding the plate of cookies. "You simply must try one of these. I know you haven't had your dinner yet, but you are legally adults after all." Merlin's brown eyes were glinting as he smiled and moved the plate right in front of their faces.

A soft giggle escaped Alex and it was followed a moment later by Arthur's deeper chuckle. The tension in the room eased as they each took a cookie from the plate and bit into it. Warm chocolate melted and spread over Alex's tongue, making her smile and make a pleased sound. Beyond Merlin, Alex saw Morgana relax slightly and a soft smile appear on her face as she devoured the fresh cookie.

"Thanks," Arthur told Merlin before he stepped back and reached for his coat. "We'll be in touch."

"Yeah," Alex agreed, licking off the tips of her fingers to get the last few crumbs. "And don't worry so much. We'll be okay."

As Alex bundled back up, her boyfriend glanced outside where large snowflakes were beginning to fall. He sighed loudly and pulled out his keys. "I'll get the car started," he told her before stepping out into the night.

Alex tightened her scarf and pulled up her hood, stepping towards the door. Alex stopped when Morgana reached out and caught her shoulder. After taking a quick breath to steel herself, Alex turned to face her teacher. She was ready to say something sharp or reassuring, but the slight shine in Morgana's eyes left her stunned.

"I am sorry Alex," Morgana told her softly. "Believe me, I know the value of time with your family. It is precious beyond measure."

"But so are the lives of everyone else," Alex heard herself say. "I do understand Morgana; I'm just disappointed is all." She forced a small smile. "Let Arthur and I be mad for a little while, stamp our feet and pout a bit and we'll be fine. We really do get it, at least to some extent. I won't pretend that we're you and Merlin, but give us some justifiable irritation and we'll be fine."

Morgana's lips curved into a slight smile and she chuckled. "Alright Alex," she agreed with a nod. "Arthur does have a point, so don't cancel your plans just yet. With some luck maybe this will all be resolved soon."

"And maybe if we're really lucky he'll attack on the solstice," Alex offered with a small smile of her own.

"Well we didn't battle Chernobog much in the past, but maybe he will be that foolish."

"Maybe," Alex agreed before she heard a car door slam behind her. "Well, I should go."

"You and Arthur have fun," Morgana said quickly. As Alex turned to leave she added, "And do get some homework done tomorrow. If Chernobog does attack soon then you don't want to fall behind."

"Really?" Alex asked as she started at the professor. "That's one of your concerns?"

There was a teasing smile on Morgana's face and her green eyes sparkled as she shrugged. "I may be a mage and a half Sídhe, but I am also a professor of this town's fine university."

"And I'm glad that I'm a literature major and not a history one," Alex teased in response before she could think better of it.

Morgana laughed a real smile on her face. She glanced out the door at the running car where Arthur waited and sighed softly. Without a word, she leaned forward and kissed Alex's forehead beneath the rim of her hood. Then she gently pushed her out the door and closed it behind her, leaving Alex on the porch feeling relieved, happy and a little sad all at once. She shook her head and put a smile on her face and went to join her boyfriend in the car.

26

Finals

"That was not fun," Aiden groaned to Alex as they left the Carlson Building.

Alex rubbed her eyes as the setting sun reflected off the white snow and nodded in agreement. She rolled her sore shoulders for a moment, hoping to dispel the last of the effects of hunching over a small desk for almost two hours.

"Why did our King Arthur final have to be last?" Nicki asked from next to her, sighing dramatically. "I mean we're wiped out from finals week and then we have to take probably the most important of our exams."

"I think the essay questions were needlessly cruel," Bran added thoughtfully as he carefully made his way down the front steps of the building.

"I don't know: the one about Camelot as a creation of the chivalry and courtly love literary movement in Europe was interesting," Arthur said with a shrug, drawing looks from everyone that merely made him smirk.

"Okay, Arthur it's official that you've been spending way too much time studying with your girlfriend," Aiden declared very seriously.

"Yeah, I think only literature majors are supposed to like that sort of stuff," Bran added with a knowing look.

"I said it was interesting, I didn't say that I liked it," Arthur insisted, putting his hands up in mock surrender. "I barely managed a reasonable essay on it."

"Really?" Alex asked, crinkling her nose slightly in the cold air. "I almost ran out of time on the last one."

"We noticed," Nicki told her with a smirk. "We were waiting for you in the hallway remember."

"You guys were there almost the whole time too," she protested with a small pout as the group started to walk towards the dorms. Already the campus was becoming deserted as students fled the area for Christmas break. "You left maybe ten minutes before I did."

"I can't speak for the others, but I didn't want to leave too early," Bran told her with a smile. "Professor Ambrose was watching us and finishing too quickly can mean bad things."

"I think I did well," Alex announced. "Hopefully all of you did too."

"I know the material," Aiden insisted quickly. "I've just never been that great at artistically arranging the bullshit."

"'Artistically arranging the bullshit?'" Arthur repeated incredulously. "Do I even want to know?"

Nicki laughed, tossing her long red braid over her shoulder. "It was a phrase one of our high school English teachers used. He said that essays were all about how to make stuff up based on what little knowledge you might have and how to present it convincingly: hence, artistically arranging the bullshit." She grinned happily, "Ah if there was a class that truly prepared me for college, it was that one."

"I'm not certain what that says about the Ravenslake public school system," Bran intoned, sharing a look with Alex as they both tried not to laugh.

"That it is awesome," Nicki said firmly. "Although, thinking back on my essay I think I misspelled chivalry."

"Really?" Aideen laughed only to get a sharp look from Nicki.

"I had to remember to write Excalibur," Bran added with a chuckle. "The professors usually refer to it by Cathanáil around us."

"Merlin wouldn't have docked points for that," Nicki assured him with a grin.

"No, he wouldn't have, but there are these things called T.A.s in college who help grade papers and confusing them is bad," Bran retorted sarcastically.

Alex smiled at the mental image of a graduate student stumbling over the word. If they knew their Arthurian mythos roots then they might recognize it as a vaguely Welsh name, but even in the Welsh stories that wasn't the sword's name. Close, but not quite.

"Let's go for a drive," Arthur suggested, reaching over and taking Alex's hand, pulling her out of her thoughts.

"Now?" Alex asked, glancing towards the setting sun. "Hon there isn't much light left. The sun will be down in like twenty minutes."

"I know," Arthur answered as he tilted his head in embarrassment. "I just need to get off campus for a little bit and driving sounds good after the last two weeks of nonstop studying."

"Oh, okay," Alex agreed with a nod before looking over at the others. "So do you guys have any plans?"

"Celebratory dinner and drinks with Gran," Nicki announced.

"You're too young to drink," Arthur pointed out with a smirk and a raised eyebrow.

"Which is why Gran has a bar at home, but don't worry I'll only have one," Nicki assured them quickly with a glance around at the few students who were sharing the sidewalk with them. "Don't want to lose control or anything like that."

"I had no plans," Bran admitted with a shrug.

"Then you and I should do something," Aiden said, throwing an arm over Bran's shoulder.

"What?"

"I don't know, we'll figure something out."

"See Alex everyone's cool," Arthur laughed, tugging on her hand. "Come on, I need a change of scenery."

"Alright, but let's run inside and drop off our stuff," Alex told him as they resumed walking towards the dorms.

Above their heads, the sky was turning a deep purple color and Alex could see one bright star out and briefly wondered which one it was or if it was a planet. On the western horizon, the sun was beginning to dip below the tops of the mountains in a brilliant red sunset that glistened off the snow. Long shadows stretched out before them and Alex kept glancing around for any sign of movement. It was cold enough that the warning system of feeling cold and seeing their breath was no longer much of a warning. The others were silent and Alex took heart in knowing that her fellow mages were on the alert as well.

Hatfield hall sat furthest to the north, near the outlet of the river into the lake with the arboretum just off to the east. Snow still clung to some of the tree branches through most was piled up against trunks due to the sunny day. The wind howled through the trees for a moment and Alex's heart jumped, eerily reminded of the cry of a Sídhe hound. Arthur squeezed her hand before pulling out his keycard and unlocking the front door with a loud click that echoed slightly off the large bricks of the building.

"Meet you back here in five?" Arthur asked as they stepped inside, stomping their shoes on the black mat.

"Sounds good," she agreed with a nod, moving so that the others could all come inside. Turning her attention to Bran and Aiden, Alex smiled and gave them a little wave. "Have a good night boys. Don't get into too much trouble," she teased.

"We make no promises," Aiden declared far too seriously, already heading for the hallway.

Bran shook his head fondly and smiled, "You two have a good night."

"Thanks," Arthur replied with a nod as he headed for the stairs on the far side of the building.

Alex looked towards the stairs just down the hall from the front door and smiled as she found Nicki there waiting for her. The pair climbed up to the third floor in silence, their footfalls extra loud in the almost abandoned dorm. As she and Nicki headed down the hall toward their room, Alex did her best to ignore the students leaving their own rooms with suitcases and excited expressions. By the unusual silence, it was obvious that most people were already gone for Christmas break. If Nicki caught onto her sudden melancholy, she said nothing and instead pulled out her card key to open their front door.

"Home sweet home, or at least close," Nicki announced as she dumped her bag on the sofa.

Alex followed suit and deposited her bag on the sofa and pulled out her wallet, keys and iron dagger. She reached over the small end table that they'd bought from a second-hand store for her purse. As she repacked her things, Alex became aware of Nicki watching her. Forcing a small smile, she looked towards her roommate who raised an eyebrow at her admittedly pathetic attempt.

"Hey," Nicki said gently. "I'm going to be staying at my grandmother's through Christmas. We have some crafting traditions, but you're welcome to join us whenever you want. I know that Bran has already accepted Christmas Dinner plans at Aiden's. I'm sure my gran would welcome both you and Arthur if you like. I wouldn't recommend trying to cook a turkey downstairs. The kitchen is decent, but the fire alarms are really sensitive."

Alex smiled and felt the frustration coiled in her chest ease a little both at Nicki's offer and humor. Smiling honestly this time, she nodded to Nicki as she wasn't quite able to form her own words. "Thanks," she choked out.

"And I'll say nothing if you and Arthur redecorate the living room for Christmas. Get a little Charlie Brown Christmas tree and some lights. This place might actually look better with some light strings, white ones, though."

"He has a dorm room too," Alex pointed out as she giggled at Nicki's ramble.

"True, but ours is better. Ours is occupied by two hot mages."

"You are terrible sometimes."

"I have my moments," Nicki agreed with a smile before she nodded towards the door. "Go on then, your reincarnated knight in shining armor awaits."

"They didn't have shining armor in Bronze Age Britain," Alex corrected with smile, none the less heading for the door.

"True, but at least he didn't have a kid with his own sister."

"If you value your life never mention that story to Morgana," Alex called back as she opened the door.

"I'm just a little crazy, not bat shit insane," Nicki told her firmly just before the door closed behind Alex.

She chuckled and shook her head for a moment before she strode towards the stairs and skipped down them to her waiting boyfriend. Arthur had discarded his backpack and was wearing his old high school letterman jacket. There was a slight bulge at his hip that alerted Alex to the fact he was wearing his iron dagger. Reaching out to grab her hand, Arthur opened the dorms front door and they stepped back out into the twilight.

"Are we going to be shoveling snow?" Alex asked, glancing around at the small snowbanks scattered around them.

"No, I had some errands to run yesterday," Arthur replied with a shrug, pulling out his car keys from a pocket.

"You did?" Alex asked with a small frown, coming to a halt. "Arthur, we're not supposed to go off alone, especially not you."

"It was twenty minutes," Arthur protested, running a hand through his hair and looking out into the parking lot. "Look I know it wasn't a good idea, but I didn't want to bother the rest of you."

"Still, you should have let me know," Alex muttered with a small glare. "I would have gone with you."

"Great, my girlfriend as my babysitter," Arthur grumbled even as he squeezed his hand.

"We just want you safe," Alex offered in a softer tone. "Sure you'd be reincarnated, but the Iron Soul is needed now." She smiled and stepped closer to him. "Not to mention I have my own selfish reasons for wanting you around."

"I thought it was only guys who thought like that," Arthur teased, a smile returning to his face.

He leaned down quickly and kissed Alex's forehead before releasing her hand and going to the far side of his car. It was unlocked in a moment and Alex climbed in, trying to keep her teeth from chattering at the chilly interior. With an apologetic smile, Arthur started the car and cranked up the heater. They sat in the parking lot for a few minutes letting the car warm up as the last rays of the sun vanished leaving behind only violet traces above the mountain. Alex tried to enjoy the color, but it was too similar to the eyes of the Sídhe for her. There was an ache in her bones that she couldn't understand and as Arthur carefully put the car into reverse she stretched out her legs the best she could in front of her.

"You okay?" Arthur asked with a glance her direction.

"I'm fine, just a little sore. Probably from not getting out and jogging or going to the gym lately," Alex told him with a shrug as she tried to settle and get comfortable.

"Maybe, but it's probably stress too. We've had a lot to worry about."

"Finals weren't that bad," Alex laughed. "Not compared to everything else. Next semester when we all have to start taking our serious classes, then we can worry."

"Hey, we had upper-level classes this semester! You and Nicki had the King Arthur class and the Enlightenment history class. Those were both 300 level."

"Yeah, but they were really interesting and that helps. Of course, Merlin teaching a class on King Arthur is hard to beat."

"And next semester he's teaching the bible," Arthur observed with a chuckle. "That should be interesting."

"I wonder how much time he or Morgana spent in the Middle East during that period?" Alex asked with a smile. "Someday we're going to have to get them to talk about stuff outside of the wars and magic."

"We've gotten them to talk about it some."

"Yeah, but not nearly enough. Three thousand years has got to produce some good stories."

"And probably some sad ones," Arthur pointed out gently.

Alex was about to reply when her phone began to chirp with a familiar ring tone. Arthur glanced her way, but Alex didn't move to retrieve the phone. Instead, she snuggled into her coat and sighed softly.

"Alex?"

"My mom keeps calling," Alex confessed softly, bumping her head back against the headrest. "I told her that I wasn't sure I was coming home, but I can't come up with a good reason."

"I hate it too," Arthur told her gently, glancing over towards her. "But it'll be okay, I promise."

"But it's Christmas and I can't even give them a lousy excuse for why I'm not coming home."

"I told my mother that you and I wanted to celebrate Christmas together," Arthur offered gently. "You could tell you your folks that."

"No, they'd just invite you to spend Christmas with us. Mom likes you and all, but I think she'd be worried about us doing something that serious after only four and half months."

"Has it really only been a few months?"

"We didn't start dating officially until school started so a couple days in August, September, October, November and the first two weeks in December. It's about four and half months."

"I count from June." Arthur smiled warmly at her. "That was a good kiss."

"I'm not going to swoon for you, even if you are the hero."

"That's one of the things I like about you."

Arthur turned them smoothly onto the smaller paved road that circled the lake before coming back into town via the older stone bridge to the east of town. The half-moon was high in the sky and provided silvery light that was glistening off the snow.

"It's so dark outside," Alex frowned as she looked up at the slowly appearing stars. "Not really a good night for a drive."

"Maybe not," Arthur agreed, tightening his grip on the steering wheel. "But we needed to get out and I just thought it would be nice to leave town for at least a little while."

"You're sweet."

"On occasion," Arthur replied with an easy going smile. "We'll just chat and drive slowly around the lake then we'll go back to town. I promise." He leaned forward and looked up at the moon with a small smile. "I know it isn't a full moon, but hopefully the half moon will look nice on the lake."

"In the summer this would be more romantic," Alex teased with a soft smile that she doubted he could see. "Without the worry about ice on the road."

"It was a sunny day, I'm sure the roads are okay, but point taken."

They didn't talk about anything in particular as Alex watched the lights of Ravenslake sparkling on the surface of the lake; mostly the conversation focused on classes and the relief of another semester being done. Directly across from them, the town looked beautiful with flashes of color from the neon signs of 4th Avenue's lakeside restaurants occasionally being visible. She thought that she could make out the Russell Gallery and hoped that Nicki was having a nice night.

As they headed further east, Ravenslake faded out of sight, disappearing behind them leaving a darker view of the lake with the moon reflecting on it. Sighing softly, Alex felt herself relaxing and smiled over at Arthur. His eyes were focused on the road, but he glanced towards the lake every few moments. All around them, the thick trees of the forest were closing around them and the hills made it feel like they were in their own little world.

Shivering, Alex paused as she heard a strange rustling sound from outside the car. Arthur slowed down the car as a flock of birds could be heard flying overhead. Her exhale misted in front of her as Alex leaned forward in confusion to catch sight of the birds flying at night. Alex looked towards Arthur and her eyes widened as his breath wafted in the air in front of him.

"Arthur, it's cold," Alex whispered, turning and looking out into the darkness.

There was a pause of total silence, the car still rolling forward on the road. Then the headlights flickered just as Arthur applied the brakes. In the corner of her eye, Alex saw a dark purple distortion through the air outside the car like a shock racing towards them. Before she could shout a warning to Arthur, it collided with the side of the car, crunching the metal. The car lurched, sending Alex sliding towards Arthur and slamming her hip against the seat belt latch as the seat belt dug into her chest and shoulder. All the air rushed out of her lungs, but she couldn't inhale as the car spun off the road, sliding into the far ditch with a shudder.

"Alex!" Arthur called just before his hand landed on her shoulder. "Are you okay?"

Shaking her head, Alex blinked and tried to inventory how she felt. Her ears were ringing, her heart was racing and her body ached from being tossed around. But she quickly answered that she was alright and began to wrestle out of the seat belt.

"I can't get free," Alex grunted as she fumbled with the latch. Next to her, Arthur climbed out of his seat belt and reached over to help her. "No," Alex protested before she fully thought out it. "Arthur something hit us, it's cold. You have to be ready to fight."

"I can't leave you like this!"

"I have my dagger," Alex told him, reaching into her bag and pulling out the sheathed weapon. "I'll cut myself out."

The headlights flickered and the engine sputtered to a stop leaving them in silence. There was a soft crunching sound outside the car, followed by a multitude of odd groans and growls that Alex couldn't identify. Arthur's eyes were wide in the light of the moon and a moment later he nodded. He pushed open the driver's side door which made a horrible scraping sound. Fighting off the icy chill settling over her body, Alex began to cut through the seat belt while keeping an eye out for anything coming at them.

Alex tore the strap off her shoulder which protested the movement. Clamoring over the middle of the car, Alex slipped out of the driver's side. Her feet sank into the snow and a shiver racked her body. Stumbling forward, Alex used Arthur's tracks to maneuver around the car. As she walked around the front, she spotted her boyfriend standing in the road, looking towards the lake. He was clutching his dagger in one hand and the other was holding something that she couldn't see.

With a burst of determination, Alex climbed out of the ditch and stepped forward onto the road as she searched around with frantic glances for the threat. She stopped short, a gasp escaping her as she caught sight of glowing red eyes peering out from the trees around them. There were eyes on the hill behind them and on the slope leading down to the lake below, dozens of them all watching and waiting.

"Arthur," Alex called in a low whisper. "Call your magic: we have to fight."

"That's not what we're here for Alex," he replied softly, his eyes locked on the lake. "It looks like Chernobog made it here first after all."

Everything stopped. All around her the world fell away into darkness as the light of the moon dimmed and everything went silent. She couldn't smell anything and only the chill of her jeans freezing around her legs and the slosh of snow in her shoes reassured Alex that the world was still there.

The shadows around them began to lift and Alex stepped forward with shaking hands. Risking a look towards Arthur, Alex swallowed at the strange gleam in his eyes. There was horror, urgency, excitement and relief. She wanted to take some heart in the expression, but her heart suddenly felt constricted and she forced herself to look back at the lake.

In the moonlight she could see strange ripples on the lake's surface right at the center where the water was deepest. A dark shape was moving beneath the water and Alex couldn't convince herself it was just a trick of the light. In the shadows around them, the monsters were making small excited sounds that sent a chill up her spine. She risked a glance back towards town and was just able to see some lights, but it was miles away.

A rumble in the water made Alex turn back so quickly her neck crunched. The ripples were turning into waves as water bubbled up violently in increasingly large circles. There was just enough light to see something black seeping up from the depths like oil onto the water's surface. A horrible smell like rotting meat filled the air making Alex gag. She could barely see the black sludge as it began to swirl together in the water. Then it vanished beneath the surface just as the bubbling stopped. The surface was still for a long moment.

The water on the shoreline retreated from the rocky beach and Alex instinctively stepped back. In the shadows around them, there was a burst of noises like cheering. A mess of strange high pitched sequels and low grumbles that made her want to cover her ears. With the sound of an explosion, water surged forward and upwards as a massive shape rose out of the water. In the soft moonlight, Alex could see a tall humanoid figure rising forth from the waves. It was a thin and twisted with long skeletal limbs. Large talons glinted in the light, seaweed hanging from them as Alex struggled to process what she was seeing.

"Chernobog," Alex gasped, the name escaping her lips against her volition.

Chernobog stood, his long form stretching out into the sky. He loomed more than twenty feet over them and slowly turned, causing waves of water to strike the shore. A sunken-in face like that of a corpse came into view; the black shining skin was stretched tightly over the bones of the face that were too sharp and wide, which gave the impression of horns growing out of its cheeks and chin. Glowing neon green eyes appeared, peering at them from the blackness. Chernobog smiled, revealing rows of sharp white teeth. A chuckle came from the creature and echoed around the valley.

Chernobog raised one of his hands and an icy wind blew all around them. High in the sky, the silvery wisps of clouds swirled together into thick dark clouds. A moment later, the clouds covered the moon and behind them, the last rays of the sun vanished beyond the mountains plunging them into horrifying darkness.

27

Broken Heart

800 B.C.E. Northern Cornwall

Dismounting from the exhausted brown horse, Arto looked
around with a thoughtful frown. His home village looked
normal, but tension was hanging in the air like a cold
mountain fog. No one was moving to greet them despite the
fact that they'd been gone for three months. His eyes scanned
around carefully, taking in a few children playing in a yard
and a woman weaving in front of her roundhouse, but none of
them reacted to his return.

He looked over at Merlin as the older mage dismounted and
swung his staff down with a soft sigh. Merlin surveyed the
village with a cautious expression despite appearing to be
relaxed. Arto knew that his mentor's brown eyes were
searching for any details that might give them some warning
as to what was happening.

There were the usual sounds and smells, not all of them
pleasant, but all expected. People were moving between the
roundhouses, tending the animals in the small enclosures and
Arto could hear the smiths at work. Smoke swirled in the area
above the village from the furnaces into the bright blue sky.

"I don't like this," Airril observed in a low voice behind him
and Arto heard the familiar metallic scraping of a sword being
pulled from a sheath.

"Calm down," Morgana ordered in a soft voice.

Arto glanced back to see Airril standing protectively next to Morgana, her hand on the hilt of his sword to keep him from drawing it further. His sister was glaring at a local woman carrying a covered basket with downcast eyes moving past them. Her green eyes were cold and a frown had taken over her face.

"What do you think?" Arto asked Merlin in a low voice. "We can't leave."

"We certainly can," Merlin corrected, leaning forward on his staff as he looked towards the hill the village was built around. "But I don't think that it is necessary."

"Arto!" a voice called in the distance and Arto quickly realized that it was Medraut.

Stepping forward, Arto patted the horse's neck and shifted towards the paths. Medraut called his name again, his voice carrying over the muted village. A moment later his cousin came into view, striding down the main hill towards them. There was a smirk playing at the corners of his mouth, but his expression soon shifted to a more neutral one. Arto couldn't help a flicker of irritation at the expression but banished it quickly. Medraut hurried over to them, the blank expression still in place. Arto watched as his cousin glanced around the village and then gestured for one of the younger men to take their horses. Again no one met his eyes even as a pair of men walked over and led the horses away.

"Medraut what is going on?" Arto demanded in a low voice. "Why is everyone behaving so oddly?"

"Arto I'm sorry," Medraut told him in a soft voice that almost quivered. "Gwenyvar and Luegáed ran away together."

The words didn't make any sense and jumbled around in his head. "What?" Arto asked after hearing Morgana inhale sharply.

"We shouldn't have this conversation here," Morgana said urgently in his ear suddenly beside him with a protective hand on his shoulder. "Let's get away from the listeners," she told him with a nod towards the curious looking villagers.

An odd look crossed Medraut's face that Arto couldn't read, but his cousin nodded and stepped to the side so they could access the path. The walk up the hill seemed to take hours. Arto could feel eyes on him with every step and even his sister's presence did nothing to ease the tension. There had to be some kind of mistake; there just had to be. Perhaps Gwenyvar had wanted to go out and harvest herbs or simply get of the village for a bit. She had grown up in the mountains of the north and maybe the views of the plains had become too dull. That was possible, so why the accusations?

Then thankfully they reached his roundhouse and Medraut pulled open the pelt and allowed them to enter. Arto couldn't even muster a smile as he spotted his mother waiting for them. She stood from his bed with a sad smile and stepped towards them. Merlin said something that Arto could not hear to Morgana and turned back to the villagers with Airril at his side just before the pelt fell back into place closing himself, Morgana, Medraut and his mother in the roundhouse.

"What is this about Gwenyvar and Luegáed running off?" Morgana demanded, turning on Medraut quickly with a furious expression. Her anger or perhaps disbelief helped pull Arto out of his stunned silence.

"Yes, how do you know that is what has occurred?" Arto asked quickly with a nod towards Morgana. "Perhaps he escorted her outside of the village. They could be injured and instead, you're accusing them of something far worse."

"I am sorry, son," Eigyr told him softly. "But I am the one who can confirm what Medraut told you." She toyed nervously with her hand and did not look at him for a long moment. "I came to see Gwenyvar and found her packing a few things for a trip. I asked her where she was going; she fumbled for an answer, but then Luegáed came in. He seemed surprised to see me and said nothing, neither of them would meet my eyes. Gwenyvar picked up her pack and they left together. That was two days ago, and they have not returned."

"We suspect they are headed south, potentially towards Rome. Gwenyvar has always been interested in it," Medraut offered quickly.

Arto was silent, completely stunned. The words kept repeating in his head, but he felt unable to grasp their meaning. Then Morgana was beside him, worry all over her face.

"Morgana," their mother called gently. "Please give your brother some space."

"But-" his sister began to protest.

"Please darling, go and make sure that Merlin has everything under control. I am sure that your good news would be well received by the village."

For a moment Arto thought Morgana might actually argue with their mother, but she nodded and stepped towards the door. She paused for a moment to glare at Medraut who returned the glare with equal disdain. Then he was alone with his mother and Medraut.

"What do you want to do about this?" his cousin asked calmly, tilting his head and giving Arto a considering look.

"What can we do about it?" Arto asked in return, barely managing a weak shrug. "It is out of our hands."

Medraut scowled, his usually attractive features twisting into something ugly that made Arto's stomach twist. He did his best to meet his cousin's condescending look with a calm expression.

"I should have known," Medraut snarled. "You'll do nothing and allow them all to think you are weak!"

"What would you have me do?" Arto demanded, anger breaking through. "Track them south across the sea? Leave the Sídhe alone for months to regain a foothold and enslave more of our people unopposed? And to what end? So I can drag my wife back and try and force her to stay against her will, using ropes if necessary? Kill Luegáed in some foolish attempt to prove myself stronger and better than him, which I might die doing by the way; his reputation as a swordsman was well earned. What is it that you think all of this would achieve?"

"Then what are you doing to do?" Medraut demanded with a clenched fist and a tight jaw as he glared at Arto. He looked like he wanted nothing more than to strike him and the feeling was mutual. Arto half-hoped that Medraut would strike and give him an excuse.

"Cousin," Medraut said with a stern expression. "We have to talk about this."

"My wife is gone, as is one of our best warriors. The situation is fairly clear, but it changes nothing," Arto said dismissively, waving a hand for Medraut to go. The only chance he had of getting through this without striking him was for his cousin to leave now.

"Of course it does!" Medraut snapped, lunging forward and grabbing his arm. "You and Gwenyvar's marriage helped secure our connections to the northlands. Her father is important and viewed having you as a son to be critical. With Gwenyvar and Luegáed running off that is thrown into disarray."

"My only goal is to stop the Sídhe," Arto reminded his cousin fiercely. "A goal that took me away from my wife much of the year. I am under no delusions as to why this occurred."

"You are now a warrior leader whose wife ran off with his best friend! Do you not understand how weak this makes you seem? How fragile your position is?"

"After everything that I have done you think I will be judged on the choices made by them?"

"Cousin.... You truly have no mind for power," Medraut sneered. "Your father at least understood that, but then I'm the one he raised as an heir."

Arto barely held the desire to lash out at his cousin in check. Only the bitter thought that he had already lost family today stayed his hand.

"Enough!" Eigyr's voice cut in sharply to the surprise of both men who turned to look at her in surprise, having forgotten she was present. "That's enough," she repeated in a lower voice, but it still rang with finality. "Medraut I know that you are only trying to help, but Arto is right that there is little that can be done now. Gwenyvar and Luegáed have made their choice and we must find a way to live with it."

"But-"

"Leave me with my son," she commanded sternly with a firm look absent of any patience for argument.

After a moment of obvious internal debate, Medraut nodded before turning and leaving the roundhouse without ever looking back towards him.

"He means well," his mother said with a sigh after the pelt fell back into place. "But I fear that boy has always carried an irrational jealousy of you. Even when your father made him the heir I think he always worried about what would happen if you ever returned to us." She shook her head, folding her hands in front of her with a weary expression. "I even caught him watching Gwenyvar on a few occasions. He has never understood the price of the power you have or the burden you bear because of it."

"I would think that the cost would be clear now," Arto snarled at his mother, anger charging through him in search of a release, but all of it centered on his cousin.

His mother wasn't distressed by him snapping at her. Instead, she looked at him sadly and said, "Arto, please calm yourself. Do not allow this to become something ugly in you. I know that you are suffering now, but Medraut is your kin." She shook her head and her eyes lowered to the ground. "And he is still here."

The words were a brutal reminder of what had started this conversation. Arto fell silent and felt the rage draining out of him despite his desire to cling to it and use it as armor, preferring anger at Medraut over the alternative. Instead, it slipped away like water inside a cracked pot and there was nothing he could do.

"Arto," his mother called gently from across the roundhouse. He ignored her and did not turn to face her, but Eigyr stepped up behind him and laid a hand on his shoulder. "Please, Arto do not be angry with me."

"Mother I-I'm not angry with you," Arto insisted as he turned towards her, careful not to hurt her hand.

His mother smiled wearily at him, her gray hair hanging mostly loose with only a few small braids around her face. Heavy lines told of her age and he was painfully struck by just how old she looked. They were both silent for a moment and then she raised her hand up to his cheek and cupped it gently.

"I saw the signs," she confessed softly. "Gwenyvar lived here too long as my daughter for me not to notice."

"I didn't."

"You were gone often; you had a duty to perform," his mother sighed. "Luegáed loved you dearly; he saw you as his brother. I thought wrongly that they would not betray you as such."

"She loved me," Arto insisted, aware of the growing ache in his chest.

"That she did, but you were both very young then and time has changed you both."

"Maybe this is for the best," Arto whispered as his eyes dropped to the floor.

"I think they tried to do the best they could," she offered gently, reaching up and gently brushing his hair. "Do not blame yourself."

Arto had no idea of what to say to that but found himself nodding to his mother out of habit. She watched him silently with a look of pity that made his skin crawl. He couldn't take that look right now, she loved him, but he couldn't.

"I'd like to be alone."

She didn't argue. Instead, she calmly nodded to him and walked towards the doorway. "I know that Morgana will be worried about you," his mother told him gently with a sad smile. "Please don't keep your sister at a distance; I don't think she could take it."

Arto stood completely still as he listened to his mother leaving the roundhouse. He was left alone to wonder as the stillness of his home sank onto him. What was he supposed to do now? The conversations seemed to be finished for now so what was the next step? Were they waiting for him to publically say something? Were the villagers waiting outside with the warriors and the smiths awaiting some explanation?

His fingers twitched to pull back the pelt and he found himself taking a step towards the doorway. Shaking his head Arto stopped himself and lowered his hand. He was being foolish he decided with a deep inhale. His head wasn't clear and his emotions felt... he frowned and swallowed thickly, uncertain of just what he was feeling. Closing his eyes, Arto took several deep and slow breaths to calm down and tried to sort out his thoughts.

There wasn't much now that his anger towards Medraut was fading, just an odd sense of numbness that was completely alien to him. Did he not care that Gwenyvar and Luegáed had run off together, that they had essentially betrayed him? As soon as the thought fully formed the odd numbness began to fall away. His knees felt weak, he realized with detachment, and he sank down on his bed.

Everything on his side was as it should be, Gwenyvar had even patched an older shirt of his and left it lying on the bed. The only thing missing from the shelves was the jet necklace that Gwenyvar's father had given her when they married. She hadn't taken any of the other valuables with her. On her side of the roundhouse, it was much the same story. Arto could tell that a few pieces of clothing had been taken, but most of it was still carefully packed in her woven baskets. Her small loom was upright with half a blanket or cloak already finished. It seemed as though she could be back at any moment. Maybe she would be; maybe she and Luegáed would come riding back in tomorrow or the next day and tell him that Medraut had been mistaken.

Maybe- Arto snorted at himself and shook his head. His eyes dropped to the pounded down dirt floor where he suddenly wished that he could see footprints. He'd been trained to track Sídhe, maybe the tracks would have told him something. Against his wishes, Arto's eyes went to the bed tucked up against the wall. Had they been there together? All those times when he was gone to fight the Sídhe and he'd entrusted the safety of his family to Luegáed had he been giving them chances to be together?

Images of entwined limbs and Gwenyvar's blissful face flashed in front of him. Closing his eyes did nothing to stop the sudden brutal assault. He inhaled deeply and tried to focus on something else, but the events were not so easily dismissed from his mind. There was a burst of anger that startled him. He wanted to find them and scream at them both, maybe fight Luegáed and demand an explanation, he wanted-

Arto shook his head and tried to dislodge the darkening train of thoughts. It was disturbing. He'd always known that he was capable of violence, he was a warrior and a leader of warriors after all, but he'd never considered raising a hand to a human or worse using his magic on one.

Time slipped away from him as Arto sat in the roundhouse. The rage seemed to have passed at least for the moment. He had no doubt that it would return in the quiet moments of the night when he turned to speak with Gwenyvar and remembered. It was almost regretful that she and Luegáed had run off and not been killed as he initially feared. Then at least his rage would have a target and he would have another motivation to destroy the Sídhe. They had enslaved his sister and killed his father, but this... they were not responsible for this. Unless he held them accountable for him being gone so frequently. If the Sídhe had not invaded then he never would have had reason to meet Luegáed or Gwenyvar. None of this would have happened.

He shook his head again and closed his eyes as he leaned back on the bed. This was... this had the potential to turn ugly. He had to keep control. There were people depending on him; they'd be watching and questioning him. His best friend and one of his chief warriors had run off with his wife. Medraut was right that many would see it as an act of weakness and they'd come too far. They were too close to have others trying to take over or worse stall or even stop the creation of the iron gates.

It was a kindness, he decided, that he hadn't known. Now he could try to cope with these convoluted emotions in peace without fear of lashing out against them. He didn't have to worry about needing to compete with Luegáed for Gwenyvar or living with her while being both in love with her and angry with her. He'd been able to enjoy the companionship of both his wife and his best friend without worry, fear or guilt over how they felt. Except now he was keenly aware of having lost those friendships, aware that if they were headed where Medraut believed that he would never see either of them again.

Movement by the doorway made Arto sit up quickly and reach towards Cathanáil abandoned next to his bed. He couldn't even remember placing it there, but at his own sluggish reaction, he was grateful. Merlin stepped into the roundhouse, letting the pelt drop closed behind him.

"I am sorry Arto," his mentor told him gently, leaning forward on his staff and looking at him. There was no pity in Merlin's eyes, but a shared sense of sadness that Arto appreciated and regretted putting there at the same time.

"What did I do wrong?" Arto asked, burying his face in his hands and dragging his fingers through his hair. "Why?"

"I suspect you will never have a satisfactory answer to that," Merlin replied gently and Arto felt his mentor move closer to him. "Gwenyvar loved you, but there are different kinds of love, different intensities. Luegáed loved you as well in his own way and I have no doubt that the love he had for Gwenyvar caused him much pain."

"I think he tried to tell me, but I wasn't listening. Was that it Merlin?"

"Arto, you aren't going to find answers this way."

"Morgana and Airril are happy!" He snapped, jumping to his feet and pacing irritably around the roundhouse. He was aware of Merlin watching him with worry, but he didn't care. "Of the suitors father offered she may have chosen him, but they weren't in love beforehand. She kept secrets from him and then spent years with us traveling and yet..." It seemed like all his energy was being pulled away from him and Arto collapsed back onto the edge of the bed. "They're happy. They love each other. Airril is devoted to Morgana and she loves and respects him. What did I do wrong?"

Merlin stepped over and placed a hand on top of Arto's head. It was a familiar gesture from his childhood, but one that Merlin had not indulged in for many years. A pained gasp escaped Arto as his fingers dug into the blankets beneath him. He felt weak and over taxed as if he'd just created two iron gates in the same night. The ache in his chest seemed to have spread all through his body making him feel old and sore. It hurt, it hurt so much. At that moment he'd have rather a Sídhe run him through than confront this. His ragged breaths turned to sobs that he did his best to muffle. Lowering his head, Arto leaned forward and hid his face. Merlin's hand never left his head and the older mage said nothing as Arto cried.

Finally, slowly, the tears began to lessen leaving a dull bone-deep exhaustion in their wake. Reaching up, Arto brushed away the last of them unsure if he felt better or worse now. He just felt raw. He glanced around the roundhouse, noting that darkness had taken hold and a fire was burning in the hearth. To his surprise, he spotted his sister standing by the doorway, her face illuminated by the last traces of the setting sun as she kept watch. The ache in his chest eased as gratitude towards his family settled in. Arto inhaled deeply, savoring the slightly smoky taste of it and suddenly aware of his hunger. He didn't want to think about how long he'd been crying, didn't want to wonder if he was really so weak. Arto managed to give Merlin a small smile of gratitude and was rewarded with another gentle brush of fingers atop his head.

Then a Sídhe horn sounded in the distance and echoed across the plains. Arto raised his eyes and looked up at Merlin who had a badly disguised look of horror on his face. His shoulders slumped for a moment, but Arto pulled back from Merlin's hand, planted his feet firmly on the ground and stood up.

"Arto-"

"The blood ward should still be active around the village," Arto cut in sternly as he reached for Cathanáil. "They're attacking despite the ward which means that this is important. This could be it."

"Let the blood ward hold them off," Morgana insisted as she took a few steps towards him.

"No," Arto replied sharply with a shake of his head. "This is still my fight and this is my home."

He saw Morgana and Merlin exchange a worried look, but ignored them and headed for the door. Arto paused for only a moment to rinse his face off in the small bowl of water near the fire. He secured Cathanáil on his back, squared his shoulders and stepped outside to the sight of the hillside in the distance on fire, illuminating a dark opening in the hill where dozens of Sídhe Riders were pouring out into the Iron Realm in formation for battle.

28

Visions of Darkness

Maybe it was just Aiden, but Ravenslake seemed too quiet. He knew that most of the university students had already left for their winter break destinations, but town even seemed to be lacking in locals. Parking in downtown had been far easier than he could ever remember it being as the sunset in the distance cast a red glow over the brick buildings.

"Violet Blaze again?" Bran asked as he climbed out and looked over at the large neon sign that was already on down the street.

"It's good food and you weren't offering any suggestions," Aiden huffed as he came around to the sidewalk and waited for Bran to get his footing. The sidewalks were mostly clear, but Ravenslake didn't have the steam piping system under the walkways that the university did.

Violet Blaze was a small buffet located off Main Street that had been through at least seven owners in Aiden's lifetime, but somehow always managed to stay in business. The menu rotated with a blend of American staples on Mondays, Wednesday, Thursday and Saturday and seemingly random ethnic dishes on the other days plus a consistent salad bar. Aiden's father loved the place while his mother hated it, but he like any good college student supported the idea of all you can eat.

It didn't take them very long to get inside and pay for their meals. It was still a bit early for dinner so there were only a handful of people scattered in the small dining room and a

long bar full of fresh steaming food. Aiden grinned, pleased to
have gotten there early enough for the first batch of the night.
They walked past the front counter with their drinks and found
a table tucked back in the corner. Aiden glanced around in the
corners quickly, checking just to make sure that there were no
unexpected monsters hiding anywhere.

"Check it out," Bran said in a low voice, gesturing towards the
other side of the dining room.

Aiden did a double take to where Bran was pointing. Jenny
and Lance were standing off to the side talking in low voices.
Judging from the expressions on their faces it wasn't an
exactly pleasant conservation. They were half blocking the
kitchen, but the staff members coming in and out were giving
them a wide berth.

"I'm surprised they're still in town," Bran observed beside
him as he put one of the little sugar packets into his iced tea.
"'Course I'm also surprised that they're talking."

"Maybe they are on a date," Aiden suggested with a shrug. He
doubted that, but still, if it were true then it would thrill Alex.
He got a doubtful look from Bran and chuckled in agreement.

"What do you think?" Bran asked curiously. "Say hi or
pretend we don't see them?"

"This place isn't that busy," Aiden remarked even as he
inwardly cringed. "Besides, I know that it means a lot to Alex
that things work out with them."

"Yeah," Bran agreed with a soft sigh and a nod. "After you
then."

"Thanks," Aiden grumbled, but he stepped forward and put on a wide smile. "Lance, Jenny," he called with a small wave. "Hey there."

The two in question turned to look at them sharply. Jenny's eyes were wide, almost panicked, but she forced a little smile. Lance recovered quickly and his stance relaxed even as he glanced towards Jenny.

"Oh hi… Aiden and Bran," Lance greeted politely with a hint of uncertainty in his voice at their names.

"Lance, Jenny good to see you both," Bran replied kindly with a soft smile. "How were your finals?"

"They went fine," Lance told them at the same time that Jenny said, "Good." They glanced at each other and Aiden nearly shivered at the tension.

"Are you going home for Christmas?"

"My flight leaves tomorrow afternoon," Jenny replied with a nod.

"I'm heading out tomorrow morning, you two?"

"I'm local," Aiden replied with a small shrug.

"I'm staying for work reasons," Bran answered calmly drawing a confused look from both Lance and Jenny for a moment.

He could tell the exact second that it dawned on them what Bran was referring to. It was almost funny how they both shifted nervously with a hint of guilt visible on both faces. Aiden couldn't help but feel both sorry for them and frustrated with the pair. It actually wasn't that different from how he'd felt about Alex at first when she was so stubborn about magic.

"So what brings you here?" Bran asked pleasantly taking over the small talk. "Are you on a date?" he asked with a little smirk that wasn't as pleasant as his tone.

"What? No!" Jenny answered far too quickly, earning a small flinch from Lance. Aiden had to wonder what it was that the guy saw in her. "We just ran into each other. My friends-" She turned and gestured to a corner, but there was an empty table with messy plates and empty glasses. "Anyway," she said quickly turning back to them and trying to hide a flash of hurt. "How are you guys doing?"

"Everyone is doing well," Bran told her gently. "Things have been… intense lately," he paused and nibbled at his lip for a moment. "It's good that you're leaving town for a bit."

They didn't ask anything further and Aiden knew that they didn't need to say anything more. He nudged Bran's elbow softly and nodded towards the buffet. The pair of them grabbed their trays and tried to ignore Jenny and Lance as they went to opposite sides of the restaurant. Lance sat back down with a small group of big guys that Aiden figured were other members of the football team. Jenny collected her jacket from the back of a chair, a sad expression on her face. He made a mental note to tell Alex to give her a call tomorrow as he reached for the spoon in the peaches.

Suddenly Bran stopped moving in the line, his breathing becoming strained as his hands shook. The plate of salad slipped from his grasp, crashing onto the floor as Bran swayed wildly. Lunging Aiden tried to grab Bran, but his friend twitched violently and stumbled back. Plates tumbled to the floor and there was a burst of noise around them. Everything seemed to slow down and Aiden was already cringing when

Bran's leg struck the side of the table with a crunch of plastic and the sharp metallic clang of the edge of the table against his brace. A look of intense pain took over Bran's features as he fell back towards the buffet once more. Then his features became neutral, and he crumpled to the ground.

Aiden dropped to his knees next to him, nearly putting a knee into Bran's dropped salad. At first, he thought his friend was unconscious; his eyes were open but glassy. His fingers were twitching very softly, but he was whispering something in too low a voice for Aiden to make out. The few other patrons in the restaurant were moving toward them, but there was a flash of purple in the corner of Aiden's eye as Jenny rushed over with Lance close behind. The football player blocked off several of the other people coming close as Jenny stood right next to him nervously tugging at the hem of her shirt.

"Aiden," Bran hissed as he grabbed onto his shoulder with a painful grip. "The lake, you've got to get to the lake. Chernobog, Alex needs help-"

Nodding, Aiden shifted closer to Bran, trying to sort out what to do as Bran's eyes closed and he groaned in pain. He glanced down at Bran's leg, noticing that the brace looked damaged from the impact and was digging into his leg.

"Oh my god is he okay?" Someone asked behind him. "I'll call an ambulance."

"No I'm fine," Bran groaned his voice tight and gravely. It was obvious that he wasn't alright, but as he lifted his eyes to meet Aiden's he understood the desperate glint shining in Bran's eyes.

"We're good," Aiden said quickly turning to look at the staff members hovering nearby. "He needs some space," he insisted as he turned to look at the small crowd that had gathered.

"That looked like a seizure," someone called from across the room.

Bran nodded and started wheezing as he struggled to breathe. Thankfully the half dozen people gathered around stepped back giving them some room. "They're in danger, Alex... Arthur, the lake," Bran groaned again, reaching up and rubbing his temples as if he had a migraine.

At Bran's words, a soft gasp escaped Jenny. She had a horrified expression on her face and Aiden couldn't but wonder which one she was more worried about: Alex or Arthur. Lance glanced her way, but then bent lower and slipped Bran's arm over his shoulder, helping him to his feet. Aiden moved back to give the football player room to maneuver Bran over to a table away from the spectators. Rushing ahead of them, he moved aside a few chairs to give Lance enough space to lower his fellow mage into a chair.

Jenny was right behind them carrying Bran's cane in hand which she handed to Bran once he was seated. Aiden shivered at the dark look that Bran gave the thing as he took it and leaned it against the wall. He knelt by his friend, trying to judge how badly the leg brace had been damaged or shifted. With some luck maybe Bran would be back up quickly.

"Can I get you something?" a member of staff asked, wringing her hands with worry. "Some water? Are you sure you don't need to go to the hospital?"

"I'm fine, but some water would be nice thank you," Bran told her with a painfully forced smile. She nodded and hurried back towards the kitchen.

"What-"

Bran turned wide wild eyes on him. "Aiden go! I'll be fine and I'll call the others. Alex needs help, she's in danger!" Bran's eyes began glassy and distant, "Something... something isn't right... I saw..." He shook his head, "The north side of the lake; you have to hurry and look out, there are shadow monsters everywhere."

"Are you-"

"I'll be fine," Bran grimaced as he tried to move his leg, a wince shaking his entire body. "But I'm out of this fight, now go."

"Go," Jenny ordered sharply in a low voice with a glance around the people who were still watching. "We'll stay with him."

"We'll get him home or wherever he needs to go," Lance added seriously, his face stern with determination.

It went against every instinct to just leave him there, but Bran's warning was ringing loud and clear in his ears. As he slowly got to his feet Bran was already pulling out his cell phone. The waitress came back with a glass of water and gave him a startled look as he pulled on his coat.

"I've got to go back to our dorm and grab his medicine," Aiden explained quickly, feeling sick to his stomach. "He's calling for extra help. Someone will be here soon, our other friends are going to stay until then."

Aiden resisted the urge to look back at Jenny and Lance; their earlier nervousness didn't fill him with confidence, but he felt helpless. Alex had faith in them, so he'd just have to hope that she was right. Everyone was watching him as he rushed out of the diner as if Sídhe hounds were at his heels. His truck was around the block and Aiden nearly slipped on a patch of ice in his rush. His fingers fumbled with his keys and he quietly repeated everything Bran had said. Taking a deep breath as he climbed into his truck and started it up, Aiden fought to keep panic at bay and pulled out into traffic.

He kept going faster and faster as the traffic thinned and he left the last of the buildings behind. Only a few side roads with scattered houses were around him now. His fingers drummed nervously on the steering wheel and he kept glancing towards the lake. The half-moon was shining down brightly and the last rays of the sun were almost gone behind the mountains. He wondered if Bran's vision was before or after Chernobog appeared; was there any chance that he'd find them before the danger even started?

Finally, the bridge appeared and Aiden sighed in relief, he was almost there and he thought he could see a car a couple of miles or so down the road. Then in the corner of his eye, he saw something changing on the lake and turned his head slightly to watch. It was getting darker all of a sudden as the last rays of the sun disappeared and a thick cloud appeared above the lake blocking the moonlight. Slowing down the truck, Aiden kept glancing towards the lake as a huge figure emerged from the surface of the water.

A strange sickening green glow was radiating off of a skeletal face. Aiden felt a chill taking over his limbs making them seem heavy and sluggish. There was a terrible sense of fear creeping into his mind, an urge to turn back, but he pulled his eyes away from Chernobog and focused on the road ahead of him. Shadows began to move outside the truck, but Aiden tried to ignore them even as he began to drive down the middle of the road. Metal scraping sounds from his truck made him shiver as another shadow monster burst onto the road and attacked. More were spilling out onto the road in front of him and turning to face him.

Slamming down on the accelerator, Aiden glared at the shadow monsters and did his best to ignore the flutter in his heart as his headlights began to flicker. The truck sped up and the shadow creatures leapt out of the way with shrieks of anger. There was another loud scraping sound as one of the larger ones swung at the truck. More and more were coming up from the lake and down from the hills.

Then everything began to sputter to a stop as the creatures swarmed around the truck. Aiden could feel the truck slowing down and glanced at the dashboard lights. They were flickering right along with the headlights. There was a hard bump against the driver's side and his truck slammed to the right, slipping on a patch of ice. The whole truck spun, the dark scenery swirling around him as Aiden slammed his eyes shut. He hit something and the truck stopped as his head knocked against the headrest. Aiden pulled his shaking hands off the steering wheel. The truck was still running, but he was in the ditch in a pile of snow. He took a slow deep breath, forcing himself to ignore the chattering and screeching sounds from outside.

Aiden pulled off his gloves and tossed them into the passenger seat before pushing open the door. It resisted for a moment, the snow piled up tight against it, but after a moment it gave way. Climbing out of the truck, Aiden avoided even glancing at the damage. Instead, he reached under his coat and shirt to the leather sheath that secured his iron dagger. He pulled it out quickly and tightened his fingers around it nervously. Aiden knew that it wouldn't do much against the shadow monsters; they weren't weak to it like the Sídhe were, but it made him feel a little better. He closed his eyes for a brief moment, quickly locating the small spark in his gut that fueled his magic. Pulling on that spark, Aiden felt it expand and felt a wave of warmth wash through his entire body. His fingers tingled pleasantly and it was easier to breathe the icy night air.

The headlights of his truck flickered completely off and Aiden was left standing alone in the dark with the cackling of the shadows closing in around him. On instinct, he summoned a flame to his hands and his magic responded instantly to the familiar command. Flames licked sweetly at his bare skin and illuminated the immediate area. He wasn't far from the road and Aiden ignored the dark shapes moving in his peripheral vision and trudged through the snow. It wasn't really that deep; he'd been lucky and hit a drift rather than a tree, but with each step, he was aware of the creatures stalking him and Bran's warning of danger. There wasn't much time. Even if Bran had called the others right away he would still be the closest. As his feet escaped from the snow and tapped against the paved road a shiver went up his spine as the creatures came closer.

From his place on the road, Aiden could see the looming figure more clearly. Chernobog was surrounded by a mass of dark clouds that looked like a billowing cloak. It was massive, his skull-like head illuminated only by glowing neon green eyes so unlike anything he had imagined. The Old One didn't seem to be moving yet, standing deathly still in the water and Aiden could only wonder just how large this thing truly was.

There were small flashes of dark silver magical light coming from up ahead: he was close to Alex and there was a shimmer of Arthur's white magic. Bran's vision may have given him enough warning to get moving, but he was too late to join them before the battle began. Swallowing, Aiden tried to find the distinct shapes of the shadow monsters circling him, but the long limbs and glowing red eyes all blurred together in the rippling darkness of their flesh. In his hand the flame flickered, the warmth draining out of it in the presence of the monsters.

If there was ever a time to get it right this was it, Aiden told himself. He could do this: he had to. Aiden could see his breath dancing on the air in soft wisps with every exhale and it felt like ice was creeping up the small of his back. With every moment the temperature around him was getting colder and more shadow monsters seemed to be spilling out of the woods.

Calling forth more magic, Aiden felt the spark in his gut grow and there was a soft thrumming in his legs and arms. The fire in his hands heightened and the creatures made a strange noise that almost sounded like laughter. He couldn't do anything to them with his fire and they knew it. Aiden considered putting it out completely, but couldn't stand the idea of the darkness. His hands were shaking, his mouth was completely dry and terror was slinking over him.

"I can do this," Aiden said out loud, his voice cracking, but the words broke through the mess of noise.

The terror receded for a moment and Aiden let the flame in his hand wither as he focused on pulling back his magic. The darkness closed in around him and in the span of a heartbeat, he expected to be ripped apart. Magic jolted to his fingers, but instead of calling on his fire Aiden allowed the tiny flickers of power to sputter from his hand. They wafted lazily in the chilly air around him and the creatures made odd sounds at the sight. The front row pulled back suspiciously giving Aiden some space.

Closing his eyes, Aiden pictured a snowy day, like the blizzard that had shut down the schools for two days when he was nine. He and Nicki had begged to go out and play together, but his parents hadn't been willing to brave the roads the first day. He could see the fat snowflakes and feel the biting wind that he'd braved for only half an hour before running back inside. Focusing everything he had, Aiden pushed that image to the front of his mind and commanded the magic: do that.

There was a sudden change in the flow of his magic, so slight that Aiden almost didn't notice it, but it was there. The warmth that he'd always associated with his magic was fading and the warm sensation was instead pulling back and swirling in his chest. He refused to let it distract him and kept the image of the snow storm he wanted in his head. It was simple, he was a native of the northwest and had seen enough snow. It was winter and snow was everywhere; he just had to build on that.

Opening his eyes, Aiden gasped softly and then grinned. Snow was swirling around him, creating a thick veil of ice between him and the shadow monsters. A soft hint of red distinguished his magical ice from the ordinary. The creatures were barely visible through the haze, but he could hear them over the howl of his own little storm. Excitement flashed through him. He straightened up, boosted by the blazing warmth in his chest as his magic lashed around him. Raising both hands, Aiden grinned and pushed more magic into the storm and looked up, watching as the blizzard created a dome over his head.

Why had this been hard? He laughed in glee as the small blizzard grew thicker and thicker as he pushed more magic out into the air. The heat he'd pulled from the magic was thrumming in his chest like a happy puppy making him feel giddy and confident. Magical snow swirled in the air around him in a thick haze of tiny ice crystals, but he wasn't feeling cold anymore. At his surprise, the magical blizzard faltered. Aiden shook his head, ordering himself to focus and not get swept up in the high of success. This storm could protect him; it was a barrier that the shadow monsters were unwilling to cross, but he'd run out of magic sooner or later. He could only do so much so how could he use this to get rid of some of these things?

"What would Nicki do?" he asked out loud, then slowly he smiled and a chuckle escaped him. After knowing her since grade school, he knew the answer all too well.

Aiden slammed his eyes shut and squeezed them tightly, willing the rest of the world to just fade away. He focused on the sounds of the small storm blazing around him and willed it inward, ordering it closer to him. The sound intensified and he could feel the snow tickling his cheeks. Pouring magic into the storm, Aiden kept repeating ice over and over again in his head. He tried to imagine every movie with ice magic he'd ever seen, every book he'd ever read or any game that had ever inspired him. His magic felt hot in his chest, sending small bursts of warmth through his arms and down to his toes. It was spiraling to the limits of his control. There was a tiny tether that he could feel connecting him to it, like the tiny fragile silk of a spider that could snap at any moment.

"Now!" Aiden shouted, pushing the magic out with all his might.

The snowy dome exploded outward, the snowflakes fusing together into shards of ice that went flying in all directions. A wave of tiny daggers rippled around him, striking the shadow monsters. Some were taller and lanky being struck in the head from the top of the dome while those that were lower to the ground took shards in their legs from the bottom. Shrieks echoed in all around him and Aiden felt his knees begin to buckle. His eyes moved to a mass of collapsed shadow creatures who were dissipating into the night air with groans and small cries of pain. The layers of darkness rippled and faded away leaving him alone in the road.

Gasping, Aiden stumbled to the side and nearly fell down. He shook his head and forced the blind spots in his vision away with several rapid blinks. It took him a moment to remember where he was, what was happening, but then he spotted the huge dark shape in the distance. Just the sight sent a spike of cold through him, making him shudder in dread, but he pushed it away.

Chernobog hadn't moved from his place in the lake; there were flashes of magic on the shores giving a clear sign that the others were fighting something, but the master of the shadow monsters was just watching. Aiden swallowed and glanced around at the shadow monsters that were coming down from the hills. There seemed to be no end to them and fatigue was already seeping into his bones. The options ran through his head like lightning and he made a decision. Stepping back, Aiden glanced towards Chernobog and swallowed. Then with a small nod to himself, he turned and started to run down the road towards the others with shadow monsters racing after him.

29

Against Shadow

Standing completely still in the darkness, Alex inhaled slowly in an attempt to calm herself. Morgana's voice echoed in her head and Alex fought off the instinctive quiver that was threatening to take hold of her. She summoned forth an orb of magic, willing it to light up the area. The small orb swirled into existence in the palm of her hand and cast a weak low light over the area, but it was like the light was being actively smothered.

Around her the shadow monsters were moving in slowly, creeping forward with gleaming red eyes. Alex wasn't sure if they were hesitant about her magic or trying to frighten her. Glancing towards Arthur, she saw his magic swirling in his hand and beginning to form something made of ice. There was a knot in her throat that kept her from yelling for him to run, but the reality of the situation was sinking in.

Moving slowly, Alex reached towards her pocket to retrieve her phone. Even a quick text could bring the help they desperately needed. But before she could reach the phone, a shadow monster shaped like a huge panther lashed out at her. Instinctively, Alex threw the energy orb at the creature and gasped softly when it snarled in pain and backed up. More creatures moved closer and Alex abandoned the idea of reaching for her phone.

She was surrounded by the swirling creatures of darkness, red eyes, teeth, and claws. Some were tall like the massive monster that was moving slowly and swinging huge long arms with long claws, others were short like the low creature that reminded Alex of a crocodile slinking towards her. They looked like twisted animals or in a few frightening cases like humans spun out of shadows. Despite the cold, she was sweating beneath her coat and her dagger felt ready to slip from her fingers.

A strange low sound came from Chernobog. To Alex's ears, it almost sounded like a growl, but there was a hint of a melodic note within it that made her feel lightheaded for a moment. Swaying on her feet, Alex shook her head and turned her face away from Chernobog. She focused on the nearest shadow creature whose red eyes were raised as it looked towards its master. Slashing with her dagger, Alex felt the flesh of the nearest shadow creature give to the blow, but there was no blood. Instead, its flesh rippled as soon as the blade was withdrawn. Alex couldn't see any sign of a wound. Around her the shadow creatures cackled, flashing their perfectly white teeth as their eyes narrowed at her.

Pulling on her magic, Alex formed another orb of energy. One of the creatures grew tired of waiting and lunged towards her. Alex shifted her position and threw the orb at the shadow creature. It struck the creature in the chest and it howled. A sharp metallic smell filled the air as the shadow creature began to vanish. The others howled, snarled and growled at her in a growing tide of noise. Alex shuddered and summoned another two orbs of energy, letting her dagger slip from her fingers to the ground.

This time she didn't wait for any of them to attack. Throwing the orbs, Alex kept pushing magic into them even after they left her hands. There was a crackling in the air as the orbs transformed into beams of magic, striking two of the shadow creatures. They vanished and more began to press forward. Alex charged up another blast, this time opening her hand and pushing it towards the creatures. Fast, but weaker bolts of energy lashed out and struck the shadow creatures. These did not vanish but were knocked backward to the ground as their comrades simply stepped over them.

She was being overwhelmed. The terrifying realization cut through the haze and the rhythm of pulling on her magic and blasting the shadow creatures. There were piles of the shadow creatures that had been blasted back and some were beginning to get to their feet, but there seemed to be no end to them. Icy tears prickled at her eyes and threatened to blind her, but the burning instinct to fight in her chest kept the tears from falling.

A risky glance towards Arthur up the hill revealed that her boyfriend was surrounded too, but there were far fewer around him. There was a sword formed of ice clasped in his hands and he was swinging it about in random patterns to keep the shadows at bay. Alex yelped as cold claws swiped her leg. Instinctively she shoved a wave of magic towards the leg as she looked down. Her jeans were slashed open and blood was oozing slowly out of the long tears in the skin. Hissing, she stumbled away from the shadow creature that had her blood dripping from its claws only to almost fall onto another shadow creature.

Alex spun around and waved her hands sending a wash of magic sparks across the area. The shadow creatures hissed as the sparks showered down on them, but they lacked enough magic to do any real damage. It bought Alex a moment to steady herself and plant her feet against a pair of rocks. She ignored the blood dripping down her leg and brought up her hands to charge another blast. This time she charged the orb up with as much magic as she dared. Three heartbeats and the shadow beasts were moving for another charge and Alex released the magic, envisioning a lightning bolt in her mind.

The magic ricocheted amongst the creatures, arcing between them as bolts of dark silver lightning. Eyes narrowed, Alex pushed more and more magic into the bolt and forced her hands to move to spread the attack. A shadow creature beside her reached forward and slashed at her side. Seeing the movement in the corner of her eye, Alex shifted her weight and avoided the worst of the attack, but heard her coat being torn open.

Panting, Alex pulled sharply at her magic and ignored her legs as they started to shake. She created another orb and released it upon another shadow creature. There was a hint of satisfaction as it faded away, but another rushed up from the shore of the lake. The swirl of magic around her was beginning to dim and she could see red eyes watching it carefully.

Magic danced over her fingers and across her palms sending a dim silvery light over the shadow creatures. Alex attacked another shadow creature and growled in frustration when it climbed back to its feet. Another wave of magic kept them at bay followed by another blast. This seemingly unending dance was getting her nowhere. She could hear Arthur fighting up the hill and glanced his way. There were far fewer around him and he was managing to keep them at bay, but the coat on one of his arms was ripped.

They weren't getting anywhere and even if they cut through all the shadow monsters there was still Chernobog to deal with. She needed more energy, the connection that thrummed inside of her to the earth felt raw. Each pull, each tug was beginning to feel painful. It was getting hard to breathe, but more shadow creatures were coming forward. In the corner of her eye, Alex could see Chernobog in the lake watching. His thin dark mouth seemed to be twisted into a smile with flashes of teeth.

Anger flashed through Alex even as she became aware of the ache developing in her muscles. Her heart was pounding as adrenaline washed through her, but exhaustion and doubt were beginning to trickle past her defenses. Alex flinched as another wave of cold washed over her and clung to her skin. Her clothes were soaked from the snow and ice and her teeth chattered violently. The air was painful to breathe, catching in her throat as more of Chernobog's magic filled the area. Alex blinked as she kicked at one of the shadow monsters.

"His magic," Alex gasped, her eyes widening and a flash of hope and excitement burning hot in her chest. "Oh my god!"

With renewed vigor, Alex forced back as many of the shadow creatures as she could with a wave of dark silver sparks. Alex opened her fingers as wide as the cold digits would allow and closed her eyes. Her heart pounded with fear as the shadow creatures moved around her and their growls filled her ears, but she pushed it all away.

Reaching out with what little magic she still had Alex envisioned a thin mist that spread out. Alex gasped as she felt an icy spark in her heart as the vapor collided with the first of the shadow creatures. It stopped moving and jumped back with a hiss, arching its back. Alex opened her eyes, fixed her gaze on the shadow monster and pulled. There was a moment of resistance, a moment of unbelievable cold gripping Alex around the heart, but she kept pulling. Chernobog's magic kept pushing back, but then suddenly it gave and the cold began to dissipate in her body.

There was a roar behind her, but Alex didn't turn her focus away from the shadow monsters. A thin shimmering stream of energy appeared in the air, glittering in the darkness. It flittered through the air towards Alex, swirling around the shadow monsters. More strands appeared and Alex laughed out loud in excitement as the strands connected to her fingers and she felt small jolts traveling up her arms.

The shadow creature screamed as thin streams of power began seeping from it and flowing to Alex's hands. It stumbled backward and hissed at her, baring its long gleaming white teeth. Around her, the cold began to recede. More energy flowed towards her and the darkness around her weakened.

The sound of sloshing in the water made Alex look towards Chernobog who was beginning to move towards the shore. She pulled harder on the cloud of energy around her and saw more streams of power appearing out of the others shadow monsters. All of them were pulling back from her with soft panicked noises as a glittery web of energy began to weave itself around her. The dark glittering strands began to shine dark silver and spun together into Alex's outstretched hands. Then cautiously she pulled her hands closer and began forming the energy, spinning the strands together into something she could control. Smiling grimly, she noted the shadow monsters pulling away from her with whimpers and whines as their magical energy was sapped and their very form was pulled away and changed.

Her whole body was shaking, but Alex kept pulling in all the power she could. Magic sparked in the air between her hands, swirling amongst the strands of energy that were arcing violently. She could barely keep her hands still, barely keep her focus on the increasing pulse of power that was threatening to explode. But she kept the energy contained. It brushed over the inside of her hands gently. Her magic traced over each jolt of energy and turned it the dark silver color of her magic.

Glancing back towards Arthur who was using the ice sword to attack one of the shadow monsters, Alex noted that he was still okay. The orb of power in her hands pulsed as the shadow creatures drew back from her. She licked her dry lips nervously and then carefully slowly drew her hands back from the orb. Then with a sigh, she let go of the magic.

There was an explosion of power that rippled all around them, illuminating the entire area in a burst of dark silver light. The air became supercharged causing Alex's arm hair to stand on end. It smelled like a thunderstorm and Alex gulped in the air greedily as she tried to control the release and keep it from harming Arthur. Alex's whole body shook as she pushed more magic outward to surround the sphere of magic, desperate to slow down the rush. Hair whipped back from her face and Alex closed her eyes against the pressure for a moment, but curiosity and fear made her open them quickly.

The shadow monsters were scattering, but many were falling to the ground as the waves of magic rolled over the area. Alex turned her eyes to one that was on the ground twisting with pain and clawing at the ground while high pitched shrieks escaped it. For a moment she felt a pang of guilt before the creature began to fade away and more of the darkness lifted. The clouds were still rolling around Chernobog, but the soft silvery glow of the moon was visible around them once again.

Dropping to her knees, Alex hissed as her knees splashed in the slush. Around her, the last of the shadow monsters were twisting on the ground and vanishing into nothing, but her sense of victory was rapidly fading. Her legs were shaking badly and her hands felt raw as if they'd been burned.

"Alex!" Arthur shouted nearby to her, but his voice sounded distant to her. She wanted to shout back to him, to reassure him but her mouth was painfully dry.

Alex began to stand only to slip in the snow and mud. Her knee hit a rock and Alex groaned in pain, frustration, and worry. Opening her eyes, she looked around wearily. The shadow monsters were almost all gone. She could see only a few pairs of glowing red eyes in the distance and far off down the road she thought that she saw headlights. Alex forced herself to her feet only to almost stumble as a shadow monster that looked far too much a like a dog for comfort rushed her with two more of its heels.

"Look out Alex!" Arthur shouted and Alex thought she heard him moving down the hill.

Alex eyed the last of the shadow monsters and mentally growled at them for surviving. The sound of the water moving made Alex freeze. In front of her eyes, the three charging shadow monsters turned into black masses of swirling darkness. Cold exploded outward and Alex shut her eyes on reflex as the icy blast hit her face. When she opened her eyes the dark swirling masses were floating through the air and Alex fearfully followed them with her eyes.

Chernobog extended one long arm, casting a shadow over the shore as he opened his hand. The masses of darkness flowed into his hand, a dark version of what Alex had done earlier. She swallowed as the giant being began to move towards the shore. His long shadow moved over her and Alex suddenly wished that the thick clouds were still surrounding him. She felt cold and frozen to the spot as the darkness surrounded her and blocked the light of the moon. Shivering, Alex pulled her eyes away from Chernobog.

Waves of water were rolling up against the shore as Chernobog moved and Alex swallowed thickly, trying to get her legs to move. She could see the large shadow stretching out on the slope of the hill around her and watched the shadow as Chernobog opened his large arms. His shadow began to become fuzzy and Alex was torn between looking to see what was happening and keeping her eyes averted. She opened her hands nervously, fighting back the pain of the cold and tried to pull more magic from the earth. The connection inside her chest ached and sparked painfully like an electric discharge at the attempt.

A strange dull but echoing sound came from Chernobog that shook the whole hillside. Alex brought her hands up to cover her ears and hunched over. Her insides were quivering and each breath felt colder and colder. Dark clouds began to roll in from around the hills, swirling and curling in the sky and casting twisted shadows down upon them. Alex raised her eyes and looked up the hill towards Arthur. He was standing perfectly still and gazing out at the lake with a fearful and nervous expression. Alex saw him glance over his shoulder towards the car and wondered if they could make a run for it.

Then Chernobog stopped the terrible noise and moved quickly through the water. Nervously Alex looked over and tried once again to call some of her magic. Chernobog was almost at the shore now, his huge form almost completely out of the water, but suddenly he stepped back into the water and sent waves crashing onto the shore. Alex frowned and scanned the lake for why Chernobog had suddenly changed his focus. Her heart was pounding and she wondered hopefully if Merlin or Morgana had done something.

Her eyes widened and Alex fumbled into her pocket to pull out her phone. With frozen fingers, she made a simple text: lake north help and sent it to Morgana and she hoped to Merlin, but her cold fingers slipped. She looked back at the lake and gasped softly as the surface of the water in the center of the lake near Chernobog began to ripple. A growl escaped Chernobog and he lashed out with one hand to strike the water. It slipped through his fingers and flowed back to the surface of the lake.

A roar escaped the being and he clawed at the surface of the water but around his long talons a wave of water began to rise up from the surface. The water swirled together, shimmering with its own light and casting back the oppressive darkness. Something gleaming rose out of the water as the water spun around it to create the rough form of a humanoid. The water dripped down the form, creating details of a gown and a face. A veil of water surrounded the form for a few seconds before it stepped through and showed itself.

It looked like a woman in a long gown, a circlet of shining droplets of water illuminating her face. What appeared to be a gown formed of water shimmered around her and Alex squinted to try and see more in the low light. The gleam once more caught Alex's eyes and her heart pounded with excitement as she took in the sword clasped in the figure's hands. It glistened in the low light and Alex could make out a golden hilt that made her heart jump. The Lady of the Lake, Cyrridven, had arrived with Cathanáil.

30

A Final Gate

800 B.C.E. Northern Cornwall

The sight of the Riders sent the village into a rush of screaming, running and calls to arms. The whispers about his family were forgotten as fear rolled over the village. Arto stood still in front of his roundhouse for several minutes and watched as the warriors rushed to their own homes for their weapons. Some were already armed and were looking about in mild confusion.

This part had been Luegáed's job, Arto reflected sadly with a shake of his head. It had been his friend who oversaw the protection of the village. Just hours ago they had been happy to gossip about him and his shortcomings, but now they were being reminded of his importance. The dark amusement he got from the situation almost made Arto feel better. A soft chuckle escaped him and he swayed on his feet as the crippling exhaustion of his breakdown hit him squarely in the chest.

"Arto!" Someone shouted in his ear as a hand jostled him sharply half catching him and half shaking him awake. "Arto?"

Blinking, Arto turned to look at his sister. She was staring at him with a pensive expression. There was a dark look on her face and a flicker of doubt in her eyes that made him feel even angrier. He looked towards Merlin only to find a similar expression his mentor's face.

"I'm going to need iron," Arto announced sternly before he looked back towards the gaping hole in the hill. He frowned; rubble was rolling down the hill from it as if the Sídhe were still digging it open. "A lot of it."

"I don't think we have that much iron in the village," Merlin answered in a tight voice. "The last gate used up much of the reserves."

"They probably knew that," Morgana growled giving Merlin a pointed look.

"Don't make such assumptions Morgana," Merlin reprimanded sternly before a worried expression took over his face. "I will gather what iron we have…"

"I need to get up there," Arto announced as he pulled his sword. He savored the sound of the metal sliding against the hardened leather.

"But-" Morgana began to protest, but Arto ignored her. He shook off her hand and strode down the hill.

Several of the warriors stopped and looked towards him, but Arto said nothing to them as his eyes scanned the horizon. More Sídhe were slipping out of the tunnel with every passing moment, but there were other creatures too. Many small creatures were ducking away from the Sídhe Riders as they headed off in the other direction. Arto frowned but pushed back thoughts of these beings. He had more pressing things to worry about then some slaves of the Sídhe who were using the huge assault as a chance to escape their masters. Silently he wished them luck and turned to a nearby warrior.

"We have to keep this fight beyond the walls!" Arto shouted, gesturing with his hands towards the hills. "If they get inside the village we won't be able to protect the people."

"What about the blood protection?" A frightened voice to his right shouted. "You said it would protect us."

"The Sídhe have decided to attack regardless of the area's protections," Arto snapped, irritation bubbling violently in his chest. "It will weaken them, you might even be able to harm them with bronze, but be careful!"

Many rushed to the gates of the village, but a few hung back and looked his direction. Arto tried to ignore their doubtful looks, but they chafed painfully. He was certain he looked like he'd been crying recently, looking exhausted and worn down and yet it changed nothing. Suddenly he envied Morgana her courage to snap at others, but he couldn't do so and walked towards the gates with as much dignity as he could muster.

The sun had set, but the hillside was blazing with Sídhe magical lights and torches that were burning brightly. Arto reached out for the soft thrum of the blood magic that he'd tied to the area and pushed more magic into it. White sparks flowed down his fingers and fell to the ground as he walked like raindrops. He felt the magic flickering with new energy and life and smirked as he saw one of the distant Sídhe horses rear up fearfully. Blood red magic seeped up from the ground beneath it and twisted up its legs as its Rider leapt off its back.

Arto increased his speed to rush up the hill, feeling his heart beating faster. His vision sharpened and he felt magic coursing through his body. Cathanáil glowed brightly in his hand and he grinned each time that he caught sight of a Sídhe being swallowed up by the blood protection, a flash of satisfaction and smugness flashing through him. One of the Riders glared at him and charged forward swinging his golden sword wildly.

Dodging the Rider's attack, Arto leapt forward to avoid the horse as it sped past. Swinging Cathanáil, Arto sank the sword into the flank of the Sídhe steed. It vanished in a flash of white light with an animalistic cry of pain, sending its rider crashing to the ground. Arto didn't give the Rider a chance to recover. He leapt forward, landing next to the Rider and put a foot on its back before bringing Cathanáil down on its neck. The Rider managed only a weak cry and an aborted movement to get Arto off of him before he vanished. Arto sucked in a deep breath and took a moment to look around.

It was chaos. It was screaming, roundhouses being set on fire, people being grabbed and pulled up onto horses without concern for age or gender as more Riders rushed through the broken gates. It was the Sídhe riding towards the humans only for their steeds to suddenly release a terrible cry of pain and vanish in a wash of blood red magic. It was the Sídhe swinging their golden blades at humans and dodging the spray of blood even as their armor began to dissolve against the blood protection on the land beneath their feet. It was warriors turning and running away from the invaders. It was every nightmare that Arto had ever suffered about a full Sídhe invasion.

Human warriors were scattered amongst the ranks of the Sídhe Riders and were greatly outnumbered as the villagers began to flee into the darkness. Morgana was slicing her way through the Sídhe with her magic, Airril at her back with his own iron sword glistening with silver blood. Merlin was nowhere to be seen and Arto could see his cousin Medraut stalking up the hill with a determined expression.

The snarl of a Sídhe hound pulled Arto back into the moment and he gave a loud cry as he swung Cathanáil. A splash of silver blood and a flash of light and the hound was gone, but another rushed to take its place with a Síd just behind it. Everything else was falling away; the pain in his heart was fading away as the battle raged around him. Arto felt sick to his stomach at the realization, but couldn't help but swing

Cathanáil a little harder than usual against the armor of a Rider. The armor glowed as he pushed magic through the sword. Magic flashed off the blade in tiny bolts of lightning making the sword look like it was aflame. The Rider screamed in pain, throwing its head back and exposing its pale neck. With a satisfied smirk, Arto ripped Cathanáil from the Rider's chest and sliced its neck. Silvery blood spurted for only a second before vanishing in the wake of the sword's magic.

He spun, ducked and bobbed his way around the Sídhe horses to take down their Riders. Around him, the blood protection was slowing the steeds before ripping them apart and on occasion taking the Riders with it. Yet for each Síd that he cut down or saw the blood protection overwhelm at least two more seemed to appear to take its place. Magic was flashing all around him and not just the familiar and comforting shade of green and silver that belonged to Merlin and Morgana.

Spotting one of the Sídhe mages, Arto charged with a roar of rage. Gold magic shot past him and he wildly sliced the air as he ran to cut down another Síd. Violet eyes glared as Arto approached and the Síd charged up a brilliantly sparking orb of gold magic. Dropping to one knee, Arto ducked the magical blast and swept Cathanáil up in a smooth arch in front of him. There was a scraping sound as the magical iron blade collided with the Síd's armor, but in a flash of white magic, the armor began to dissolve. Pushing himself forward Arto used the momentum of standing up to thrust the sword through the Síd's chest. It gurgled for a moment before it vanished.

He was in front of the tunnel now. His fingers itched to keep swinging Cathanáil about and destroying the Sídhe invaders, but he had to focus. A few Sídhe were still coming out of the tunnel on foot, but many stopped just before the entrance with wide and fearful violet eyes at the sight of Cathanáil glowing in his hands. Frowning, Arto watched as they began to pull back and linger further back in the tunnel. A few brave ones rushed forward with their swords drawn. Arto spun quickly to avoid their attacks and lunged to the right with Cathanáil to strike the first Síd. Its armor began to dissolve with the first hit and it stumbled. He was panting as he impaled the second Síd and then turned back to the first as it took a swing at him.

Metal struck metal and Arto's knees almost buckled at the forces of the Síd's attack, but he held firm. The Rider was stronger than he was with several inches on him and the higher position on the slope of the hill. Glaring at the Síd, Arto pointed at it and pushed a jolt of magic through the finger. A spark of magic arched off his fingertip and struck the Síd in the face. It snarled and stumbled back, clawing at its face as the spark of white magic jumped over its skin leaving a trail of burnt flesh. Arto swung Cathanáil and cut the Rider down with a short snarl of his own. Panting softly, he turned and looked into the tunnel with a frown.

He risked a glance towards the village where he could see the fires spreading over the thatch roofs of the roundhouses. Worry for his mother filled him, but Arto forced it down brutally and forced himself to look back at the tunnel. It was larger than usual with a rougher mouth. There were no elegantly placed rocks to form an archway and support the flow of magic. Instead, this was rough and messy; this was a last tunnel of desperation. Arto considered it with distress simmering in his gut, his heart beating too quickly in his chest.

More Riders were moving towards him and those hiding in the tunnel seemed emboldened and began to move forward. A soft growl escaped Arto, a knot of rage tightening in his chest. Anger, hurt, grief and doubt all warred and he tightened his fingers around the hilt of Cathanáil in an effort to keep some level of control.

He screamed tugging at the knot and letting it unravel in a collapse of his control. The air around him exploded outwards in a burst of white swirling magic. For a moment Arto could feel nothing, see nothing and hear nothing. Slowly awareness returned to him and he was staring into the darkness of the tunnel as wisps of his magic danced around the entrance. The Sídhe who had been approaching him were gone. A bitter chuckle escaped him and Arto nodded to himself as the magic around him began to weaken.

"Alright then," he murmured letting his eyes fall closed.

Gripping Cathanáil's hilt with both hands, Arto pulled viciously on his link with the magic of the world, gathering the power in his chest. With an exhale he released it in another burst of magic that rippled out around him, brushing over the humans and crashing into the Sídhe. Underneath him, the earth thrummed with the combination of his unleashed power and the blood protection even as he pulled on the raw power of the Iron Realm. Slowly, Arto raised his hands. There was a glimmer at the edge of his senses as he felt the world stretching out around him. He could see the burning village, the roundhouses on fire as people threw water on them or grabbed their possessions and ran. He could see the workshop with chunks of iron lying about under the flames. The forges where the iron of the gates had been created and formed. Cathanáil pulsed in his hands, the magic woven into its metal flashing in response to his thoughts.

Raising Cathanáil into the air, Arto pulled on the magic all around him directing it through the sword. He closed his eyes tightly and focused all his being on calling the iron to him. Everything iron in the whole of the isles that wasn't already part of a gate was here and he needed all of it, even the weapons. A shock ran through his body as a wave of magic washed up through his feet and rushed up his body to the glowing Cathanáil. The sword in his hands flashed white and then the color began to change to a dark silver like the color of the iron blade itself. Arto struggled to breathe as the magic swirling around him became a storm.

Swords flew through the air towards him, iron axe heads were torn off their handles and smaller objects swirled above him. There were small pots, spearheads, arrowheads and dozens of small pieces of iron that were decorative, but any artistic value was lost on Arto. His hands were trembling as he pulled and pulled on the magic all around him and cast it into the iron. Around him, he could hear the sounds of battle and feel a strong wind whipping around him keeping everyone away from him. Distantly he thought he heard Medraut scream his name. The mere sound of his cousin's voice brought their last conversation crashing back to the forefront of his mind.

The glimmering connection to his magic inside of him was vibrating violently and felt like it was on fire. Now he could smell the smoke of the burning village and gagged as he caught the hints of burning flesh. Hopefully, it was livestock, but in his mind's eyes, he could see the carnage. They'd been swarmed and overwhelmed: there had been no real way to protect the village. Not and close up the tunnel. Arto was struck by doubts; if they'd stayed in the village could they have held it and protected everyone? Could they have fought back the Sídhe and then closed the tunnel? Luegáed would have known how to handle-

He shook his head quickly and glared at the tunnel entrance. He pushed everything aside; he banished his thoughts about Gwenyvar and Luegáed. He couldn't be distracted, not now. He couldn't be that weak, that broken at this moment. This was everything now; they didn't matter anymore beyond how the hurt could keep him going. He kept pushing more of the magic out into the swirl of iron above his head. Sparks of white magic danced over the various pieces and slowly they all began to glow as the magic seeped into them. Slowly, a small smile of triumph appeared on his face and Arto felt a stirring of confidence in his chest.

There was a sharp pain in his side so sudden and overwhelming that for a moment there was nothing else. He forgot everything as he stumbled to his knees, Cathanáil slipped out of his falling hand. The magic around him wavered, the pieces of magically enhanced iron falling to the ground with dull thuds. Slowly he came back to himself. It was hard to breathe and for several long moments, his entire being did not exist beyond the pain.

Weakly Arto brought his hands up to his side, reaching blindly for the source of the agony. His fingers became moist as a new sharp pain jolted through his body pulling him harshly back to reality. Arto brought his hand forward and looked at it dumbly. Red blood, human blood, his blood was smeared across his hand. He felt and heard someone behind him and wanted to turn, but the wound in his side made that impossible.

"I'm actually sorry that your wife ran off and left you," Medraut's voice announced calmly as he stepped around in front of him, a vicious sneer on his face. There were long cuts and burns across his cheeks and his tunic was badly torn. "I had designs on her myself; thought it would be a nice way to usurp you. I already took your family's base of power, and then I'd take your wife."

"Medraut?" Arto asked weakly, his mind stumbling over what was happening.

"Hello cousin," Medraut greeted coolly, raising his bronze sword up so Arto could see the dark red blood covering it. Medraut shifted his blade to let the blood drip off on the ground. Arto saw small flashes of red as the blood magic absorbed more of his blood, but it did not activate against Medraut. "This tunnel has been ready for months, just short of the final connection to this realm," Medraut said in a conversational voice as he gestured to the tunnel entrance behind him. "The place for the final battle when you were vulnerable. Tonight I made contact and gave the order and the Sídhe finished breaking through."

"The gates are all over the place, they can't go far!" Arto reminded him a tight voice, nearly chocking on his words.

"Those little bits of metal can be broken easily enough," Medraut hissed with a glint of victory and pride. "If you have the right weapon."

Against his will, Arto's eyes flashed over to Cathanáil. Everything they'd done couldn't truly be undone so easily, could it? He'd channeled his magic through Cathanáil every time he'd made an iron gate and the sword itself was even stronger than any of the iron used in the gates. Maybe... he tried to reach for his sword, but the pain in his pain made it almost impossible to move.

"I suppose there is one last secret you should know Arto," Medraut told him seriously. "Think back to the day your father died. All that chaos all around you and you used a blood spell... think about where your father was, who was nearby."

Clutching at the wound in his side, Arto stared at Medraut barely able to still see straight much less attack him.

"Can't manage it huh, I suppose a side wound isn't quite as good as a back wound, but allow me to clarify." Medraut leaned closer to him, a twisted little smile on his face. "I stabbed your father in the back."

He should have expected it, but he hadn't. A gasp escaped him and he stared at his cousin completely dumbstruck. He'd hoped… he'd hoped that maybe the betrayal was recent, the result of simple jealousy or the Sídhe making him an offer but…

"No," the word spilled with blood from his lips.

With gleaming eyes, Medraut stepped towards Cathanáil with his hands extended. Arto's eyes jumped to his sword lying forgotten in the grass only a foot away from him. Weakly he tried to reach for it once more but felt something tearing in his side. His vision went black for a moment and his lungs constricted. As he regained awareness Medraut knelt and began reaching for the sword's hilt, his fingers twitching eagerly. Arto knew suddenly with perfect clarity that Medraut would undo everything. He'd willing hand over hundreds of people to the Sídhe and help them expand to the south and the west and however far the world went. He'd surrender everything if only for the sake of holding some grand title. Arto tried to gather more magic, but his connection was barely flickering.

Medraut's fingers brushed the hilt of the sword. White magic enveloped the sword and lashed out to strike Medraut in the chest. He screamed and was thrown back towards the tunnel as white magic danced over his body like lightning. Arto nearly laughed in relief, but instead blood and spit spilled out of his mouth and he gasped painfully for air.

Raising his eyes, Arto stared into the tunnel entrance and into the darkness beyond. He could see violet eyes in the distance as more and more Sídhe marched to invade his world. Arto could hear the sounds of battle, the clash of metal on metal and the sounds of the dying. The scent of smoke was tainting the air and the red glow in the night sky confirmed the worst.

Screams echoed up the hill from the village far behind him. They had failed.

"Luegáed," Arto sobbed softly, blood filling his mouth at the effort of speaking. Tears were rolling down his cheeks. "I needed you here." His vision was becoming hazy from his tears even as darkness crept into the edges of his vision. "Gwenyvar…" he whispered her name sending blood trickling from his lips.

Bowing his head, Arto felt a sob rising his chest. It was agony, only adding to the pain that was slowly dulling as he lost feeling in his body. Gone was his early rage, his earlier determination, and stubbornness. Even the earlier exhaustion from sorrow was gone. Now all he felt was a strange sense of resignation and relief. It didn't matter. He didn't need to survive now. Those hopes of a peaceful life with Gwenyvar were gone, that desire for children to hold and be there for had vanished and there would be more no happy moments with Luegáed. Morgana had Airril and Merlin would be alright. He could… no, he would do this.

White magic exploded forward, sweeping over the Sídhe warriors bearing down on him and pushing Medraut back towards the tunnel entrance. Briefly he watched his cousin fight to stand, but his movements were sluggish. Taking a desperate breath, Arto raised himself up onto his knees. His wounded side screamed at the movement and for a moment the pain blocked everything else, but he pushed through it. His hands were shaking and covered with his own blood as he brought them up. Arto pulled on his connection to the earth and felt magic flooding into his body. The connection, the thin thread that he could feel binding him to the ground was stretching painfully tight. It felt raw and ready to snap.

"This is it then," Arto whispered to himself, closing his eyes for a moment and savoring the soft warm sensation that was buried beneath the pain in the connection. Another tear slipped from his eyes, born not from pain, but this time from a bone-deep sorrow. "I'm sorry," Arto said to no one in particular and everyone all at once. "I tried."

Another breath and another heartbeat then he pushed all of his magic forward towards the tunnel. Streams of fluid magic twisted and turned in the air, scooping down and collecting all the iron that Arto had summoned earlier. Each piece of iron began to glow faintly as it flew through the air. The metallic forms began to change, stretching out and glowing brighter with each passing moment. Molten iron shimmered as it flowed past Arto and into the hole in the hill.

Arto kept gasping through the pain and the shaking of his body. He couldn't hear anything other than the beat of his own heart in his ears as it began to slow. In the corner of his eye, all he could see were dark shapes and flashes of silver magic. Morgana was fighting to get to him; the thought made him smile softly. Closing his eyes, Arto visualized the magical iron flowing together and weaving into the familiar iron gates. He'd made so many over the last decade that he knew the beautiful way that the gates came together. His magic began to fade away and Arto opened his exhausted eyes.

The gate was shimmering with magic as the iron bars carved their way into the rocky tunnel walls. He took in a shallow breath that made his chest convulse painfully. Arto licked his lips weakly, tasting the iron of his blood as more trickled from his mouth. Each inhale was becoming harder and harder. The heartbeat in his ears was slowing. He could barely see anything except for the brilliantly glowing white bars of iron as they wove themselves into a barricade. Medraut was slowly climbing to his feet, a heavily bleeding gash on his head.

"You!" A sharp vicious female screamed near him cutting through the din in his ears, but it wasn't familiar to him.

He couldn't support his weight anymore; everything hurt too much. Closing his eyes, Arto lowered himself to the ground and dug his weak fingers into the dirt. He couldn't move anymore and the unyielding pressure of the earth against his chest and stomach felt strangely pleasant. It was familiar; the feel and smell of the ground and he suddenly remembered lying here with Morgana and watching the clouds as a child. For a moment he regretted that he wouldn't speak to her, that he couldn't reassure her one more time that he didn't blame her for anything. He wished that he could tell Airril to look after her, that he could thank Merlin and tell the old mage that he loved him and he'd been a great father.

A soft breeze washed over him and Arto shivered. A few tears leaked out of his eyes as he tried to open them, but he couldn't see anything more. His chest ached as a sob tried to escape him, but he lacked the strength to make even a single sound. Silently, he curled his fingers deeper in the dirt and wished for his sister or Merlin to get to him even if he couldn't speak. Just having them there… a soft smile at the memory of him playing with Morgana on this very hill when he was young and another clench of his fingers in the bloody mud forming under his hand as the pain in his side became unbearable. Then the pain was gone, he felt faint, and then nothing.

31

Guardian Cyrridven

Alex was in a daze as she stared at the magical figure. She was both in awe and disappointed by the sight of the mythical lady of the Lake after hearing Merlin talk about Cyrridven so much. The figure was tiny compared to Chernobog but seemed unconcerned as the sword in her hands cast light all around her. Silence had descended over the lake. The shadow monsters were gone and Alex suddenly found their absence disconcerting. She wanted to turn and look towards Arthur, maybe start putting distance between them and Chernobog, but she couldn't bring herself to turn away. Inside her chest, the thread that tied her to magic was beginning to hum as the burning sensation of exhaustion began to fade away.

Cyrridven moved along the surface of the water, the soft sound of the lake rippling was suddenly the only noise in the area. Alex stared at the feminine figure as she moved and her eyes dropped to the sword that she was carrying in both hands. Cyrridven floated around Chernobog, seemingly unconcerned as the massive creature turned and kept his glowing green eyes on her. Then she stopped in front of Chernobog, placing herself between Chernobog and Alex and Arthur on the shore. Alex felt the air becoming warmer with a sweet smell wafting around her. It smelled like fresh grass, flowers and something that she couldn't put her finger on, but it was familiar.

Slowly Cyrridven raised the sword, shifting it in her hands so that the blade pointed towards the sky. Water dripped off of it and the sword began to glow brightly with a brilliant white light. Around Chernobog the dark clouds began to break apart leaving the massive skeletal form exposed in the moonlight.

Its glowing green eyes turned down to the lady with the sword, but then Chernobog began to chuckle. The very human laugh rolled over the shore of the water making Alex shuddered.

"Cyrridven," a deep, but soft voice echoed through Alex's body making her shudder. "You still stand with the humans."

"You stood with them once long ago," a smooth female voice announced. "Before you lost yourself."

It took Alex a moment to realize that she wasn't hearing the words in her ears, but rather they were echoing in her head. There was a moment of desperate panic before the uncomfortable reality that she could do nothing about it settled in.

"Depart from here," Cyrridven commanded sternly, her hands tightening on the sword she was holding.

"I will not," the dark voice whispered in her mind. "There is power here."

"That is the power of the Iron Soul and it belongs to this realm. Return to your slumber. Sleep here in these waters and perhaps you shall be cleansed."

"Cleansed?" An incredulous laugh rolled over Alex and she instinctively stepped back from the lake. "You are but a pet dog to the humans Cyrridven, you and the others who resign themselves to slumber."

"This is not our world."

"No, but here we are gods!"

"You have not always thus!" Cyrridven shouted even as Chernobog made a threatening step towards her. "Is Belobog truly dead?"

Chernobog did not answer her and instead brought up a hand in front of his chest as shadows began to swirl around his long fingers. Cyrridven rose up in a wave of water with a rushing sound as she reached out a hand towards Chernobog. The huge dark creature released a deafening roar leaning towards Cyrridven as the shadows in his hand burst forth in a stream of black magic. The Lady of the Lake took one hand off of Cathanáil and raised it gracefully. All around her water rose up in a flowing curve putting a wall between Cyrridven and Chernobog that his black magic crashed into and dissipated in. Then the wall surged forward striking Chernobog and forcing him to stumble back in the waters of the lake. Water surged up around Chernobog, wrapping around his legs and solidifying into ice. Cyrridven from her perch high above the surface of the lake on the fountain of water was moving her free hand and directing the water in a swirl of sea green magic.

Chernobog raised his right hand towards the sky. The temperature began to plummet as dark clouds gathered in a rush of shadows and icy wind above them. Swirling like a tornado the clouds churned down through the air and into Chernobog's open hand. Black magic flashed ominously and Chernobog's left hand reached up and clawed viciously at his own chest. The dark mass of flesh gave way to shimmering gold blood.

Alex's stomach heaved as Chernobog gathered the golden blood in his palm before the dark magic spun into his bloody hand. He closed his palm with a strange smile twisting his face. Moving his arm in a lazy motion, Chernobog flung his hand towards the shore. Droplets of gold turned black in midair as they sailed through the air, the darkness seeping into the blood. They twisted into strange shapes over the water.

"Look out!" Arthur shouted behind her.

The black shapes hit the shoreline and in jerky movements finished taking form. Six shadow monsters were snarling at her, three shaped like giant sabretooth cats, one long and lanky like a human, one hunched forward like an ape with horns and the last low to the ground with a huge hinging mouth. There was a sound of alarm from Cyrridven as Alex stumbled back.

Two of the shadow monsters were caught in a wave of water that surged up onto the shore and dragged the hinged jaw creature and one of the cats out into the lake. There was a shimmer of sea green magic beneath the surface of the water.

Dark silver magic flickered in Alex's hands as she dove away from the first of the shadow beasts and kicked the second one in the head. Alex couldn't pull on any more magic, the ache in her body was making her sluggish. In the corner of her eye, Alex saw flashes of black magic colliding with sea green magic. Alex glanced towards Cyrridven hoping for more help as a tiny orb of dark silver magic finally materialized in her hands. She threw it at the ape-like creature and twisted to avoid one of the cat-like shadow monsters as it rushed past and up the hill.

"Arthur!" she called frantically in warning as one of the shadow monster swiped at her arm shredding her coat and slicing into the skin. "Look out!"

Then Cyrridven raised Cathanáil and turning her back on Chernobog, she threw it towards the shore. The sword sang as it sailed through the air, a soft haunting sound that spurred Alex into action. Rushing forward she nearly slipped in the snow but paid no mind to the shadow creatures or to

Chernobog as the massive figure reached towards her. The sword's hilt hit the palm of her hand and Alex tightened her fingers around the grip. One of the creatures slashed at her, slicing into her arm, but Alex barely felt it as magic surged through the sword. It was a heady feeling, but the chill of the shadow monsters around her kept Alex grounded in the moment.

"Arthur!" she called, turning and extending her arm to throw the sword, but a loud snarl made her spin on her heel.

The tall shadow creature lunged at her with a wide open hand and Alex forgot all plans of handing off the sword. Swinging the sword in front of her body, Alex felt off balance for a moment as the blade collided with the flesh of the shadow creature. It screeched and vanished in a burst of light that almost blinded Alex.

With wide eyes, Alex looked at the sword in her hands. White sparks were dancing over the surface of the blade as dark silver flickers of magic from her hand swirled around the hilt. The pain in Alex's magical connection began to ease and she felt her body relaxing. She spun with Cathanáil raised and swung at the other shadow monsters with a shout. The shadow monster tried to dodge but vanished in a flash of white light. Inside her chest, Alex could feel her heart racing and her own magic flaring. The third shadow creature began to move back, but Alex jumped forward and slashed at the creature. She looked over her shoulder in time to see Arthur kill the last of the shadow creatures with a spear of ice.

A cry of pain from the lake made Alex spin towards Cyrridven and Chernobog once again, the sword still clutched in her hand. Black magic crashed through a wall of ice cracking the structure and sending chunks splashing into the lake. On her pillar of water, Cyrridven waved both her hands in a rush of sea green magic and pushed the cloud towards the dark creature. Chernobog raised both hands and a dark cloud appeared between them. It formed into a lance and blasted through the cloud of magic striking Cyrridven.

A cry of alarm ripped from Alex's throat as the Lady of the Lake fell from the pillar of water which splashed back into the lake. Chernobog lunged forward, a long bony arm reaching for Cyrridven. Her cloud of magic lingered on his skin and Alex could see ice forming, but the dark being resisted her spell. He caught the falling Cyrridven in his large hand and tightened his fist around her. Chernobog's fist began to shimmer as magic sparked around it both sea green and black.

Cyrridven threw her head back as she screamed sending waves of pale hair falling over her back, but then the waves of hair began to melt into water. A dark laugh rippled through the air before another blast of black magic enveloped Cyrridven. Forgetting to breathe, Alex could only stare as the form of Cyrridven began to turn black and melted into a thick dark ooze that slid down Chernobog's arm.

Alex couldn't move as her eyes stayed locked on the dark ooze that dripped into the lake. She waited for the ooze to reform into Cyrridven upon contact with the water, but nothing happened. A pained sob caught in her chest and Alex opened her mouth, but no words came out. Chernobog laughed and Alex looked up at him in alarm. Darkness was swirling in his left hand and he was looking straight at her with glowing green eyes. Then before she could fully process what was happening the darkness spun through the air straight at her.

The wisps of darkness swirled around her, turning into a fog that Alex couldn't see anything through. Then glowing neon green eyes flashed in front of her. Alex gasped and felt the dark clouds rush in through her mouth and slide down her throat before she could do anything. Raising her hands, Alex uselessly batted at the darkness and tried to cough. For a terrible moment, she couldn't breathe at all and couldn't see anything beyond the dark wisps. Everything went black as the darkness encased her face.

Suddenly she could cough again and Alex proceeded to try to cough up whatever she'd swallowed. Her fingers brushed around her mouth and she spit a few times in a desperate attempt to rid herself the sensation of the oily shades slipping down her throat. Alex raised her head and looked around only to gasp in shock. She was in the Sídhe tunnels.

Alex tried to call forth her magic, but the small spark was gone. She couldn't find it, couldn't feel it. Panic thrummed at the edges of her mind and Alex looked around frantically. The tunnels were just as she remembered them, seeming to stretch forever and then curving out of sight, but how had she gotten here? Alex frowned and rubbed at her head as a sharp pain jolted through her head, she couldn't remember, but something was very wrong.

At that thought, Alex shuddered. The dark tunnels were closing in. There was no breeze of fresh air promising freedom. There was no crying in the distance or voices of the Sídhe. There was only silence around her. She was alone and lost in the carved tunnels of Sídhe magic and earth. Alex began walking down the corridor, but her phone slipped from her hand and fell to the ground with a terrible cracking sound. Everything became dark and even as she dropped to her knees, Alex couldn't find the phone anywhere.

She tried to use her hands to guide her along the ground as she slowly crawled, but then the ground began to change. Holes were suddenly everywhere, threatening to swallow her as she blindly tried to find her way. Then there was a terrible howl in the distance that rang down the tunnel and violet eyes appeared just ahead of her. Alex couldn't see them, but she heard a sword being drawn and remembered with a thick swallow the sight of the golden Sídhe blades.

Her hand began to feel hot, a strange warmth was spreading through her skin and Alex tore her gaze away from the violet eyes watching her. But there was nothing in her hand, she lifted it off the floor and looked at it. Alex gasped softly, she could see her hand, but there was no light. She was glowing... somehow. Sparks of magic appeared in her hand illuminating the tunnels, but then the tunnels began to dissolve around her. In a brilliant flash of light, Alex found herself back at the lake in front of Chernobog, gripping a glowing Cathanáil in her hands. The sword was hot in her right hand and Alex sighed in relief even as a deep growl escaped Chernobog.

On instinct Alex raised Cathanáil in front of her, sliding one foot back like she'd learned in fencing club. It took both of her hands to keep the sword steady and it was unlike any foil or sabre she'd held, but the heat of it coursed through her body. She could feel the ache in her body fading and felt the soft thrum of magic in her stomach and chest. Chernobog didn't move and everything seemed to slow down as Alex tried to think of what she could do against the Old One.

She needed more power, more magic than she could call on by herself. In her hands, Cathanáil pulsed as if picking up her thoughts. Mindful of the pain she'd suffered earlier Alex began to reach out around her searching for more magic and power once again envisioning the thin mist spreading over the air to find her sources of energy. There were small flickers of power all around her in the air that Alex didn't fully understand, but she pulled on them. Wisps of magic began to appear in the air, coming out of the ground and out of the lake all around her. They swirled towards her and Cathanáil began to glow once more as the first spark touched the blade. More and more appeared and came rushing towards her, the pounding of her heartbeat in her ears almost completely drowning out Chernobog's roar.

In the wave of tiny lights, Alex couldn't see the new shadow beasts appear on the shore, but she felt them as their cold rushed over her. It lasted only a moment before she grabbed onto their magic and began to pull it sharply. Three strands of magic flowed into Cathanáil while soft cries of pain echoed around her followed by a roar and the sound of something crashing through the water.

Alex couldn't breathe anymore; the pulse of the energy was pounding into her chest and suppressing her lungs. In her ears, she could both feel and hear her heart racing as her arms brought the sword up. Cathanáil glowed brightly as more and more of the energy spun into the iron blade. Distantly she heard shouting and growling, but her focus was locked on the sword and the flow of the energy around her. Alex had no idea where it was all coming from but with every beat of her heart, she could feel more draining into the sword from around them.

She'd closed her eyes at some point. Alex forced them open as the sound of water crashing became too loud to ignore. Chernobog was just off shore and reaching towards her with a large bony hand. Fear flashed through her chest at the memory of Cyrridven dying in that hand. Cathanáil shuddered in her hands and fighting back a shudder, Alex pushed the magic at Chernobog.

Energy burst from the tip of the sword and arched through the air like a giant dark lightning bolt. The force shook Alex's entire body and she fell to her knees, but she kept the sword pointed at Chernobog. Everything smelled of ozone as the energy lashed across Chernobog's body. The huge creature was writhing and roaring in pain. Alex grit her teeth together hard. Her muscles ached and she was ready to collapse, but

Alex arched her back to keep herself upright. The hilt of the
sword was growing painfully hot, but Alex clung to it to hold
the chill of Chernobog's presence at bay. Tears leaked from
her eyes, a blend of fear and physical pain at the effort.

Chernobog lurched backward, his dark body trying to twist
away from the energy forcing Alex to adjust the sword. The
stream of magic resisted her, but then gradually the stream
adjusted to continue its assault on Chernobog. Her arms and
legs shivered violently as the heat in Cathanáil began to fade
as the magic supply waned. Alex was just beginning to fear
that it wasn't enough when a split in Chernobog's dark flesh
appeared, but instead of golden blood spilling from it golden
light blasted out dissipating the dark clouds. Chernobog's
mouth was open in a silent scream as he clawed at the air and
his own flesh. Another crack was ripped in his body and more
gold light streamed forth. A low pained sound echoed across
the lake, so desperate and sorrowful that Alex lost control of
the magic. Lightning flashed over the lake and she was thrown
backward, Cathanáil still clutched in her hands.

Hearing choking Alex looked up at Chernobog sharply. The
black creature was swaying in the lake with widening golden
cracks appearing over his body like a crumbling statue. A soft
sound like a sob escaped it before the body broke apart into
pieces. The golden light lingered for a moment as the chunks
fell through the air. Alex watched them turn to dust before
they hit the water. A dark shadow lingered on the lake for a
moment before the last of the dust began to sink. Moonlight
sparkled on the surface of the lake as the last evidence of the
battle vanished.

Everything was still and Alex gasped for air. Her arms felt hot
and heavy even as she sank into the snow and mud beneath
her knees. She pried her left hand off of Cathanáil's hilt and
looked down at it, surprised that there was no sign of a burn.
In her right hand, she was still clenching Cathanáil tightly with

the blade laying across her thighs. The moonlight shined off the blade, but the glow was long gone. Yet it was still humming with some kind of magic in Alex's hand and sent pleasant tingles through her skin. Smiling, Alex tilted the sword slightly and watched as it caught the light of the moon.

"Alex," Arthur's voice called next to her.

Turning Alex found her boyfriend staring at her with wide eyes before his eyes dropped to the sword she was holding. Suddenly Alex felt nervous and started fighting to get to her feet. Arthur reached out and caught her arm letting her leverage herself off him. His body felt cold and she glanced over him to check him for injuries. His arm was bleeding, but otherwise, he looked in much better shape than she was.

"Arthur," Alex sighed, leaning against him as he wrapped one arm around her. Cathanáil hung loosely from Alex's hand by their sides and she groaned as the last of the fear and tension finally drained away. "We're alive."

"Yeah we are," he whispered gently, kissing her forehead.

"But Cyrridven…" Alex struggled with the words as she remembered Chernobog destroying the Lady of the Lake. Guilt twisted in her gut and Alex found herself blinking back tears. She wasn't sure if she was mourning for the Old One, happy to be alive or if it was just a release of the tension and fear that had been building ever since Bran's vision.

"I know," Arthur told her, bringing his hand up to cup her cheek. "I know." He stepped back a little and gave her a small smile. "At least she got the sword to one of us."

Alex blinked at the sudden change in the conversation but looked down at the sword in her hand. From the wound in her arm, a little bit of her blood was dripping onto the hilt. Flushing slightly, Alex brought the sword up and carefully shifted her hands so one of them was holding the blade and the other the guard of the hilt. She turned it and presented it to Arthur.

"Your sword," she announced dramatically, unable to keep herself from smiling even as a few stray tears spilled from her eyes.

"At long last," Arthur whispered as he reached out with a gloved hand. He looked at the blood on the hilt just long enough for Alex to feel nervous about not wiping it, but Arthur turned his palm and glanced down at a smear of blood on his glove. She was about to ask Arthur about it when he gripped the sword's hilt.

It sparked with white magic, beginning to glow and vibrate in Alex's hands. Gritting her teeth Alex tried to stay still and keep the sword steady. Arthur's face was pained for a moment before he exhaled with a grin. Releasing the sword carefully, Alex smiled and stepped back as Arthur lifted the sword in front of his face the point towards the sky.

"This is a huge moment Alex," Arthur told her as his eyes trailed over the sword lovingly. Alex resisted the urge to tease him and instead reached for her phone.

"We should let the others know that we're okay," Alex reminded Arthur and she fumbled with her phone.

"In a moment," Arthur said as he took one hand off the hilt of the sword and reached towards her.

Smiling softly, Alex stepped towards her boyfriend. She inhaled the chilly air and closed her eyes as Arthur brought his hand up to her face. Once again she could hear sounds in the forest around them and thought she could hear someone calling their names nearby. Alex opened her eyes and looked towards the road.

"Did you hear that?" Alex asked in a low voice as she tried to listen. "I think someone is nearby."

Arthur looked towards the road, his smile fading for a moment and he nodded to himself. Looking back at Alex, he brushed a finger over her lips.

"I am a little sorry about this," Arthur told her gently, caressing her face with his fingers and smiling.

Alex frowned slightly at him in confusion, and then he moved faster than Alex had ever seen before swinging Cathanáil in his hands. Stepping back on reflex, Alex gasped in alarm as Arthur thrust the sword forward stabbing her in the side.

32

Revelation

The pain was so sudden and overwhelming that nothing penetrated her mind: she wasn't aware of anything other than a sharp agonizing ache in her gut. Then slowly she became aware of something warm and slightly sticky oozing over her hands. Breathing hurt and suddenly her legs gave out and she tumbled to the ground. Alex gasped in pain as her knees hit the icy ground with a thump. Her fingers jarred into her stomach sending more of the sticky stuff over her hands. Alex looked down and her heart stopped when she saw the gash in her stomach. She looked up as Arthur moved around in front of her and spotted the sword in his hand with blood flowing off of it slowly.

"But-" she tried to say, but it came out a gurgle.

Blood began to fill her mouth and the edge of her vision was beginning to darken. Desperation clawed at her chest, but she couldn't even summon the energy to cry or crawl away. The pain was pushing her instincts to the forefront, but Alex's mind was still trying to make sense of what was happening, why her boyfriend had just-

"But I'm Arthur the Iron Soul," he laughed cruelly above her. Then he knelt down and tilted her chin up so he was looking straight at her. "Sorry darling, but wrong answer." He chuckled once more and reached into the pockets of his coat pulling out three plastic vials with screw on caps a moment later. Without a word, he pulled one of her hands away from her wound and pushed the first vial into the wound.

Alex fell forward and Arthur caught her in his arms. He made a small shushing noise that almost sounded comforting but kept the vial pressed into the wound. Alex was torn between fear and confusion as Arthur pressed a soft kiss to her forehead. The aggravation of the wound made her whimper weakly and she tried to pull away only to have Arthur's grip on her tighten.

"Think back Alex. Think back to that conversation about Mordred," he whispered in her ear with a wide smile. "And don't die just yet sweetheart, I need more of that blood of yours. After all, you can't beat the blood of the real Iron Soul." He pulled back to watch her face but must have been disappointed because he frowned. Staring at him, Alex mentally stumbled over what he was saying. Arthur shook his head at her and sighed dramatically. "Don't look at me like that, it's just business. If I thought that I could convince you to help us instead then I would, but I know that would just be a waste of time."

"Merlin and Morgana," Alex whispered as the vial was removed from her wound. Arthur capped it with a loud popping sound but quickly shoved another into the wound. Alex shuddered and gripped his shoulder tightly at another jolt of pain, tears leaking out of her eyes.

"I gave them the Iron Soul they wanted; I played the part beautifully don't you think? They knew the Iron Soul would be here and I fit what they were looking for. I'll admit even I was surprised at a female Iron Soul incarnation, congratulations sweetheart you're a first.' Course that only made things easier for me since Merlin and Morgana never looked at you twice."

"This isn't real," Alex coughed, "Chernobog... nightmare. You can't be Mordred."

"No this is very real, I needed the sword. If Scáthbás and I are going to take back control of the Sídhe then we need to control the gate. I show up in Ravenslake with Jenny as my girlfriend and make friends with Lance and what else could anyone think, but that I'm the Iron Soul. Well, Cyrridven seemed to know the truth, but she showed up only at the last moment."

Alex panted against his shoulder, her brain jumping between random memories and she caught sight of her dagger a few feet away. Weakly she tried to reach out with her magic, but the connection was dimming and nothing happened.

"And I am sorry to tell you this, but Jenny is much better in bed than you," Arthur informed her with a soft laugh as he snapped the lid on the second vial and slipped it into his pocket. The vials slid in his blood-slicked fingers, but a moment later another vial was being pushed into her wound and collecting her blood.

"How?" she managed to whisper, the word slipping off her lips with several drops of blood.

"Your blood of course," Arthur laughed, tilting her body and pushing the vial at a painful angle. "I have magic myself this time around, but when I charge it with your blood it gave me that little extra kick I needed to fool Morgana and Merlin." He leaned forward and pressed a quick kiss to her lips and then licked the blood off his own with a grin. "Thank you for donating with me so often; it was such a lovely couple thing to do."

Then as he pulled the last vial out of her wound, Arthur twisted out from beneath her letting Alex fall to the ground. He nudged her with his toe and chuckled as Alex tried to curl into a ball. Rolling onto her back, Alex sobbed as the skin around the wound tore at her movements. Bringing her hands up to the wound, Alex tried to put pressure on it and ignore

Arthur's cold blue eyes watching her. She tried to move, but all she could manage was a weak sound. Then Arthur reached down and picked Cathanáil up in his bloody hands. This time the sword didn't even spark and he grinned wickedly at her.

Arthur turned away and Alex forced her head to turn so she could watch what he was doing. He stepped closer to the lake and raised both hands, Cathanáil still gripped tightly in his right hand. Sparks of white magic swirled around him and the blood on the sword's hilt and blade began to shimmer. A wave of water burst up from the surface of the lake and for a moment Alex thought that it might be Cyrridven. But instead of striking Arthur the water began to arch over the lake as even more water rose up and began to swirl. White magic flowed into the water and a vortex began to form in front of Arthur.

Alex could hear only the sound of the water churning and the slowing beat of her heart in her ears. Arthur was completely still in front of her and once again Alex found herself grasping for her magic, but the pain made it impossible to focus. The edges of her vision were darkening, she was so thirsty and a cold terror was settling into her chest. Around her fingers, the blood was slowing, but she could still feel some oozing out. Distantly she wondered if the cold was keeping her alive and a bitter laugh almost escaped her. Arthur's white magic began to fade away as the swirling portal of water seemed to calm to a gentle slow swirl. He moved slightly and Alex couldn't help but gasp as she stared into the slow vertical whirlpool. Every few seconds she thought that she could see a shoreline or a fish, but it all flowed by too quickly for her to be sure.

Arthur moved again, stretching out his left hand towards the portal and he began to take a step towards it. Suddenly there was a shout nearby and there was a flash of red light that cut through the darkness as a ball of fire hit Arthur in the shoulder. Arthur snarled in pain and shouted, "Too late Aiden, the Iron Soul is dead!" and started to turn around. Another blast of fire erupted out of the forest, this time striking the sword. Arthur stumbled to grab it, but the sword slipped from his grasp and into the swirling water. Alex heard someone shout her name as Arthur dove into the swirling passage of water, grasping for the vanishing sword.

She began to turn her head as the water portal shimmered and then splashed apart. The breeze sent a few drops of water swirling through the air and they hit her face. Alex took a shuddering breath as she listened to someone crashing down the hill. Her eyes closed for a long moment as a relief began to bubble up inside of her only to be banished as the ache in her body intensified. She coughed violently which sent spasms of pain through her chest and down all her limbs.

"Oh God Alex," Aiden's voice gasped beside her. "It's okay Alex," Aiden said in a shaky voice. "Help is on the way, you're going to be okay."

Forcing her eyes open, Alex looked up at Aiden's shadowy face. Between the low moonlight and her darkening vision, she could barely see him, but she could feel the despair radiating off of him. She wanted to tell him she was sorry; give him some sort of message for the others or at least some decent dying words. But it didn't work like that, she realized darkly as the cold took over her legs. You couldn't just keep talking, didn't linger until you'd said what you need to. Sometimes you couldn't speak at all.

Tears leaked out of her eyes and slid sideways into her hair. Terror clutched at her and she tried to move her hands to cover her wound again: maybe she could hold on. The cold was seeping into every bit of her body and she was so scared. If she could have Alex knew that she'd be sobbing. She wanted her Mom or her Dad or her brothers, she just wanted someone she loved there.

"Alex," a distant voice was calling, but she couldn't focus on it anymore. Everything was fading away, even her fear.

Then there was a warm feeling in her stomach like a heater had been placed beside her. Alex wanted to roll into comforting heat, but instead, only a soft sigh escaped her. The cold began to recede slowly and she took a small breath that didn't hurt. Above her, Alex could hear someone panting and tried to open her eyes, but the warmth seeping through her body made it difficult to focus. She inhaled again and coughed slightly to clear the blood that had been building up in her mouth. Trying again, Alex felt her lungs expanding without pain.

Alex opened her eyes and blinked several times to dispel the fog that had taken root. The darkness that had been creeping into her vision was quickly receding. Aiden was leaning over her with a look of intense concentration on his face. His hands were glowing red casting a fiery color over his face. Opening her mouth Alex felt her lips begin to crack and licked them quickly.

"Aiden," she whispered, her brow furrowing in confusion as a nagging sensation that she forgetting something poked at her.

Aiden's brown eyes met hers as the fire red glow in his hands vanished. He smiled, but as she began to sit up Alex could see exhaustion weighing him down. Aiden opened his mouth to say something but only a low pained groan came out as he pitched forward. Opening her arms, Alex did her best to catch Aiden and gently rolled him over so he was lying on the ground. Snow sloshed beneath them and Alex leaned over him with wide worried eyes, pushing away her own panic over what had just happened.

"Aiden thank you! Come on wake up," Alex croaked out painfully, reaching out and touching his face gently before her fingers slid down to check his pulse.

He was breathing, but it was slow and irregular and Alex swallowed back a cry of alarm. She tried calling his name again and touched his hands, but he didn't react. The sound of a car distracted her and Alex looked up sharply. She tried to cry out for help, but her mouth and throat were still painfully dry.

The vehicle stopped with the engine still running and Alex heard a door slam. She looked up as Morgana came rushing down the slope from the road. A sob escaped Alex as the professor slid down next to her and wrapped an arm around her even as she reached for Aiden with her other hand.

"Alex, it's okay I'm here now," Morgana told her gently as she leaned over and tightened her grip on Alex in a one armed hug. Morgana's expression was fearful as she looked down at Aiden and looked around in alarm. "Where is Arthur?"

Another sob ripped out of Alex's throat and she started to shake. "Arthur he-" another sob as the memory of his smile as she was dying flashed through her mind. "He stabbed me with the sword!" She forced out, wrapping her arms around herself.

"What?" Morgana gasped staring at her in shock.

"Mordred," Alex whimpered as fresh tears spilled down her cheeks. "Mordred stabbed me. Aiden tried to stop him. Knocked the sword away and saved me. Went into a water tunnel."

"He saved you from a stab wound from Mordred," Morgana repeated to clarify with wide eyes before she leaned back and looked down at Alex's ripped and bloody coat and shirt. "Oh by the ancestors," Morgana marveled as her eyes jumped back to Alex's face. "I'm a fool."

"Aiden," Alex whispered breaking the stare to look back at her friend.

Another car door slammed and Alex could hear people moving above them. Merlin appeared at the top of the hill and Morgana released her hold on Alex to stand up.

"Help me get Aiden into one of the vehicles," Morgana shouted up to him. "We have to get him to the hospital."

"Can't you help him?" Alex asked after licking her lips. "Can't you heal him?"

"Alex," Morgana started to say turning back to her. Morgana's face was conflicted and sad. "We'll do what we can, I promise, but please stay close to me and let us get him to the hospital."

Merlin quickly joined them and glanced around with worry at the lake. "Morgana-"

"Later," she said quickly. "Merlin the Iron Soul is safe and the foes are gone."

Merlin's confusion was apparent, but he nodded and followed Morgana's lead in creating a swirling cloud of magic. Streams of silver and green magic wrapped around Aiden and gently lifted him off the ground, keeping his body level. Alex watched hopefully, but he didn't wake up. Morgana reached over and grabbed her hand tightly as the two older mages slowly began to trudge up the hill with Aiden suspended between them.

33

End of an Era

800 B.C.E. Northern Cornwall

Instinct roared to life as he threw his magic rapidly at any violet-eyed target and Merlin felt anger flaring in his chest each time a Síd or a hound attacked one of the villagers. There were so many of them, more than Merlin had ever seen at any one time. He was struggling between satisfaction in knowing that their efforts had alarmed the Sídhe so much that they mustered such a force and fear that they might fail to stop them now.

Riders were rampaging through the village and throwing torches on the roofs of the roundhouses. They burst into flames sending pillars of smoke curling into the air. The smell and sounds of people running and screaming sent him back to the Sídhe attack on his own village and his mother's death. A Rider's screamed as his horse was consumed in a swirl of blood red magic rising out of the Earth and Merlin smiled viciously. He had to remind himself of his mission and forced himself to ignore the screams and shouts as he sought out what iron was in the forges.

The Sídhe became a blur of violence and magic as he'd rushed the large bag of iron up the hill only to drop it when a pair of Hounds surprised him from the right. He'd killed them both in short order with his magic, but then the iron objects had flown from the bag and up the hill in a swirl of white magic. It had been easy to know where Arto was at that moment and he'd busied himself with destroying hounds and Riders as they poured into the Iron Realm. Then the world had slowed down as from a distance he'd watched Medraut stab Arto and send his pupil falling to the ground.

Merlin charged a blast of magic only to have a Síd warrior swing at him with a golden sword. Terror and rage warred in his chest as Merlin stuck down the warrior only to be swarmed by three more. The blood protection swirled around one of them and slowed the other two down long enough for Merlin to send a bolt of green magic into the first one's chest. Pushing magic into his staff, Merlin swung it sharply through the air and struck the second Síd's head with a satisfying crack.

The metal of the gate was still glowing and pulsing with power as the magic settled into the rocks, plants, and dirt all around the tunnel. Merlin could feel some of it washing over him as he dropped to his knees beside Arto. Dropping his staff, he reached out with a shaking hand and placed it tenderly on the boy's head and embraced the swell of grief inside of him.

It eclipsed the pain he'd felt at his mother's passing all those years ago. This was sharp and bitter and cut much deeper. His fingers shifted through Arto's messy hair as the world around him faded away for a moment. Gently he rolled him over so his face was turned towards the sky and searched for any sign of life, but the man was not breathing. There was no heartbeat and the flow of blood from his wound had stopped.

"No," Merlin cried. The words slipped from him and cut the fog that was weighing down on him. "Arto," he called as icy panic surged through him. "Arto!"

But the young man didn't move. He didn't grumble and open his eyes. He didn't roll over and curl up into a ball like he had as a child when he didn't want to get up. There was just... nothing. The shard of denial that had risen through him melted away in the face of the truth. Merlin kept moving his fingers through Arto's hair as he forced himself to look up and take stock.

The swarm of Sídhe had lessened around the tunnel and they were spread over the hills around the village. He could see a few warriors still on the feet, but without their iron weapons they were holding off their attackers at best. One of the bolder ones was holding a Rider down on the ground as the blood protection destroyed it. Most of them were running away from the remaining Sídhe or scooping any fallen weapons they could find. A flash of pity went through Merlin's chest, but he couldn't bring himself to move from Arto's side.

He heard a scream that drew his attention sharply back to Morgana and saw the Queen of the Sídhe throwing an orb of golden magic towards Morgana with flashing violet eyes. Queen Scáthbás was dressed in golden armor with a dark purple cloak about her shoulders and a pair of hounds flanking her. A golden spear was gripped in one of her hands and he saw her look toward Medraut who was collapsed near Arto. Merlin shivered at the look of utter rage and hatred on Morgana's features as she glared at Queen Scáthbás who was glaring back just as fiercely.

Silver magic lashed through the air crackling with power and illuminating the area. Merlin stilled and watched as the magic sailed through the air and collided with the Queen's golden spear. The magic wrapped around the spear and he saw it pulse as Morgana pushed more magical power forth. The spear began to dissolve as the Queen created an orb of golden magic. Merlin began to cry out a warning to Morgana, but she reached out her left hand and sent a bolt of silver magic straight into Scáthbás' chest.

Queen Scáthbás hit the Iron Gate with a sharp cracking sound. A scream escaped her as Morgana's magic wove around her and bound her to the Iron Gate. Writhing, the Queen clawed at the silvery magic with her golden nail guards in a desperate attempt to free herself. Merlin frowned momentarily torn between ending her life and allowing Morgana's torment, but he was distracted by Medraut stumbling towards the sword. As the other man reached for the blade once more with a cautious expression Merlin felt rage rising in his chest.

Before he even thought about it, Merlin lashed out with a swirl of green magic. It struck Medraut in the chest and the man crumbled to his knees. Merlin wasn't aware of commanding his magic, his mind was simply thrumming with the desire to hurt Medraut. Queen Scáthbás may have been the root of all of this, but it had been Medraut who stabbed Arto. His blood was on his own cousin's hand.

The scream that ripped from Medraut's throat made Merlin shiver and he pulled back his magic. As Medraut crumbled to the ground Merlin looked towards Morgana who was still lashing Queen Scáthbás with a whip made of her silver magic. Glancing around Merlin's stomach turned at the sight of human bodies lying all around them, some dead and others dying. The village was aflame and in the orange glow, he could see people running.

"Morgana," he called with a thin and weak voice that startled him. "Enough."

"She's the reason for all of this!" Morgana screamed unleashing another blast of magic that forced the queen harder against the iron.

Even at his place by Arto Merlin could smell the Queen's flesh beginning to char and could see it turning black and cracking. The rage had not vanished from Morgana's face and now her green eyes seemed to be glowing with grief. He felt for the girl; far more than he ever had. It had been simple to be angry with her when she was younger and had put her brother at risk even as he felt pity for the poor little girl that the Sídhe had stolen, torn apart and put back together. He'd felt proud of her from time to time in the past decade when she was impressive with her magic or proved her devotion to Arto. Now he only saw the small little girl who had just lost her brother and was facing a monster from her past.

Rising to his feet, Merlin pulled his hand off of Arto's cooling body with a heavy heart. He glanced down at Medraut and reached down to pick up Cathanáil. The sword felt heavy in his hand and tears pricked at his eyes, but he stepped forward until he was beside Morgana. Reaching out with his free hand he placed it on Morgana's shoulder.

She tensed but stopped her magical attack on the Queen. Stepping closer, Merlin shifted his hand around her shoulder and hugged her gently. It was awkward, but slowly the woman relaxed and dropped her hands to her sides. A loud sniffle escaped her and tears began to spill from her eyes. He eased his hold on her, not wanting her to feel trapped, but hoping that she could feel that he was there.

A sound to his right made Merlin turn his attention away from Morgana in time to catch sight of Medraut lunging at him with a sword in hand. Raising his right hand Merlin began to call for his magic only to feel the weight of Cathanáil in his hands. Slashing out with Cathanáil, Merlin heard and felt the sword sing as it sliced into Medraut's chest. As blood spurt from the traitor's chest in a long deep slice in his flesh, Merlin felt a stab of relief and vindication. Medraut screamed in pain and fell back from Merlin. His sword dropped from his hands and he brought his fingers up to press on the wound in vain attempts to stop the bleeding.

White sparks of magic were still dancing over Medraut's skin and something inside of Merlin ached at the sight of Arto's magic still attacking Medraut. He hoped it killed the little bastard. Limping away from Merlin, Medraut looked towards the Queen and opened his mouth to speak to her. Blood spilled out from between his lips and Merlin knelt next to Arto once again, no longer fearful of anything that Medraut might do.

"This isn't over," Scáthbás hissed at Morgana. "One day these gates will fall and the Sídhe will sweep over your world." She cackled before subsiding into coughs and little sounds of anguish. "You won't be here to stop it and your precious Iron Soul is dead."

Morgana raised her hand and silver magic coiled tightly around her palm like a serpent. Instead of throwing the gathering magic, she stalked forward and placed her hand on the Queen's chest. The magic jumped off her hand and burrowed into her chest cracking the remnants of her golden armor.

"You won't be here either," Morgana hissed in a low dark voice. If she said anything else Merlin couldn't hear it. Then she stepped back leaving the silver magic attacking Scáthbás from the inside out.

Rising to his feet, Merlin took a tentative step forward as Scáthbás screamed and the gate's glow brightened. He could see small threads of white magic connecting the Queen and the iron of the gate and frowned in confusion. The Queen began to dissolve in a burst of golden light and the gate's glow brightened for a moment. She reached out a hand towards Morgana, her lips moving silently as dark violet eyes bored into them both. Medraut stumbled towards the queen with wide fearful eyes, but he collapsed against the gate. His bloody fingers gripped the iron bars which flashed in response. The Iron Gate pulsed with magic, sending white flashes of magic sparking around it. Beyond the gate, Merlin could see violet eyes and retreating figures. Scáthbás vanished with a silent scream and Medraut's hands gripping the Iron Gate caught fire. His screams cut through the air and Merlin shuddered at the sound as Medraut's entire body was consumed.

Covering his eyes, Merlin looked away from the gate as it began to glow a blinding white. Everything around them seemed to fall away for a moment and the air smelt like a thunderstorm had just rolled in. Merlin carefully turned back towards the gate, bracing himself. He could see the gate clearly, the iron looked polished and was shining slightly in the light of the distant fires, but the glow of the magic had faded. There was no sign of Scáthbás or Medraut and Merlin took a tentative step towards the gate. He could feel the soft hum of the magic, but it was light and soft as it finished settling in. Glancing back at Morgana he found her staring down at her brother's body with a look of complete devastation. Her fingers were gripping her cloak tightly by her sides and shaking badly.

Deciding to give her a moment, Merlin turned and surveyed the surrounding area. The smoke in the air reflected the fires in the village illuminating everything with a dark red glow. He could see a few surviving Sídhe running west and briefly considered following them. They would be trouble, he could feel it in his bones, but Merlin couldn't bring himself to leave Morgana. In the distance, the sounds of laughter and glee echoed down the hills and he wondered just how many of the poor creatures enslaved by the Sídhe had escaped. They also might be trouble in the future he realized with a sigh. He'd never felt so much his age before, he'd been very lucky to maintain his health and vitality, but now he just felt worn out.

"How did this happen?" Morgana asked in a low broken voice. "We were so careful for so many years. We had them cornered."

"An animal is most dangerous when wounded and trapped," Merlin observed sadly. "You were right Morgana: there was a traitor. I am sorry." He stepped towards her, reaching and gently placed his hand on her shoulder.

"It doesn't really matter now does it?" she remarked sadly with another sniff. "Arto is dead, but the war is won." She raised her head and looked towards the Sídhe that were vanishing out of sight in the night. "They are trapped in the Iron Realm; I wonder how long it will take them to die."

"We'll deal with them another day," Merlin assured her. "Not tonight."

"No, not tonight," she agreed, swaying on her feet.

The sound of someone coming made them both tense and Merlin turned quickly with Cathanáil raised. Airril came into view, blood trickling down his face from a small cut on his forehead. He was unsteady on his feet, but a smile spread over his face at the sight of Morgana. It faded a moment later as he caught sight of Arto. Merlin's heart swelled slightly at the recognition of how much this man cared and he deeply wished that Medraut could have been half such a man.

"Morgana," Airril said gently as he moved to his wife.

She tensed but allowed her husband to slip his arms around her. After a moment a small sob escaped her and she turned to bury her face in her husband's chest. Merlin watched them for a moment using the sight of Airril stroking his wife's hair as a distraction. When he became aware of his staring he looked around the area.

Bodies were collapsed all over the hillside with red blood staining the ground. He could see the blood protection shimmering softly and absorbing the blood of those who had given their lives in the battle. Merlin tried to take comfort in knowing that their sacrifice would only strengthen the defenses of this place. This area by the shoreline would be protected from the Sídhe for generations even if the gate were to ever fail. He exhaled slowly, trying to calm his churning emotions before he lost control of his magic.

"We should return to the village," Morgana told him weakly. He said nothing about her red eyes or the tracks left down her dusty cheeks by her tears. Then in a softened, almost childlike voice, she asked, "Will you help me with Arto?"

Merlin nodded, giving her what he hoped was a gentle smile. She bristled slightly at the look and took a determined step away from Airril. He lingered close to her, his bronze sword in hand as he glanced about. Morgana brought up both her trembling hands slowly. Silver sparks began to dance in the palms of her hands. Merlin stepped up next to Arto's body and called forth his own magic. It lazily swirled out of his fingers as if sharing his sense of exhaustion.

Silver and green magic swirled together in a soft breeze around the pair of them before the glimmering sparks of magic spun down to surround Arto's body. Morgana made another small sound of grief as his body slowly lifted off the ground and revealed the large pool of blood that was seeping into the ground. Reaching over, Merlin took her hand and squeezed it tightly. They said nothing as the body slowly rose into the air until it was at the level of Morgana's chest. With a shaky breath, Merlin took out his water flask and wet the edge of his cloak. Gently he washed away the blood around Arto's mouth and cleaned his hands. A soft flash of green magic sent sparks flooding around the wound to clean and mend the fabric, hiding the deep gash.

Airril knelt down and collected his staff and Merlin nodded his thanks to the younger man, tightening his fingers around the hilt of Cathanáil. They moved down the slope of the hill slowly, each of them lost in their own thoughts. Even as he kept his magic gently flowing into the air to support Arto's body Merlin couldn't bring himself to look at the lad. The loss didn't seem real, didn't seem possible, and even now he knew that he was waiting for the land to do something to help its champion. Arto had been created by the raw power contained in their realm so why, how could he be gone? But as they slowly walked towards the dying flames of the village nothing miraculous happened and Merlin felt his hope fading.

Over half of the village was gone with the ashes already blowing away in the wind. Villagers were moving around with jars of water and dowsing what flames still remained. Piles of red coals outlined what used to be homes and Merlin shook his head sadly as he watched a few survivors poking through the devastation. He wished them luck in finding a few valuables as he saw a couple of women placing some objects in a basket.

His eyes went up the hill towards the site of Arto's former roundhouse and glanced towards Morgana. There was no sign of her mother and Merlin doubted that Eigyr would have fled the village while her children were fighting. Morgana's expression was neutral, but her green eyes were darting around and her jaw was tight. The next few days were certain to be amongst the most difficult that either of them had ever faced.

Airril led the way to an intact roundhouse and with care they lowered Arto onto the surviving bed. Merlin looked around and saw that almost everything had already been scavenged from the roundhouse and sighed softly. Exhaustion was weighing down on him, but he couldn't bring himself to sit on the bed next to Arto. Merlin took his staff back from Airril and gently laid Cathanáil over Arto's chest. A sad sound escaped Morgana as she leaned over and kissed her brother's forehead and brushed a strand of brown hair from his face.

Merlin managed a small smile as Airril wrapped an arm around his wife and Morgana leaned against him. The roundhouse was still and silent as all three looked down sadly at the body of Arto while outside the roundhouse the villagers were already at work putting their lives back together. Leaning forward on his staff, Merlin rested his forehead against the smooth wood. As he looked at the man's face he couldn't help but feel angry once again at Gwenyvar and Luegáed. Perhaps them being here could have saved him, and if not then at least he wouldn't have died broken-hearted. Holding back tears, Merlin thought back to the first day he'd met Arto when he'd first come to the village to meet the remarkable young boy.

Time slipped away from them. Airril left the roundhouse eventually to help with the efforts of the villagers, but Merlin and Morgana remained in their vigil. Neither of them spoke and Merlin was certain that Morgana was as lost in memories as he was. For the first time, he felt guilty for having taken Arto away all those years ago. At the time he'd doubted her love for her brother, but now... he almost laughed; time did indeed change everything.

Rays of sunlight slipped into the roundhouse through the empty doorway and cast a soft glow over the body. Morgana moved first. She reached down and gently took Cathanáil off of Arto's chest and with shaky hands unbuckled the sheath from his shoulders. A soft sound escaped her as she slid the sword into the sheath and gripped it tightly. Without a word, Merlin unclasped his cloak and draped it over Arto's body.

He could hear birds outside and more people moving about. The survivors were returning home and it was time to begin rebuilding. Merlin inhaled slowly before raising his eyes to look at Morgana. She swallowed thickly and looked up to meet his eyes, raising her chin bravely. With a small smile, Merlin shifted his staff to his left hand and held a hand out to Morgana. After a moment of hesitation, she removed her left hand from Cathanáil and accepted his hand. Together they stepped away from Arto and stepped outside into the daylight.

34

Helpless

As she sat waiting and trying not to think about Arthur, Alex reflected on the fact that hospitals are strange paradoxical places. In one room a father of two gets told that he beat cancer while just a few meters away a woman loses her baby girl. Even as soft chimes sound the arrival of a new baby in one part of the hospital there is crying and suffocated whimpers as a loved one passes in another. Alex had never spent much time in hospitals. There had been a few trips to visit relatives and friends after some kind of surgery, but this felt different. She'd gone to the recovery rooms then, where there were bright balloons, complaints about the food and one or two machines at the most.

Now she was in a small waiting room by the intensive care unit. Her seat gave her a view of the main nurse's station. There was only one other person in the room and he was staring at the wall with a completely dead expression. Her chair let her look out into the hallway and into the ICU where Aiden was being cared for. His parents had burst in only a short time ago and she'd watched Merlin and Morgana speak with one of the nurses as doctors went in and out of the small room that Aiden was in. Curtains blocked her view into the room, but with each moment more machines were coming in. Once again she was left feeling like a silly stupid kid who didn't know anything about the world.

She'd expected Merlin and Morgana to be able to help Aiden themselves, but instead, they'd come straight to the hospital and Aiden had been handed over with a quick story about wild dogs. Neither of the older mages had asked her about what

Arthur had done and she hadn't even told them about
Cyrridven yet. Her thoughts were jumping all over the place,
but always circling back to Arthur.

Was this really real or was it a nightmare conjured by
Chernobog? She wanted it to be, desperately wanted it even as
the sense that this was very real settled on her shoulders. Little
things that Arthur had said and done over the last year and a
half kept replaying in her head. Only Alex had ever formed a
Connection with him, but the others never had. Maybe it was
because they were related or they had been. Her stomach
turned at the very idea and Alex shivered. She pulled her legs
up and curled up as tightly as she could on the chair. There
were so many little things, but they added up and she felt so
stupid. Worse than stupid, she'd helped him and encouraged
him. She'd thought that she'd saved him when he'd taken off
after finding out about Jenny and Lance but it was all just a
show. Everything had been a show.

Shuddering, Alex hid her face in her knees and tried to push
away all the little memories of them. She'd been crazy over
him and so damn happy when they got together. It had almost
seemed like a fairy tale except that she got to save him. She
nearly laughed at herself and sniffed loudly to control the urge
to cry.

Her side still ached. Alex reached down and brushed her
mended shirt over where she'd been stabbed. There wasn't
even the smooth skin of a scar, but she could still feel how
much it had hurt. Tears stung her eyes and Alex took in a
shaky breath as she tried to control them. Guilt rose up in her
chest at her feeling sorry for herself when Aiden had hurt
himself saving her.

Then the old man stood up and headed back into the ICU area
leaving her all alone in the room. Soft slow music was playing
in the background and the television was showing scenes of

waterfalls, fields of wheat and baby animals, but Alex just felt like shit. She leaned forward to rest her elbows on her knees and held her head in her hands. Even with the music playing the ticking of the clock on the far wall seemed to echo in the room as Alex's sense of time slipped away.

Rapid footfalls made her look up in time to catch a flash of red hair as Nicki rushed up the nearby nurse's station. She felt herself begin to rise from her chair, but then stopped as fear crept to the front of her mind. Sitting back in her chair, Alex dropped her eyes and tried to ignore the sound of Nicki's voice asking after Aiden. The nurse didn't give Nicki an answer she liked and for a moment the redhead tried to argue. Alex glanced up in time to see Nicki's shoulders slump and her nod.

Nicki stepped back from the counter slowly. Her movements were sluggish and Alex saw her swallow thickly. She wanted to reach out and grab her hand or hug her, but she couldn't make herself move. Her own limbs felt heavy and cold. It was almost like she was back on that shore and dying. As she stepped into the waiting room, Nicki stopped and stared at her with wide eyes like she was seeing her for the first time. Neither of them moved and Alex wondered how much Nicki knew or had guessed. Then the redhead crossed the waiting room and sank into the chair next to her, but made no move to touch her.

"Hi," Alex offered softly.

"Hi," Nicki whispered before she looked over at Alex. "They won't tell me about Aiden's condition."

"Morgana and Merlin are in there; officially they brought him in," Alex offered carefully. "His parents are already here too."

"Good," Nicki fidgeted in her seat for a moment. "I just missed you guys at the lake. I found Aiden's truck and was trying to find you when Merlin called. He gave me the highlights," Nicki explained softly. "Is it true?"

"Which part?" Alex asked in a low voice.

"That you're the real Iron Soul and Arthur was Mordred."

"Yeah," Alex managed around a lump in her throat. "The Lady of the Lake showed up to help us; she gave me the sword before Chernobog killed her." Nicki reached over and brushed her pinkie against Alex's limp hand. "Arthur stabbed me with the sword." A small sound escaped Nicki and Alex looked up to see Nicki staring in shock. "Aiden saved me with healing magic," Alex choked out, flinching into herself.

If Nicki was going to say anything it was lost when the sound of more footfalls in the hallway made them both tense up and look towards the doorway. A few moments later Alex heard Bran's voice. She forced herself to stand up, nearly collapsing at the effort. Nicki stood up beside her and reached over to link their fingers for a moment. She breathed in a little more easily and headed for the doorway. Together they stepped out into the hallway and spotted Lance, Jenny and Bran coming up the hallway.

Bran was pale and shaking with each step he took and looking far too old. Lance was hanging close to his side and kept glancing towards him and adjusting his position. Jenny was trailing behind them looking confused, worried and lost all at once. She caught sight of Alex and visibly sighed in relief before she dashed over.

"Alex! Thank goodness!" Jenny said with obvious relief.

Jenny slung her arms around Alex before she could move. For a moment Alex was completely still. She waited for the world to go funny or for her to have some kind of flashback or something, but all she felt was the warm hug. Slowly she released Nicki's hand and brought her hands up to return the embrace as a few tears leaked out of the corners of her eyes.

"I was so worried," Jenny told her as she released Alex and stepped back. She glanced around nervously and then frowned. "Where's Arthur?"

Alex froze at the question. Whatever warmth and reassurance the hug had given her flitting away like pollen on the wind.

"Haven't you told them?" Nicki asked Bran with a pointed look towards Lance and Jenny.

"No," he admitted with a small flinch. "Merlin called while they were taking me home. I didn't... I didn't want to be the one to explain," Bran finished with an apologetic look.

"Tell us what?" Jenny asked with widening eyes. "Oh no! Is Arthur okay?" She looked around frantically. "You said Aiden was the one who was hurt!"

"He was," Nicki snapped so violently that Alex instinctively reached over and gripped her shoulder. "He is the one who is hurt. He's in the intensive care unit."

"Then what is going on?" Lance asked in a soft calm voice.

His lower tone made it obvious how loud the rest of them had gotten. Alex gave him a grateful look and was suddenly aware of everyone looking at her. Nausea washed through her and Alex felt her knees locking up. Swallowing Alex tried to think of some way to avoid this conversation.

"Uh… well…"

"Alex is the Iron Soul, not Arthur," Morgana's clear voice cut in behind them.

Alex almost fell over in relief as Professor Cornwall stepped up next to her and placed a hand on her shoulder.

"What?" Lance questioned with obvious confusion while Jenny's jaw slackened and she stared at Morgana in stunned silence.

"Arthur was really the reincarnation of Medraut," Morgana provided before shaking her head and adding, "Mordred. He was just pretending to be the Iron Soul so that he could steal Cath- Excalibur."

"But- but," Jenny stuttered before she gestured to herself and Lance. "But-"

Morgana raised an eyebrow at Jenny with a tight expression. "You were tools in the masquerade. Obviously Merlin and I were on the lookout for the love triangle so he played it through with the two of you."

"Jenny was dating him for years before this," Lance pointed out with a worried glance towards the pale Jenny. He put his arm around her and this time she didn't try to shake it off. Instead, she leaned weakly against Lance who looked torn between relief, worry, and shock.

"That is one of many worrying things," Morgana agreed with a nod to Lance. "None the less, Cath- Excalibur was given to Alex by the Lady of the Lake and she used it to destroy a dangerous Old One to protect Ravenslake. Arthur himself admitted to her that she was the real Iron Soul."

"He just told you that?" Lance asked doubtfully, trying his attention towards Alex.

"After he stabbed me and I was dying," Alex managed to say earning looks of horror from Jenny and Lance. "Aiden saved me," she added in an even lower voice. She forced herself to look at Morgana. "How is he?"

Morgana opened her mouth to answer but paused as Professor Yates strode out of Aiden's room and headed over towards them. His brown eyes lingered on Jenny and Lance for a moment before he exchanged a glance with Morgana. Stopping next to Morgana he slid his hands into the pockets of his jacket.

"Aiden's parents are with him," Merlin informed them softly as he looked at all of them in turn.

"And his condition?" Nicki asked urgently, looking between Morgana and Merlin frantically. "We've done the explanations to Jenny and Lance, but how is Aiden!" She demanded impatiently.

Alex desperately wanted Morgana to say something optimistic, to reassure them that Aiden would be fine, but she knew that her expression meant that wasn't going to happen. Morgana shook her head sadly. "The doctors are at a bit of loss to explain Aiden's collapse I'm afraid. They are already seeing to the marks left by the Shadows he fought off, but he's in a deep coma. The doctors have put him on mechanical support to make sure that nothing shuts down and he'll be going in for some tests soon to determine how much function he has left. There is a chance that he will recover, but…" Morgana trailed off, her eyes dropping to the ground as she broke eye contact with them.

A sharp gasp escaped Nicki and she stumbled back, her
expression completely stricken. Lance caught her gently as her
knees threatened to buckle and Jenny looked at her with
sorrowful eyes. Alex just felt numb for a moment before guilt
began to claw at her chest. Tears pricked at the corners of her
eyes, but she forced herself to look at Morgana's face.

"Is he going to die?" she asked softly, nearly choking on the
words. In her chest, her heart jumped and her lungs felt
constricted.

"I don't know Alex," Morgana told her gently turning her sad
green eyes towards her. "He's in very fragile condition right
now." She reached towards Alex, but she stepped back from
Morgana. "Healing magic requires a mage to pour their magic,
their energy into another and transform it. Aiden pulled you
back from the brink of death."

"We warned you about healing with magic," Merlin reminded
them all sadly with a shake of his head. "If he remembered the
warning then Aiden made a very brave choice."

"What exactly has happened to him?" Lance asked calmly
with a neutral expression and Alex was suddenly very grateful
that he was there.

"When Aiden healed Alex he poured his own magic and much
of his life force into her due to how close she was to death. His
organs were beginning to shut down when we arrived here."

Jenny had a small sound of alarm, reaching over and gripping
Alex's arm tightly. Alex just felt sick to her stomach as she
wondered if someone in a coma could become brain dead. She
wanted to look over at Nicki, but couldn't bring herself to.

"The bottom line is that you children need to prepare
yourselves," Merlin told them softly, reaching towards Alex

who stepped out of his reach. "The odds of Aiden recovering from this are not good."

"Are you saying that you can't help him?" Nicki asked in a soft thin voice. "Not at all? Isn't there a spell that will keep him from slipping away?"

"Nicole," Merlin said gently turning to look at her. "Healing magic has its limits. I'm afraid that even if all of us combined what magic we could safely muster to help him the shock to his own system at receiving magic from different sources could harm him."

"Merlin and I will be slipping in when we can and giving him some magical power," Morgana informed them all softly. "With the help of modern medicine and a little magical boost, there might be a chance."

"Can I see him?" Nicki asked in a small quivering voice.

Alex forced herself to look over at her friend, reminding herself that she deserved whatever guilt and pain she felt for it. Nicki was ghostly pale with her freckles standing out sharply and her watery eyes shimmering in the lights of the waiting room.

"There is a limit of two people inside the rooms at a time," Merlin told her gently. "Let Aiden's parents stay with him for now."

"But you were in there!" Nicki protested gesturing towards the room.

"I used magic," Merlin told her in a low voice. "The doctors and his parents didn't notice me, but you don't have the control for that."

"Great so you can go invisible now?" Bran asked with a frustrated chuckle.

"No, not invisible," Merlin replied with a small smile at the attempt. "I simply suggest to them that I'm not there. Cameras can still pick me up and it doesn't work on other beings with magic."

"It's really only good for sneaking around a bit," Morgana said with a small nod towards Bran. "You kids can go home, we'll keep you informed," Morgana added, but no one moved earning a small sad smile from her.

Lance and Jenny shifted nervously as they stood on the edge of the group as if uncertain if they were supposed to be there or not. Alex wanted to tell them it was okay, but her mouth went dry as she looked at them. She was staring as her mind tripped over the realization that if she was really the real Iron Soul then it meant that she was one they betrayed. There was no rush of anger at the thought, but instead a pang of sympathy.

It occurred to her that they really shouldn't just be standing in the hallway. Alex was about to suggest to the other that they go into the waiting room where they could sit down and have more privacy when Morgana's phone chirped. The professor reached into her pocket to reject the call, but a moment later it rang again drawing everyone's attention. Morgana gave Merlin an apologetic look. She pulled it out and her eyes widened at the number on the screen as her face contorted with rage.

"Morgana," Merlin called as the phone rang once more.

"Arthur," she growled earning a wide-eyed look from Merlin who looked at Alex and the others.

He glanced towards the waiting room door and waved his hand. Green magic shimmered around him earning a soft gasp of surprise from Lance and Jenny. Morgana pressed a button on the phone and then with a beep the speakerphone turned on.

"Hello Morgana," a crisp female voice laughed over the phone.

Alex shivered at the sound of the voice and looked at Morgana only to see a look of shock and horror on her face. Merlin began to reach for the phone, but Morgana tightened her fingers around it.

"Can't be," Morgana whispered. Her voice was weak with complete shock. It was disturbing.

"What's wrong my precious girl?" the voice cooed to Morgana.

Alex felt a wave of anger that pushed away all the complicated emotions that were churning in her gut. She grabbed onto the anger and clung to it desperately as she looked at Morgana and watched the older mage swallow thickly.

"Hello Scáthbás," Morgana choked out earning a soft gasp from Merlin. "May I ask how you are alive?"

"It seems that we both are here to see the fall of the Iron Gates," the voice on the other end of line said imperiously. "I suppose I should have known that things like you and Merlin couldn't die like proper humans."

"How are you alive?" Morgana asked with a strong voice as she gave all of them a warning look.

Nodding, Alex stepped back from the phone a little and gently tugged Nicki back who was glaring at the phone with murderous eyes. Jenny looked ill as she stared at the phone and Alex wondered what was going through her head.

"Don't you remember my dear little mage? I was bound to the Iron Gate when you murdered me. All around me the magic of the Iron Gate was still settling. I became a part of it." The cheerful and pleasant tone in the voice faded away and turned sharp and cruel. "Imagine it, my sweet Morgana, the Queen of the Sídhe surrounded by iron for three thousand years. Constant agony, but I escaped when the gate began to fail, and I will make you suffer for it."

Merlin's expression darkened and Morgana's expression hardened, but she forced a small smile on her face. Her face was so tight that it looked ready to crack or maybe even shatter.

"So did your boy make it out of the water tunnel?" Morgana questioned in a light voice. "I understand that he went diving in after a certain sword."

"Of course he did; I'm calling from his phone after all. No need to worry about Arthur, he found his way home."

"But he doesn't have the sword," Morgana declared with a victorious smirk. "He lost that."

"Yes, well, you lost your Iron Soul. Maybe I can't open the gates right away, but they will fall soon enough and you can't create any more."

Alex wanted to speak up, but a warning look from Merlin kept her silent. She tightened her fists so hard that her nails dug into the flesh of her palm. To distract herself she looked over at Jenny only to see her friend looking very ill and clutching Lance's arm tightly.

"We'll just have to see how this story plays out, won't we Morgana?" Scáthbás sneered. "Tata darling."

The other end became static and a moment later the call ended. Morgana glared down at her phone for a moment before putting it back in her pocket with a dark expression. Jenny made a strange small sound and tightened her grip on Lance's arm.

"This is insane," Jenny said in a thin almost hysterical voice. "That was-"

"Not now!" Morgana hissed without even looking at Jenny. "Ambrose we need to-"

"You don't understand," Jenny insisted quickly in a stronger voice with a shake of head that sent her long curls flying. "That was Arthur's mother!"

"Are you certain?" Morgana asked with wide eyes, reaching out to grasp Jenny's shoulder.

"Yeah, I grew up with him remember?" Jenny offered weakly looking sick to her stomach. "That's definitely his mother's voice." She swallowed weakly and with a pale face added, "And she used to call me dear Jenny or precious Jenny exactly like that after my mother died."

Something flickered over Morgana's face as she studied Jenny's face for a long moment before she finally released her shoulder. Morgana reached over and gripped Alex's shoulder before looking over towards Merlin.

"Do you think there is any point in going to California to find them?"

"No, she wouldn't stay at the Pendred home. I suspect they just dumped the phone so tracking that wouldn't be of much help to us. If she is indeed his mother then they have been planning this for a long time."

"They set us up," Alex added dropping her eyes. "All of us." Jenny looked ready to be sick and Alex more than understood the sentiment.

"Indeed; Arthur dating Jenny was a brilliant move," Merlin observed with sigh. "Morgana and I assumed that since he had powers and a connection to Jenny and Lance that he was the Iron Soul."

"He was using my blood too," Alex offered, wrapping an arm around herself a chill spread through her body at the thought. "That's how he was able to do magic with iron." She swallowed back a shudder. "He collected three more vials of it before he left."

"What do you mean collected?" Bran asked looking very ill. Alex gave him a look and he grimaced. "Shit, he's a sick bastard."

Jenny made another small sound of distress and Alex almost echoed it. She shivered despite herself at the memory of the vials being forced up against her wound. The phantom pain returned and Alex grimaced as she tried to calm down. Everyone politely looked away.

"We need to deal with Arthur's car and arrange for him to have departed from school so next semester doesn't bring any questions that the kids can't answer," Morgana observed with a sigh, reaching up and massaging her temple lightly.

"Ambrose, can you keep an eye on Aiden? If Arthur did escape the water tunnel and discovers what happened he might come back."

"I'll stay here," Merlin agreed with a nod before looking over at Alex. "But Alex, you do need to rest. Your body may have healed, but you used massive amounts of power tonight and have been through severe trauma."

"I'm staying," Nicki announced and Alex noted that her roommate didn't look at her.

"You shouldn't be alone-" Morgana began to protest.

"I'll be fine," Alex interrupted quickly, pushing a strand of blonde hair out of her face.

Returning to the waiting room, Alex grabbed her coat and pulled it on. Alex fingered the fabric that Merlin had mended to keep it from attracting attention. She desperately wanted to turn around and storm into the ICU, demand to see Aiden and try to help him. Looking down at her hands Alex could still see some traces of blood despite Morgana using some kind of wipes on her hand while Merlin got Aiden into the SUV. Without looking at the others, Alex left the waiting room and began to walk down the hallway only to stop as she realized that she had no car. As she began to turn around she found Lance standing behind her with a soft smile that carried too much pity for Alex's comfort.

"I'll take you home," Lance told her with a small reassuring smile, his tone not really leaving any room for argument as he reached out and put a hand on Alex's shoulder. He turned and looked back towards the others. "Any others need a ride?"

"That'd be good, thanks," Bran agreed with nod. He looked over at Nicki, reaching out and squeezing her hand. "Text me if there is any news."

Nicki said nothing but nodded with her eyes still downcast. Jenny looked torn, but then walked towards them placing herself on the other side of Lance. Bran walked over and stayed by Alex, moving with short and slow steps as they made the trek out of the hospital. Unable to think of anything to say, Alex stayed quiet the whole drive back to campus from her place in the back seat next to Jenny. They stayed on opposite sides of the bench seat of Lance's truck and never touched.

When they got to campus Alex said a quick thank you to Lance only to get another smile and a nod from him as he tried to help Jenny out of the back. Jenny wasn't having it and quickly jumped away from him and headed off towards Upham Hall. Lance sighed and shook his head, but Alex couldn't think of anything to say. She slowed down enough for Bran to walk with her to Gallagher Hall, but once they were inside she headed up to her room without a word.

The dorm room felt alien to her as she stepped inside and Alex decided against turning the lights on. She felt her way down the hallway and used her card key to open her bedroom. Stepping inside, Alex kicked off her shoes and shrugged out of her winter coat. A fog of exhaustion began to creep over her mind and with a grateful sob Alex collapsed forward onto her bed. Tears spilled from her eyes into her pillow as her fingers twisted in the fabric of her comforter. She cried and screamed into the pillow until somehow she fell asleep only to be greeted by nightmares.

35

Worth the Sacrifice

The sunlight made the ripples of the lake shimmer and in the trees, Alex could hear the birds singing. There was the soft sound of water dripping around her as snow melted off the branches of trees and dripped to the ground. It was a beautiful winter morning, but Alex only felt cold and sore as she stared out over the water. There was no sign of the battle beyond the trodden down snow and rocks: there was nothing that indicated that two ancient beings so powerful they were held as gods had fought and died last night. It felt empty, like the world was already trying to forget.

Alex shifted as a sigh escaped her and pushed a strand of hair that had escaped her messy braid behind her ear. Exhaustion weighed down on her, but Alex couldn't bring herself to leave. She knew that she wouldn't sleep even if she did return to her dorm. The sunlight caught something metal a few steps away from her and Alex moved to retrieve the dagger she'd dropped the night before.

The blade felt cold against her palm as the memory of Cathanáil in her hands made her shiver. Alex pushed away the small wave of sorrow and longing that the thought of the sword being lost brought forward. She tried to think of Aiden and Cyrridven, determined to think of something that she could do. It was tempting to march into the hospital and see just how much magic she could give back to Aiden, but she knew that Merlin or Morgana would be nearby to prevent just that. She didn't find the idea of being wrestled out of the ICU by her professors a pleasant one as it would likely get her banned.

"Shit," Alex muttered as she slipped the dagger back into the sheath hidden in her purse. The bag dropped to the ground and Alex shoved her hands in her pockets. "Now what?" she asked out loud, glaring at the water. "Look, I'm not hero material world." Alex paused and shook her head. "Okay maybe I'm hero material, but I'm not The Hero material."

Alex kicked a stone into the lake and watched the ripples with a dejected sigh. She'd been happy with Arthur being the Iron Soul and being with him. His face with cold eyes and that cruel smirk flashed before her eyes and Alex shuddered. Shaking her head, she wrapped her coat tighter around herself. The sound of a car on the road made Alex tense and she glanced up the hillside cautiously. Her own car was pulled off onto the shoulder on a straight stretch to keep it out of the way. She waited for the car to pass by, but instead, the red sports car pulled off behind her own car. A weary sigh escaped Alex, but she watched as Morgana climbed out.

The professor made her way down the slope calmly, not seeming at all worried about slipping in the snow. Morgana's boots crunched in the mix of slush and rocks that the battle last night had mixed together. Alex turned and looked back over the water as a cloud slipped in front of the sun and dimmed the harsh light.

"Any change?" Alex asked softly as Morgana came to a stop next to her.

"No, he's still in a coma. The nursing staff seems to be very good though and are keeping a close eye on him. They even bent the two-person rule and let Nicki in to see him late last night."

"That's good to know," Alex managed to say. "I know she's worried."

"We all are," Morgana told her gently before she shivered at a sudden blast of wind. Morgana buttoned up her long coat. "You did kill Chernobog right?" Morgana teased.

"Well he turned to dust, which is the only remotely good thing that happened last night, so I really hope so." Morgana sighed at Alex's response and she felt a little guilty. "I suppose winters are colder here than in the Britain where you grew up," she said in a more cheerful voice that came off just sounding pathetic.

"Somewhat. The isles are affected by the Gulf Stream," Morgana informed her with a chuckle. "And when I was young it was quite warm there comparatively." Morgana paused and glanced towards Alex. "It wasn't until the last Iron Gate was created and the Sídhe were forced out of our world that I learned how cold it could be." Alex threw Morgana a confused look at the conversation change. "Something about what we had done triggered a period of much colder weather in the isles. That combined with all the iron in the whole of the isles, not that there was much of it yet, being used on the last gate and Arto's death meant that everything descended into chaos pretty quickly."

"So no happily ever after then."

"No, Medraut stabbed my brother like he had Arto's father, my stepfather Uthyrn, and Arto died of that wound and magical exhaustion. Not a happy ending."

Lost once more, Alex struggled for something to say. Morgana seemed content to let her lead the conservation and waited silently.

"Did you scry for me?" Alex asked, trying to sound calm even as she held back a shiver.

"I didn't have to," Morgana informed her, stepping up next to Alex and joining her in looking out over the lake. "Merlin doesn't blame you, Alex, no one does."

"I'm not sure about that."

"Nicki is hurting and afraid of losing her best friend," Morgana said gently. "She knows that you'd never harm Aiden."

"But it's my fault that he had to heal me. I was an idiot. I trusted Arthur! I lo-" Alex stopped herself and squeezed her eyes shut tightly.

"Merlin and I are much older than you; we have a great deal more experience than you," Morgana informed her sternly. "And we were fooled. We allowed ourselves to assume that just because it looked like what we expected that it was real. I didn't pay attention to the fact that I've always felt a strong kinship with you while Arthur irritated me. I didn't notice that Arthur and you were giving blood like clockwork or test that the blood he was using on his spells was his own. We failed, Alex, and we had a much greater responsibility and foundation to draw from. We made the bad assumptions that Arthur wanted us to make." A loud sigh escaped Morgana sending a wisp of curling white breath into the air. "I should know better than to simply believe that history is repeating itself."

They were both silent. Alex felt a little better after the near rant from Morgana, but the silence felt unnatural. It felt like she needed to acknowledge what Morgana had said somehow. Licking her lips, Alex gazed out over the lake and tried to think of what to say.

"I thought that history did repeat itself," Alex finally remarked, turning just enough so that she could see Morgana's face.

"Patterns and themes are repeated," Morgana agreed with small knowing smile. "But it is never exactly the same. There are always a few tiny changes that are easy to miss. At first glance it seems to be the same; it seems to be the same story replaying itself and that lures you into thinking that you know how the story ends. However, those little details build and build and change the course of the story into something you never expected."

"Are we talking about history or literature?"

"They are both stories Alex. Some are simply believed to be accurate."

"I get the feeling you're trying to tell me something," Alex said around a soft tired chuckle. "But I didn't sleep worth shit last night and I can still feel phantom pains in my side so pretend that I'm five."

"Don't assume that you know how this story is going to go. Don't assume that you know your place in it. Be prepared to be surprised," Morgana informed her with a knowing look. "What comes next… well, I may be three thousand years old and a professor of history, but I'm not going to pretend that I know that."

"I'm not sure if that's comforting or not," Alex sighed as she tilted her head. "That doesn't offer me any idea of what I do next."

The slamming of a car door made Alex and Morgana both turn and look up the hill. Morgana stepped forward slightly placing herself between Alex and the road. The action made Alex want to scream or hit something, but she stayed silent. Lance walked into view a moment later with Jenny on his heels. They looked around on the shoulder of the road for a second before Jenny poked Lance's arm and pointed down towards them.

Alex as rooted to the spot as she watched the pair descend the hill. Lance held Jenny's arm gently to help her keep her footing and shy glances kept passing between them. Her lips twisted into a small smile and something loosened slightly in her chest as they came to a stop in front of them. Lance let go of Jenny and the pair stepped apart from each other, but it was a hesitant move.

"I thought you guys were going home this morning," Alex said weakly as she regarded the pair with trepidation. "It's Christmas time and you should be with-"

"Alex," Lance's clear gentle voice called cutting her off.

Alex swallowed and silently stared at them for a long moment. Both were looking at her with expressions that were a mixture of pity, guilt, confusion and determination. Jenny stepped forward and before Alex could move wrapped her arms around her and hugged her tightly.

"I'm so sorry," Jenny whispered in a soft almost broken voice. "God honey, I'm so sorry."

Bringing up her own arms, Alex embraced Jenny and lowered her face into Jenny's shoulder. Alex inhaled the rich vanilla scent of Jenny's shampoo and body wash. It took her back to some of their Sunday mornings where they'd be in bathroom together getting ready; Jenny for church and her for soccer practice. Things had been simpler then and for a moment Alex ached for those days.

"Thanks," Alex managed weakly. "I know that this has got to be hard on you too."

"It's hell," Jenny agreed with a watery laugh. "All sorts of questions that I can't answer and way too many memories that went from bittersweet to creepy." Jenny released her and stepped back, wiping at her own teary eyes. "I tried to call the Pendred residence, but the number has already been disconnected." Jenny swallowed and shook her head. "I just... I needed you to know that I'm sorry."

She was supposed to say something now, she knew that, but Alex simply couldn't think of anything to say. This was a situation that she had no clue about. Morgana was standing nearby watching them, but her expression was much softer than it had ever been before when regarding Jenny. The sound of another car made them all look up the hill. Two doors were closed and Bran and Nicki walked into view. They both lingered on the shoulder of the road with Nicki watching Bran before he carefully stepped onto the slushy hillside. Alex quickly began to climb back up the hill and Morgana was only a few steps behind her.

"Was there an ad saying where I was?" Alex managed to say with weak laugh.

"You weren't answering your phone," Bran told her. "It wasn't hard to guess where you'd go. Plus your car kind of makes it easy." Bran paused on the hill and regarded Alex for a moment.
"You look like shit," he greeted with a shake of his head.

"Thanks, you're so sweet," Alex grumbled but without any real sting as she looked at Bran. The bags under his eyes actually looked darker than hers and his face was pale and drawn like he was in great constant pain. "You look really bad yourself," she said in a teasing tone though she couldn't keep the worry from her voice.

She looked over at Nicki who was pale with her long red hair in messy pigtail braids and dark rings under her eyes. Bran snorted and tilted his head in slight agreement as he moved over to one of the larger rocks on the hill. He waved Alex back and lowered himself onto the edge of the rock. Bran steadied himself by leaning forward on his cane and in the corner of her eye Alex saw Morgana smile. Nicki stayed nearby but was silent as Jenny and Arthur moved away from the mages.

"Thanks, Alex," Bran replied with small forced smile and a glance towards Jenny and Lance. After a moment he nodded towards the lake. "Nightmares," he muttered as he looked out over the lake. "Kept seeing a skull and some kind of weird old cup in a small cave. Really creepy and I kept waking up, but then promptly saw it again as soon as I closed my eyes."

Morgana straightened up and looked thoughtfully at Bran. For a moment Alex was certain that the older mage was seeing something that she wasn't. Nicki raised her head with a flicker of curiosity in her eyes.

"Did this cup have the triskele symbol on the center of the stand?" Morgana asked carefully. "Shaped like a chalice except with a large bowl and smaller stand?"

"Yeah," Bran replied with a small frown of surprise and worry. "Why? What did I see?"

A brilliant laugh escaped Morgana as lifted her face towards the sun as the clouds finally moved to reveal its warmth. She made a soft happy sighing sound before she turned towards Alex and smiled. "It would seem that the Iron Realm has decided on your next course of action."

"What are you talking about?" Alex demanded, concerned about Morgana's sudden change of attitude. She exchanged a glance with Bran, "What did he see?"

"It's like the sword," Morgana answered with growing excitement in her voice sounding younger that Alex had ever heard before. There was a hint of giddiness in her tone. "Maybe we can turn this around."

"But the sword is gone!" Alex protested as a mixed wave of anger, confusion, and guilt washed over her again. "It's probably on the bottom of the Indian Ocean by now!"

"That would be in our favor," Morgana observed with a soft chuckle. "We have significant allies in India amongst the Hindu Pantheon. Shiva especially." Alex wanted to ask what she meant but had a feeling that she wouldn't like or understand the answer and there was just too much going through her head right now. "Besides," Morgana continued. "The sword is just the first of the Iron Treasures, not the only one."

"What?" Nicki asked in a soft voice as she stepped towards Morgana.

"Cathanáil was made by the first incarnation of the Iron Soul, but that was not the only life of the Iron Soul or the only time they faced battle." Morgana smiled and looked sideways towards Bran with a curious expression. "Another notable Iron Treasure is the Iron Chalice."

"Iron Chalice?" Bran repeated looking at Morgana like he was ready to run or be ill.

"Indeed. It is most likely the mythological basis of the Holy Grail and several objects in Celtic mythology. The Iron

Chalice was the creation of an incarnation of the Iron Soul who lived around 680 B.C.E. and had the power to heal any wound when charged with the power of the Iron Soul."

"Heal any-" Alex gasped as she jumped towards Morgana. "Where is it? Why didn't you mention it last night?"

"Can it save Aiden?" Nicki asked urgently almost tripping on the rocks.

"Because when that Iron Soul incarnation died the Chalice was hidden away. Cathanáil's magic is weak, but it is always present with or without the Iron Soul which is why it was placed in Cyrridven's care," Morgana explained thought she sighed and bit her lip. "Sadly, Merlin and I never even saw the Chalice. We only learned of it after the fact and its location was never revealed to us," she added delicately with a tight expression. "It can't be found by scying and outside of digging up the whole of Wales I have no idea of how to find it," Morgana said before looking back at Bran. "But perhaps there is someone who can find it now."

"Me?" Bran squeaked, clutching his cane tightly in both hands. He looked ready to tumble off the rock onto the ground if it got him a little further from Morgana.

"You saw it in a vision."

"I saw an old cup; how does that lead us to it? I haven't a clue of where the cave is."

"Wales most likely," Morgana answered, "But potentially as far east as Stonehenge. During the Celtic Age after the bronze trade ended, travel became much rarer. I can't imagine he went much further."

Again questions bubbled up inside of Alex, but she couldn't seem to give them voice. Glancing towards Nicki, Alex could tell that the other girl felt the same way.

"Do you think we can find it?" Nicki asked Morgana in a tightly controlled voice.

The older mage turned and looked at each of them in turn. Then Bran clutched at his head as his eyes slid closed and he swayed on the rock. Lance moved the fastest of them all grabbing his shoulder and keeping him steady. Nicki moved towards him and dropped down on his other side.

"Damn that's getting old," Bran cursed as he blinked and shook his head.

"What did you see?" Nicki asked urgently.

"A skull and a cup!" Bran snapped shaking his head and shifting on the rock. The metal of his leg brace squeaked slightly and a soft groan escaped him. "I saw the cave again, but..." he frowned and licked his lips. "But then I saw this guy with a brown beard and an axe in a field for a second. It was weird." He looked around at the others. "Am I the only one worried about there being a skull?"

Morgana nodded and made a small sound before she turned and started walking up the hill. "Try Wales and see where Bran's visions lead you," she called back casually. "It may very well be that Merlin and I overlooked something else."

"Wait!" Nicki shouted as she moved away from Bran and towards Morgana.

The professor stopped and turned back so she was facing the group. She stood above them on the slope with a raised chin.

"Arthur believes that he killed Alex," Morgana observed in a calm voice even as her green eyes glinted with anticipation. "He and Scáthbás won't be able to move against the old Iron Gates without the sword just yet and won't be plotting how to destroy you right now. We have a brief window before the lack of news of a murder in Ravenslake alerts them that you're alive." Morgana paused and frowned. "And unless Aiden's condition improves then his parents are going to be having to make some hard decisions soon. You don't have much time so do what you need to do quickly."

Morgana gave them a smile before she turned away and started walking up the hill. Alex stared after her torn between laughing and asking more questions. It was clear that Morgana wasn't going to do this with them and the very idea sent both fear and exhilaration through her.

"Wales," Alex whispered to herself.

"Uh, are we really considering this?" Bran asked Alex with wide eyes. "Go on a quest for the proto Holy Grail with nothing more than Wales as a starting point?"

Alex laughed at the phrasing even as she wished that Aiden could have heard the little joke. He'd have found it funny. "Yeah," Alex managed to say with a nod. "I think we are." She brushed some blonde hair behind her ear. "And I say we ban King Arthur and the Quest for the Holy Grail jokes right now."

"Yeah... no," Bran replied with a hesitant smile. "If I've got to deal with disturbing dreams and visions to make this insanity work then I get to make Monty Python jokes."

"Fair enough." Alex agreed softly before she looked over at Jenny and Lance. "You don't have to come. This isn't your problem."

It was Jenny who answered the statement first to Alex's surprise. Her former roommate straightened up to her full barely over five-foot height and gave Alex a stern look. "You're not the only one with something to prove Alex," Jenny informed her with flashing dark eyes. "Arthur didn't stab me, but he used me for years and made me believe-" Jenny cut herself off as her expression faltered. "Besides, I'm the one with Daddy's credit card unless you mages have some other way to get to Wales."

"I'm in," Lance said simply as he ignored a look from Jenny. "I may not be a mage and I may not have a lot of experience yet, but I know something about geology and traversing difficult areas which you may need."

"Nicki?" Bran asked as he turned to look at the silent redhead who was staring at Alex. "Are you coming or do you want to stay with Aiden?"

"Morgana and Merlin will look after him and Ravenslake," Nicki replied still not taking her eyes off Alex. "We have to try. Aiden deserves that from us."

"Yeah," Alex heard herself agree. She took a step towards the others so they formed a circle. "Look Nicki, Bran, I'm sorry about Aiden. You're closer to him than I am and I can't imagine how hard it is for you to have him hurt like this."

"Alex, don't," Nicki ordered, crossing her arms over her chest.

"No," Alex said as she looked out over the lake as a strange blend of anticipation, determination and fear rose in her chest. "I'm not worth Cyrridven and Aiden's sacrifice, not yet, but I'm going to be. That's a promise."

CPSIA information can be obtained
at www.ICGtesting.com
Printed in the USA
LVOW10s0238271117
557668LV00032B/2404/P